# CAPTIVE
# HEART

ALSO BY SARAH McKERRIGAN

*Lady Danger*

# "I AM NOT AFRAID OF ANYTHING," HELENA SAID BETWEEN CLENCHED TEETH, "NOT MEN, NOR BATTLE, NOR DEATH, NOR YOU."

She braced herself as if for a powerful punch. "Go ahead."

"Go ahead, what?" Colin asked.

"Kiss me."

"Nay. 'Tis not my way to frighten fainthearted ladies."

She growled in frustration. "Bloody hell! Kiss me, you irksome knave."

"Not unless you ask nicely."

"Son of a . . . For the last time. I am not. Afraid. Of you." And to prove it, she bent forward and crushed her lips against his in a hard, dispassionate kiss.

At least it started out dispassionate . . .

## REVIEWS FOR SARAH McKERRIGAN'S *LADY DANGER*

"Four stars! Will heat the room and melt any woman's heart. You couldn't ask for much more."
— *RomanceReaderAtHeart.com*

"A fine historical tale."
— Harriet Klausner, *Midwest Book Review*

Please turn the page for more reviews and don't forget to turn to the back of this book for a preview of Sarah McKerrigan's next novel, *Knight's Prize*.

# CAPTIVE HEART

## SARAH McKERRIGAN

NEW YORK   BOSTON

Copyright © 2006 by Glynnis Campbell
Excerpt from *Knight's Prize* copyright © 2006 by Glynnis Campbell
All rights reserved. No part of this book may be reproduced in any form or by any electronic or mechanical means, including information storage and retrieval systems, without permission in writing from the publisher, except by a reviewer who may quote brief passages in a review.

Warner Forever and the Warner Forever logo are trademarks of Time Warner Inc. or an affiliated company. Used under license by Hachette Book Group, which is not affiliated with Time Warner Inc.

*Cover design by Diane Luger*
*Cover illustration by Craig White*
*Book design by Giorgetta Bell McRee*

Warner Books
Hachette Book Group USA
1271 Avenue of the Americas
New York, NY 10020
Visit our Web site at www.HachetteBookGroupUSA.com.

Printed in the United States of America

First Printing: October 2006

10 9 8 7 6 5 4 3 2 1

For
Grandma Edna,
who raised four boys,
outlived six husbands,
flew airplanes,
rode a red Indian motorcycle,
and owned a beauty parlor,
long before kick-ass women were in fashion.

With special thanks to
Melanie, Helen, and Lori,
for their faith.

# Acknowledgments

Warm thanks to . . .

"America," Kathy Baker, Dr. Barbara Barnett,
Orlando Bloom, Brynna Campbell, Dick Campbell,
Dylan Campbell, Richard Campbell, Carol Carter,
Lucele Coutts, Karen Kay, Hudson Leick,
Lauren Royal, Betty and Earl Talken,
Shirley Talken, Charles and Nancy Williams,
and everyone who plays "Starcraft"

## Chapter 1

### The Borders
#### Summer 1136

HELENA WAS DRUNK. Drunker than she'd ever been in her life. Which was why, no matter how she struggled against the cursed brute of a Norman oaf wrestling her down the castle stairs, she couldn't break his hold on her.

"Cease, wench!" her captor hissed, stumbling on a step in the dark. "Bloody hell, you'll get us both killed."

She would have grappled even harder then, but her right knee suddenly turned to custard. Forsooth, if the Norman hadn't caught her against his broad chest, she'd have tumbled headlong down the stone steps.

"Ballocks," he muttered against her ear, his massive arms tightening around her like a vise.

She rolled her eyes as a wave of dizziness washed over her. If only her muscles would cooperate, she thought, she could wrench loose and push the bloody bastard down the stairs.

But she was well and truly drunk.

She'd not realized just *how* drunk until she'd found

herself in the bedchamber of her sister's bridegroom, Pagan Cameliard, dagger in hand, ready to kill him.

If she hadn't been drunk, if she hadn't tripped in the dark over Pagan's man, slumbering at the foot of the bed like some cursed faithful hound, she might have succeeded.

Jesu, 'twas a sobering thought. Helena, the daughter of a lord, and an honorable Warrior Maid of Rivenloch, had almost slain a man quite *dis*honorably in his sleep.

'Twas not entirely her fault, she decided. She'd been up until the wee hours, commiserating over a cup, indeed *several* cups, with her older sister, Deirdre, lamenting the fate of Miriel, their poor little sister, betrothed against her will to a foreigner. And under the influence of excessive wine, they'd sworn to murder the man if he so much as laid a hand on Miriel.

It had seemed such a noble idea at the time. But how Helena had gone from making that drunken vow to actually skulking about the bridegroom's chamber with a knife, she couldn't fathom.

Indeed, she'd been shocked to discover the dagger in her hand, though not half as shocked as Sir Colin du Lac, the brawny varlet over whom she'd tripped, the man who currently half shoved, half carried her down the stairs.

Once more, Helena had become a victim of her own impulsiveness. Deirdre frequently scolded Helena for her tendency to act first and ask questions later. Still, Helena's quick reflexes had saved her more than once from male-factors and murderers and men who mistook her for a helpless maid. While Deirdre might waste time weighing the consequences of punishing a man for insult, Helena wouldn't hesitate to draw her sword and mark his cheek with a scar he'd wear to his grave. Her message was clear. No one tangled with the Warrior Maids of Rivenloch.

But this time, she feared she'd gone too far.

Pagan's man grunted as he lifted her over the last step. Damn the knave—despite his inferior Norman blood, he proved as strong and determined as a bull. With a final heave, he deposited her at the threshold of the great hall.

The chamber seemed cavernous by the dim glow of the banked fire, its high ceiling obscured by shadow, its walls disappearing into the darkness. By day 'twas a lofty hall decked with the tattered banners of defeated enemies. But by night the frayed pennons hung in the air like lost spirits.

A cat hissed and darted past the hearth, its elongated shadow streaking wraithlike along one wall. In the corner, a hound stirred briefly at the disturbance, chuffed once, then lowered his head to his paws again. But the other denizens of the great hall, dozens of snoring servants, huddled upon mounds of rushes and propped against the walls, slumbered on in oblivion.

Helena struggled anew, hoping to wake one of them. They were *her* servants, after all. Anyone seeing the lady of the castle being abducted by a Norman would send up an alarm.

But 'twas impossible to make a noise around the wad of the fur coverlet her vile captor had stuffed into her mouth. Even if she managed, she doubted anyone would rouse. The castle folk were exhausted from making hasty preparations for the travesty of a wedding in the morn.

"Cease, wench," Sir Colin bit out, giving her ribs a jerk of warning, "or I'll string you up *now*."

She hiccoughed involuntarily.

Surely 'twas an idle threat on his part. This Norman

couldn't hang her. Not in her own castle. Not when her only crime had been protecting her sister. Besides, she hadn't killed Pagan. She'd only *attempted* to kill him.

Still, she swallowed back the bitter taste of doubt.

These Normans *were* vassals of the King of Scotland, and the King *had* commanded that Pagan wed one of the daughters of Rivenloch. If Helena had succeeded in slaying the King's man . . . 'twould have been high treason, punishable by hanging.

The thought made her sway uneasily in Colin's arms.

"Whoa. Steady, Hel-fire." His whisper against her ear sent an unwelcome shiver along her spine. "Do not faint away on me."

She frowned and hiccoughed again. Hel-fire! He didn't know the half of it. And how dare he suggest she might faint? Warrior maids didn't faint. 'Twas only her feet tangling in the coverlet as they shuffled through the rushes in the great hall.

Then, as they lurched across the flagstones toward the cellar stairs, a different, all-too-familiar sensation brought her instantly alert.

Sweet Mary, she was going to be sick.

Her stomach seized once. Twice. Her eyes grew wide with horror.

One look at the damsel's beaded brow and ashen pallor told Colin why she'd stopped in her tracks.

"Shite!" he hissed.

Her body heaved again, and he snatched the wad of fur coverlet from her mouth, bending her forward over one arm, away from him, just in time.

Fortunately, no one was sleeping there.

Holding the back of her head while she lost her supper, he couldn't help but feel sorry for the miserable little murderess. She obviously wouldn't have tried to slay Pagan in his sleep if she hadn't been as drunk as an alewife.

And he certainly didn't intend to have the maid hanged for treason, no matter what he led her to believe. Executing the sister of Pagan's bride would destroy the alliance they'd come to form with the Scots. She'd obviously done what she'd done to protect her little sister. Besides, who could drop a noose around a neck as fair and lovely as hers?

Still, he couldn't allow the maid to think she could attack a King's man without consequence.

What Colin couldn't fathom was why the three sisters of Rivenloch so loathed his commander. Sir Pagan Cameliard was a fierce warrior, aye, a man who led an unparalleled fighting force. But he was kind and gentle with ladies. Indeed, wenches often swooned over the captain's handsome countenance and fine form. Any woman with half a brain would be ecstatic to have Pagan for a husband. Colin would have expected the sisters, sequestered so long in the barren wilds of Scotland, to vie eagerly for the privilege of wedding an illustrious nobleman like Pagan Cameliard.

Instead, they quarreled over who would be *burdened* with him. 'Twas perplexing.

Poor Helena had ceased heaving, and now the pretty, pitiful maid quivered feebly, like a storm-tossed kitten locked out of the barn. But Colin dared not let compassion override caution. This kitten had shown her claws. He let her up, then instantly drew his dagger, placing it alongside her neck.

"I'll spare you the gag now, damsel," he told her in a

stern whisper, "but I warn you, do not cry out, or I'll be forced to slit your throat."

Of course, if she'd known Colin better, she would have laughed in his face. 'Twas true, he could kill a man without a moment's hesitation and dispatch an enemy knight with a single expert blow. He was strong and swift with a blade, and he had an uncanny instinct for discerning the point of greatest vulnerability in an opponent. But when it came to beautiful women, Colin du Lac was about as savage as an unweaned pup.

Happily, the damsel believed his threat. Or perchance she was simply too weak to fight. Either way, she staggered against him, shuddering as he wrapped the fur coverlet tighter about her shoulders and guided her forward.

Beside the entrance to the buttery were a basin and a ewer for washing. He steered her there, propping her against the wall so she wouldn't fall. Her drooping eyes still smoldered with silent rage as she glared at him, but her pathetic hiccoughs entirely ruined the effect. And, fortunately, she hadn't the strength to lend action to her anger.

"Open your mouth," he murmured, using his free hand to pick up the ewer of water.

She compressed her lips, as contrary as a child. Even now, with fire in her eyes and her mouth tight with mutiny, she was truly the most exquisite creature he'd ever beheld. Her tresses cascaded over her shoulders like the tumbling froth of a highland waterfall, and her curves were more seductive than the sinuous silhouette of a wine-filled goblet.

She eyed him doubtfully, as if she suspected he might use the water to drown her on the spot.

He supposed she had a right to doubt him. Only moments ago, in Pagan's chamber, he'd threatened to, what was it? Take her where no one could hear her scream and break her of her wild ways at the crack of a whip? He winced, recalling his rash words.

"Listen," he confided, lowering the ewer, "I said I wouldn't punish you until the marriage is accomplished. I'm a man of my word. As long as you don't force my hand, I'll do you no harm this eve."

Slowly, reluctantly, she parted her lips. He carefully poured a small amount of water into her mouth. As she swished the liquid around, he got the distinct impression she longed to spew it back into his face. But with his blade still at her throat, she didn't dare. Leaning forward, she spit into the rushes.

"Good. Come."

When they'd first arrived, Pagan's betrothed had given them a tour of the Scots castle that would be their new home. Rivenloch was an impressive holding, probably magnificent in its day, a little worn, but reparable. The outer wall enclosed an enormous garden, an orchard, stables, kennels, mews, and a dovecote. A small stone chapel sat in the midst of the courtyard, and a dozen or more workshops slouched against the inner walls. A grand tiltyard and practice field stood at the far end of the property, and the imposing square keep at the heart of the holding was comprised of the great hall, numerous bedchambers, garderobes, a buttery, a pantry, and several cellars. 'Twas to one of the storage rooms beneath the keep that he now conveyed his captive.

Placing Helena before him, he descended the rough stone steps by the light of a candle set in the stairwell's sconce. Below them, small creatures scuttled about on

their midnight rounds. Colin felt a brief twinge of remorse, wondering if the cellars were infested with mice,
if 'twas cruel to lock Helena in there, if she was afraid of
the creatures. Just as quickly, he decided that a knife-
wielding wench prowling about in a man's chamber, prepared to stab him in his sleep, was likely afraid of very
little.

They'd almost reached the bottom of the stairs when
the damsel made a faint moan and, as if her bones had
melted away, abruptly withered in his arms.

Knocked off-balance by the sudden weight against his
chest, he slammed into the stone wall with one shoulder,
cinching his arm around her waist so she wouldn't fall. To
prevent a nasty accident, he cast his knife away, and it
clattered down the steps.

Then she slumped forward, and he was pulled along
with her. Only by sheer strength was he able to keep them
from pitching headlong onto the cold, hard flagstones
below. Even so, as he struggled down the last few steps,
the fur coverlet snagged on his heel and slipped sideways
on her body. He lost his grip upon her waist and made another desperate grab for her as her knees buckled.

His hand closed on something soft and yielding as he
slid off the last step and finally found his footing at the
bottom of the stairs.

Colin had fondled enough breasts to recognize the soft
flesh pressed sweetly against his palm. But he dared not
let go for fear she'd drop to the ground.

In the next instant, she roused again, drawing in a huge
gasp of outrage, and Colin knew he was in trouble. Luckily,
since he'd received his share of slaps for past fondlings,
he was prepared.

As her arm came around, not with a chiding open palm, but a fist of potent fury, he released her and ducked back out of range. Her swing was so forceful that when it swished through empty air, it spun her halfway around.

"Holy . . . ," he breathed. Had the maid not been drunk, the punch would have certainly flattened him.

"Y' son of a . . . ," she slurred. She blinked, trying to focus on him, her fists clenched in front of her as she planned her next strike. "Get yer hands off me. I'll kick yer bloody Norm'n arse. Swear I will. S—"

Her hands began to droop, and her eyes dimmed as she swayed left, then right, staggering back a step. Then whatever fight she had left in her fizzled out like the last wheezing draw on a wineskin. He rushed up, catching her just before she collapsed.

Cradled against his flank, all the fury and fight gone out of her, she looked less like a warrior maid and more like the guileless Helena he'd first spied bathing in Rivenloch's pond, the delectable Siren with sun-kissed skin and riotous tawny hair, the woman who'd splashed seductively through his dreams.

Had that been only this morn? So much had transpired in the last few weeks.

A fortnight ago, Sir Pagan had received orders from King David of Scotland to venture north to Rivenloch to claim one of Lord Gellir's daughters. At the time, the King's purpose had been a mystery. But now 'twas clear what he intended.

King Henry's death had left England in turmoil, with Stephen and Matilda grappling for control of the throne. That turmoil had fomented lawlessness along the Borders, where land-hungry English barons felt at liberty to seize unguarded Scots castles.

King David had granted Pagan a bride, and thus the stewardship of Rivenloch, in the hopes of guarding the valuable keep against English marauders.

Despite the King's sanction, Pagan had proceeded with caution. He'd traveled with Colin in advance of his knights to ascertain the demeanor of the Rivenloch clan. The Normans might be allies of the Scots, but he doubted they'd receive a hearty reception if they arrived in full force, like a conquering army, to claim the lord's daughter.

As it turned out, he was right to be wary. Their reception, at least by the daughters, had been far less than hearty. But by God's grace, by midday on the morrow, after the alliance was sealed by marriage, peace would reign. And the Scots, once they were made merry with drink and celebration, would surely welcome the full complement of the Knights of Cameliard to Rivenloch.

Helena gave a snort in her sleep, and Colin smiled ruefully down at her. *She'd* offer him no word of welcome. Indeed, she'd likely prefer to slit his throat.

He bent to slip one forearm behind her knees and hefted her easily into his arms.

One of the small storerooms looked seldom used. It held little more than broken furnishings and tools, piles of rags, and various empty containers. It had a bolt on the outside and a narrow space under the door for air, which meant it had likely been employed at one time for just this purpose, as a gaol of sorts. Indeed, 'twas an ideal place to store a wayward wench for the night.

He spread the fur coverlet atop an improvised pallet of rags to make a bed for her. She might be an assassin, but she was also a woman. She deserved at least a small measure of comfort.

After he tucked the coverlet about her shoulders, he couldn't resist combing back a stray tendril of her lush golden brown hair to place a smug kiss upon her forehead. "Sleep well, little Hel-hound."

He closed and bolted the door behind him, then sat back against it, crossing his arms over his chest and closing his eyes. Perchance he could steal one last hour of sleep before morn.

If all went well, by afternoon the deed would be done, and the rest of the Cameliard company would arrive. Once Pagan was decisively wed, 'twould be safe to release Helena.

He marveled again over the curious Scots maid. She was unlike any woman he'd ever met—bold and cocksure, yet undeniably feminine. At supper, she'd boasted of being an expert swordswoman, a claim none of her fellow Scots had disputed. And she'd regaled him with a tale of the local outlaw, trying to shock him with gruesome details that would have unnerved a lesser woman. She'd exhibited the most unbridled temper when her father announced Miriel's marriage, cursing and slamming her fist on the table, her outburst checked only by the chiding of her older sister. And her appetite . . . He chuckled as he remembered watching her smack the grease from her fingers. The damsel had eaten enough to satisfy two grown men.

And yet she inhabited the most womanly form. His loins swelled with the memory of her naked in the pond— the flicker of her curved buttocks as she dove under the waves, the gentle bounce of her full breasts as she splashed her sisters, her sleek thighs, narrow waist, flashing teeth, the carefree toss of her sun-streaked hair as she cavorted in the water like a playful colt . . .

He sighed. There was no use getting his braies in a wad over a damsel who currently slumbered in drunken oblivion on the other side of the door.

Still, he couldn't stop thinking about her. Helena was unique. Intriguing. Vibrant. He'd never met a woman so headstrong, so untamed. As fresh and wild as Scotland itself. And as unpredictable.

Indeed, 'twas fortunate Pagan had chosen quiet, sweet, docile Miriel for a bride, and not Helena. *This* wench would have been a handful.

*More* than a handful, he considered with a wicked grin, recalling the accidental caress he'd enjoyed moments ago. Jesu, she had a delectable body. Mayhap he could eventually charm the maid into allowing him to take further liberties. His loins tingled at the thought.

Earlier, when he'd foiled her assassination plans, imprisoned her in his arms, and, in the flush of anger, threatened to break her, she'd skewered him with a green glare as raging hot as an iron poker. But she'd been besotted and desperate and not in her right mind.

By the time she awoke in the morn and recognized what she'd done in a drunken furor, she'd likely blush with shame and weep with regret. And when, by the light of day, she realized the mercy this Norman had shown her—his patience, his kindness, his compassion—she might feel more agreeable to his advances. Indeed, he decided, his mouth curving up in a contented smile as he drifted off to sleep, mayhap then she'd *welcome* his caress.

# Chapter 2

Helena hated Colin du Lac. With all of her heart. With every fiber of her being. Forsooth, if she didn't hurt so much this morn—all that loathing on top of the terrible throbbing in her head—she would have manifested that hatred by slamming her fist against the oak door and screaming at the top of her lungs.

But today her rancor had to be of the silent, smoldering kind, for too much wine had left her with a sour taste in her mouth and a dull headache that threatened to crack her skull.

Sitting on the pile of rags her gaoler must have heaped into a rude pallet for her, she dropped her head onto her bent knees and pressed at her aching temples.

Why had she gotten so drunk last night? And why had she been so damned impulsive? If she'd only bided her time, she might have been able to think of a better way to prevent Miriel's wedding. A cleverer way. One that didn't entail trying to murder the bridegroom in his sleep.

But now, as Helena languished, powerless, in the cursed cellar, no doubt poor Miriel stood trembling beside her churl of a groom, shyly murmuring the vows that would make her his chattel forever.

Helena shuddered. She'd caught a glimpse of Pagan Cameliard last night as he rose naked from his bed. The man was easily twice Miriel's size, broad of bone and thick of muscle. Forsooth, he'd vowed not to take Miriel against her will, but Helena didn't trust the Norman. And when she imagined her innocent sister being mauled by such a brute, she felt sick.

"Shite!" she barked in frustration, wincing as the oath sent sharp pain streaking through her head.

If only she hadn't swilled so much wine.

If only she hadn't tripped over that meddlesome Colin du Lac.

If only, she mused with grim villainy, she hadn't missed with her dagger.

She pressed her closed eyes with the heels of her hands. She knew better than to think she could have committed cold-blooded murder, drunk or not. Fierce warrior she might be, but she was no assassin. Even if she *hadn't* tripped and gone sprawling across Pagan's bed, she'd have found some excuse not to stab him.

But the Normans had caught her with a knife in her hand and bloodlust in her eyes. Now she'd never convince them she was both incapable and inculpable.

She shivered as she remembered Colin's words. *'Tis treason. You should hang for that.*

Her hand went involuntarily to her throat. Surely 'twas an idle threat. A foreigner couldn't simply ride up to a Scots castle, marry the lord's daughter, and then execute her sister. True, once Pagan wed Miriel, he'd become steward of Rivenloch, a position of significant power, especially considering Lord Gellir's sadly lapsing wits of late. But the three sisters had managed the keep well enough without their father's help. They didn't need Pagan's help either. And they certainly didn't need him to, as his first stewardly obligation, hang her for treason.

But even if he didn't drag her to the gallows, Pagan had left her in the clutches of his partner in perfidy, Colin du Lac. Already the man had threatened her with bodily harm. Already he'd hinted at chastisements of a lingering nature. And last night, wrestling her down the stairs, the cur had put vile hands upon her, clutching at her breast as if she were a harlot for the taking.

She hadn't trusted the knave from the moment she'd glimpsed him at supper, his green eyes sparkling with devilry, his black hair as irreverently overgrown and riotous as his humor, his lips subtly curved with ever-present amusement. He was cocky, the Norman was, and brazen and sly, the kind of man who felt he was entitled to whatever he desired. He'd already helped himself to Rivenloch's wine and hearth.

She'd be damned if he'd help himself to her.

She narrowed her eyes at the door, as if she could burn a hole through it and sear him on the other side. Of course, he wasn't there. By now everyone would have gathered at the chapel in the courtyard to attend the wedding.

Muttering a soft oath, she rose slowly to her feet to scour the dim cellar, looking for something, *anything,* she could use to free herself.

The room to which he'd brought her was naturally the one stocked with utterly useless items—chests with broken hinges, stools with broken legs, dusty bottles and crockery and vials with naught in them, cracked pots, torn parchment, and scraps of cloth too small and worn to be used for anything other than polishing one's dagger or wiping one's arse.

Her belly growled in complaint, and she scowled, rubbing her hand over the sunken spot.

One door farther along the passageway was a storeroom filled with cheese and bacon, oats and salted fish. Beyond that was a cellar packed with sugar, spices, and sweetmeats. But, of course, the Norman had locked her in the room with no food.

Mayhap, she thought sullenly, he planned to starve her to death.

She eyed the generous crack at the bottom of the door, where faint light streamed in, taunting her. Then she frowned. If she could slip her arm through that crack . . . somehow lift the bolt out of its latch . . .

She'd need a sword or a long stick, but it just might be possible.

Revived by hope, she dropped to the floor to peer under the door, then inched her hand through the crack. But though she pushed and strained, she couldn't squeeze past her elbow.

"Ballocks!"

She scraped her arm back in and tried another spot. The floor was uneven. Mayhap the crack was wider elsewhere.

But again her arm jammed.

Twice more she tried, earning naught more than a red and abraded forearm for her efforts.

Then as she squinted under the far left edge of the

door, she spied some small object lying on the floor. 'Twas too dark to tell what it was or even if 'twas within her reach. But the possibility that it might be edible convinced her to make the attempt.

Using her left arm this time and pressing her cheek to the cold floor of the cellar, she stretched as far as she could, patting the ground with splayed fingers, trying to locate the object, to no avail.

With a groan of pain and effort, she managed another inch, and her middle finger contacted something cold and hard. Breathless with triumph, she scrabbled at the thing until she managed to maneuver it closer. A series of flicks and urging finally edged the object near enough to grasp. And when her hand closed at last about the familiar contours, she smiled, forgetting all about her aching head.

Colin shook his head as he made his way back down the cellar steps. This day had been strange indeed. Awakening early, he'd checked the bolt on the storeroom, then left to help Pagan prepare for his wedding. And what a wedding it had been, with thunder and lightning cracking the sky and rain pelting the earth with a vengeance, the bride's handmaiden a shriveled, unmannerly crone from the Orient, the bride's father an addled old man with the bearing of a Viking invader, and the bride . . .

That was the biggest surprise of all. And to Colin's amazement, Pagan didn't seem to mind in the least that he'd wed the wrong sister.

As if all *that* weren't enough excitement for one morn, Rivenloch's guards had spotted an army approaching on the horizon, an army Deirdre was convinced was English. Of course, Colin and Pagan knew better. 'Twas none other

than the Knights of Cameliard. But Pagan had chosen not
to reveal that fact to the Scots. He'd decided to use their
arrival as a drill, a test of Rivenloch's defenses.

And now Colin had been sent to summon Helena, who,
Deirdre informed him, was the second-in-command of
the guard.

A woman in command of the guard. He shuddered.
What would the Scots think of next?

Of course, he had no intention of setting Helena free.
He wasn't about to put the fighting force of Rivenloch in
the hands of a wench who'd tried to slay his captain. She
was likely to order her archers to open fire upon the
Knights of Cameliard.

But though he had no plans to release the bloodthirsty
damsel yet, he couldn't let her languish uncomforted in
her gaol. She was but a maid, after all, young and foolish.
Besides, she was doubtless suffering this morn from
pangs of overindulgence, remorse, and hunger. He smiled
as he unwrapped the still-warm, fragrant loaf of currant-
studded bread he'd snatched from the kitchen. He could at
least assuage *one* of her discomforts.

Musing over what his compassion might earn him in
the way of thanks, he rapped upon the cellar door. "Good
morn, little Hel-fire. Are you awake?"

There was no response.

He pressed his ear against the oak. "Lady Helena?"

She suddenly threw herself against the door with a thud.

Startled, he jerked back.

"Help," she wheezed through the crack in the door.
"Help . . . please . . . I can't brea— . . . can't brea— . . ."

Alarmed, he let the bread drop to the floor, then lunged
forward, shoving the bolt from the latch and flinging the

door open. His heart knifing painfully in dread, he quickly scanned the dim room.

She had flattened herself against the wall, and as he stepped in, before he even had time to regret his lack of caution, she charged at him, pinning him against the wall with a knife at his throat.

"Make a sound, and I'll cut you," she bit out. "Move a muscle, and I'll cut you. Even *think* of resisting, and I swear I'll spill your reeking Norman blood all over the cellar floor."

Still reeling in shock, he muttered, "Where did you get—"

He felt a sharp sting as the point dug into his flesh. He winced. Jesu, the wench was serious, as serious as her sister, who'd marked Pagan with her blade yesterday.

"'Tis your own dagger, fool," she purred.

The dagger he'd dropped on the stairs last night— somehow she'd acquired it.

With her free hand, she irreverently searched him, patting him about the waist and hips, finding and discarding his eating knife, leaving him the coin he'd won off her father last night. Under different circumstances, Colin might have enjoyed such aggressive handling by a woman. But there was naught seductive or affectionate about her touch, and to his chagrin, he began to sense, as incredible as it seemed, he might indeed be at the wench's mercy.

Men could be such half-wits, Helena thought, tucking a hastily scratched missive into her bodice as she prodded the Norman forward, her knife at his ribs. They always assumed women were defenseless creatures, devoid of muscle and slow of wit. Helena was neither. Aye, like many women, she was impulsive, but this time that impulsiveness would bear sweet fruit.

"Slowly," she told him as he climbed the stairs. She needed time to assess the situation in the great hall before they emerged.

To her surprise, as she peered out from the stairwell, she saw the household was alive with activity. Men took up arms. Miriel rounded up the women and children. Servants rushed to and fro with arms full of candles and cheese and blankets. Preparations were taking place for something far more serious than simple wedding festivities. Forsooth, it looked as if the castle prepared for siege.

Before the Norman could make his presence known, she hauled him back by his tunic and pressed him against the wall of the stairwell, placing the point of the dagger against the vein pulsing in his neck. She drew close enough to hiss into his face, "What's happened?"

Despite the fact that she held his life in her hands, his eyes glittered with some secret amusement, and one side of his lip curved unbelievably upward, as if he was enjoying every moment. Which incensed her.

"Speak!" she snarled.

He complied. "An army is approaching."

Her heart raced. "An army. What army?"

He hesitated.

"*What* army?" she demanded.

"The Knights of Cameliard."

She frowned. Could it be true? Did Pagan *truly* command a company of knights? Deirdre and she had speculated that his title was a ruse, that Pagan was a mere knight-errant with neither land nor coin, who had somehow convinced the King to wed him to a Scotswoman with both. "Pagan's knights?"

"Mm."

But Rivenloch was preparing for battle. Why would the Knights of Cameliard assail the keep wherein their commander resided? Unless . . .

Perchance Pagan wasn't content with mere *stewardship* of Rivenloch. Perchance the devil intended to claim the castle for his own.

She cursed under her breath as she realized the truth. "They're laying siege."

Colin was silent, but his eyes twinkled darkly.

This put a twist in her plans.

She'd intended to steal Colin away and hold him hostage at the cottage in the woods until Pagan agreed to annul his marriage to Miriel. But if Cameliard's men were attacking Rivenloch, she was needed here to command the men-at-arms.

On the other hand, she might be able to use her hostage for an even greater purpose.

How valuable was Colin du Lac to the people of Cameliard?

She gave him a quick, assessing perusal. He was undeniably sturdy and strong, long of bone and broad of shoulder, probably a competent fighter. But he was also a pretty-faced, cocksure, poetry-babbling knave, the kind of varlet the Scots scorned. Mayhap the Normans measured a man's value in different terms. If so, was Colin du Lac worth the return of Rivenloch?

'Twas a risky wager, but one she was compelled to take.

"We're going on a journey," she decided.

He lifted his brows. "Now? But—"

"Hist!" She raised the blade a notch, forcing him to lift his chin. "You will not speak again until I grant you leave. We're going to walk through the great hall, across the courtyard, and out the front gates. Take care you do not draw attention to us in any way, for I'll have this dagger at your ribs, and I warn you, if you disobey, you'll not be the first man to feel my blade pierce his flesh."

In the midst of all the chaos, 'twas fairly easy to skirt along the edge of the great hall undetected. Colin gave her no trouble, aside from making small grunts of pain when her blade dug a little too deeply into his side. Even crossing the courtyard wasn't difficult, though she was dismayed to find the weather unfavorable for travel. Rain had made the ground soggy, and the brooding clouds looked as fitful as a lad with a bloodied knee, deciding whether or not to cry. Neither of them had a cloak, and she wished she'd thought to snatch the fur coverlet from the cellar.

The challenge was getting out the front gates. As the Rivenloch guards had been trained for siege, once the cows and sheep were gathered inside the castle walls, the gates were secured. Thinking quickly, she called up to the guard manning the portcullis. "Open the gates! Three of Lachanburn's cows have wandered onto our land. We'll bring them inside as well."

The guard nodded. Lachanburn was Rivenloch's closest neighbor, and the relationship between the two clans was one part alliance, two parts rivalry. The one thing they battled over with almost childish glee was cattle. Thus the guard would be understandably glad to raise the portcullis in the hopes of acquiring a few more of Lachanburn's cows.

Once outside the gates, Helena steered her captive

quickly toward the woods. Already an impressive number of Normans crested the hill. She didn't dare risk discovery. One slip of vigilance on her part, and she could just as easily become a hostage for the Normans.

At last, under cover of the thick pines and oaks of Rivenloch's shadowy forest, she felt safe.

'Twas tempting to remain at that vantage point at the verge of the woods, to spy on Cameliard's army, to watch what transpired. But for leverage, she had to go deeper into the forest, to a place only her sisters knew. She nudged him onward. "Move."

A sly smile stole across his face. "Ah, I see now." He clucked his tongue. "You know, if you wished to ravish me in the dark of the woods, all you had to do was—"

"Quiet!"

The last thing Helena needed was the distraction of a pompous Norman who believed he was God's gift to womankind. Perchance Colin du Lac's dancing eyes and beguiling grin seduced other maids, but Helena was not a woman easily fooled by such transparent ploys.

She shoved him forward.

A path wound through the woods, one the sisters kept carefully hidden. Leaf fall camouflaged the trail, and in places, overgrowing branches obscured the passage. But the Rivenloch sisters had used it for as long as Helena could remember.

The abandoned crofter's cottage at its end, roughly five miles hence, had served over the years as both a rendezvous and a refuge.

They'd traveled perhaps two hundred yards when she pulled her captive up short. She needed to take one more precaution. "Lie down."

The varlet's eyes sparked with mischief as he arched a brow at her command. To her credit, she resisted the urge to smack the smirk off his face.

"On your belly, with your hands behind you."

He gazed at her with lusty amusement. "As you wish."

While he lay helpless on the ground, she rummaged beneath her surcoat and used the knife to cut two strips of cloth from the bottom of her linen underdress. One of them she twisted and knotted about his joined wrists, roughly enough to make him grimace.

"Easy, wench. No need for brutality," he chided, adding smoothly, "I'm quite amenable to your pleasure."

"'Tis *not* a matter of pleasure, sirrah."

This time there was a hint of sarcasm in his voice. "In such sweet company, who could *not* find pleasure?"

She didn't care for the speculative gleam in his eyes. She wound the second cloth about his head, securing it with a knot at the back, effectively blinding him. In the event he escaped, she didn't want him to know the path home.

He clucked his tongue. "Now you deprive me of the sight of you. Alas, you cut me to—"

"Up!" She had no time for his flowery nonsense. What she'd heard about Normans was true. They were as soft as babes, with dulcet tongues and downy curls and perfumed cheeks.

She wrested him to his feet, then stole a clandestine whiff of him. He *did* smell different from the men of her country, but 'twas neither womanly nor unpleasant. Indeed, an agreeable spice lingered on his skin, like the cinnamon Miriel sprinkled on apple coffyns.

"If you'd only let me know your desire . . . ," he murmured coyly.

The man was incorrigible. "If you continue your prattle, my desire will be to gag you as well."

"Fine," he said with a sigh of surrender. "I'll rest my tongue." Which he did, though the knave's suggestive smile never completely faded from his face.

Colin was mystified. Norman women never asked him to be quiet. They *loved* to talk. And they were always charmed by his flirtations. Every damsel he encountered, from crinkle-faced crones to babes in the cradle, giggled and cooed over Colin's flattering turn of a phrase.

What was wrong with this wench?

She dug her fingers into his upper arm, maneuvering him forward, and he shuffled blindly through the leaves, his gait awkward.

'Twas the Scots, he decided. They must all be mad. Their men wore skirts, and their maids carried swords. And *this* maid apparently had a heart as impenetrable as armor.

Not only was she unrepentant of her violence of last night, but she seemed bent on continuing it. He grunted as she poked his ribs yet again with the dagger. God's blood, did the maid plan to administer a slow death of a thousand nicks?

As they wandered farther into the forest, Colin discovered his other senses grew sharper. Now he could hear Helena's labored breathing, her light footfall, the soft rustle of her skirts. He took a breath of cool, rain-pure air. Layered over the pungent fragrance of pine was the faint aroma of his captor, an indefinable scent that was simply clean and womanly, as unpretentious as the maid herself. The place where she gripped his arm grew warm, from a touch as deceptively intimate as a lover's.

They traveled for what seemed like miles without speaking, until Colin began to wryly wonder if she might be marching him all the way back to Normandy.

Helena's abduction of him had been startling at first, then amusing. But now the wench was taking things too far. If they strayed much farther afield, the people of Rivenloch and Cameliard alike would begin to worry about them, with good reason. After all, bound and blind-folded, Colin was unable to protect the damsel from whatever bands of miscreants lurked in the Scots wilds.

Deciding he'd had enough, he pulled suddenly against her grip, halting in his tracks, earning himself an acciden-tal jab of her knife. "Jesu!"

"What?" she demanded.

"I would speak."

She sighed heavily. "Go on."

Charm didn't work on her. Perchance candor would. "What exactly do you intend, my lady?"

"'Tis not your concern."

"On the contrary, I'm the one at the point of your dag-ger. *My* dagger."

"True."

"So?"

Her smug delight was almost palpable. "You, sirrah, are going to be my hostage."

If those words had come at another time, they would have stirred his blood. Abductor and hostage. It sounded like one of the games of seduction he enjoyed—the stable lad and the milkmaid, the sea reiver and the buried trea-sure, the Viking and the virgin. But he suspected this was no game. "Your hostage?"

"Aye," she gloated. "If it should happen that the

Knights of Cameliard seize Rivenloch, I intend to hold your life as forfeit against its return."

For a moment, he was struck speechless as he digested her words. Then he realized her mistake. "You think the knights have come to seize the castle."

"What do you mean, I *think?*" she snapped. "You said yourself they were attacking."

"I did not."

"You did!"

He shook his head. "I said they were *approaching*. You assumed they were attacking."

"What?" she whispered. He could almost hear her Scots blood beginning to simmer.

"Curious. Your sister, too, made the same mistake. 'Twas she who gave the order to prepare for siege."

The point of the dagger suddenly jabbed under his chin, and he flinched in surprise. Perchance, he thought as his vein pulsed beneath the cold steel, he should not have told the warrior maid the truth.

~~

# Chapter 3

HELENA'S HEAD WAS throbbing again. "They're not attacking," she reiterated.

"Hardly," he said with a smirk. "Why would they attack? We came to form an alliance."

She ground her teeth. The Normans had been here but a day, and already they were turning her world awry.

She narrowed her eyes while her brain worked furiously. If the Normans weren't attacking, then she didn't need Colin du Lac to ransom Rivenloch after all.

But that didn't mean she couldn't continue with her original plan to save Miriel. The ransom note she'd scratched out in the storeroom was still tucked between her breasts. All she needed was a messenger.

"Come." She lowered the dagger and pulled on his arm. "I have another use for you." He lifted his lips in a speculative grin, but before he could open his mouth to make a bawdy suggestion, she pushed him forward. "Not a word!"

They had to hurry. The detour would add another hour to their journey, but with luck, she'd find a trusty messenger for her pains.

A solitary monk lived in a little cottage at the western edge of the woods, a meek servant of God who made daily rounds of the outlying crofts, caring for the sick, blessing the poor, living on what the crofters provided him. Helena knew she could rely upon him to deliver her missive.

They quickly traversed the forest, following a narrow deer trail that wound through the firs and fern toward the monk's lodgings. As they hied along, Helena noted that her talkative prisoner had grown curiously subdued. Perchance he'd resigned himself to capture. Typical Norman. Forsooth, she wondered if they had any backbone at all. If it had been *her*, she would have gone kicking and bellowing all the way.

In hindsight, she should have suspected from his silence that something was afoot.

Just as she reached a small break in the trees where the sunlight had given birth to a patch of violets and cowslips, her captive stuck out his foot and tried to trip her.

She was agile enough to catch herself before she fell. But he had successfully dodged out of her dagger's reach and now twisted his head this way and that, trying to dislodge the blindfold as he shuffled awkwardly away from her and into the gorse ahead.

She cocked her hands on her hips. "Where the devil do you think you're going?"

He successfully manipulated the blindfold enough to peer beneath it with one glittering green eye. "Back."

She shook her head. "You'll have to go through me."

He sniffed and bent his knees, ready to charge. "I'd suggest you move aside."

In the next moment, he barreled forward.

She stood firm until the last possible moment, then sidestepped him. As he passed, she gave him a gentle lateral nudge.

His momentum was unstoppable. He stumbled over the brush and fell, hitting the sod shoulder first with a thud that made even Helena cringe.

"Bloody . . . ah!" he cried out, grimacing as he rolled off his shoulder.

She frowned. God's eyes, had he injured himself? She hoped not. Not that she cared if a Norman suffered a few bruises. But the last thing she needed was a hostage who required a physician.

He twisted to the side, then gasped. "My arm, I think it's . . ."

She glanced warily at his arm. "Broken?" It didn't seem to be. At least his elbow was bending the right way. Then again, he'd fallen with his arms bound behind him. He might have thrown his shoulder out of joint. She'd done that once. 'Twas horribly painful.

He tried to sit up, then spewed out a foul oath, dropping back down to the ground.

She sighed in self-disgust. Ruthless warrior she might be, but she had no appreciation for needless suffering. She supposed she'd have to cut him loose and make him a sling or something. While he gasped in pain, she approached, wincing in involuntary empathy, tucking the knife into her belt. "Lie still. I'll see if anything's bro—"

Before she could hunker down beside him, his legs swung suddenly around, catching her behind the knees to sweep her off her feet and knocking her backward into the wildflowers. As her elbows banged into the dirt and her skirt flew up over her head, shock took the breath from her.

God, she *hated* the Norman.

For a moment she lay stunned, trying to imagine how she'd fallen into his trap. Then she shook off the absurdity of the moment like a hound shaking off water. Angrily flailing her arms to free herself from the tangle of her skirts, she scrambled up, spit a lock of hair from her mouth, and drew the dagger.

He saw her coming, but he didn't have enough time to get his knees under him. His one visible eye widened as she stalked toward him with murder in her eyes, and he struggled for purchase.

Before he could rise, she planted a foot upon his buttocks, pressing him back down to the ground. "A broken arm? *I'll* give you a broken arm."

He squinched his eye shut and braced for impact.

She had no intention of breaking his arm, of course. She wasn't the kind of warrior who would wound a man when he was down, despite what he thought. Besides, though she was furious at him for outwitting her, she was more furious with herself for being outwitted.

"Never mind," she muttered. "I have no stomach for cowardly caterwauling. Besides, 'twould render you *completely* useless as a hostage."

Colin frowned, humiliated by the fact that this imp of a maid had her boot planted on his arse like some hunter gloating over a kill. He'd almost outfoxed her. Almost.

If only he'd been able to shake the blindfold completely free.

If only he'd had time to maneuver himself to a crouch.

If only, he thought ruefully, he hadn't been paralyzed by the sight of Helena's long, luscious legs splayed haphazardly as she fell, revealing the tantalizing fact that she wore not a stitch underneath her skirt.

While she continued to disparage his worth, he heard someone coming down the path. Mayhap 'twas The Shadow, that nefarious woodland outlaw she'd spoken of at supper, the one who moved at the speed of a devil, leaving his victims stunned and penniless. Or perchance 'twas one of those infamous Highlanders, a half-naked savage come to rape and pillage. Whoever 'twas lurking in the remote depths of the forest, chances were he was up to no good.

Colin's chivalrous instincts rose to the surface. Despite their current circumstances, despite Helena's treachery, despite the fact that an ignoble part of him longed to toss her over his knee and thrash the arrogance out of her, Colin was first and foremost a knight, sworn to protect ladies.

"Cut me free!" he hissed. "Someone's coming. Cut me free."

She lifted a dubious brow.

"'Tis no trick, I swear, my lady. Cut me free, and I'll defend you."

"Defend me?" she scoffed. "*You'll* defend *me?*"

"Hurry," he said urgently. "Can you not hear? Someone comes."

"I hear," she assured him with what Colin deemed inappropriate calm.

Mayhap he could frighten her into cutting him loose. "What if 'tis The Shadow?"

She shrugged. "Too noisy." Then she annoyed him greatly by hunkering down beside him and giving him a wink. "Don't worry, little one. I'll keep you safe."

The last person Colin expected to see ambling up the deer trail was a monk. But once he beheld the coarse brown cassock and tonsured head, he knew 'twas not trouble, but salvation that had arrived.

Quickly, before Helena could open her mouth and betray him, he blurted out, "Brother! Praise God, my prayers are answered."

The young monk had frozen on the path, looking much like a startled deer.

"I beseech you, kind brother, free me," Colin pleaded. "I fear this poor, misguided woman has mistaken me for another and intends to"—he affected a dramatic gulp—"slay me."

The monk glanced nervously between the two of them, blinking rapidly. "I beg your . . .?"

"She seems to be," Colin confided in a whisper, "addled."

He expected Helena to burst out in vehement protest.

She didn't. Instead, she gave him a condescending smirk, then rose to face the monk. "Brother Thomas. How nice to see you."

Colin's hopes dropped with his shoulders.

"I know you," the monk said, bobbing his head upon his lanky neck. "Lady . . . Lady . . ."

"Helena."

"Aye. You're one of the ladies of the keep. But what . . ." The monk's mouth gaped as if he wanted to say more but couldn't quite find the words.

"I need your help," she purred.

Her entreaty seemed to bring the man to life, as if she'd

uttered some sorcerer's incantation. The monk straightened his narrow shoulders. "I am God's servant and yours, my lady."

Colin rolled his eyes, silently cursing the power beautiful women had, even over men of the cloth.

She fished in the top of her bodice and withdrew a scrap of parchment. "I'd like this delivered to Rivenloch, to my sister, Lady Deirdre."

The monk reached for the missive.

"Do not," Colin warned.

To his satisfaction, the monk hesitated.

"Go on," Helena coaxed, waggling the paper like a bone in front of a dog.

"If the lady means me no ill, then why has she bound me?" Colin asked. "And why does she wield a dagger?" The monk frowned in confusion. Colin used that advantage to further his cause. "I tell you, she means to kill me."

He expected Helena to beguile the priest then by feigning innocence or bursting into false tears or lamenting the state of Colin's diseased mind. The last thing he expected was for her to tell the truth.

"Aye, I'll kill him," she said evenly, "if this missive doesn't reach my sister."

The monk looked as shocked as Colin felt.

"And if you force me to commit murder, Brother Thomas," she told him, "and my eternal soul is forever damned, I fear 'twill be upon your head."

Colin's jaw dropped. Her convoluted logic was dizzying. For a long moment, neither man could reply.

"Oh, n-nay, my lady," the monk sputtered at last. "I'll take it. There's no n-need for you to . . . to . . . no need for you to hurt him at all." He glanced at Colin with a worrisome forced smile that was anything but reassuring.

Colin scowled as the monk snatched the parchment from Helena's hand.

"God . . . God bless you, my lady," the monk said with a nervous dip of his head. As he skirted by Colin, he murmured, "And God save you, my lord."

Then the scrawny, useless man of the cloth scurried down the narrow path, taking Colin's best hope with him.

As Colin gazed after Brother Thomas in disbelief, Helena almost felt sorry for the bewildered Norman. After all, he'd made a valiant effort. He couldn't help it if his wits were no match for hers.

"That's done," she said, satisfied that Brother Thomas would deliver her message. She crouched to take hold of Colin's shoulder. "Let's go."

"Nay," he said, pulling away. "Not until you give me some answers."

She frowned. Did he truly think he was in a position to barter with her? Why could he not accept that he was at her mercy? Mayhap she'd not made herself clear. With the point of the dagger, she lightly flicked his earlobe. "You know, I could call Brother Thomas back," she mused. "'Tis not too late to send a token along with the missive." He stiffened visibly. "An ear . . . or a finger or . . ." She pretended to deliberate, letting her eyes course over his available features.

Then she noticed he was staring at her with that one exposed eye, as if he measured her, judged her, wagered upon her soul. And though he lay helpless upon the ground, completely at her mercy, it suddenly seemed he gazed with his glittering, perceptive, all-seeing eye, straight into her heart.

Unsettled, she reached out, yanking the blindfold back down.

He lifted his chin nobly, not an easy feat for one lying on one's belly. "You will do as you please, of course. But I think you should know, I have no tolerance for pain, so I'll probably scream like a stuck pig."

She lifted a brow.

"And bleed?" he continued. "I once pricked my finger on a thorn and bled for three days."

She'd never heard anything so absurd. "Three days," she drawled.

"Aye. But I'm willing to make a bargain with you, my lady, and save us both the trouble of disfiguring me."

A more ruthless woman would have sliced his ear off at once to show him how little trouble 'twas. But Helena was only savage when she was forced to be. And at the moment, with the Norman trussed up like a goose, she could afford to be merciful. Besides, though she hated to admit it, she was intrigued by his cunning. 'Twas rare she met a man so quick of wit.

"Indeed?" she said, stooping down beside him again. She hadn't noticed before, distracted by the gleam of his eyes, how pleasantly formed his mouth was. His lips looked soft, yet firm, and where they parted, she saw the white tips of his teeth, one in the front slightly askew, just enough to lend the brawny knight a vulnerable quality. His nose was perfectly sculpted as well, not too narrow, not too wide, with nostrils that flared as he awaited her reply.

"My lady?"

She gave her head a hard shake, scattering her errant thoughts. "You're hardly in a position to bargain, sirrah."

"Nonetheless, you seem a reasonable woman."

She raised both brows. No one called Helena reasonable. She was anything but reasonable. The Norman was either feebleminded or lying through his teeth. "Go on."

"If you answer one question, my lady, I'll cease fighting and come willingly with you."

"One question?"

"Aye."

"Ask it."

"If you don't intend to ransom me for Rivenloch, what is it you intend? What did the missive say?"

She blinked. Why should he care? 'Twould not alter his fate. 'Twas up to Pagan what happened to him. On the other hand, 'twas no great secret. And if Colin meant what he said, that he'd cooperate . . . "If I give you answer, you'll come with me willingly?"

"Aye."

"And you'll try no more trickery?"

"No trickery. I vow it upon my honor as a knight."

She smirked. Perchance he was not so clever as she imagined. 'Twas a bargain too good to pass up. She would give him naught, and he would give her everything.

"Very well," she said, sheathing her knife. "The note said, 'I have taken the Norman hostage. I will not return him until the marriage is annulled.'"

"What!"

She repeated, "'I have taken the Norman—'"

"Aye, I heard you, but what . . . how . . . ah, bloody hell . . ."

She chuckled smugly. "Now he'll *have* to give my sister back."

"He won't do it."

"Oh, I think he will."

The Norman's pleasantly formed mouth turned down at the corners. "You don't know Pagan Cameliard."

"And you don't know the Warrior Maids of Rivenloch."

He shook his head, as if some great jest had been played upon him, but he said no more.

She helped him to his feet, and they continued along the trail without speaking. True to his word, he went willingly, but for Helena, his silence cast a dark pall upon her rousing adventure.

With each mile they marched away from Rivenloch, Helena's sense of unease grew. Could Colin be right? What if he wasn't as valuable to Pagan as she assumed? What if Pagan deemed the loss of his man a reasonable price to pay for wedding the bride of his choice? What if he tore up the missive before Deirdre could see it? What if, God forbid, she never heard from her sister? How long would she have to wait in the woods? How long could she hold Colin hostage?

And most critical, how long could they survive without food?

Her belly was already grumbling when they finally reached the copse of gnarled oaks in which the cottage nestled. 'Twas sufficiently overgrown with ivy and moss and ferns that its walls appeared to be made of foliage, and in the deep shade of the leafy trees, the structure was hardly visible. The door of the dwelling sagged, and the pair of rotting shutters dangling over the sole window looked as if they might blow away at the slightest breeze.

The roof was more hole than thatch, but vines had climbed across to fill in the gaps, rendering the cottage relatively safe from the elements.

At one time the hovel had belonged to a crofter, and nearby was a clearing where barley had been planted. But that, too, had long since filled in with gorse and heather, wildflowers and weeds. Not far away, a spring trickled out of the hillside to become a brook, then a stream, then a rivulet, ultimately emptying into one of the twin lochs for which Rivenloch was named.

"We're here," Helena announced, stopping at the threshold of the cottage to remove Colin's blindfold.

Colin didn't know what he expected to see. A holy sanctuary perchance. Or a neighboring castle. Or the modest home of one of Helena's allies.

He certainly didn't expect a veritable hovel in the midst of the darkest part of the forest, a decrepit cottage that looked like it might harbor light-fearing goblins and wart-covered toads.

"Oh, this is lovely," he drawled.

Peeved at his sarcasm, Helena gave him a shove forward. "You'll be glad enough of its shelter when the wolves come, sirrah."

He scanned the garlands of ivy and fronds of fern and patches of moss smothering the walls and wondered if there were indeed walls beneath the foliage.

"I doubt any wolves would brave this hovel," he muttered.

"They may already be here," she said. Then she did something extraordinarily heroic, something that took him aback. Grabbing a fistful of his shirt to keep him within reach, she placed herself between him and the entrance and used the haft of the dagger to nudge the door open a crack. If a beast did lurk within, it would charge her first.

Which disturbed him greatly.

"Wait," he said. "Allow me."

"I don't think so." She shook her head. "I don't intend to lose my hostage to a charging boar."

"And I don't intend to lose my spurs for lack of chivalry," he insisted. "Besides, how much experience do you have in fending off wild animals?"

One side of her mouth curved up in a sly grin. "Including you?"

Under any other circumstances, he would have found that smile inviting. The fact that she'd called him an animal didn't bother him in the least. Women called him many things—knave, varlet, beast—always with affection. But this was neither the time nor the place for flirtation. Dangerous creatures might prowl beyond the door. And he wasn't about to use a lady as a shield against them.

"Cut my bonds and give me the knife. I can—"

Without warning, completely ignoring his directive, she gave the door a hard, reckless shove. It swung wide and slammed against the inner wall with a loud bang and a puff of plaster dust.

His jaw slackened. If there *was* a wild animal within, 'twould attack them after that alarming jolt.

Fortunately, all he heard from within was the skittering of tiny creatures fleeing the light. And aside from a couple of spiders that frantically scrambled up their damaged webs across the doorway, no beasts sprang from the shadows. But when Helena turned to assure him 'twas safe, he was so simultaneously horrified and livid that he couldn't speak.

Noting his apoplexy, she raised a challenging brow. "You Normans are not afraid of mice, are you?"

Colin was too shaken to reply. As Helena hauled him into the cottage, he had only one thought.

This woman was trouble.

She was careless and savage and far too daring for her own good. That kind of impulsiveness was going to get her killed. 'Twould likely get *him* killed as well.

"'Tisn't what you Normans are used to, with your perfumed pillows and silk sheets," she said with thinly veiled disgust as he surveyed the interior, "but 'twill suffice."

Perfumed pillows? Silk sheets? Colin had no idea what she was talking about. His bed was made with linen—coarse, plain linen—unless he was on campaign, and then he counted himself lucky to bed down on a flat spot with his cloak and a pallet of leaves. Where the wench got her ideas about Normans, he didn't know.

The inside of the cottage was surprisingly tidy. Though a thin layer of dust covered everything, the hard-packed dirt floor was strewn with yellow rushes, few vines grew between the cracks in the plaster walls, and the sparse furnishings in the room appeared sturdier than the lodging itself.

The hearth was stocked with split wood, and three iron cooking pots hung on a rod suspended above the fire. Beside the fireplace clustered a pail, a pitcher, a coil of rope, three cups, and a clay vessel full of spoons of various sizes. A three-legged stool stood watch over a small pine chest, and an empty lantern with a flint was suspended from the wall on a hook. Shoved against one wall was a wooden-frame rope bed furnished with a reasonably clean pallet. The exterior of the hovel might be overgrown, but someone had used the inside recently.

"Do you bring all your hostages here?" he asked her.

She smirked, then nodded toward the pallet. "Lie on the bed."

He shot her a lusty glance. "If you insist."

While he laid back awkwardly on his bound arms, she fetched the coil of rope from beside the hearth, slicing off four yard-long pieces.

She seized one of his ankles and began to tie it to the wooden leg of the bed. While he understood her desire to keep him prisoner, he didn't like the idea of being left defenseless.

"My lady, is this absolutely necessary?"

"I can't have my hostage escape."

"But what if there's a fire? What if wolves come? What if—"

"I told you before," she said, tying off the knot, "I need you alive. I'm not going to let anything happen to you."

He ground his teeth as she began to secure his other leg. He'd been raised to be self-reliant. 'Twas difficult enough for him to depend upon his fellow knights. But putting his trust in a woman, and an impetuous one at that . . .

"What if I give you my word that I won't escape?"

She leveled her gaze at him. "Your word? A Norman's word?"

"I kept my word to come willingly," he reasoned.

"You kept your word because I was still holding the knife."

She was only half-right. Once he'd given her his vow,

he'd never considered attempting escape, though there'd probably been a dozen opportunities to do so. He was, after all, a man of honor.

He twisted on the bed, trying to relieve the numbness in his hands, caught beneath him. She snatched his bound wrists and sliced the linen away, freeing his arms. But she was careful to return her weapon at his throat.

"Arms up," she said.

"I hope you're right," he grumbled, spreading his arms in compliance. "I hope your sister comes before thieves do."

She secured his right arm to the wood frame. "Let me worry about the thieves, Norman."

As she leaned over him to seize his left wrist, he was tempted to make one final attempt at escape. One unexpected blow of his fist could probably knock her senseless.

Two things stopped him.

The first was chivalry. Colin always treated women gently. He never raised his hand in anger to a maid. Indeed, he seldom raised his *voice* to a lady. The thought of intentionally hurting a woman was unconscionable.

But the second thing that gave him pause was the fact that as Helena reached across his body, she lost her footing on the rushes and stumbled forward against his chest. He stiffened, sure he'd feel the dagger plunge into his throat. Fortunately, her instincts were lightning-swift. She pulled back the blade before it could do damage.

But for one instant as she lay there, crushing his ribs, their eyes caught, and an awareness of mutual vulnerability passed between them. She could stab him. He could disarm her. Instead, they remained paralyzed at some curious impasse. And in that moment, as he gazed into her startled green eyes, unable to move, unable to breathe, he glimpsed, beneath her bravado and flippant manner, a gentle heart.

In the next moment, 'twas gone. She closed her eyes and her soul to him and pushed up off his chest with a dismissive frown.

Then she anchored his last hand.

Colin fought back mounting unease. 'Twas not the first time he'd been tied to a bed by a woman, but Helena was the first to make the knots inescapable. If anything happened, he'd be helpless to defend himself . . . or her.

Helena, her task completed, nodded in satisfaction. Sheathing her knife, she took four steps and sank onto the three-legged stool. She was still rattled from nearly stabbing her hostage. At least she tried to convince herself 'twas the source of her breathlessness. The fact that Colin's gaze had for a moment lost its mocking cast and seemed to glow with admiration had naught to do with the way her heart was racing.

"My lady, this is unwise and—"

"Hush." She didn't want to listen to his arguments. Now that her captive was secure, she could rest easy in the knowledge there would be no more excitement today.

Colin complied with her command and seemed to be absorbed in thought as he lay staring at the crumbling ceiling of the cottage. Now she would just sit and wait.

And wait.

And wait.

Her stomach growled loudly, and she glanced in chagrin to see if Colin had heard the sound. He had. Though his eyes never left the ceiling, the corners of his mouth turned up in amusement.

She scowled. "Mayhap if you'd locked me in a cellar with *food* . . ."

"My apologies," he said.

She chewed at her bottom lip. Lord, she was hungry. There were those who mocked her ravenous appetite, but they didn't realize how much fuel her warrior existence required. "Deirdre should send word before nightfall," she said, half to herself.

"And if she doesn't?"

Helena didn't want to think about it. In her impulsiveness, she'd brought no provisions. If they were forced to stay the night, in the morn she'd have to seriously reconsider her plans.

She continued to wait, as restless as a caged wildcat, prowling the small room, then plopping down upon the stool, roaming now and then to the window to peer through the sagging shutters, only to witness the shadows growing deeper and deeper.

By her twelfth trip to the window, she could see only the vague silhouette of the trees against the twilight sky. The air was heavy with evening mist, and she shivered against the chill. No one would come now. Though Helena was fearless when it came to the forest, cautious Deirdre never roamed the woods after dark.

She sighed, turning away from the window. She supposed they'd have to spend the night in the cottage, then.

She rummaged through the contents of the pine chest. There was a wool coverlet with moth holes in it, and this she tossed atop Colin. He had to spit part of it from his mouth, but the rest of it covered him from shoulders to shins. She dragged out the two remaining blankets, as threadbare as the first, and used one to make a mattress for herself on the floor beside the pallet, bunching straw beneath it.

'Twas a travesty, she thought, sleeping on the hard ground while her hostage took the pallet. But the bed frame was a more solid place to secure him than the walls of the hovel, which might collapse if he tugged on them with enough force.

Stretching out with her feet in the direction of Colin's head, she pulled the remaining coverlet over herself and watched the cottage slowly fade to dove gray, then to slate, then to ebony.

Just as she was about to give up on ever falling asleep, across the darkness, Colin whispered, "Are you awake?"

'Twas tempting not to answer him. She didn't want to hear him gloat about how he was right, that no one had replied to her missive.

But she was fitful and hungry and bored. Conversation would be a welcome respite from ennui. Even if it 'twas with a Norman.

"What do you want?"

"Tell me, Hel-fire, are you afraid of *anything?*"

She bristled at his pet name for her. "Aside from being stuck in a cottage with a chattering Norman all night?"

He laughed. "Aye, besides that."

"Fear is a waste of time."

"But surely you fear something."

She shrugged. "What is there to fear?"

"Wild beasts. The dark." He paused, then added pointedly, "Starvation."

She snorted. "Don't fret, Norman. I won't let us starve." She smirked in the dark. "Though you could stand to lose a bit of softness about the edges."

"Softness?" he blurted. "I am naught but muscle, you wicked wench, and you know it."

"Then how is it I was able to overcome you in the cellar?"

His laughter seemed to warm the room. "'Twas a clever ploy, little vixen, luring me into your lair that way."

She furrowed her brow, wanting to be irritated, but secretly pleased by his praise, which for once seemed genuine.

"Where did you learn such wiles?"

"Trafficking often with half-witted men," she said dryly.

"Ah."

As soon as she said the words, she regretted them, for her cutting remark silenced Colin. And as much as she claimed to despise the man, discourse with him was not unpleasant. He was a man of appreciable wit, even if most of it was wasted on fawning flattery. At supper, he'd seemed educated, well traveled, and somewhat interesting. And on a cold and empty night such as this, stimulating speech was welcome.

So after a lengthy silence, she relented and gave him a gentler reply. "My sister and I have always battled men of greater size and strength. We've learned to rely as much upon our minds as our muscle."

When he didn't answer at first, she suspected he might have drifted off.

Finally, he gave her a soft reply. "If your muscles are half as able as your mind, my lady, you must be a worthy foe indeed."

She was glad of the darkness, for his compliment brought a blush to her cheek. Surely 'twas just another piece of empty Norman flattery. Flustered, she felt the silence thicken again, and she searched for words to fill it. At last she grudgingly replied, "That trick with your shoulder . . . 'twas . . . 'twas clever as well."

His chuckle eased the tension. "That? 'Twas inspiration born of desperation. The fall was accidental."

She smiled. The poor fool probably *had* injured himself.

Quiet descended again, and she was sure this time her captive had settled into sleep. As the night lengthened and the stars wheeled slowly through the heavens, Helena's thoughts began to drift back to Rivenloch.

Had Deirdre received the missive in time? Would it serve to delay the consummation? Or was poor Miriel even now languishing in her marriage bed?

"You're restless," Colin murmured, startling her.

"Perchance because someone keeps waking me."

"What troubles you?"

How he'd guessed she was troubled and why she should disclose her most secret thoughts to her enemy, she couldn't fathom. But the truth seemed to slip off her tongue as easily as butter from a warm knife. "If he hurts her . . . if he harms her in any way . . ."

"Pagan? By the Rood, my lady, he is no ravager of women. Aye, he has a fierce reputation as a warrior, but all the maids claim he is the gentlest of lovers."

"All the maids?" Her mouth soured. "So my sister is wed to a philanderer?"

"Nay," he hastily replied. "Far from it. God's eyes, Pagan hasn't had half the women *I* have."

Helena rolled her eyes, a gesture completely wasted in the dark. "Ah. So you're a worse philanderer."

"Nay. I only meant—"

"And just how many women have you *had?* Do you notch your saddle for every—"

"Bloody hell! 'Tis not about me. 'Tis about Pagan." He sighed in exasperation as he tried to climb out of the pit he'd dug. "He's a good man, a better man than I am. And he's a man of his word. He swore to you last night he'd not take your sister against her will. He will not."

Helena wished she could believe that.

"I swear it on my own spurs," he added. "She won't be forced to do anything."

With that feeble assurance, Helena rolled onto her side and pulled the thin coverlet over her shoulders. But 'twas not worry for Miriel that kept her awake now. 'Twas the image of Colin counting the women he'd swived and the appalling fact that she should even care.

Finally, as the creatures of the night slowly emerged, the mice skittering along the cottage walls, the owls hooting from beyond the shutters, a lone wolf baying in the distance, she laid the dagger beside her head, falling asleep with one hand on the haft.

## Chapter 4

COLIN WOKE IN the quiet hours before dawn to the sound of Helena's breathing. 'Twas not exactly a snore or a shudder, but something between the two. The room was still as dark as the grave and cold enough to turn breath to mist.

His chivalrous heart went out to the shivering maid. Bending his head forward, he caught the edge of his coverlet in his teeth and, inch by torturous inch, dragged it off himself, until it finally fell atop her. There was a snort and a rustle as she woke enough to rearrange herself, then slipped back to sleep.

Meanwhile, he lay awake and shivered, wondering what the day would hold.

He was sure if Pagan intercepted Helena's missive, he'd think it a great jest that Colin was being held at the mercy of a wench. Pagan would be in no hurry to ride to his rescue, and Colin might languish here for days. Which, given the comeliness of his abductor, might not be a terrible thing.

But they were hardly provisioned to stay any length of time. She'd brought no food, and her only hunting weapon was his dagger. He had coin, but 'twould do them no good in the wilds of the woods.

Would she reconsider her demands? Could he convince her that Pagan would never agree to them? That while Pagan was not unreasonable, he was resolute? That he was a wise leader with Rivenloch's best interests at heart?

Any other woman, Colin would have had eating from his fingers with just a wink. But this maid was a challenge. She was no simpering bud to bloom at his touch. Helena was more akin to the thistle of Scotland, bright and lovely to look at but fraught with treacherous thorns.

Despite the cold, Colin drifted back to sleep, dreaming he searched for a prized purple thistle in a vast field of pale daisies.

He wakened some hours later when the door closed. 'Twas Helena, returning from outside. She must have gone to answer the call of nature, something he'd have to do soon.

Sunlight struggled through the forest flora now, enough filtering down through the patchy roof to lend a dim golden hue to the room. Emerging in the hazy glow, dressed in her surcoat of pale saffron, the Scots beauty looked as magnificent as Apollo, still warm from the chariot of the sun. She drew near, and he noticed she held something cupped in her hands.

"Morning," he mumbled, squinting to adjust to the daylight.

"I found a patch of strawberries," she said. "You'll need your strength for the walk back."

That brought him fully awake. "They've come?"

"Nay. But they will. Soon."

"Hm." He wished he had her optimism.

"Open," she said, bringing her hands close. The alluring fragrance of ripe berries made his mouth water.

They were as luscious as they smelled. As she dropped the tiny berries one by one into his mouth, like the adoring concubine of an Arabian prince, it took all Colin's will to resist lapping the sweet juice from her fingers.

"Deirdre should come by midmorn," she predicted.

Colin thought not. When Pagan successfully seduced a woman, as Colin was sure he had, she lay abed with him for hours.

Helena tucked another berry betwixt his lips, and he playfully nipped the tip of her finger, earning a scowl. As he crushed the strawberry between his teeth, he suddenly noticed that his coverlet had been returned to him. She must have replaced it before she went outdoors. He grinned. Little Hel-fire was not half as heartless as she pretended to be.

When she offered him another berry, he turned away. "You take the rest. You must be famished."

She wasted no time, wolfing down the handful with zeal.

"Let me ask you something, my lady." Now that her hunger was momentarily staved off, perchance she'd listen to reason. "If you win, if you have this marriage annulled, what do you hope to gain by it? After all, this alliance is decreed by your own King."

She smacked the juice from her thumb. "I don't think my little sister should be a pawn in the King's game."

"'Tis no game. 'Tis a true union. The Normans and the Scots *are* allies, you know."

"Nonetheless, 'tis not Miriel's place to be a sacrifice. She's too young and too—"

"Wait." Colin blinked. "Miriel. You said Miriel?"

"Aye, my sister."

He shook his head. "But Miriel did not wed Pagan."

Her eyes widened. "What?"

"She didn't wed him."

"What do you mean?"

"She. Did not. Wed him."

Understanding finally dawned in Helena's eyes, and she gave him a solid shove. "Why didn't you tell me this? You let me abduct you for naught?"

"*Let* you?"

"So Miriel is untouched. And Pagan is not steward of Rivenloch."

"Not exactly."

"What do you mean, not exactly?"

"Pagan *is* steward." He braced himself for another possible shove. "*Deirdre* married him."

"What?"

"Deirdre disguised herself as Miriel and wed Pagan."

A curious expression evolved on Helena's face, first shock, then outrage, then anger. "That conniving vixen! She planned this from the start. She got me drunk a-purpose and . . ."

"You're not pleased?"

"Nay, I'm not pleased!"

"But Miriel has been saved from wedding Pagan."

"'Twas *I* who was supposed to wed the bastard," she snarled.

"You?" He burst out laughing, which was a grave mistake.

Fire blazed in Helena's eyes, and she drew her dagger, brandishing it before his eyes. "Aye, me. What of it?"

"Naught," he said, making a poor attempt to control his laughter. "Only . . ."

"Only what?" she bit out.

He could have flattered her, told her she was far too beautiful and sweet to be wasted on Pagan. He could have. He *should* have, considering she held a sharp blade not three inches from his chin. But Helena was bright. She'd smell his deception in an instant. He'd have to tell her the truth, or at least a diplomatic version of the truth.

"Pagan likes his women more . . . malleable. Weak-willed. Weak-kneed. Weak-minded."

"Hmph."

"Neither of you would be content in such a marriage."

"'Tis not necessary to be content. I'm certain Deirdre will not be so." She sheathed her knife and backed away again. "And if Pagan believes for one moment she is weak-willed . . ."

Colin frowned. The last time he'd seen Pagan and Deirdre together, they'd been arguing over castle defenses. Perchance Helena was right. Perchance they'd have an unhappy marriage. But he didn't think so. 'Twould not take much for that spark of rivalry to flare into a heart-consuming fire.

Suddenly he realized that with Miriel saved, Helena no longer needed a hostage. "Does this mean we can return now?"

"Return? Nay. I would still have the marriage annulled."

"But why?" Colin was beginning to see why King David had sent the Knights of Cameliard to take over the keep. He doubted the three rivaling sisters could stop quibbling long enough to agree on a way to lower the portcullis.

"Because *I* intend to wed him." Helena sniffed. "'Twas supposed to be *my* sacrifice."

"'Sacrifice.'" Colin shook his head. "Where we come from, Pagan Cameliard is considered a prize."

"Mayhap to a crofter's wide-eyed daughter."

He quirked up the corner of his lip and narrowed his eyes, goading her mercilessly. "Oh, nay," he said, nodding. "I see now. You've secretly grown fond of the warrior captain and want him for yourself."

Her mortified shudder was priceless. "You're mad. Why would I willingly wed a . . . a . . ."

"Norman?"

She shuddered again.

"Tell me, my lady, why do you hate Normans so?"

She smirked. "We won't be here long enough to count the ways."

"You're a cruel wench," he said, clucking his tongue. "Very well, tell me just *three* things you hate about Normans."

She sighed. "Normans are soft. They're spoiled." Her eyes slitted spitefully. "And they have no ballocks."

Helena expected *that* would chip through the Norman's cheerful demeanor. Mayhap now she'd see his composure crack.

She was wrong.

He chuckled. "Indeed? And how many Normans have you known?"

Her brows converged in a frown. "Your reputation precedes you."

"You've never actually met a Norman, then." His eyes sparkled with amusement. "Before me."

"What is your point?"

"You *do* know the Normans conquered the Saxons?"

Her scowl deepened.

"And that your King David calls upon Normans to fight for the Scots?"

She fumed.

"Oh, aye," he continued, "we're quite renowned for our—"

"Perfumed hounds," she blurted out.

"What?" After a stunned silence, laughter bubbled out of him, and though 'twas at her expense, the sound made the dark cottage seem brighter.

"I know all about Normans," she grumbled testily. She'd heard tales from Scots travelers who claimed Normans were so soft they couldn't grow a proper beard, that they dined on naught but sweetmeats and subtleties, and that they scented everything from their pillows to their animals. 'Twas not difficult to believe, given Colin's blithe manner, though she noted that the black stubble shading his jaw this morn contradicted at least one of the rumors.

Once the knave's laughter subsided, the smile he gave her was gentle. "Ah, my lady, you know little about Normans, and you know naught about *me.*"

His smile was disarming. She raised her chin defensively. "I know that you're arrogant and vain and, oh, aye, philandering," she said, reminding him of his boast.

He winced. "I'm really not philandering. And I do need to dispel that myth for you, my sweet." He frowned. "At the moment, however, I'm afraid I have a more pressing need."

She folded her arms in challenge. She wasn't about to fall prey to one of his tricks again. "Indeed?"

"A *pressing need?*" he said pointedly, raising his heavy brows.

She stared at him, waiting.

"Bloody hell, wench," he muttered. "I have to *piss.*"

Her arms fell out of their fold, and she felt a blush heat her cheeks. Of course. Here was another thing she hadn't considered when she'd become an abductor. She'd expected she could just tie him up and be done with him until Deirdre arrived. It hadn't occurred to her that she'd be responsible for his human needs. What would she do now?

As if he read her thoughts, he said, "You could bring me a chamber pot, but since you've bound my hands, I might need some . . ." He gave her a wink. "Help."

To her annoyance, her face grew even hotter. 'Twas not as if she'd never seen a naked man. By the Rood, she practically lived in the armory, where men stood about in all manner of undress. But the thought of this stranger, this *Norman* . . .

"Mayhap," she threatened, "I'll just let you piss your trews."

He shrugged an eyebrow. "I suppose you may. But I shudder to think what penance Pagan will have you pay if you treat his favorite knight so cruelly."

"'Twill not be up to him. He'll no longer be steward."

"Hm. So you say."

Helena's lips twisted with displeasure. 'Twas another thing she hadn't anticipated in a hostage—having to listen to his opinions. "Deirdre *will* come. And the marriage *will* be annulled."

"I still need to piss," he said dryly.

She glowered at him as if he'd intentionally planned this inconvenience. But she knew 'twas not so.

Inspired, she drew her dagger. "See that knothole in the chest?"

Perplexed, he said cautiously, "Aye."

With a lightning-quick flick of her wrist, she sent the blade skimming through the air to lodge in the exact center of the knothole. Then she looked to gauge his reaction.

He whistled low. "Impressive."

She crossed to retrieve the weapon. "I can pin a coney at five yards," she told him. "You won't be that far away, and you'll never be out of my sight."

She cut his wrists free, letting him untie his own ankles while she stood with her dagger poised. Then she made him walk slowly out of the cottage to a patch of gorse.

She stood two yards back while he turned away to untie his trews, jerking them down enough to relieve himself. What made her blush was not the loud trickle upon the sod. Nor the fact that a Norman pissed on Scots soil. What flushed her cheeks with warmth was the small measure of hip he revealed as he did so, firm with muscle and the same tawny color as the rest of him, and the brief glimpse of his cock nestled in fine black curls as he fastened his trews again. And what truly unnerved her was the fact that the forbidden sight made her heart race.

Prickly with distress, she prodded him back to the cottage at the point of her dagger.

"I'm grateful, my lady," he said with a sardonic grin as they passed through the door. "I'm sure Pagan will be lenient with you for your kindness."

She frowned as she sat Colin on the floor to tie his hands behind him, then secured one ankle to the base of the bedpost so he couldn't wander far.

"Perchance if you found something more for me to eat," he suggested, "Pagan would be even more merciful."

She didn't tell him that was exactly what she'd planned. She didn't appreciate his manipulation. And she *really* didn't relish the possibility that he might be right, that Pagan wouldn't ransom him after all. The wretched man had sown seeds of doubt in her mind, and now she couldn't shake the suspicion that they might be sentenced to this hovel for longer than she'd anticipated. Worse, Deirdre might be forced to tell Pagan where they were, and he'd come for her himself.

Such dismal thoughts dogged her from the cottage to the patch of brush fifty yards away, where she crouched beside a narrow trail of bent grass, dagger in hand, waiting for a coney to appear.

As far as Pagan was concerned, she was a traitor to the King. And now she'd complicated matters by holding his man hostage. If things didn't work out the way she'd planned, if conniving Deirdre refused to annul the marriage, which was likely, considering she'd sacrificed herself for Miriel, then Helena would be held accountable for her misdeeds. And one of those misdeeds was treason.

Despite fingers made shaky with doubt, Helena managed to kill breakfast within an hour. When it came to coneys, she was the best hunter at Rivenloch. And now, she thought as she flung the limp carcass over one shoulder and hefted the pail she'd filled earlier at the stream, at least one of her problems was solved.

In the cottage, while Colin watched her from his spot on the floor, she made a fire on the hearth and skinned and cleaned the coney, skewering it on a dead branch she'd picked up in the forest. Soon the aroma of roasting meat filled the room, and her belly began to growl in earnest.

As she held the coney above the fire, she reflected again on her options regarding Colin and Pagan and the King. Even if the worst possible thing happened, if Deirdre refused the annulment and Pagan retained his stewardship, surely he wouldn't do something as rash as executing the sister of the bride. Christ's bones! She'd been drunk. That was obvious. And she'd done what she'd done in defense of her sister, not in defiance of the King. Surely anyone with half a brain . . .

"Pardon me."

She glanced over at Colin. A furrow of worry lined his brow.

"The coney," he said. "'Tis too near the fire."

He was right. She'd absently let the branch droop too low. She lifted it again.

Still staring at the flames, she murmured, "The other night, the night I came into your chamber, you know I was besotted."

"Oh, aye, well and truly besotted."

"So besotted I shouldn't be held accountable for my actions." At his silence, she leveled her gaze at him.

A slow, calculating grin bloomed on his face. "That depends." Then he glanced sharply at the fire. "Take care!"

She pulled the coney up out of the coals. It had a black smudge on one side, no more. Fat dripped onto the fire with a sizzle. She tried to focus on the hearth. "You wouldn't execute me."

Colin gazed at the breathtaking Scots warrior, fascinated by the curious blend of strength and vulnerability in her bearing. She hadn't asked a question. She'd made a statement. But clearly 'twas triggered by uncertainty.

She had cause to doubt him. He'd made some awful threats the night he'd waylaid her, threats about keeping her on a leash until he was ready to hang her for treason.

'Twas tempting to assuage her fears, to confess that he'd spoken in the heat of the moment, to let her know he was anything but brutal when it came to women. And yet it better served his purposes, considering that he was currently at her mercy, to make her believe he was capable of anything.

"You *should* be executed," he said, "if you refuse to do as the King wills."

"But *you* wouldn't hang me."

He didn't answer, captivated by the sight of her lovely profile against the flickering fire.

"Would you?" she asked, turning to him with eyes like liquid emeralds.

With every fiber of his being, he longed to shout nay and ease her anxiety. But her uncertainty was the best tool of negotiation he possessed.

"I would have to weigh the evidence," he said. "Consider the circumstances. Measure your remorse. Calculate future menace." With a sniff, he added, "And much depends upon the manner in which I am treated in your keeping."

She looked disgruntled at his response. He suspected

she didn't much care for being kind to a Norman. But now her own fate relied upon it.

"I've not treated you badly," she said in her defense. "I haven't hurt you. I gave you the pallet while I slept upon the floor. I let you go off into the woods to piss. And I'm cooking your breakfast."

"Burning," he corrected as gray smoke rose from the underside of the roast.

"What?"

"*Burning* my breakfast." The coney flared up with a flash of light.

She turned in time to see the dry stick crack in half and the carcass plop onto the coals, igniting like a ball of Greek fire. "Shite!"

Before he could shout a warning, she reached into the fire and yanked the roast out. In her haste to unhand the hot thing, she dropped it to the floor, then smothered the flames with one of the coverlets.

The carcass was incinerated beyond recognition.

Still, when it was cool, Helena picked up the thing and tore off a haunch, offering him a bite.

He wasn't sure he should be grateful. After all, 'twas barely palatable fare. But he was a gentleman. Courtesy prevented him from telling her, as he tore off a piece with his teeth, that the burnt exterior was bitter, the interior stringy and nearly raw.

"Mm." But he feared his face revealed the truth, for as he chewed and choked down the tough morsel, he couldn't suppress a shudder of distaste.

She snorted and tore off a haunch for herself, and though

she tried to pretend 'twas perfectly delicious, she, too, gagged on the meat.

"I suppose *you* could do better." Her voice dripped with sarcasm.

He smiled to himself. Of all the absurd traits she'd endowed him with, she'd missed the one that was oddly true. "Didn't you know? Normans are the best cooks in the world."

# Chapter 5

HELENA LOOKED AT him with such skepticism that he laughed out loud. "Come, come. You believe I—what was it—perfume my hound and sleep in a silk bed, and yet don't think I can cook?"

"'Twould seem a Normanly trait," she admitted in a mutter.

"I'll make a bargain with you. Since you're so adept a hunter, you bring me game, and I'll roast it properly for us."

She glanced at the burnt carcass in her hand, considering his offer. "'Tisn't a trick?"

"I'm as ravenous as you are."

After a moment, she tossed the ruined roast onto the fire and brushed the black char from her hands. "Very well." She whirled to go back outside, paused, then wheeled back to shake a warning finger at him. "But know this. I am not out of hearing. If someone arrives, I'll know it. You won't have time to sob to anyone about how I'm mistreating you."

"Sob? I don't sob."

She arched a brow of disbelief, then turned to go.

"Oh," he said, "I'll need a bit of wild onion to go with that."

She stopped in her tracks.

"And rosemary if you can find it."

She stiffened. "Would you like some spun gold while I'm out?"

He ignored her jibe. "And if you happen upon a patch of borage or mint . . ."

She spoke over her shoulder. "This had better be worth it."

He grinned. She'd be surprised at what a Norman could do with but a few herbs. After all, ranging the wilds of England and France, waging war, and living on little, one learned to be creative.

As Helena slammed the door behind her, Colin, for the first time since he'd arrived, actually hoped rescue wouldn't be too forthcoming.

She'd been gone nigh an hour, during which time Colin entertained himself—at first by visually examining the entire cottage until he had every knothole and crevice memorized, then by humming ballades that Pagan's squire, Boniface, oft sang at supper—when a curious sensation gripped him and stopped him in midsong. Silently scanning the room, he could see naught had changed, and yet a sort of prickling awareness crept up his spine, a sense that something was different. Strange as it seemed, he was almost convinced a knothole had moved or a spider had suddenly vanished from its web. For one fleeting moment, he wondered if the place was haunted by spirits.

While the air around him seemed to shimmer expectantly, he thought he saw something flicker past the gap in the shutters. But when he cocked his head to look, 'twas gone.

He swallowed back the sudden dread that a wolf might lurk outside, looking for a way in, that Helena might be in danger out there. He quietly twisted against his bonds, mentally cursing the wench for leaving him so helpless.

But studying the narrow crack of light, waiting for whatever was outside to pass by again, he never detected the figure that mysteriously materialized within the cottage. When he finally glanced toward the hearth, he drew in a shocked gasp and scrabbled backward, colliding with the pallet.

"Jesu!"

How the man had come to be in the cottage he didn't know. He'd appeared as if by magic. And now Colin knew whereby the thief had gotten his name.

The Shadow.

He was slight in stature and clad head to toe in black. His legs were sheathed in black cloth. His hands were gloved in black leather. Even his head was swathed in black wrapping, which was tied at the back, leaving only one tiny gap for breathing and two small holes for sight. He wielded no weapon, but 'twas possible he hid something in the elusive folds of his surcoat.

While Colin might have been startled, he was not afraid of the intruder. Of all the horrific tales Helena had told about the notorious outlaw, none of them had featured mortal injury. And though The Shadow had slipped into the cottage with unearthly stealth, he was clearly human.

When Colin's heart calmed, he asked, "What do you want?"

The Shadow ignored him, instead studying the interior of the hovel, much as Colin had for the last hour. So Colin used the moment to study his foe in turn.

The man moved across the floor without a sound. His boots must have been made of very supple leather, for his steps were as fluid as a wildcat's. Like a well-trained warrior, he held his arms slightly up and away from his body, ready to grapple or to move in any direction in the blink of an eye.

The Shadow returned to the smoldering fire, depositing a black satchel beside the hearth. He crouched beside the three-legged stool, eyeing the burnt roast, then picked up something from the floor, a single long strand of hair. Helena's. Turning and rising in one graceful movement, he stretched the strand between the thumbs and fingers of his hands, holding it out to Colin in askance.

To protect Helena, Colin said, "She's gone. She won't be back before nightfall."

Satisfied, The Shadow let the strand fall.

Then he wasted no more time, drawing near to discover the pouch of coins Colin wore upon his hip, silver he'd won gambling from Lord Gellir.

But The Shadow had apparently overlooked the fact that one of Colin's legs was free. As soon as the thief began to tug on the leather pouch, Colin swept his leg out to trip him.

What happened after that Colin could only recall in a blur. Somehow The Shadow jumped over his swinging leg, then seized Colin's ankle, giving his leg a sharp twist and turning him instantly over on his belly. As he planted a foot on Colin's back to anchor him there, Colin yelped, the knee of his bound leg strained nigh to breaking.

Then, to his amazement, as he cursed in pain, The Shadow bent close, wagging a scolding finger in his face.

"All right," Colin wheezed in surrender. "All right."

The varlet lifted his foot then and nudged him back over, releasing the strain on his knee. As Colin exhaled in relief, The Shadow withdrew a tiny knife from his surcoat and cut loose the satchel of coins. Mayhap 'twas best Colin hadn't succeeded in overcoming the robber. That knife was honed to a parchment-thin edge.

Colin would have sworn The Shadow gave him a gloating wink before tucking the bag into the front of his surcoat. Then, with a deft flip of his wrist, he sent the tiny blade flying across the cottage. Colin followed the knife's path as it thumped into the wood of the shutter, its black haft quivering when the blade came to rest.

By the time Colin looked back, the outlaw had vanished again. Only a subtle flicker of light in the room, the swiftly shifting shadows on the floor, made him realize that somehow, defying the earth's pull, the man must have escaped through a gap in the roof.

For several moments, all Colin could do was stare in amazement. Listening to Helena's tales of the elusive Shadow, he'd thought them an exaggeration. But now he'd witnessed just how slippery the robber was. 'Twas no wonder he'd never been caught.

But the ordeal was not yet over. Helena was still outside. If The Shadow found her . . . Jesu, there was no telling what the villain might do, confronted by the intrepid Scotswoman. Nor what reckless Helena might do to endanger herself.

Colin wrenched at his bonds with renewed determination. But no matter how he twisted his wrists against the tough rope, he only succeeded in scraping away his flesh.

By the time he heard a noise at the door, his brow was dripping with sweat, and his forearms stung where the skin was shredded.

The door swung open to reveal Helena, unharmed, thank God, a coney slung over one shoulder and a clump of herbs in her hand.

"Sweet Mary, you're safe," he said in a rush, breathless with relief. "Did you see him? Is he still outside?"

"Who?"

"The Shadow."

"The Shadow?"

"Aye. He was just here."

She smirked. "Indeed?" She closed the door with a nudge of her hip.

"He was! He stole my silver. If you cut me loose, I may still be able to catch him."

She shook her head. "You can't be serious."

If not for his bonds, he'd have hauled her forward by the front of her surcoat and showed her just how serious he was. "Curse it all, wench, 'tis true! Now cut me loose before he gets away."

She gave him a knowing smile and moved with infuriating nonchalance toward the hearth.

Frustration boiled inside him. "You don't believe me."

"That's right."

"Then how do you explain that?" He jutted his chin out toward the satchel the thief had unwittingly left behind.

She followed his gaze, frowning down at the black cloth

bag. Slowly, she dropped the herbs into one pot and slung the coney over another. "Where did this come from?"

He growled. "I've just told you."

"The Shadow?" She glanced over at him. "Forsooth?"

"Aye!"

"You're certain 'twas him?"

He let out a long-suffering sigh. "All in black? Small? Nimble? As quick as lightning?"

At last, to his great relief, Helena seemed to believe him. She nodded, drawing her dagger.

"Good wench. Cut me free." He twisted to give her access to the ropes. "Stay in the cottage," he commanded. "He won't look for you here. If I'm not back . . ."

But Helena didn't appear to be listening. Nor was she moving from the spot. He scowled. What was going through that wayward head of hers? She still gripped the dagger in her hand, but she seemed in no hurry to come sever his bonds.

"I pray you, damsel. Time's a-wasting. By now, he's probably halfway . . ."

She stared at the door, her eyes narrowed with grim intent. Suddenly he knew exactly what she was thinking.

Bloody hell. She couldn't mean to . . .

"Wait!" He felt like a knight discovering his horse was charging toward a precipice. "Wait!"

"Which way did he go?" she demanded, clenching her fingers around the haft of the weapon.

"Oh, nay. You're not going out there yourse—"

"Which way?"

He clapped his mouth shut, refusing to answer. He'd be damned if he'd help her get herself killed.

"Fine," she said. "I'll track him on my own."

"Nay! Wait!"

"I have no time for this, Norman. As you said, time's a-wasting."

"But I . . ." He blurted out the first thing that came to mind. "I lied."

"What?"

He sighed and stared at the ground. "I lied," he muttered, shrugging. "'Twasn't The Shadow at all."

She hesitated, weighing his words. "You lied."

He nodded.

"You *lied?*" She glanced at the abandoned bag. "Then who—"

"There *was* a thief," he amended, "but he . . . He left an hour ago. I was hoping . . ."

Her gaze slowly curdled with disdain. "Aye?"

Lord, how it bruised his pride to have her look at him that way, as if he was a spineless churl. But her scorn was a small price to pay for her safety. "I thought . . ."

"You were hoping," she finished for him, "that I would cut you free so you could run away." She sheathed her dagger again, and he exhaled an invisible sigh of relief. "Like I said, Norman," she sneered, "no ballocks."

He scowled. It rankled him to play the coward. God's wounds, he was a bloody Knight of de Ware! And even within those illustrious ranks, Sir Colin du Lac was renowned for his valor. He'd led the charge at the Battle of Moray. He'd won countless trophies in tournament for his bravery. Once, he'd even rushed into a burning demesne to save a bevy of harlots. No ballocks, indeed.

Helena sighed, strangely disappointed. She'd almost begun to think this Norman was different, that he might possess some small sliver of courage. But nay, he'd proved himself as craven as the rest of his countrymen.

She supposed 'twas just as well he was a coward. After all, cowards were easier captives to manage than heroes. Still, she couldn't help but be displeased.

With a disapproving smirk, she crouched beside the black pouch the outlaw had left behind and loosened the drawstring. She should have realized the Norman was lying. The Shadow was scrupulously cautious. He'd not be so careless as to leave behind a satchel. Indeed, the only evidence anyone had ever recovered of The Shadow was the signature black knife he sometimes lodged in a wall after the commission of his crimes.

Helena opened the satchel. Inside were several small parcels. Perchance the robber had left behind something of value. She gingerly unwrapped one of the cloth-covered packages. It contained two kinds of cheese. Another parcel held a dozen oatcakes. The third cloth enveloped a sizable hunk of salted pork. And bundled loosely into a knotted rag were ripe cherries. The thief had unwittingly provided a veritable feast for them.

"Mayhap your coin was well spent after all," she called to Colin. "There's enough provender here for another day at least."

"Provender? *That's* what he left?"

"Aye, and 'twill serve him right to suffer an empty belly tonight for his crime."

"At the price I paid, it had better be gold-encrusted swan's eggs," he sulked. "I had six shillings on my person."

She raised a brow. "Shillings won off my father, no doubt."

Lord Gellir had a weakness for gambling he indulged

almost nightly. The folk of Rivenloch had made a habit of secretly surrendering the bulk of their winnings to the sisters, to be returned to the castle treasury. In that way, the lord's frequent losses didn't affect the coffers. Strangers, however, were a different matter. They took their winnings with them, sometimes only to lose them to The Shadow.

"Anyway," she said, setting out the packages, "now we won't starve."

"I'll get started on that coney if you'll loose me."

"Loose you? After you tried to run away?" She shook her head. "Nay, I don't trust you."

"But I give you my word—"

"Your word? The word of a liar?"

His jaw tightened with shame, and she almost felt sorry for him, but damn his eyes, he'd brought mistrust upon himself.

"You must free me," he insisted. "You left me helpless before, at the mercy of a thief. What if he'd been a murderer? What if he'd decided to kill me?"

She swallowed. 'Twas not something she'd considered. What if Colin *had* been slain? What if she'd returned to find him dead? Grisly images of Colin in a pool of blood and Pagan at the gallows, calling for vengeance upon her, squirmed through her mind like a menacing serpent.

"Listen, my lady. 'Tis true I lied to you before," he confessed, "but no more. I swear it on my honor as a Knight of Cameliard."

She hesitated. Knights did not bargain lightly with their honor. Still, 'twas a fool who trusted a liar.

"My lady, with thieves loose in the wood, we ought to, both of us, have our limbs free."

"Why? So I can fend them off while you flee?"

He scowled at the ground, muttering, "I'm not the coward you believe. I would never leave a woman defenseless."

Helena smirked. She'd seen little proof of that thus far. Still, Colin had a point. The two of them were adversaries, but against a common enemy, 'twas a better defense to band together. Nonetheless, 'twas with some reservations that she finally decided to release him.

"I'll keep the dagger," she informed him, squatting to slice the rope from his ankle.

When she circled behind him to cut his wrists free, she saw that he'd torn his flesh on the bindings, trying to escape. Guilt furrowed her brow. The poor, spineless wretch must have been in fear for his life when the thief arrived. And 'twas partly her fault for not realizing she'd left him so vulnerable.

As the ropes dropped off, he flexed his fingers and cursorily scanned his abraded wrists.

"There may be a salve in one of the chests," she offered.

He shrugged. "They're only scrapes. I've done worse sparring." He rose and rubbed his palms together. "Now let me at that coney. I promise you a feast, my lady," he said with a slight bow and a twinkle in his eye, "to make your mouth water and your tongue sing Norman praises."

She shook her head at his nonsense. Forsooth, she was so hungry, she'd sing praises for pig slops.

While Colin acquainted himself with the cookpots and jabbed the coals on the hearth to life with a stick, Helena kept watch, half-reclining on the pallet, slowly twirling the dagger between her hands. She'd been able to find him rosemary and mint, but no wild onion. He didn't seem to mind. According to him, a Norman could make soup from a stone.

"I need a knife," he said.

She stopped spinning the dagger. The only knife she had was the one in her hands. Was it wise to surrender her only weapon?

"Don't worry. I'll give it back when I'm done." Then he added pointedly, "Even if 'tis *my* dagger."

She vacillated, her belly growling in anticipation of the feast, her heart uneasy with the idea of arming him. Just before her belly won the argument, he volunteered, "If you don't trust me, why don't you borrow the thief's knife?" He gestured toward the window. "He left it in the shutter there."

Helena's heart dropped when she beheld the familiar black blade with its lightning-keen edge and slim haft. Rivenloch possessed three of the curious weapons. They had all come from the same source, confiscated from victims of The Shadow.

## Chapter 6

Hᴇʟᴇɴᴀ ғʀᴏᴡɴᴇᴅ, ᴅᴇᴇᴘ in thought, as she ran a finger over the silk-smooth haft of The Shadow's dagger. If the notorious outlaw *had* been here, why had Colin changed his story? Why had he claimed 'twas another thief?

There was only one possible answer.

He'd been telling the truth.

And he'd only varied his tale when Helena had threatened to go after The Shadow. He'd lied to protect her.

She should have been insulted. His intervention meant that he considered her incapable of defending herself.

But try as she might, the only emotion she could muster was grudging admiration. In order to protect her, Colin had made himself look a coward when he was clearly nothing of the kind. He'd sacrificed his pride to keep her from harm. 'Twas the sort of thing only an exceptionally gallant knight would do.

She glanced sidelong at the inscrutable man as he tended the coney, turning it slowly over the flames. Was he truly the fainthearted weakling she'd assumed? Or did his flowery speech and uncanny skill with a cooking spit have naught to do with the man inside? Was it possible he was so chivalrous that he'd lie to protect even his foe?

"Shame we haven't neeps and peas," Colin murmured, distracting her from her musings. "A good, strong mead to go with it. Peach tarts to finish."

Done with the dagger, he handed it back to her, haft first, and she tucked it into her girdle.

The savory scent of the roasting meat wafted past her nose, rich with rosemary and a light touch of mint. True to his word, the fare was making her mouth water. She cast him a dubious look. "You can cook all that?"

His smile exuded confidence. "Oh, aye. No Norman knight worth his spurs cannot cook. 'Tis in our blood."

Helena frowned. She couldn't cook, not well. Cooking required too much patience, too much attention. Her impulsive nature wouldn't let her sit still long enough to tend to a meal. "If you prove yourself worthy, mayhap I shall let you continue with your kitchen duties."

Colin suppressed a grin. The wench wasn't fooling anyone. She was about as familiar with a cookpot as a monk was with a broadsword. *Let* him continue, indeed. After she tasted this meal, she'd be *begging* him to cook for her. Already he'd caught her twice, licking her lips.

He ladled the drippings he'd collected over the coney again, drenching the roast with the herb-infused liquid and making the coals beneath sizzle.

"Pity we have no fine white pandemain to sop up the juices," he said.

"We have oatcakes."

He screwed up his features in distaste. "Oatcakes? Those bland atrocities you Scots are always packing about? The ones that suck all the spit from your mouth?"

She straightened indignantly, her green eyes burning fiercely. "There's naught better when you ride into battle. A Scot can bake an oatcake on his shield, have it for breakfast, and still have the strength by afternoon to lay a foe flat with that same shield."

Her pride was admirable, but 'twas her passion that fascinated him. "Peace, little Hel-fire. We are not at war."

"Don't call me that, Norman."

He smiled as he lifted the spit from the fire and inspected the roast. "Don't call me Norman."

*Checkmate,* he thought as she stewed in silence.

"Is it done yet?" she grumbled at last.

He grinned. "To perfection."

Despite his own hunger, as they sat together beside the fire, 'twas all Colin could do to concentrate on swallowing as he watched Helena enjoy the meal. She ate with relish, smacking her lips, licking her fingers, and, though she tried to hide it, making small sounds of pleasure in her throat. He wondered wickedly if she made those same moans when she coupled.

"Why aren't you eating?" she asked, pausing to lap the juice from the corner of her lip.

He wasn't eating because, watching her devour the roast, he suddenly craved something even more appetizing than food. His loins ached with a hunger he hadn't fed in weeks. But he didn't dare tell her that.

"I was just wondering," he hedged, pulling a morsel of meat from the bone, "how long you plan to keep me here."

She frowned thoughtfully, then popped her thumb into her mouth, sucking off the last of the grease with sensual leisure. The sight stirred the beast in his braies. "However long it takes," she said, casting her half of the stripped carcass into the fire.

However long it takes. He wondered how long 'twould take to tame a wild wench like Helena. How long would it be before he had her eating from his hand?

"Did you," he asked, "enjoy the coney?"

"'Twas . . ." Her answer was guarded. "Adequate."

"Adequate?" He nodded ruefully. He supposed 'twas the highest praise she could offer an enemy. But he knew the coney was superb. And before his time as a hostage came to an end, he determined he'd win over his captor, if not with his turn of a phrase, then with the turn of a spit. "My skills are prized among the Knights of Cameliard." He neglected to mention that his most prized skills had naught to do with cooking but with swordplay.

"If you're so prized, then why has no one come to ransom you?"

He opened his mouth to reply, then closed it again. How could he explain that his captain likely thought the whole ransom affair a grand jest?

"Nay," she continued, "I think you must be worthless."

"Worthless!" He chuckled. "Oh, nay, little Hel-cat," he taunted. "No one comes because no one wishes to. Trust me. By now, Pagan has thoroughly seduced your sister. I would wager they lie abed still—the master," he said, dabbing grease from the corner of his mouth, "and his tamed bride."

If he'd blinked in the next instant, Helena's punch would have knocked him backward into the fire. But luckily his reflexes were swift. He brought his arm up in time to deflect the blow, losing his half of the coney in the process. On instinct, he made a grab for Helena's wrists.

She instantly twisted against his grip. "No one," she spat, "*tames* a Warrior Maid of Rivenloch."

Her proud declaration sounded like a challenge to Colin's ears, and the passion of her claim kindled his blood to new heat. Forsooth, so startled was he by her sudden attack and her vehement oath that it took a moment for him to realize that he now held her in his power. And another moment for *her* to realize it.

Her eyes widened, and she began to fight in earnest.

He could have overpowered her. He could have crowed in triumph and asked her, "Who's the captor now?" He could have trussed *her* up and tied her to the bed for the night to see how *she* liked it.

'Twas tempting.

But he was a noble Knight of Cameliard. He was a man of chivalry and honor. Mostly, he was Colin du Lac.

"Let me go!" She struggled against his stronger hold.

He held firm.

"Let me *go!*"

"On one condition."

He knew she had no leverage. She knew it, too. He could see it in the desperation of her gaze.

She spoke through her teeth. "Name it."

"You will not tie me to the bed tonight."

She emitted a humorless chuckle. "And will you slay me in my sleep, or will I awake to discover the cowardly pigeon has flown?"

"Neither. You will trust me."

"Trust you," she sneered. "A Norman?"

"A Norman."

Helena might have been a spirited fighter, but she knew when she was beaten. Narrowing her eyes with loathing, she bit out, "Fine."

Then he released her.

She tumbled backward with the shock of sudden freedom, but when she rolled to her feet again, by some miracle, she held The Shadow's knife in her grip.

By the Saints, he thought in grudging admiration, the maid was agile. Almost as agile as The Shadow himself.

*Lord, he was fast,* Helena thought, her heart pumping as she cautiously advanced with the knife. He'd blocked her punch almost before she realized she'd thrown it. He'd seized her wrists in one lightning-quick movement. And for a long, terrifying moment, he seemed to hold her at his mercy, his knowing gaze burning into her soul as if to say, you are mine.

'Twas unsettling.

He'd rattled her, caught her off her guard, used her impulsiveness against her. Which both ashamed and enraged her.

And yet, just as quickly, he'd let her go. His gloating grin of victory had faded. He held his palms up now in a gesture of peace.

She scowled in confusion, tightening her fist around the dagger. What new trickery was this? She sensed 'twas more than sleeping arrangements he bartered for.

One thing was certain. Colin du Lac was an enigma.

"Sheathe your claws, kitten," he said, casually retrieving his dropped coney from the floor and wiping the dirt from it with his sleeve. "You trust me now, remember?"

Helena frowned. She was a woman who liked the feel of cold steel in her palm and chain mail on her shoulders. They were things of substance, physical proof of power, of control. His oaths of honor and trust seemed as insubstantial as mist and as mutable as the moon. She *couldn't* trust him . . . not truly. Nay, she would hold on to the knife, for it gave her the security that vague promises did not.

He shrugged, then, to her amazement, pulled his dagger from his own belt and began carving up the coney, eating slices from the blade. She patted her girdle, where she thought she'd tucked the dagger for safekeeping. Bloody hell! How had he managed to reclaim it?

She decided he must have seized it as she went toppling backward. Which meant they were on equal ground now.

Reluctantly, she lowered her knife.

"Do you like trout?" he asked abruptly.

"What?"

"Fish. Trout. Those wiggly creatures that swim in the—"

"I know what trout are." Jesu, he was vexing. 'Twas almost as if he enjoyed confounding her wits. She stuffed The Shadow's knife into her girdle.

"Well? Do you?"

"Aye. I suppose."

"Good." He resumed eating in silence for several moments, as if 'twas the end of their conversation.

"Why do you want to know?" she finally demanded.

"Know what?"

"The trout," she muttered. "Why do you want to know if I like trout?"

He shrugged. "I wouldn't make it if you didn't."

She definitely got the impression he was thoroughly savoring her confusion. "You're going to make trout?"

He finished off the meat and tossed the bones into the fire, where they kicked up fresh sparks. "Aye. Why not? On the morrow, you and I will go fishing, catch a few trout. I'll fry them up for supper. Mayhap we'll find some watercress or purslane for a—"

"On the morrow," she told him firmly, "we'll be on our way back to Rivenloch."

"You've changed your mind about the ransom?"

"Nay." Then she added with a confidence she only half felt, "Deirdre will come today."

"Ah."

'Twas patronizing, that "ah," and it piqued her ire. "She *will*. You'll see."

"Very well." He crossed his arms and cocked his head at her. "But if she doesn't, you owe me a fishing trip on the morrow. Agreed?"

She let out an annoyed sigh. "Agreed."

Helena couldn't decide what 'twas about Colin du Lac that made her feel so . . . prickly. Perchance 'twas his smug glances or knowing grins, his smooth-as-honey voice or the lithe way his body moved. 'Twas as if each time he spoke, he blew a sultry, warm breath across her skin, making every hair stand on end. 'Twas not a pleasant sensation. It left her feeling edgy and guarded and off-balance.

She would be glad when Deirdre came, even if she refused to give up her new husband. Helena was anxious to return to her life at Rivenloch, where she was second-in-command of the guard, men cowered in fear of her blade, and no one sent shivers across her flesh with mere words.

Unfortunately, Colin's predictions proved accurate. Deirdre never came. As Colin regaled her with tales of

Pagan's exploits, and she recounted some of her father's grand battles, the shadows lengthened with the passing hours. While they nibbled at their cache of cheese and cherries and shared a cup of water, the last of the sun's rays faded.

At least, when the forest finally darkened to a forbidding gloom, Colin had the decency not to mock her hopes.

"Go on," she muttered, packing up the cheese and stuffing it back into the satchel. "Say it."

"What?"

"She didn't come," she said tightly. "You were right. I was wrong."

He could have gloated then, but he didn't. He only shrugged. "Perchance on the morrow." He yawned. "Meanwhile, I'm for bed. If we get an early start, we could be feasting on trout by midday." He rubbed his palms together and winked at her. "Mayhap we'll even share some with your sister if she arrives in time."

Colin's childlike enthusiasm admittedly took some of the sting out of her disappointment. She did love trout. And if it wasn't for the fact that Colin was her hostage, that she was in the midst of political bartering, and that time was of the essence, she might indeed enjoy the challenge of hooking a fish or two.

Colin took the singed coverlet for himself and stretched out beside the hearth. "You can take the bed tonight."

She creased her brow, not at his offer, but at his audacity. Was he actually dictating terms to *her?* Not that she minded the terms. The bed was preferable to the floor. "You're sure your frail Norman bones can withstand sleeping on the ground?"

His lips curved up in a lazy grin. "Forsooth, I'd much prefer silk sheets and perfumed pillows, but 'twill do."

He closed his eyes then, and she dragged the remaining coverlets to the pallet to make her own bed. Despite the welcome comfort of the straw-stuffed mattress, she was prepared for a sleepless night. She slid the slim knife from her girdle and wrapped her fingers about the handle.

She might have agreed not to tie Colin to the bed, but she'd never promised she wouldn't lie awake all night, watching him. Which she fully intended to do.

Indeed, the last thought she had as her drooping eyelids fluttered shut was that she'd ultimately be much more alert if she allowed her eyes to close for just a brief moment.

## Chapter 7

"HELENA," COLIN WHISPERED across the shadowy room.

Her soft snoring continued.

"Helena, psst."

No response.

Dawn already lightened the sky. They should arise now. Their best hope of catching trout was to fish in the early morn, when the trout were hungriest.

"Helena, wake up."

Still no answer. Lord, the woman slept like a rock. No wonder she'd wanted him tied up. He could have easily walked out the door, shouting a cheery farewell, while she dozed blissfully on.

He rubbed the sleep from his eyes, then tossed back the coverlet and lurched to his feet. He arched his back, releasing the inevitable pops that came from sleeping on the ground, then ran a hand back through his messy hair.

"Hey, little Hel-fire," he teased, "I think your hostage is escaping."

Still she drowsed.

He smiled, then took a step closer, gazing down at her. How innocent she looked, her lashes lush against her cheek, her lips parted like a babe's, her fingers curled harmlessly beside her face.

"Is that cherry tarts I smell?" he whispered. "And smoked ham? Currant buns, warm from the fire, and sweet cheese flan?"

Her brow wrinkled slightly, but to his amusement, she didn't stir.

His grin widened. "Wake up, wench! The Normans have come. Hurry, before they force you to wear perfume and sleep on silk sheets."

To his amazement, even *that* didn't rouse her. Shaking his head, he decided that as long as she dozed on, none the wiser, he might as well take advantage of her compliant state. He eyed her mouth, so supple, so inviting, then lowered his head to taste her soft lips.

As soon as he made contact, she awoke, lashing out with the knife coiled in her fist. He recoiled and sucked in a breath of shock as the fine point sliced across his cheek. God's bones! If his reflexes had been any slower, he might have lost an eye.

"Jesu!"

Helena looked as startled as he was. "Get back!"

"Bloody hell!" He pressed a thumb to the edge of the wound. It stung like the devil. Why was it the tiny cuts that hurt the worst?

"Back!" She brandished the knife before her.

"I only—"

"*Back!*"

He obliged, staggering back a step, and she sat up,

sweeping the hair out of her face with her free hand. Lord, he could see by the glaze in her eyes, she wasn't even fully awake. She'd attacked him purely on reflex.

"By the Saints, wench! Put your weapon away. I was only trying to wake you." He examined the smudge of blood on his thumb. "Lucifer's ballocks, you sleep like the dead."

"If I sleep so soundly, then why are you bleeding from my knife?"

He furrowed his brows. "You must have been *dreaming* of killing Normans."

Apparently deeming him harmless, she slipped the knife back into her girdle. "Next time, try calling my name."

He only shook his head.

"You owe me a fishing trip," he grumbled.

His cut turned out to be shallow. 'Twould not even leave a scar. But the memory would be forever engraved upon his mind. Never again would he attempt to rouse a sleeping Scots serpent with kisses.

The sun shot quarrels of light through the pines as Helena led him along the stream, crude fishing poles of stripped branches perched on their shoulders. Scotland was truly beautiful country, Colin decided, with its rocky crags and magnificent waterfalls, its vast moors of purple heath and glens thick with fern. But Rivenloch, she was a jewel set in its midst, lush with forest and meadow, fed by a myriad of springs and brooklets that traversed the landscape like threads of silver cleverly embroidered on a surcoat. He saw now why the King wanted the land defended.

Helena seemed to know the countryside well. She led

him to a spot where the stream widened into a deep pool, perfect for fishing.

Earlier, he'd carved primitive hooks out of wood, and now he attached them to the poles, knotting together fibers from the reeds growing beside the water to make lines.

As Helena baited her hook, skewering a squirming worm with nary a shudder, Colin had to smile. He wondered if all Scotswomen were so intrepid.

Soon they sat side by side upon the great boulder at the water's edge, as companionable as lifelong friends, their lines tugging in the lazy current. No one would have guessed they were abductor and hostage.

A quarter of an hour later, Helena caught the first fish. With a satisfied cock of her brow and an expert flick of her wrist, she flipped the trout onto the grassy bank.

He couldn't help but laugh in delight. "You've been fishing *before*."

"A time or two," she said, rising to retrieve her fish.

"Well, I was trying to be gallant, letting you make the first catch," he teased. "But I see now you're a wench to be reckoned with. I think I may have to issue a challenge."

"A challenge?" She held the wriggling trout in one hand and casually dislodged the hook, as if 'twas something she did every day.

"Oh, aye. I challenge you to match me, fish for fish."

"Match you? Already you lag behind."

"Not for long," he vowed.

"I've fished these streams all my life," she boasted, tossing her catch upon the grass and returning to her post. "What would a Norman know about the ways of Scots trout?"

He stroked his chin thoughtfully. "I suspect they are much like Scots wenches."

"Hmph."

"Slippery. Elusive. Stubborn. Impulsive." He dabbled his line above the dark shape circling gracefully beneath the water. "But tempt them with just the right bait . . ."

And at that instant, to Helena's consternation, the trout took his line, and he hauled the wiggling fish up out of the water. "You see?" he said, grinning wide. "'Tis as easy as seducing a maid."

Her mouth had opened in surprise. Now she clapped it shut. "Aye, if the maid's as stupid as a fish."

He chuckled, unhooking the fish and pitching it beside hers. "Well, we are *even* now."

She caught the next two, though he argued they should only count for one since they were so small.

Forsooth, Colin couldn't ask for a more pleasant time than passing the morn in friendly rivalry with a beautiful maid. He stared surreptitiously at the lovely damsel with the flashing emerald eyes and sultry lips and wild mane of tawny hair. She was a prize indeed, a beauty made to grace a man's bed. She bit at her bottom lip in concentration, and as he continued to watch her, her straw-colored skirts bunching about her bare ankles where she crouched on the rock, her gown gapping slightly to reveal the upper curve of her breast, he reconsidered. Oh, aye, there was something that could make the morn even more pleasant, something the starving beast in his braies had done too long without.

"Are you going to pull it out," she asked, "or are you just teasing the poor thing?"

Given the bent of his thoughts, her question stunned

him. For a moment, he could only stare at her, wondering at her candor. Then he followed her gaze toward the water. A large trout tugged at his line, swimming in figure eights beneath the surface.

Bemused, he quickly dragged it from the stream. It took far longer for him to drag his thoughts back to fishing.

Meanwhile, the impudent wench, in the time it took him to unhook the fish and unearth a worm for bait, caught two more trout.

As she sent yet another worm to a watery grave, he asked, "Shall we make the challenge more interesting?"

She smirked. "Sounds like the desperate ploy of a man about to lose."

"Mayhap," he agreed. "But what about this? Whoever catches the most trout by the time the sun reaches the tops of the trees . . ."

"Aye?"

A thousand sinful possibilities flooded his mind, but he voiced none of them. Helena still wielded The Shadow's knife, and he was in no mood to be skewered. "Wins a rousing song of victory from the loser."

"A song?"

"Aye, something triumphant and stirring."

She shook her head. "I don't sing."

"If you win, you won't have to," he said, grinning.

"True."

"Is it a wager, then?"

"Very well." The hint of a smile played about her mouth. "But you'd better not frighten away the Scots trout with your Norman singing."

"When I sing, my lady," he bragged, "the woodland creatures gather round to give ear."

A bit of a laugh escaped her, and he suddenly longed to hear more of the sound. There were few songs as enticing as a woman's heartfelt, carefree laughter.

Forsooth, a new challenge reared its head, one that piqued his sense of competition. He might owe Helena a song by midmorn, but in turn, he'd see that she rewarded him with a laugh.

Colin du Lac *was* amusing, Helena had to admit. Even if he was a varlet. And a Norman. And a philanderer.

He'd also been true to his word. Of course, she would have expected as much from any of her knights of Rivenloch. But Colin's honor came as a surprise, given that he was a foreigner and her hostage. He'd made no attempt to escape, though he could have when she'd carelessly dozed off last night in the cottage. And he'd not harmed her. Indeed, she regretted she'd lashed out at him in surprise this morn. He'd obviously meant to kiss her, and a very wicked part of her was curious as to how a Norman's kiss differed from a Scotsman's.

Still, she couldn't afford to feel the way she was beginning to feel. Companionable. Empathetic. Merciful. Humane.

She had to remind herself, as she stole fleeting glances at the handsome knave with the brawny shoulders, unruly black mane, and dancing eyes, that he was the enemy. They might pass the hours in blissful leisure now, but when Deirdre arrived, Colin du Lac had to become a sacrificial pawn in her game, no more.

By the time the sun topped the trees and their contest was over, Colin had snagged two more trout. But 'twas still one less than Helena's catch for the morn, making her the victor.

He grumbled in jest. "I still say those two fry can hardly be counted. They wouldn't fill a child's belly."

"If you don't want to sing . . ."

"Nay, nay, nay. I'm a man of honor. I owe you a song, and a song I shall give you." He set aside his fishing pole and furrowed his brow. Sitting cross-legged beside her on the boulder while she dangled her legs idly over the edge, he stared pensively into the water. "Ah, here it is." He cleared his throat and began to sing. His voice was not unpleasant, though he certainly was no minstrel. But what he lacked in melody he more than made up for in volume.

*"All praise to Helena of Trout*
*Who's proved her worth this day!*
*She boldly took her pole in hand,*
*Ere any could say her nay.*
*And bravely braved the deadly deep—*
*Sea monsters for to slay. . . ."*

A giggle escaped her. Sea monsters?

He paused to glare at her with mock severity, then resumed his song.

*"The first foul fish to find its fate*
*Lay hidden in a shoal.*
*But Helena, the clever maid,*
*Knew how to bait a hole.*
*While Colin languished troutless,*
*For no trot would touch his pole."*

She gave him a chiding shove for his obvious vulgarity.

"Trout," he corrected, though there was no mistaking the mischievous glimmer in his eyes. "I meant trout." His lips twitched as he continued.

> *"The second two she proudly hooked,*
> *A-fishing from the rock.*
> *Though Colin did contend they must*
> *Have come from lesser stock.*
> *For the two of them, set end to end,*
> *Were no longer than his—"*

She gasped before he could say it and gave him another shove.

He grinned and shoved her playfully in return.

Then, with a wicked gleam of vengeance in her eyes, she pushed with full force, tipping him off the boulder and into the water.

He fell in with a great splash. When he popped to the surface, his shocked sputtering was sweet reward.

She stood up, looming over him in triumph. "That should cure your vile tongue, Norman."

He shook the water from his head and squinted up at her. "Don't call me Norman."

Then, without warning, he began barraging her with splashes of water. Before she could even take a single step in retreat, she was thoroughly drenched.

Her jaw dropped, and she gasped in awe, peering at him through the dripping strands of her hair. How dared he? And yet instead of feeling outrage, she was struck by humor.

Men usually responded to her aggression in one of two

ways. They shied away from a fight, fearful of either injuring her or losing to a woman. Or they attacked with uncommon rage, seeking to kill what they didn't understand. This Norman . . . Colin, she amended, had no qualms about simply giving as good as he got. And something about that was . . . fascinating.

So he wanted to spar? She'd spar with him. Gladly.

A grin blossomed on her face, and she flexed her knees, preparing to dive into the stream.

But just then she heard a branch move behind her, the softest brush of pine needles, yet enough to alert her to an intruder. Her hand shot instinctively to her knife, and she wheeled about with her weapon drawn.

# Chapter 8

SHITE!

'Twas no intruder. 'Twas *five* intruders.

A cursory glance told her they were strangers. Foreigners. Miscreants. They were heavily armed, and their skin was dark with filth, as if they'd been traveling a long while.

"Look, lads," one of them growled as he slowly perused her from head to toe. "'Tis a drowned rat."

"Nay," another chimed in. "She's one o' them Siren creatures, a mermaid."

They guffawed in chorus. Glancing at them one by one, Helena doubted they possessed a score of teeth between them.

English. They were English. What the bloody hell were the English doing in Rivenloch?

By the piecemeal look of their leather armor and the maces and swords and flails hanging from their belts, they were mercenaries. Not only that, but she could tell they were not the sort of men who shied away from a fight . . . even with a woman.

Five ordinary men she could take. But these brutes warred for a living. Armed with only The Shadow's knife, her odds against them were slim.

She glanced briefly toward the pond. 'Twas empty.

"Are ye out here all alone, wench?"

Her eyes narrowed to cold slits. Apparently so. Curse Colin's Norman hide! The cowardly knave had scampered away, leaving her to battle the English herself.

"She's no common wench," one of them realized. "Look at her. She's a proper lady."

"Mm," the first said. "I believe ye're right. A proper lady out here all by herself." He eyed her in curious speculation, pulling at his grizzled beard. "Are ye lost?"

Helena might not have the advantage when it came to weaponry, but she had mettle, and in her experience, that could count for much. She eyed them grimly, each in turn, and spoke between her teeth. "Hear me well, you English bastards. I am not lost. I am one of the Warrior Maids of Rivenloch, and I am here with my army. If you do not turn about this instant and get off my land, I'll summon them to finish you off."

For a moment her ruse worked. For a moment they froze, staring at her in awe.

Then the grizzled man asked, "The Warrior Maids o' what?"

They exchanged a few nervous giggles, then dissolved into gales of laughter. All except for one man at the back, who suddenly found himself squirming at the point of a dagger.

"Rivenloch," Colin said distinctly as he pressed the tip of his knife against the Englishman's throat.

'Twas about time, Helena thought. Relief coursed through her. She wasn't sure if 'twas because her odds had just improved or because Colin had proved no coward after all. The clever man must have floated downstream and slipped out of the water to steal up behind the intruders.

"Do as the lady says," Colin bargained. "Leave quietly, and I won't have to mince up your friend here."

Helena frowned. She had no patience for Colin's negotiations. These weren't the type of men to negotiate. Besides, now that the Norman was here, the two of them had a fighting chance against the mercenaries.

So with a bark of "Now!" to alert Colin, she swept up her fishing pole with her left hand and swung it in a wide arc before her, backing off the intruders.

"What?" Colin replied.

"Now! Now!" What was wrong with him? Didn't he understand that battle was at hand? She took a step forward and swung again, this time catching one of the Englishmen alongside the head.

"Bloody hell!" Colin cried, joining her. He shoved his captive away, but not before stealing the man's sword. Then he spread his arms wide, sword and dagger in hand, to fend off the mercenaries.

By then, the Englishmen had drawn a vast array of weapons. Even the man Helena had struck recovered. He jerked a studded flail from his belt and advanced on her, swinging it over his head.

She hastily tucked the pole under her arm and jabbed forward, using it like a lance to catch the man in the belly. 'Twould have taken the wind from him, too, if his leather breastplate hadn't softened the blow. The buffet only slowed his advance.

Meanwhile, Colin fought the remaining four.

A quick glance told her he was a respectable enough swordsman. Still, she dared not rely upon his skills at fighting four at once.

Retracting the pole again, she stabbed forward at a second man's back. "Here, you stinking English swine! Turn and fight me!"

It worked. Her goading effectively distracted one of the men from Colin. Now he faced her, with murder in his eyes.

Colin's first thought when Helena rashly shouted "Now! Now!" and started waving her fishing pole about was that she'd lost her mind. If only she'd had a little patience, they might have been able to talk their way out of a skirmish.

His second thought, glimpsing the madwoman, armed with that feeble pole and a tiny knife, facing one giant with a flail and another brandishing a sword and a mace, was that if she survived this brawl, he was going to give her the thrashing of her life.

And then he could watch her no more. The remaining three men attacked him at once, armed with a full complement of swords, daggers, and war hammers.

He took one wide swipe with his blade, forcing his foes to retreat, and quickly decided that there could be no good end to this battle, not for him or for Helena. These Englishmen were clearly mercenaries, as practiced as knights, but with less honor. The best he could hope for was reasoning with them, as he'd tried to do before impetuous Helena had forced his hand. Unfortunately, he thought, blocking one man's blade and ducking under a war hammer that missed his head by an inch, he'd have to do it while fending them off.

"What do you want?" he shouted, using his dagger to deflect the point of a sword and engaging a second man with his sword.

"Whatever's in your purse!" replied a man with a scar across his eye as he swiped forward with his war hammer.

Colin stopped the weapon at the haft of his dagger, and the resulting clang jarred the bones of his arm all the way to his shoulder. "I have no purse!"

"Oh, aye, and we've no weapons!" one of them sneered, slashing out with his blade.

Preoccupied with dodging two daggers, Colin suffered a cut as he tried to block the sword with his arm. He gasped in pain and retreated a step.

Helena yelled, "You're too late, you half-wits!"

From the corner of his eye, Colin saw her spin and thrust with the fishing pole, effectively catching the flail-wielding combatant in the groin. Then she swung one foot around, faster than a well-oiled quintain, and kicked the other man in the ribs.

"Another thief came before you!" she informed them.

Their opponents were only daunted for a moment by this revelation before they advanced again. Colin was forced to take up his weapons and divert a sword attack from two sides. This time he managed to snap the tip of one sword with his dagger. But the second blade swung lower, clipping his hip. The steel cut through his surcoat, stopping short of his flesh, but 'twould leave a considerable bruise, he was sure.

"Ye're nobles!" the grizzled man fighting Helena cried. "Someone's bound to pay a fat purse to see ye safely returned!"

Colin stabbed forward with his sword, wounding the shoulder of one of the Englishmen, who cursed as the blade receded. But the man whose sword he'd cropped a moment ago now drew a vicious mace, replete with steel spikes. If ever there was a time for reasoning, 'twas now.

"You cannot ransom me!" Colin exclaimed as he kept a keen eye on the man with the mace. "I'm already being held for ransom . . . by this lady." As the man with the sword hacked forward again, Colin stepped in to bring the pommel of his sword down hard upon the man's wrist. The sword clattered to the ground. "I cannot be ransomed twice!"

"Aye!" Helena shouted. "He's *my* hostage! Keep your bloody hands off of him!"

"*Your* hostage?" the grizzled man sneered. "We'll see about that!"

The mace came toward Colin's head, and he thrust up his dagger to check its path. The blade was no match for the sheer weight of the mace, and it snapped beneath the blow, but not before glancing the weapon away from Colin. Now he had but one sword against the three of them.

The middle opponent thrust his blade forward, and Colin turned sideways just in time. But the first man's dagger found lodging behind Colin's shoulder blade. Colin gritted his teeth against the sudden gouge and lunged away.

He glanced about to see how Helena was faring. Blood dripped down her dagger arm, but the cut wasn't dire enough to hamper her movements. She lunged forward again with the pole, but this time the branch broke on her opponent's leather breastplate, leaving her with a stick no longer than a short sword and far less intimidating. Nevertheless, she wielded it as if it were made of the finest Toledo steel. It broke, of course, under the onslaught of the flail.

Colin meant to plunge toward her attacker, to defend her against the nasty weapon that could shatter her skull as easily as it had the pole. But because of that instant of inattention as he watched Helena, when he charged forward, 'twas onto one of the mercenaries' blades.

The sword sank deep into his unprotected thigh, and for a moment there was no pain, only thwarted movement. He tried to advance, stretching his blade out toward the man who was already swinging for a second strike at Helena. Then the man drew his sword back violently from the muscle of Colin's leg, and Colin felt the breath ripped from his lungs with the same force. He staggered, trying to take his weight on his good leg and hold on to his sword.

"Lucifer!" Helena spat, shoving the remains of her pole into the chain of the circling flail, tangling it and rendering it harmless. "You bastards!" She ceased fighting for an instant to stare at Colin, who felt the air swim before him. His eyes widened as he saw the man with the mace raise his arm behind her, but she stopped the attack as casually as a stable lad swatting a fly, spinning to drive the point of her knife into his wrist. The man screamed and dropped his weapon, clutching his bleeding forearm, and Colin didn't know whether to be impressed or mortified. Above all, he was relieved. Until Helena glared at the remaining Englishman and said, "What have you done to my hostage?"

"'E's not yours anymore, wench." The man who'd stabbed him held a dagger to his throat now, and Colin swayed on his feet. Damn his eyes! The threads of consciousness were breaking, strand by strand.

"The hell he isn't!" Helena shouted. "And now you dolts have ruined him. How much do you think I'll get for a lamed Norman knight?"

Colin had just enough awareness left in him to feel utterly betrayed. He'd risked his life to help the ungrateful wench, and she didn't care a whit about his sacrifice or his pain. Her only concern, as his blood dripped steadily onto the ground, was his diminished worth.

Helena bit the inside of her cheek and forced her gaze away from Colin, willing her bones to hold firm. She hoped the mercenaries couldn't see her shaking. Seeing the noble Norman wounded so cruelly had affected her far more deeply than she dared show, and the sight of his lifeblood seeping out of him was dizzying. Black spots floated at the edges of her vision.

Jesu, she hated to surrender. She hated it more than losing. As her Viking father had taught her, 'twas better to suffer a grievous wound and fall to the ground with sword in hand than lower a blade and hang one's head in shame. But when Helena saw the steel go deep into Colin's thigh, 'twas as if the sword had pierced her own flesh. Her heart seized, and she knew if she didn't stop fighting, Colin would die.

So, resisting every impulse she had to continue the battle, putting on a brave face despite her quivering nerves, she surrendered her last weapon, lodging it in her attacker's wrist, and turned on the mercenaries with defiance in her eyes.

"You bloody swine! What good is a dead hostage," she hissed, "to any of us?"

"'E's not dead," the man supporting Colin said. "'E's not even damaged. Not that bad."

He *was* hurt badly. Nausea rose in her gorge as she watched blood well from the wound. But she dared not reveal her concern for Colin, for that might prove her undoing.

As the mercenaries seized her, it taxed all her instincts not to fight back. Even now, she thought, she might have been able to take them with a kick to the ballocks. A well-placed sweep of her foot. A hard punch to the leader's bulbous nose. But while Colin's life hung in the balance, she couldn't risk any of it.

She told herself 'twas for selfish reasons. If Colin returned to Rivenloch damaged or, God forbid, dead, Pagan Cameliard would hold her accountable.

And yet within her heart, something had taken seed, some small bit of respect for the Norman, a respect that bordered dangerously on affinity.

She put up little struggle as they bound her wrists behind her, then wrested her through the forest, though she was tempted to make the journey as difficult as possible for them by dragging her feet and twisting in their grasp. Her attention instead riveted upon Colin, who had grown as silent as death.

"If he dies . . . ," she said tightly.

"He won't."

"But his leg . . ."

"Will mend."

"Not if it doesn't stop blee—"

"God's eyes! Ye sound like my bloody mother."

One of them snickered. "You mean your bloody *dead* mother?"

"Aye."

The second man leaned close to her and gleefully confided, "Otis here, he got tired of the wench's flapping jaws and shut her up for good."

The man had hoped to shock her. But Helena wasn't shocked. Men like these who roamed the countryside, hiring themselves out to the highest bidder, their loyalties as mutable as the wind, did so not by choice, but by circumstance. Most of them had criminal pasts too grievous to absolve.

Which gave them all something in common, she thought ruefully, wondering if Pagan Cameliard was readying the gallows for her even now.

For several hours, the English forced them to march. They journeyed perhaps ten miles west, deep into the woods, past the border of Rivenloch, where Lachanburn land began. By late afternoon, Helena's belly was growling like a wild boar. The mercenaries had gathered up their morning catch of trout, but it didn't seem they ever intended to eat it. Not that Helena's mind was on food, despite what her stomach told her.

Her thoughts centered on Colin.

His face had grown as pale as alabaster. Sweat beaded his brow and stained his shirt. Thankfully, the bleeding from his wound appeared to have stopped. But he hovered between waking and sleep, grimacing every time he put weight on his leg.

Helena knew enough about wounds to realize he might lose that leg if he didn't receive proper treatment. 'Twas clear these mercenaries didn't know the first thing about caring for injuries. One of them had a crooked arm that had been broken and healed badly. Another wore a broad scar across his cheek where he'd neglected to close a knife slash. Otis was missing the tip of a finger. They weren't going to dress Colin's wound unless she intervened.

"Aren't you going to do anything about that cut?" she asked as they stopped in a clearing where they apparently intended to set up a crude camp.

"What are you jabbering on about now?" Otis groused.

"The Norman. He's losing value every moment you delay."

"What's it to you? He's not your hostage to ransom."

She smirked. "Oh, aye, good luck there. You don't even know who to ransom him from." Not that that would help, she thought. *She* certainly hadn't had any luck with ransoming him.

Otis peeled his lips back in a sneer, exposing his three front teeth. "I'm sure you'll tell us what we need to know."

"Forsooth?" She spit pointedly on the ground. "And where's the advantage to me?"

She should have expected violence, but it caught her by surprise. Otis nodded to the brute beside her, the one whose wrist she'd mangled with the knife, and before she could flinch, he clouted her with his good fist, exploding stars across her vision as he caught the top of her cheekbone.

She swayed, struggling to stay upright as the sunlight dimmed around her. Otis's voice seemed to come from a distance, down a long tunnel.

"There's your advantage, my sweet. No more of Dob's tender caresses if you tell us what we want to know."

Pure anger was the only thing that kept her conscious, anger at herself for not anticipating Dob's blow. Her cheek throbbed. Though the bone hadn't cracked, she expected there'd be a black bruise there on the morrow.

"But for now," Otis said with false magnanimity, "let's set aside our grievances, eh? My gut's as empty as a nun's womb."

Helena and Colin were secured to the trunks of neighboring trees at the camp's edge, about six feet apart, while the Englishmen built a fire and began cooking supper. Colin dozed in oblivion against the tree, but Helena's mouth watered as the tantalizing aroma of roasting trout wafted through the clearing.

Of course, the hostages were not to be fed. 'Twas no matter that Helena had caught most of that trout. The greedy English bastards took it all for themselves. As the mercenaries huddled by the fire in the gathering darkness, their features demonic in the flicker of the flames, she watched them in sulky silence, her eyes smoldering.

"'Twould not have been good anyway," Colin suddenly volunteered in a weak whisper. "They're terrible cooks."

She snapped her head around, a smile touching the corner of her lips. Colin's voice was feeble and breathy, but the fact that he was awake and capable of levity was a good omen. Mayhap, she hoped, he was not as gravely wounded as she suspected. Still, in the fading light, she could see he was weary, his mouth tense with strain. The usual spark in his eyes was muted, like stars glimpsed through the fog.

"What happened to your eye?" he murmured.

She shook her head. A bruise was of little consequence. "Are *you* all right?"

He sighed, and his mouth took a doleful turn. "If you mean have I been . . . diminished in value . . . nay, I don't believe so. Yet."

She frowned. That wasn't what she meant at all.

"Or do you want to know if I'll live long enough," he continued, "to tell Pagan 'twas not your hand that killed me?"

"Nay, 'tis not that. I ask, because—"

"Quiet, wench!" Otis shouted from across the fire. "Enough conspiring. 'Tis time to consort with the enemy." He chuckled at his own jest, then rose to trudge over to where she sat, Dob trailing after like a loyal hound.

Otis would expect her to name their ransomer now or suffer Dob's pummeling. Despite the swelling beneath her eye, proof of Dob's brutal fist, all of her instincts told her to refuse him. After all, one never gave the enemy what they wanted.

But for once she thought before she acted.

"Listen," she told him, "I'll give you what you want."

Otis gave her a smug smile, as if he expected as much. "That's a good lass."

"But only if you grant me a favor."

Behind the now-scowling Otis, Dob grinned and massaged his knuckles, eager to cuff her again.

Otis's frown turned to a sneer. "A favor? What makes ye think ye're in a position to ask for a favor?"

"*I'll* give ye a favor," Dob chimed in. "I'll clout ye where it won't show this time."

"Shut your jaws, Dob," Otis said. "What's this favor?"

"Let me treat his wounds," she said, nodding toward Colin. "His ransomers won't pay for a lame warrior. Crippled, he's no good to either of us."

Otis scratched his grizzled chin, glancing at Colin, who sat frowning in concern. "So I let ye tend to his wounds, and ye'll give me what I want?"

"Aye."

Colin had heard enough. Helena might be a betrayer of the worst kind. She might be selfishly motivated. She might be the most reprehensible mercenary of the lot of them. But she was still a woman, deserving of his protection. And he had the sick feeling that she was bargaining away something she might later regret.

Bloody hell, if she'd promised to bed the bastard . . .

"Wait!" he shouted, earning a twinge of pain from his thigh for his efforts. He turned to Helena. "Do not, my lady!"

"Silence, Norman!" the leader bellowed. "'Tis between the wench and me."

"'Tis not worth it," he told her. "You'll only regret—"

The rest of his words were cut off by a sudden buffet to his chin, delivered by Dob. His head knocked painfully against the tree trunk, and bright bursts exploded against the dark night.

"Go on, wench," the leader urged.

"Nay!" Colin cried, his head throbbing.

"You'll let me dress his wound?" Helena asked.

"Nay!"

"Aye," the leader agreed.

She nodded in assent. But she didn't disrobe, as Colin had feared. Instead, her voice as clear as a cathedral bell, she replied, "Rivenloch. Those who would ransom him are at Rivenloch."

For a moment, Colin was speechless. Helena hadn't bargained away her body after all. She'd only supplied the English with the name of the ransomers.

Jesu, she'd supplied them with the name of Rivenloch! She hadn't even bothered lying. She was leading the enemy to the gates.

The best that Colin could do was to try to muddle her response by shouting, "Macintosh!"

She glared at him. "Rivenloch."

"You must tell him the truth," Colin told her, trying to confuse their captors. "Otherwise, we'll never be ransomed. 'Tis Macintosh, my lord. Macintosh."

Her eyes flared with incredulity. "What the bloody hell are you trying to—"

"Macintosh," he repeated. "'Tis north of here about twenty miles. In the Highlands."

"Macin— " She shook her head, wanting no part of his deception. "He's lying, Otis. The ransomers dwell at Rivenloch, some ten miles south."

Colin ground his teeth. If his hands had been free, he might have throttled the cursed Scots wench. How could she be so careless? She'd revealed the one location where the English might have leverage. Pagan never negotiated with enemy mercenaries, even when it came to his own men, and the Knights of Cameliard understood well his position and their duty. But Helena's people were another matter. They might well surrender the keep for the safe return of Lord Gellir's daughter. Which would be an intolerable sacrifice, as well as a failure for Cameliard and the King.

And for what? So she could see to his wound and mayhap preserve his value as a hostage, *her* hostage.

He frowned. 'Twould never happen. Now that the English knew the name and location of their ransomers, they'd hie there with all haste. And once they beheld the extent of Rivenloch's wealth, the mercenaries would surely not be satisfied until they received an enormous ransom for Helena. As for Colin, he'd be lucky if he escaped with his life. That is, if Helena's ministrations didn't kill him first.

## Chapter 9

HELENA HOPED SHE wasn't doing more harm than good. She'd rinsed out Colin's wound with fresh water, pulling away the cloth that was stuck to the cut. He hadn't said a word, but she could tell by his occasional quick intake of breath that 'twas painful for him.

She'd treated numerous of her own wounds over the years, so she knew all about stitching and bandaging, using shepherd's purse to stop bleeding, sprinkling dill seed and yarrow into an open cut to speed its healing. But restoring a foreigner might be a different task altogether. What cured a Scotswoman might poison a Norman.

For better or worse, none of the Englishmen knew hemlock from hellebore, nor were they interested in searching for herbs in the dark of night. So all she had to work with was water, a rag, a bit of ale, and a needle and thread one of the mercenaries carried to mend tabards.

"Here," she said when she'd threaded the needle, handing the aleskin to Colin.

He took a hearty drink, bracing himself, then returned the ale.

She took a swig. Then another. Then a third.

"Is that wise?" Colin asked in concern, eyeing the needle winking cruelly in the firelight.

She swallowed. "Oh, aye." She wiped her mouth with the back of a shaky hand, then tossed her head, steeling herself. "You aren't going to faint on me, are you?"

"Nay."

"You won't sob and carry on?"

He shook his head.

"Or scream?"

"I don't scream."

She hesitated. "If you lash out, kick me with your foot or—"

"God's eyes! Have mercy, wench. Get on with it."

Somehow she managed to do it. She tried to imagine 'twas only a bit of mending. It helped that Colin spoke not a word the entire time. His breathing was ragged, and sweat poured from him, but he didn't flinch once, despite what must have been pure torment.

After she knotted up the last stitch, her fingers began to quiver in delayed reaction to the ordeal. She mopped her moist brow with her sleeve and let out a rough sigh of relief.

Colin looked pale, even in the warm glow from the fire. His eyes were half-closed in fatigue, his jaw lax. Involuntary tears of pain had slipped silently down his cheeks, and they dried now upon his face. His chest rose and sank with rapid, shallow breaths, and his hair fell in damp tangles across his forehead. He reminded her of the hero in the Viking tale her father liked to tell, the one in which long-suffering Odin hung speared in an ash tree for nine days.

But what Helena saw when she looked at Colin was more than the physical manifestation of suffering and more than the masculine beauty she now had to acknowledge. She perceived an inner courage, a strength in him that made her reevaluate everything she'd ever heard about Normans. Colin du Lac was no mewling, swooning, faint-hearted coward. He was as brave as any of the knights of Rivenloch, mayhap braver.

She only prayed he'd live long enough to get back into fighting form.

As she perused his weary face, she was tempted to smooth the hair back from his troubled brow, to bathe his fevered skin with a damp rag, to wipe away the stains of his tears. 'Twas a disconcerting desire. She hardly knew this man, and certainly she bore him no great love. Before her hands could betray her, she busied them with tearing linen from her underskirt and bandaging the wound.

When she finished, she felt his gaze upon her, hot and penetrating.

"I know I should be grateful," he croaked, "but I suspect you enjoyed every poke of the needle."

She boldly met his stare. "Then you suspect wrong."

Something charged the air for an instant, arcing between them like lightning. Their eyes locked, and 'twas as if their spirits synchronized, forging a mysterious bond as potent and eternal as the melding of steel and iron.

Even when their gazes parted a moment later, a vestige of that union remained, an understanding and a truth so profound that Helena found it difficult to speak or look at him again.

"On the morrow," she finally murmured, gathering up her supplies, "I'll need to change the bandages."

"Good." Then the incorrigible Norman managed to slip in one last word of impropriety, breaking the tension with his ribald humor. "A few more days of making bandages, and you won't have a stitch of clothing left."

Colin dozed fitfully. Partly because of his aching wound. Partly because his senses were fully alert, given that he slept among the enemy in the wilds of Scotland. And partly because his emotions concerning the beautiful, scheming Scots abductor dozing a few yards away roiled about in his head like boiling oil.

Was Helena angel or demon? Did she care for his welfare, or was she only concerned with his worth? He thought he'd uncovered her true nature, that she'd aided him for purely selfish reasons. After all, if he perished, she would not only lose her hostage and thus her bartering power, but she'd also be held accountable to Pagan for his death. Naturally she'd want to treat his wound. Her own well-being depended upon it.

But then she'd stitched him up, and though he'd been distracted by the painful trial, biting back groans of agony, blinking back the tears that leaked unbidden from his eyes, he grew dimly aware that 'twas an ordeal for her as well.

And afterward, when he'd caught her gaze, when she'd denied feeling pleasure at his pain, he'd never glimpsed a face more innocent, more honest, more vulnerable. Sincerity pooled in her eyes, and he felt in that instant the same closeness of spirit he sometimes experienced when making love with a woman.

'Twas absurd. Helena of Rivenloch was not to be trusted, no matter what he saw in her eyes. She was impulsive and conniving and unpredictable. And she hated Normans. She'd started this venture with treachery in mind, and though things had progressed far beyond her intentions, 'twas still her fault they were here. She would say anything, *do* anything to advance her own cause.

Including, he thought ruefully, bewitching him with those wide green eyes of hers.

Helena woke before the others. The ground was wet with dew, her belly ached with hunger, and her wrists were numb where they were bound behind her. She peeked over at Colin. Thank God, no wolves had devoured him in the night. He seemed to be breathing, and no blood oozed through the bandage on his leg. She hadn't killed him with her doctoring after all.

Arrows of sunlight shot through the pines, and she knew the mercenaries would rouse soon. Meanwhile she needed to sharpen the strategy that had been taking shape in her brain.

Colin had thought 'twas a mistake to give the English the name and location of Rivenloch, but Helena knew better. She wasn't so foolish as to lead the enemy up to the castle walls. Still, the closer she was to allies when she overpowered her abductors, the better their chances were for survival, and the more likely a party of knights from Rivenloch could ride out afterward to hunt down the English. 'Twas a risk, aye, but like her father, she found it nigh impossible to turn down a wager. Hopefully, her luck would run more favorably than Lord Gellir's.

She glanced again at Colin, whose brow furrowed in

his sleep. The Norman didn't trust her judgment. Despite all she'd done to save his leg, to say naught of saving his neck, still he had no faith in her. It cut her to the quick.

She sighed softly. On the other hand, perchance 'twas for the best Colin didn't comprehend her plans. At least when the time came for deception, he wouldn't give her away.

The rest of the camp woke gradually. The mercenaries passed out a breakfast of coarse maslin bread and watered wine to their captives, not out of kindness, but in preparation for the long journey ahead.

'Twas a long journey, especially when Helena measured it in Colin's limping gait, in the ashen pallor of his face, in the sheen of sweat that glistened upon his throat as he struggled along the makeshift path between his two captors.

By late afternoon, 'twas clear she'd have to take action sooner than she expected, though they were yet miles away from Rivenloch. Colin could not endure much more travel. Already blood seeped from his wound again, staining the linen bandage. Forsooth, the only good news was that the mercenaries' southward path had brought them close to the cottage in the wood. When she did manage to secure their escape from these savages, they wouldn't have far to go for shelter.

"His bandage needs changing," she told Otis as they entered a clearing in a thick copse of sycamores. "And I need to find herbs to stop the bleeding."

Otis frowned. "Doesn't look all that grave to me."

"If he loses much more blood, you'll have to carry him." As if to lend credence to her statement, Colin's knees buckled, and only the quick reflexes of the men beside him kept him from completely collapsing.

Otis spat, obviously irritated with the delay. "Very well," he growled. "Dob and Hick, take her to look for her damned weeds."

She took her time finding the shepherd's purse, though it grew rampant along the path. The English wouldn't know the difference, and the delay would buy her time to put her strategy into play. After a long while, she at last pretended to spot the plant and directed Hick to cut several pieces for her.

When she returned to the clearing, Colin was propped against a tree, dozing, and Otis paced impatiently, eyeing the setting sun.

"What delayed ye, wench?" he snapped. "We could have been there by now."

A hundred acid retorts sprang to her mind, but she bit her tongue.

"I'm no more happy about this than you are," she told him companionably. "I'd hoped to drain Rivenloch's coffers by now."

Otis's brows shot up. "Indeed? And why should ye wish to drain its coffers? Ye said ye belonged to Rivenloch."

"Aye," she said with a snort, "I *belong* to Rivenloch. For years he's kept me as a slave." She gazed dreamily off into the distance. "This was my chance to take revenge, holding his favorite Norman hostage." She emitted a bitter little laugh. "Now instead you'll ransom the both of us and return me to my slavery."

Otis's brows converged as he considered her words. Helena turned away then, satisfied. She'd planted the seeds of doubt. Though the deception had only begun, 'twas enough for now that she'd got the Englishman to thinking.

"Will you loose me now so I can dress his wound?"

Otis cut her free, but kept her well guarded as she changed Colin's bandages.

She swallowed back trepidation as she beheld her handiwork of the night before. Though her stitches had held, blood still leaked from the wound. She crushed the shepherd's purse and pressed the leaves gently against the cut, tearing another strip of clean linen from her garment for binding. Colin was probably right. Before a sennight passed, she'd have ripped all of her underskirt to make bandages for him.

Just as she tied up the ends of the linen, Colin's eyes fluttered open. "Water," he grunted.

She nodded. "Otis, have you fresh water?"

She saw Otis flinch at her use of his given name, but he nonetheless complied, tossing her a half-filled skin of water he'd collected earlier from the stream.

She tipped the skin back for Colin, helping him to drink. Their eyes met, and she felt once again that curious alliance, the feeling that they could read each other's minds, that they had known each other forever. But she couldn't afford to be seduced this time by his fellowship. Her success tonight depended on a great deal of deceit, and she dared not let Colin's perceptiveness stand in her way. So she averted her eyes before he could steal her thoughts from her.

When he was finished drinking, she returned the skin to Otis. She intentionally let her fingers brush those of the Englishman, resisting the urge to shudder as she contacted his grimy calluses. While the others occupied themselves building a fire, she engaged him in private conversation, hoping their intimacy might disarm him and make him forget to tie her up again.

"So how much were you planning on asking for the Norman?" she murmured.

Otis shrugged. 'Twas clear he hadn't thought about it.

"He's Rivenloch's best knight," she confided.

"Fifty pounds?" he guessed.

"Fifty?" She chuckled softly. "Oh, he's worth far more than that, I assure you. Rivenloch's coffers can afford a much higher ransom."

He narrowed his eyes conspiratorially. "Ye *do* want to cripple the Lord of Rivenloch, don't ye?"

She let murder infest her gaze. "More than anything."

He leered at her then, as if he understood her motives all too well, and she leered back.

"Huh," he said, studying her face for signs of deceit. She was careful to show none. "And how much would ye have asked for him?"

"A hundred and fifty."

"A hundred and . . . ," he barked. Then he lowered his voice. "Ye could get that much?"

"Aye." Lord, she hoped he believed her. The Scotsmen she knew wouldn't pay a shilling for a Norman knight.

He rubbed at his stubbled chin, digesting this information.

She wanted to give him time to think, so she rubbed her palms together, and asked, "Do you have something a little more potent to quaff, Otis?"

He eyed her suspiciously. "I might."

"I could use a strong drink after having to play nurse to that despicable Norman." She shuddered.

But Otis wasn't as stupid as he appeared. "Ye fought beside him earlier. He didn't seem so despicable then."

She dipped her eyes in a demure imitation of her youngest sister, the only one of the three who came by her feminine wiles honestly. "At the time, Otis, I thought you meant to kill me." She pressed one hand to her bosom, as if the thought left her breathless even now. "I mean, when I saw your broad shoulders and grim face and . . . and the length of your sword . . ."

Otis straightened, obviously pleased with her flattering impressions.

"What else could I do," she continued, "but call upon a knight sworn to defend me?"

She let her fingers stroke subtly along the edge of her neckline, willing him to look there.

He did, and she saw a gleam of lust enter his eyes.

"Well, ye needn't fret, m'lady," he purred. "I don't think I'll have to kill ye."

"Indeed?" She allowed her gaze to roam over his chest, pretending interest where she felt revulsion. "I'd be ever so . . . grateful . . . if you did not."

With a one-sided smile that bared a patch of naked gums, he hunkered down to pull a leather bottle from his pack. She could have kicked him in the face while he was down, but she stifled the urge. He uncorked the top and, wiping it with his sleeve, offered her a drink. She took it with a coy smile, trying not to grimace as she brought the filthy bottle to her lips.

Colin scowled, twisting his wrists against his bonds. What the devil was that vixen up to now? He couldn't hear what she said to the Englishman, but 'twas clear they were forming some sort of alliance.

This was bad. Very bad.

Helena of Rivenloch was surely the most foolish wench in all of Scotland. Not only was she throwing in with a bunch of dishonorable mercenaries, but it appeared she was attempting to seduce their leader.

He ground his teeth. He knew better than to believe the lass was honestly attracted to the grizzled, toothless oaf. Nevertheless, disappointment clouded his vision as he watched her sidle up to the drooling Englishman, her breasts all but toppling out of her gown.

And then she made the worst mistake of all. She began drinking.

He'd already seen what drink could do to her. If she drank herself senseless tonight, there was no telling what might happen.

But he was helpless to intervene. Tied to the tree, he could only watch as she imbibed more and more with each passing hour. By the time the sky grew dark and the stars emerged, she was exchanging bawdy tales with the mercenaries around the fire. Before long, they were singing together, raising their cups in drunken salutes to their favorite harlots, and in Helena's case, stable lads.

Colin chewed at the inside of his cheek, wondering if she'd really bedded the dozen or so lads she mentioned by name. He scowled. To think she'd had the gall to call *him* a philanderer.

Eventually their revelry took an all-too-predictable turn. As Helena twirled unsteadily in a spontaneous dance, accompanied by the men's clapping, Otis took the liberty of giving her buttocks an overly familiar squeeze.

Colin smiled grimly, knowing the lass would wheel about now and flatten the man with a hefty punch. After all, that had been her reaction when Colin had mistakenly clutched at her breast. But to his displeasure, the cursed wench only giggled and swatted playfully at Otis's offending hand.

Instant rage simmered Colin's blood. What was *wrong* with the maid? She'd shown naught but contempt for *him*, a Norman, her ally. And now she caroused, nay, *consorted* with the English, her enemy. 'Twas little wonder the King had wanted Pagan to take command of Rivenloch. *This* Scotswoman, at least, had no concept of loyalty.

He watched in sickened silence as she weaved in and out among the mercenaries, swinging her hips close to their groping paws, bending forward to give them taunting glimpses of her bosom. Colin clenched his jaw. He only hoped she'd be prepared for what would inevitably come of her seduction. And he hoped he'd not have to witness the ensuing debauchery.

"Wait!" she cried, chuckling and skipping out of hand's reach of one of the knaves seated on a log beside the fire. She tucked the half-flattened wineskin between her breasts and held her hands up for silence. The men complied as best they could, reduced to drunken grunts and lusty panting. "Before we get too . . . ," she said with a lascivious grin, "d'stracted . . ."

The men sent up a vulgar cheer, and Dob rubbed suggestively at his groin.

She sidled up to where Otis sat, uncorked the wineskin nestled in her bosom, and leaned forward, letting the wine pour into his open mouth. His palms came up to cup her breasts, and she gave a coy little squeak, cutting off his wine and dancing out of his grasp.

Colin didn't want to watch, but he couldn't help himself. He'd played such games himself, games of seduction and withdrawal that piqued desire to a fever pitch. But 'twas different watching Helena play them. It made his skin burn, and he wasn't sure if 'twas from desire or disgust, from envy or rage, from lust or disappointment or shame. But all of those baffling emotions coursed through him as he fought to tear his gaze away.

"'Tis too late, m'lady," Otis slurred. "'M already distracted."

She dipped down to brazenly pat his braies. "I c'n see that."

Otis growled.

She grinned. "But firs' we nee' to make sure our li'l dove won't fly the coop." She rose, swayed for a moment, then started toward Colin. "I'll jus' check the knots."

Colin lowered his eyes. He couldn't bear to look at her as she staggered up. His emotions had congealed into one now. All he felt was disgust. He had naught to say to her. Naught.

Yet he couldn't help himself. "I hope you realize what you're doing," he muttered.

He smelled the wine on her breath, but she didn't seem all that drunk as she whispered, "Oh, aye," then circled behind him.

"Because they won't be gentle with you," he warned. "Their kind never are."

She chuckled as she labored over his bonds. "I wasn't expecting them to be gentle."

He frowned. Mayhap she was one of those odd creatures who *liked* to be handled roughly.

She gave his hand a patronizing pat. "But I think I can handle them."

He growled in distaste. Never had his judgment been so flawed. He'd truly believed Helena was a respectable lady, that she possessed scruples and honor and virtue. 'Twas obvious now that she was not at all the woman he'd imagined.

"'Ey, wench!" Otis bellowed. "Methinks ye tarry too long wi' the pris'ner. Ye aren't swivin' 'im, are ye?"

The rest of the company chortled.

"What? An' mix Norm'n blancmange with good Scots pottage?" she called back, making them laugh uproariously. "Nay, love. I'm savin' m'self for you."

Colin stared coldly at the ground. Christ's bones, the maid had a tongue more vile than a dockside harlot's. Now he *knew* he didn't want to witness the vulgarities to come.

As if she read his thoughts, she murmured to him, "Keep your eyes open."

Not for a shipload of silver, he thought as she left his side to saunter toward the fire. And yet he couldn't help an occasional glance as the wench began to work her wiles on the willing targets of her seduction.

"Otis, m'lad," she purred, "where've you put tha' long steel dagger o' yours?"

"'S right here, wench," he replied, loosening the ties of his braies.

"Oh, my, but I didn't mean *that* dagger, love. I meant *this* one."

In a flash, she reached past his gaping braies toward his

sword belt and whipped his dagger out of its sheath. While Otis blinked in confusion, she reared back her foot and kicked him squarely between the legs. Colin, momentarily stunned, now cringed. But as Helena spun toward another mercenary, suddenly completely sober, Colin straightened in amazement. And when he did, he discovered something astonishing. The ropes around his wrists were loose.

## Chapter 10

"RUN!" HELENA SHOUTED at Colin. "*Run!*" God's eyes, what was taking him so long? Aye, he was injured, but she'd given him plenty of time to prepare. She'd spent well over an hour getting the men drunk. And now one of them was off in the woods, pissing. 'Twas an ideal opportunity for her to make a stand and for Colin to make his escape. God's hooks! Hadn't she told him to keep his eyes open?

She shoved Hick from his log seat with her left hand, sending him sprawling into the pine needles. Then she leaped over the fire, narrowly missing igniting her skirts, to face Dob with the dagger.

From the corner of her eye, she saw Colin had finally made it to his feet, though he was moving at a hobble.

Her thirst for revenge fueled by the pathetic sight, she raised her dagger high, then stabbed it hard into the top of Dob's thigh. "That," she bit out, "is for wounding my hostage."

He screamed and scrabbled at the wound, but she felt no remorse as she yanked the blade free. The man had shown *her* no mercy, after all. He'd blackened her eye and ruined Colin's leg, likely crippling the noble knight forever.

She glanced up, hoping to see Colin limping off to safety, but instead he staggered into the fray.

"Go! *Go!*" she cried.

He ignored her and began to engage the fourth Englishman, armed with only his bare hands. He threw a powerful punch that caught the man's jaw, followed by a blow to the belly that folded him in half.

Meanwhile, Hick had scrambled up from the other side of the log. He drew his dagger and came toward her with a leer. "So ye want to play rough, do ye?"

She narrowed her eyes. "Oh, aye," she assured him.

She took a step backward to brace herself, not realizing that Otis had recovered enough to reach out and wrench her ankle out from under her. She lost her balance and fell backward, nearly into the fire. Worse, the weapon shot out of her grip when her wrist hit the ground.

Hick was still advancing, and as she caught her breath, Otis hunched over her with murder in his eyes. She swung her fist around with all the force she could muster, catching Otis's nose with a sickening crack. The blow made her knuckles throb with pain, though likely not as much as Otis's face did.

When she whipped her head around, Hick was already there, brandishing The Shadow's confiscated knife. It gleamed as it made its descent toward her chest. She twisted aside enough so that the blade just missed the back of her ribs before it lodged in the dirt. Then she scooped up a handful of hot coals and flung them toward his face.

Hick shrieked and leaped backward, scrubbing madly at his eyes. In the chaos, Helena rolled to her hands and knees to see if Colin had fled yet.

She had to admit, for a crippled nobleman, he was putting up an impressive battle. Instead of fighting like a proper knight, he was doing the clever thing. He was using his fists and feet and even spittle to badger his opponent.

But he wouldn't last long. Already she saw fresh blood seeping through the bandages. And if his foe took even one swipe at that vulnerable spot . . .

She wrenched The Shadow's knife from the earth and closed in on the battling men. But there was no need for her intervention. Just as she stood poised to use the knife, Colin threw a hard punch that rocked the man's head backward and sent him to temporary oblivion.

Whether she was alerted first by the quiet scrape behind her or the widening of Colin's eyes, she didn't know, but she suddenly realized they were outnumbered. The fifth man had returned.

There was no time to defend herself, no time to turn, no time to even look. The best she could do was to stab blindly backward and pray she hit something vital.

But when she thrust the knife behind her, it whisked through empty air.

"Down!" Colin yelled.

Without thinking, she dropped to the ground, thank God. For in the same instant, Colin's hand shot forward, firing a dagger that missed her by mere inches. Behind her, she heard a grunt, then staggering footfalls, and she knew the knife had met its mark.

Without a backward glance, stealing a mislaid dagger

and a full wineskin left near the fire, she clambered to her feet and ran toward Colin. "Let's go!"

They bolted from the battlefield into the forest, shuffling through the darkness as best they could. Helena helped him, slinging his arm across her shoulders and taking some of his weight. Mayhap the Englishmen followed them. Mayhap not. But after a mile or two, they lost whatever pursuit there was, nearly losing their own way as well.

Her lungs burning, Helena was finally forced to halt. She sagged forward, bracing her hand on her knee, drawing in huge gulps of air. Colin, winded as well, leaned against a tree. Their mingled gasps grated against the quiet of the woods.

As they caught their breath, Colin said, "Make me an oath."

"Aye?"

"Never do that again."

"Do what?"

"Take such a foolish risk. Challenge foes who outnumber and outweigh you. Pit yourself against unscrupulous mercenaries."

She frowned. "You're welcome."

"Plan an escape," he added pointedly, "without consulting your ally."

"I *did* consult you. You were just too thickheaded to understand."

"Run, you said? *Run?*" He shook his head.

She shrugged. "You're a Norman."

He scowled. "I'm a *knight*."

"Besides," she said as they set out again at a more leisurely pace through a familiar grove of oaks, "everything turned out for the best."

"But what if it hadn't? What if you'd lost the battle? And what if one of them . . . or *all* of them . . . had decided to take you up on your offer?"

Helena stopped in her tracks. "Sweet Mary, do you truly believe me so helpless? Every woman knows a man is most vulnerable when his trews are about his ankles." God's eyes, 'twas the reason she'd spent half the evening seducing the mercenaries.

Colin furrowed his brows and sighed.

Still, he was right about one thing. She hadn't really considered the consequences of losing. She seldom did. But then, if she thought too much about the possible outcome, she'd *never* draw her sword.

Colin's braies weren't about his ankles, not yet anyway, but that didn't mean he didn't feel every bit as vulnerable as the English mercenaries. He'd watched the same temptress they had, after all, and he was hardly immune to her charms.

With her arm around his waist and her breast nestled far too cozily against his chest, Helena helped him limp back to the cottage. 'Twas a miracle they found it, considering how much she'd drunk over the course of the evening, but she seemed surefooted and aware of her bearings. Once inside the shelter, she took great pains to make sure he was comfortable, insisting he take the pallet.

"The floor is fine," he argued.

"Nonsense." She pushed him back onto the bed, then leaned close to tuck the coverlet around his shoulders, forgetting her gown was loose about the neck. Her breasts swelled above the cloth and, by the flickering light of the fire, looked as golden and delectable as loaves of honey bread.

Fighting nature, he forced his gaze away. Still, his voice cracked as he said, "I insist."

She crossed her arms under her bosom, which only made the problem worse. "And just how are you going to insist when you can scarcely stand upright?"

*He* might not be able to stand upright, but another part of him was having no trouble at all. Despite the painful throbbing of his wound, a more pressing ache clamored for his attention.

"Nay," she continued. "You'll take the pallet. I won't have that wretched captain of yours saying I didn't care for you properly."

That jarred some of the desire out of him. For a moment, he'd forgotten Helena's motives. Aye, she wanted him to heal, but only because 'twould better serve her purposes. The woman was as greedy as the mercenaries.

"You're wasting your time," he said bluntly. "He won't pay a farthing for me."

She clucked her tongue. "Why, Sir Colin, even I know you're not *that* worthless."

It took him aback, hearing her call him by name. He liked the way it lilted off her tongue.

"Besides," she continued, "I'm not asking for a farthing. I'm asking for my sister."

He shook his head. "Sir Pagan will not be manipulated."

"*Everyone* can be manipulated."

"Ah," he said, a sour taste in his mouth. "You mean the way you manipulated the mercenaries?"

She only gave him a sly smile, then moved to begin tending to his leg.

"And you called *me* a philanderer," he grumbled.

"I'm not a philanderer."

He smirked. "I can't quite recall. How many stable lads was it?"

She chuckled as she carefully unwrapped his bandage. "You believed me?"

"Where else would you learn all those . . . those . . . ?" Images of the breathtaking beauty, swinging her hips and fluttering her lashes and exposing her velvety bosom, wound their way through his mind again, heating his blood.

"Oh, aye," she told him, her voice laced with sardonic humor. "I've slept with all the stable lads. And I've bedded all the knights of Rivenloch as well."

She might think 'twas amusing, but he did not. Not tonight. Not when she'd displayed such expertise at seduction. Not when she'd risked her body to set him free. And most especially not when he'd begun to grow perilously fond of the Scots maid.

She propped her foot up on the pallet, then proceeded to cut yet another swath from her underskirt. If he didn't know better, he'd suspect she did it to provoke him, for his gaze couldn't help but wander up the enticing length of her exposed calf.

He scowled. "'Tis just as well Pagan will not surrender his bride."

"And why is that?" She lowered her foot. Wetting a rag in the nearby bucket of water, she began swabbing at his wound. Her touch was surprisingly gentle for a woman who had just stabbed a couple of outlaws without blinking an eye.

"You wouldn't last long as his wife."

"Indeed?"

"Sir Pagan would demand fidelity."

"Ah." She frowned, pretending to consider his statement. "So he'd have no patience for my stable lads?"

He lowered his brows. The wench wasn't taking him seriously at all. "He'd kill them."

"Pity." A hint of a smile hovered about her lips. "Of course, I'd have to kill all his mistresses in turn. Then who'd be left to tend to the castle?"

Helena could feel the frustration roiling off Colin like the heat off a new-forged sword. She found his attitude half-amusing and half-irritating. Why was it that men assumed they could bed whomever they desired, but women had to be faithful? 'Twas hardly fair.

Not that she was interested in bedding *any* man, including the man she planned to make her husband. Forsooth, if Pagan wished to be a philanderer and swive every maidservant in the castle, 'twas fine with her.

"There," she said, finishing off the bandage and dusting her hands together. "Now where's that satchel of food? I'm starving." She spotted it by the fire. Picking it up, she batted it a few times to see if any vermin had crawled in. "What about you? Are you hungry?"

There *was* hunger in his eyes, but 'twas hunger of an entirely different sort. His gaze smoldered with desire, like a banked fire waiting to be roused. God's bones, he, too, had been affected by her seduction. She hadn't noticed before. Of course, it probably didn't help that she'd just spent several lingering moments tending to a wound located mere inches from . . .

She glanced at his trews. There was no mistake. He was as solid as a lance primed for the joust. And for some curious and disturbing reason, that sent a thrill of excitement through her veins.

'Twas absurd. She was accustomed to such sights. In the company of men for most of her life, she'd been exposed to all sorts of manly displays, from loud belching to arse scratching, from proud farting to vile swearing. She'd witnessed men snorting and pissing and, aye, swiving.

But something about Colin's manifestation of desire, and knowing 'twas for her alone, gave her an intoxicating sense of power and playfulness.

She sauntered toward him with the satchel of food, a sultry smile playing about her lips. "So do you not think I can win Pagan's devotion?"

He looked uneasy, as if he didn't want to think about it. She perched beside him on the pallet, then popped a cherry into his mouth.

He chewed for a moment, then spoke around the pit. "Pagan is not as gullible as that pack of mercenaries."

Impulsively, she leaned forward to whisper, "*All* men are gullible when it comes to their trews," then gave his ballocks a light pat.

As quick as a falcon snatching its prey, his hand shot out and caught her wrist. He turned his head and spit the cherry pit onto the floor. She expected him to blush with shame and cast her hand away as well.

She never expected his grim smile. Or his smoky gaze. Or that, completely unabashed, he would press her palm against his erection and hold it there against her will. At least, she supposed 'twas against her will. She didn't make much of an effort to resist.

He looked at her through slitted eyes. "Don't begin what you're unwilling to finish, little temptress."

Her heart beat at her breast like a wild bird flapping against its cage. Lord, his cock was firm and full, and she could feel the heat of it through his trews. But 'twas what resided in his gaze that took her breath away. In his eyes was an invitation to high adventure, the promise of unimaginable pleasure. Her own loins tingled in response, her skin flushed hot, and the blood sang in her ears. Indeed, if she hadn't heeded the warning voice in her head, the one that sounded much like Deirdre's, telling her she was being dangerously impulsive, she might have leaned forward to see what Norman lips tasted like.

Colin could feel Helena's desire like a palpable thing. 'Twas intense and powerful. Forsooth, if he'd known just how powerful, he'd never have forced her hand against him.

He'd thought to issue her a stern warning, to awe her with the consequences of her teasing, to teach her that though he might be a noble knight, he was also a man.

But she wasn't heeding his warning at all. Instead, she seemed drawn to him. Her emerald eyes sparked with fierce longing, their lids dipping as if the weight of desire was too heavy to bear. Her lips, looking more delicious than the cherry, parted as she lowered her sultry gaze to his mouth. And her hand remained where it rested upon his groin. Indeed, her thumb brushed brazenly along the length of him, eliciting from him a groan of pleasure.

Every nerve in his body instantly craved her touch. But he knew it could not be. She was too drunk, and he was too vulnerable. If they consummated this desire, then he'd be no better than the mercenaries.

Using all his force of will, he released her wrist and tore his gaze away.

It took Helena a moment to revive from her languid haze and realize he'd let her go. Lifting her hand, she blinked away the veil of lust, then stumbled awkwardly backward, knocking the satchel from the bed.

As she gathered up the food that had spilled, she seemed agitated, and he wondered if he *had* shocked her after all. He hoped so. 'Twas difficult enough, battling his *own* passions, without having to temper hers.

Finally, without meeting his eyes, she shoved the satchel at him. "Here. You need your strength."

"But what about you? You must be—"

"I'm not hungry."

With that, she made her own bed on the ground, then climbed under the coverlet, facing pointedly away from him.

Colin suddenly wasn't hungry either, not for cherries and cheese. He set the satchel aside. While the fire dimmed, he stared up at the ceiling, unable to shake the provocative images of Helena from his mind—her flashing eyes, her coy smile, her voluptuous breasts, the gentle curve of her hip.

Mayhap on the morrow, he thought, when she was less intoxicated, and he was more in control of his appetite . . .

As the flickering light slowed its dance upon the splintered beams, he closed his eyes and let sweet anticipation lull him to sleep.

All night he dreamed of Helena—cavorting in the pond with her sisters, struggling in his arms down the castle stairs, grinning in triumph as she caught a trout, battling the mercenaries, swaying and whirling seductively in the firelight, tenderly bandaging his wound.

By morn, he thought he'd be weary of her image, but he was wrong. Especially since the first thing he saw when he cracked his eyes open was the object of his dreams, completely and unabashedly naked, washing by the fire with a rag and a bucket.

For a long while, he stared in silence, afraid to make a sound lest he rob his eyes of this lovely feast. She ran the rag over her shoulder and down one arm, then switched hands to wash the other. As she bent to dip the rag in the bucket again, her breasts swung gently forward, and his loins responded to the sight, swelling with desire. She bathed her throat, then her breasts, shivering as the cold water stiffened her nipples. He stiffened as well, and low in his belly grew a familiar ache, an ache he'd not relieved in too long a time.

When she laved between her legs, he almost let out an audible sigh. God's eyes, he envied her hands. She performed the task with nonchalance. But he knew how to touch a woman there to make her sob with passion.

She progressed down her legs, the long, silky length of them, and he wondered what they would feel like, wrapped around his waist, her heels digging into his buttocks as . . .

"Good morn," she said casually, as if she wasn't naked and lovely and tempting. And naked.

Few things left Colin speechless. He could seduce the most reluctant maid with a clever turn of phrase. He could summon up verse as quickly as a jongleur. He could talk his way out of a jealous husband's chamber with ease. But this—this tied his tongue in knots.

# *Chapter 11*

HELENA THOUGHT SHE might be the most wicked woman in all Scotland. She knew very well what effect she had on men, and this morn she intentionally provoked Colin.

Why she taunted him, she wasn't certain. Mayhap to regain the upper hand she'd lost last night. Colin's intimacy had unsettled her, left her out of control, and she was a woman unaccustomed to feeling vulnerable.

Today she'd prove she was master of her own emotions.

"When I'm done, I'll fetch a fresh bucket of water for you, if you like," she offered, propping her foot up on the stool to scour the dirt from her ankles and show off her shapely legs.

He made no reply, but she felt his gaze stroking down the length of her. 'Twas a heady feeling indeed.

Ever since they were children, she and her sisters had bathed outdoors, in a pond near the castle. They'd never developed a sense of shame about their bodies, nor had they realized their own attraction. But in the last few years of bathing so openly, Helena had discovered a secret. She could wield more power in her natural state than she could while fully clothed. Men were left stunned and stuttering when they glimpsed her in all her naked glory.

She scrubbed at her other foot and cast a quizzical look at him over her shoulder. "That is, if you wish to bathe."

His expression, predictably, was dazed. Now she had him under her heel. He might have made her pulse race last night, but this morn, she dominated the game.

Smiling to herself, she flipped her head, tossing her hair forward, then used her fingers to comb out the tangles. "Has your voice escaped you in the night, Sir Colin?"

"Nay." He cleared his throat. "Nay." After a moment, he asked hoarsely, "Are you not . . . cold?"

"Oh, aye, a bit. I could add a log to the fire." She flung her hair back once more and felt his gaze lock on her. "Or mayhap you'd like to come closer to the hearth?"

For a while, he continued to stare at her in disbelief, and she enjoyed his riveted attention, stretching her arms above her head in a way that she knew favorably displayed her breasts.

But her triumph was to be short-lived. As he watched her, his eyes gradually narrowed, and the hint of a smile began to soften his lips. The varlet had guessed her ploy. "Oh, aye," he murmured, "I'd like to come closer."

She tried to remain nonchalant, but his sudden confidence unnerved her. She was accustomed to men groveling and drooling at her feet. Colin du Lac did neither. Though he'd been rattled at first, now he was self-assured, unaffected by her beauty. And for the first time in her life,

Helena's nakedness made her feel, not supremely power-ful, but horribly vulnerable.

As Colin swung his legs over the side of the pallet and sat up, wincing in momentary pain, she pressed the rag to her throat, casually covering her breasts with her arms.

"I *would* like to wash," he decided. "Get the stink of the mercenaries off me." Without preamble, he pulled both his shirts over his head and cast them aside.

Helena couldn't draw breath. She'd seen men's bare torsos before, but none to compare with his. By the Saints, he was well made. His chest was broad, and his waist was flat. His arms and shoulders swelled with muscle. A thin white scar traversed his stomach, and below his navel, fine black hair traced a slim path to what lay lower. Her heart fluttered.

'Twas not lust, she told herself. And 'twas certainly not panic. She was still in control. But suddenly she tired of the game and wished to get dressed. Dragging her gaze away from his magnificent body, she grabbed her abbrevi-ated underdress from the hearth and quickly slithered into it.

He stood up carefully, favoring his injured leg, and began loosening the ties of his trews. Her eyes widened. Lord, he meant to expose himself, here and now. With an invol-untary squeak, she seized her surcoat and tugged it down over her head, allowing the fabric to block her vision. But curse her curiosity, she couldn't resist a peek.

He was beautiful. Unlike the fair-skinned men of her clan, his flesh was golden all over. He was perfectly pro-portioned, his legs long and sturdy, his hips lean. Though his body was that of a warrior, large of frame and hard with muscle, parts of him appeared not menacing, but intriguing. The nest of curls at the juncture of his thighs looked soft and lush, and the rigid staff protruding there seemed made of velvet.

She found her mouth sagging open, and she closed it with a snap. A quick glimpse into his eyes told her he knew quite well what he was doing. Somehow the knave had beaten her at her own game. Now she was the one drooling at his feet. 'Twas infuriating.

With a scowl of self-disgust, she wrenched tight the laces of her surcoat and began tying them. So overwrought was she that she broke off one of them.

"Do you need help?" he asked casually.

"Nay!" she barked. She didn't want him coming any closer with that dangerous body of his.

As nonchalant as she had been, he sauntered toward her, his legs flexing and his . . . She bit her lip. He didn't so much display that part of his anatomy as brandish it. Now she couldn't deny that the quickening of her breath had everything to do with panic. What she feared, she couldn't name, but before he could draw any closer, she snatched up the bucket and headed for the door.

Her voice was high and brittle. "I'll just go and fetch you clean water, then."

Colin chuckled as she tore out the door, her feet bare and the bodice of her surcoat askew. When she'd gone, he leaned against the hearth and grimaced as lightning seared his thigh. It had taken all his self-discipline to walk toward her without grimacing in pain, but it had been worth it to see the shock in her eyes.

The naughty wench had thought she was the only one who could play at seduction. She didn't know with whom she dealt. Colin was favored among the ladies for his skills at lovemaking, for his inventiveness and patience and devotion. He knew how and when and where to touch a woman to leave her pleading for more.

Helena might think she'd learned a great deal from the stable lads and knights she'd bedded, but Colin knew things about women that most men did not. Before they returned to Rivenloch, he intended to teach the impish Scotswoman just what talents her Norman hostage possessed.

But by the time she returned, her eyes carefully averted, Colin's thoughts had strayed by necessity to his wound. It ached more than it should have, and he suspected it might have worsened.

"I'll check your bandages after you've finished," she muttered, setting the bucket on the floor and shoving a dagger into her belt. "Meanwhile, I'm off to fetch a coney."

After a hasty washing, he donned his undershirt again, added wood to the fire, then climbed onto the pallet.

He gingerly peeled back the linen bandage on his leg. True to his fears, the flesh around the stitched wound was red and swollen. He cursed under his breath.

There was little he could do. He'd have to cut the stitches loose and drain the infection, or worse, cauterize the wound. Either option was a wretched choice. But the longer he waited, the worse 'twould be.

Using The Shadow's sharp knife, he took a deep breath and slipped the point under the first stitch. Just as he sliced upward, Helena came in the door, one fist full of greens and a coney slung over her shoulder.

"What are you doing?" she demanded, dropping her burden onto the pine chest.

"The wound festers."

"Nay! Stop!"

Now that he'd begun, he wasn't about to stop, even for the woman who'd painstakingly sewn all the stitches. He sliced another one.

But she was having none of it. She marched over and knocked the knife from his hand with her fist.

"Hey!"

"Don't you dare ruin my handiwork." She fetched the wineskin she'd stolen from the English. "There's a better way."

"Indeed?" He arched a brow at the wineskin. "And what is that? Get so drunk I no longer care about the pain?"

"Hardly," she said, uncorking the skin. Then she hesitated, as if thinking better of it. "Mayhap you had better have something to bite."

"To bite?"

"'Twill sting like the Devil."

He frowned. Was it wise to rely upon the cures of a Scotswoman? For all he knew, she used powdered frogs and raven's claw.

"Don't worry. I've done it myself before." She pulled aside her neckline and showed him a jagged scar near her shoulder. "'Tis unsightly, but the wine killed the infection and saved me from losing my arm."

Colin didn't find it unsightly at all. Forsooth, he had to resist the urge to place a kiss on the patch of puckered flesh. But if she'd endured the pain with good results, so could he. "Very well. Do it."

"If you'd like a leather belt . . ."

He shook his head.

"Lie back, then," she said.

When the liquid poured onto his cut, burning like fire, folding him nearly in half, he almost wished he'd accepted the belt. A groan was wrenched from him, followed by the foulest oath he knew.

"Sorry," she mumbled.

"Bloody hell, are you trying to kill me?"

"I'm trying to save you."

The wine was like searing acid, etching away at his flesh, and he fought to breathe through the pain.

She corked the wineskin again. "Next time I'll give you the belt."

"*Next* time?"

"It should be done every few hours."

"Bloody hell it should."

"Do you want it to heal or not?"

He speared her with a look full of loathing. "I think you're enjoying this."

"You think wrong."

He supposed 'twas unfair to accuse her of inflicting hurt upon him intentionally. After all, she was caring for him as best she could, even if 'twas ultimately for her own designs. But 'twas hard to think fairly, squirming in pain while she calmly rose to retrieve the coney. He wondered how she could have endured such agony.

While he waited for the sting to subside, Helena skinned and dressed the coney. He'd almost forgiven her when she asked over her shoulder, "Is there anything else you need?"

He lifted his brows. Was she feeling guilty for the hurt she'd wrought? Did she wish to make amends? He grinned. Physician and patient. 'Twas a game with which he was very familiar. Most ladies liked for him to play the physician, but he was only too willing to bend to Helena's wishes.

"When I was a lad," he called out softly, "my mother would always kiss my cuts. She said it made the pain go away and healed them faster."

She turned around, her face a mask of perplexity. "I meant, anything else you need to make supper? I found wild onions and rosemary."

His grin faded. Was food all she could think about? He supposed he'd have to create some clever meal out of the small beast. One, he thought slyly, that included the remainder of that cursed wine.

"Nay." He sniffed. "But I still could sorely use a woman's healing kiss, soft and tender and sweet upon my flesh."

"I'm not going to kiss your cut." She raised a scolding brow, but he noticed a smile tugging at her lips. "No matter how pathetically you beg."

He affected a pout. "'Tis the least you could do, my lady, considering how much pain you've inflicted."

"Hmph."

"Forsooth," he said, crossing his arms over his chest, "I think I should get a kiss every time you pour that Devil's fire upon me."

She clucked her tongue. "You *are* a knave."

He pretended affront. "And now you call me names. Is there no end to your abuse, my lady?"

She shrugged. "I'm not making you eat my cooking."

He smiled. She'd made a jest. And he'd thought she was too serious to match wits with him.

With her help, he managed to make it to the hearth,

cooking while he sat on the three-legged stool. He put the coney in water and added the wild onions and a generous sprinkling of rosemary to the pot. While she wasn't looking, he poured in a small measure of wine. Soon a rich stew bubbled over the fire.

Helena ate with relish, though she still spared him no word of praise, and they shared the last of the cherries afterward. But with only a bit of cheese left from The Shadow's cache, she'd have to find something for the evening meal. Colin offered to help her, but she insisted he stay in bed, threatening to tie him there if he moved from the spot.

She managed to trap a pair of quail and brought back a pot brimming with blackberries, but between her rounds of foraging, she returned to dole out her torturous cure to his wound.

Every time was as agonizing as the first, and his cursing was just as vehement. After a meal of roast quail with blackberry sauce and a salat of herbs, she gave him the last treatment of the evening. But this time she did something that made him forget all about the pain. She leaned forward and very softly, very tenderly, very sweetly placed a kiss upon his thigh.

He looked at her in awe, but her brow furrowed, as if she wondered why she'd done it.

He closed his eyes and caught her hand in his. "'Tis feeling better already."

He fell asleep like that, holding her hand, pleasantly weary, a vague smile on his lips. And he would have slumbered peacefully till morn, but in the middle of the night, he heard the unmistakable sound of a damsel in distress.

\* \* \*

Helena shivered violently in the darkness. It seemed winter had chosen to visit on this midsummer night. Her jaw ached from clenching her teeth for the past several hours, and she blew on her hands, trying to warm her numb fingers.

She'd given Colin two of the coverlets. It seemed the right thing to do, considering how much pain she'd made him suffer. Besides, he needed a solid night's rest to help him heal. But now she was paying for her kindness.

Naught was left of the fire but a dim glow. She'd made the mistake of letting the supply of wood run out. Now 'twas so cold, she'd begun to consider burning the furniture.

She curled into a tight ball and let out a long, chattering sigh.

"God's eyes, wench," came a growl from the bed. "Why didn't you say something?"

She heard him rustling the coverlet, but she was too stiff to move or speak.

"By the Saints, 'tis colder than a nun's . . . 'tis freezing," he amended. "Come here, my lady."

"I'm fine," she managed between her teeth.

"Nonsense. I can hear your bones rattling from here."

"'T-t-tis naught."

"Come, lady. I'll share the pallet. We can keep each other warm."

"Oh, aye, you'd like that, w-wouldn't you? Ph-ph-ph-philanderer." Lord, even half-asleep, the knave had naught but bedding her on his mind.

He was quiet for a moment, and she wondered if he'd drifted off to sleep again. When he spoke again, his voice was solemn. "I am a knight, my lady, a man of honor. I will sleep beside you and keep you warm, 'tis all."

His offer was tempting. She was so cold that her breath made mist upon the air.

"Come, Hel-cat. Who will ransom me if you freeze to death?"

She wondered if she *might* freeze to death. She couldn't remember being this cold, even when she bathed in the pond at Martinmas.

"I swear by my sword I'll be a gentleman. Come up."

With great difficulty, she managed to uncoil herself and hobble to the pallet. He lifted the coverlet to make room for her. She climbed in, careful not to touch him. But her efforts were for naught. In an instant, he threw a possessive arm around her and hauled her back against his chest, enveloping her in delicious warmth.

"Of course," he murmured against her hair, "if you *wish* me to keep you warm another way . . ."

She tried to elbow him, but his arm held her fast.

"Shh, little Hel-fire. You're safe with me."

She *did* feel safe. She should have felt trapped, smothered in his embrace. Instead, there was calming comfort in the circle of his arms, a curious contentment, as if she was protected . . . and cherished.

She slept so soundly that the sun was already up when her eyes finally trembled open. The first thing she noticed was that Colin's palm cradled her breast. The second was that his loins pressed against her backside. The third, the thing that saved him from her wrath, was that he was sound asleep. Soft snores issued from his parted lips, and his body was as limp and heavy as a coat of chain mail.

She knew she should move. 'Twas not gentlemanly at all, the way he touched her, surrounding her, violating her. She would move at once. At least she *planned* to move. Then again, as long as he was sleeping . . .

His hand felt rather pleasant there. It fit her perfectly, as if 'twas made to encircle her breast. 'Twas curious how it fell at just the right place when his forearm rested upon her hip. She took a deep breath, and the subtle movement made a sweet friction between her breast and his hand. 'Twas as if he stroked her there, and she felt her nipple swell as her bosom rose and fell beneath his palm. A wave of warmth suffused her blood, and her nostrils flared as she savored the sensation.

She felt him breathing, his broad chest expanding and contracting against her back, while his loins nestled against her buttocks. Sweet Mary, he was so hot there, like a coal waiting to be stirred to life. She wondered what would happen if she moved against him?

He must have read her wicked intent, for he roused in his sleep then and rolled away from her onto his back. And though she'd never lain with a man before, though she always slept alone, her body felt instantly bereft of his touch.

She carefully turned toward him so as not to wake him and lay on her side, studying his profile. He was quite a handsome man. For a Norman. He hadn't the rugged quality of her countrymen. Their faces were scarred by weather and battle, their skin ruddy, their hair as brown as the heath in winter. Colin's features were almost delicate in comparison, and yet there was naught feminine about him. His mane was a much richer color, not quite black, but as dark as wet oak. His skin was golden, as if he'd been dipped in honey. His brow was heavy, but the lashes falling upon his cheek were as fine as new grass.

She lifted herself onto her elbow to get a better view. Something had happened to his nose, mayhap a brawl, mayhap an accident, but there was a tiny nick across the bridge where the bone might have been chipped. His jaw was wide and strong and covered with a light growth of coarse black hair, proof that Normans could indeed grow beards.

She gazed at his lips. Even they were different from those of the Scots. Rivenloch men had grim mouths, mouths meant for frowning and feasting and bellowing in battle. Colin du Lac's mouth looked as soft and yielding as pandemain fresh from the oven. She'd seen his lips curl in displeasure, curve in amusement, and grimace in pain. But now, while he slumbered, they parted slightly, making him look as sweet and innocent as a child.

'Twas a mouth made for laughter, for sipping wine, for reciting verse, for all the carefree pleasures of life. 'Twas a mouth, she thought, made for kissing.

She supposed it made sense. After all, he *was* a philanderer. No doubt he applied potions and salves to his lips nightly to keep them supple for all that kissing.

She wondered just how soft they were. She bit her own lip. Did she dare try? She'd kissed plenty of Scots lads, mostly on a dare or to distract them so she could follow up with a hearty punch. Once, when she was twelve summers old, a kitchen lad had wagered she could not kiss his sleeping friend without waking him. She'd won the wager. But then the lad's lips had been wind-chapped and as dry as dust. She doubted he could have felt a teat shoved between them.

She ran her tongue over her bottom lip, wondering if she could kiss Colin without waking him.

On impulse, before she could change her mind, she leaned over him, hovering inches away as his breath brushed across her mouth. Then she closed her eyes and, holding her breath, pressed her lips ever so softly to his.

## Chapter 12

THIS TIME, SHE would have lost the wager, for the moment their mouths met, Colin woke, seized her by the shoulders, and slammed her back down onto the pallet. Blinking the sleep from his eyes, he frowned down at her. "What are you doing?"

"Naught." She gulped. She'd forgotten he was a warrior, trained to sleep with one eye open, a man accustomed to reacting first and reasoning later. She'd also forgotten how strong he was. God's bones, he'd flipped her onto her back faster than she could suck in a startled breath. And he still held her pinned there.

"What were you doing?" he demanded again.

His threatening tone tweaked her ear. Her awe turned to anger, and she sneered, "I was trying to suck the life from you."

He sighed. "Don't you know better than to wake a sleeping soldier?"

"I didn't think something as . . ." She seized his

forearms, trying to push him away. 'Twas hopeless. He was as strong as a warhorse. "Something as insignificant as a ki—" As soon as the words left her mouth, she regretted them.

"As a what?"

The silence seemed thunderous.

Then crinkles slowly formed at the corners of his eyes, and an infuriating smile replaced his scowl. He clucked his tongue. "Lusty little Hel-cat. You were trying to *kiss* me."

"Nay."

"Oh, aye."

"I was trying to . . . to *kick* you."

"Indeed?" He lowered his gaze to her mouth, and God help her, her lips tingled almost as if he touched her there. "And did you enjoy it? That *kick?*"

Naught enraged her more than mockery. She'd show him a kick. She twisted her left leg free, intending to boot him in the shin.

But he guessed her intent and slung his heavy thigh over her before she could move. "Take care, my lady. I am yet a wounded man."

Spitting mad, she nevertheless heeded his warning. The last thing she needed was to deal him a blow that would make his recovery take longer.

And yet he insisted on testing her temper. "You know, if you want a kiss," he told her, his eyes sparkling mischief, "all you have to do is ask."

"I don't, you overgrown, oversexed son of a—"

"My lady!" he exclaimed, feigning shock. "'Tis *you* who wished a kiss from *me*. I was sleeping blissfully when you came to ravish me with—"

"Ravish you? I did no such—"

"By the Saints, you practically threw yourself at me and—"

"Oh!" Fury built inside her, the kind of fury that made her speak without thinking, but she could no more stop her tirade than one could stop ale flowing from a cracked keg. "'Twas only to see if 'tis true what they say," she snarled, "that kissing a Norman is like kissing a toad!"

Most men cowered at her outbursts. Colin only laughed. "And have you kissed many toads?"

Rage blinded her. Words eluded her. The only reaction she could summon up was a scream of pure wrath.

But before she was finished, his lips descended to cut off her cry, muffling the sound in the recesses of his mouth.

Her blood boiled, and she struggled against him, trying to twist away from his insistent lips. But she could no more shake him loose than a hound trying to shake loose a tick. He slanted his mouth across hers, but she managed to seal her lips shut to prevent his entrance. His heavy breath blew across her cheek toward her ear, sending an unwelcome shiver through her. So forceful was his kiss that she couldn't even maneuver her teeth to bite him.

But she could use her fists. 'Twas awkward with his hands holding her down, but she pounded on the sides of his shoulders as hard as she could. She might just as well have been patting a well-performing horse. He gave no outward indication that he felt a thing. Indeed, his kissing grew even more unrelenting.

Colin meant to stop. Though he was a master of seduction, he was no ravisher. Unless, of course, 'twas the game his mistress wished to play.

He'd only meant to silence her scream.

But now that he was engaged, now that he could taste the sweet, wild honey of her lips and feel the heat of her anger, so like passion, 'twas difficult to extricate himself.

Desire seized him betwixt the legs, sending a current coursing through his body. He distantly noted Helena pummeling at his shoulders, but 'twas naught compared to the pounding of his heart as lust roused him with a vengeance. He deepened the kiss, trying to coax her lips apart, and a groan of pleasure rolled up from his throat.

Her small mewl of protest finally awakened his conscience, and he forced the raging beast within to calm. By the Rood, he thought, he was a gentleman. No matter how great the temptation was, Colin du Lac never forced a woman to his will.

But in the next moment his world was turned awry. As he softened his kiss, the intensity of her pummeling lessened, and to his shock, she began tentatively kissing him back.

Somewhere in the midst of her rage and resistance, Helena stopped thinking. That was the only way to explain her diminishing lack of will and the way her limbs seemed to turn to custard. She acted, or more accurately, reacted, not from reason, but from instinct.

Lord, his lips were soft and warm, warmer than she'd imagined. Where they touched hers, they left her flesh hot and tingling. His beard was coarse against her cheek, but she scarcely noticed it as his tongue brushed lightly across her lips. His breath caressed her face, and his low growls of contentment called to something primitive inside her.

'Twas as if every nerve in her body convened at that one point of contact. Her breasts ached, her belly fluttered, her loins burned. His kiss seemed to bring her to life. 'Twas an empowering sensation, one that left her feeling nigh omnipotent.

But when he lessened the pressure and backed away briefly, giving her a respite from his onslaught, some of the sensual haze dissipated, and she became almost capable of rational thought. 'Twas when he smugly murmured, "*You* enjoyed that as well, didn't you, Hel-fire?" that her vision cleared. Her pride instantly rose in defense, and she ground her teeth, incensed by his male arrogance.

Did he think she was so easily conquered? That he was every woman's desire? That she would now turn to clay in his hands? She refused to give him the satisfaction. Trying to look as bored as possible, she offered him an insulting shrug.

He chuckled warmly and rubbed his nose against her cheek. "Liar. Open your mouth, and I'll make it better."

Contrary to a fault, she clamped her lips together. Kissing him might be a breathtaking experience, a lofty thrill, much more pleasurable than any she'd had before. But she'd not be mastered by her emotions. And she'd definitely not be bested by a cocksure Norman.

"Are you afraid?" He arched a brow.

"I'm afraid of naught," she said, thrusting out her chin.

His gaze lowered to her lips. "Then open your mouth."

"Nay."

"I think you're afraid you like Norman kissing."

"Hardly."

"In fact, you prefer it to your Scots stable lads' unskilled pecks." His eyes sparkled. "Or all those toads you've been kissing."

She smirked. "Are you going to let me up?"

"Eventually."

"I never knew Normans were such tyrants."

"I never knew Scotswomen were so stubborn."

"We're only stubborn when our virtue is threatened."

He laughed. "I'm not threatening your virtue. All I'm offering is another kiss."

"I wouldn't kiss you again if you were the last man on earth."

"And yet 'twas *you* who woke *me,* little wanton."

She felt her cheeks grow hot. "I'm not a wanton."

"Oh, aye, right." His lips curved up in a sly smile. "You're afraid."

Her temper, never stable to begin with, simmered perilously close to eruption. "I am *not* afraid of anything," she said between clenched teeth, "not men, nor battle, nor death, nor you."

"Prove it."

"I don't have to prove anything."

"True." Amusement made his eyes glitter. "But I'll forever know in my heart you're afraid of kissing me."

Then he smiled and let her go. Rolling off her, he fell back onto the pallet and laced his fingers behind his head, staring smugly up at the ceiling.

She should have been satisfied. After all, she'd won. He'd released her. And yet the glimmer in his eyes told her that somehow he believed he was the victor.

"Wait!" she said, knowing even as she said the word that she was about to get herself into trouble. Nevertheless, she fixed her eyes on a beam overhead, blew out a hard breath, and braced herself as if for a powerful punch. "Go ahead."

"Go ahead, what?"

She shuddered. "Kiss me."

After a moment's consideration, he sniffed. "Nay."

She whipped her head around. "What do you mean, nay?"

He shrugged. "Nay. 'Tis not my way to frighten faint-hearted ladies."

"I am *not* fainthearted."

"So you say."

She growled in frustration. "Bloody hell! Kiss me, you irksome knave."

"Not unless you ask nicely."

"Son of a . . ." She threw back the covers and flounced over till she loomed above him, then bit out, "For the last time. I am not. Afraid. Of you." And to prove it, she bent forward and crushed her lips against his in a hard, dispassionate kiss.

At least it started out to be dispassionate. But when he wove his fingers through her hair, caressing her ear and the nape of her neck, then wrapped his arm around her back, pulling her closer, her body began to melt into his embrace like iron in a crucible.

He seemed to surround her, stroking her, cradling her, murmuring wordless urgings. And slowly, gradually, inevitably, she resonated to his play, like a lute to a minstrel's touch.

"Open for me," he bid her softly.

And, cursing herself for a fool, she did.

She'd thought his lips were supple, but they were naught compared to the soft, wet explorations of his tongue. His invasion was gentle, but she found herself longing for more. She delved further into the kiss, letting him swirl his tongue around hers in a languorous dance that sent her reason spinning wildly away.

His hand slipped lower, cupping her buttocks, pulling her firmly against his obvious need. The rigid staff pressed upon her woman's mound, and she gasped as the pressure sent a jolt of pleasure through her.

He caught her gasp within his mouth and answered it with a moan. The sound affected her like thunder sometimes did, sending a thrill of excitement along her spine. Only half-aware of what she did, she thrust her hands into his hair, burying her fingers in the lush treasure, and deepened the kiss.

His hand came around to her jaw, holding her steady, and his fingers dug gently into her cheek. Beneath her, his chest rose and fell rapidly, and the thought that they shared the same turmoil magnified her exhilaration.

His thumb teased at the corner of her mouth, and she turned her head to nip at it. Sliding it farther inward, he eased it between her lips. She grazed it lightly with her teeth, then lapped at it, then took the whole thumb in her mouth, sucking hard.

He rasped in a ragged breath and shuddered, and she peered at him through slitted eyes, relishing the effect she was having on him. His mouth hung open in naked desire, and his brow furrowed as if he suffered great pain. Why he should be thus aroused, she didn't know, but 'twas a heady feeling to be in command.

That sense of command lasted but a few moments. Colin, like a novice knight deciding he was outmatched, growled and slipped his thumb from her mouth.

"Lucifer's ballocks, you're a wicked wench," he said breathlessly.

She frowned, unsure what he meant. But when he pushed her, gently but firmly, off of him, evidently done with her, she felt insulted and unsatisfied. 'Twas as if he'd challenged her to combat, then withdrawn just as she was about to win.

Forsooth, her displeasure went beyond disappointment. 'Twas a palpable disquiet. Her entire body tingled with expectation, the way her nose did before she sneezed. Her heart raced with anticipation, and her skin was as uncomfortably hot as the instant before she dove into the cool waters of Rivenloch in summer.

As Helena bounded from the pallet, Colin bit the inside of his cheek, willing his desire to subside. Sweet Mary, what was wrong with him? Had it been so long since he'd lain with a woman that he'd lost all restraint?

God's eyes, 'twas but a few kisses. He'd kissed a hundred women—ladies, kitchen maids, millers' daughters, harlots. But none had affected him so deeply. Nor so quickly.

From the first contact, his blood had simmered faster in his veins than a shallow pan of blancmange over a hot fire, roiling out of control and threatening to boil over. But when she took his thumb fully into her mouth in blatant suggestion, sucking at it as if . . .

Lord, he dared not let his thoughts wander there. His loins already swelled in urgency, demanding appeasement. Only reason saved him from disavowing his chivalry.

Curse her teasing, the little vixen knew what she did. The triumph was obvious in her smoldering eyes. She tormented him, making lascivious promises with her body that she had no intention of keeping.

He wondered if she tortured her stable lads thus. He wondered if she'd ever been taken against her will because of it.

Luckily for her, Colin was as expert at reining in his passions as he was at reining in an unruly warhorse. But watching her as she flitted about the room in agitation, her cheeks flushed, her breathing rapid, her hair whipping over her shoulders in alluring disarray, 'twas hard not to wish her back in his bed.

"I'm going fishing," she suddenly announced.

"Alone?" He raised up on one elbow. "Is that wise?"

"I *want* to be alone."

Her reply probably had a deeper meaning, but at the moment, he paid it little heed. "I don't think you should go by yourself."

"I told you," she said, tucking both blades into her belt, "I'm not afraid of anything."

"That is foolhardy."

She pulled the door open. "Nay. Letting you kiss me was foolhardy." She slammed it behind her before he could get in a word.

Muttering a string of foul oaths, Colin shoved the coverlet back and threw his legs over the side of the pallet. He might be wounded, but that didn't keep him from his knight's vows. He'd sworn to protect ladies. Even if 'twas from their own foolishness.

By the time he put on his boots and managed to hobble out the door, a heavy iron spoon—the only weapon he could find—clenched in his fist, she was long gone. But by her obvious trail, she'd returned to the same fishing spot.

"Damn!" Did the woman seek trouble? Or was she just attracted to it? If the English *did* come after them, where else would they go but to the place they'd first found them?

He limped along faster, wondering if he'd fare any better against the mercenaries with a cooking spoon than he had with a fishing pole.

By the time he came crashing through the brush to see Helena gingerly dipping her line in the water, his leg throbbed, his face dripped with sweat, and he was in no mood for her defiance. "Damsel, are you *trying* to get yourself killed?"

"Hush."

"Don't hush me!"

"There's a fish circling the bait," she whispered. "That's it. That's . . ."

"I don't care if there are mermaids circling the bait! We have to get out of here."

"Shh!"

He limped forward. He might be injured, and she might be stubborn, but he outweighed her by half, and if he had to remove her bodily, he would.

"Oh, curse you, Norman!" She let the pole drop. "It's swum away now." Then she turned and glared at him in outrage. "What do you think you're doing? You were supposed to stay in bed. Get back to the cottage!"

"*You* get back to the cottage!"

"Do not order me about!"

"Do not order *me* about!"

She blew out a harsh sigh. "You're injured. You should not be taxing your wound."

"And you're a woman. You should not be baiting mercenaries."

She gave him a long-suffering roll of her eyes.

"Damn it, wench!" A muscle ticked along his neck. "What if the English return?"

"They won't." She hauled the line in on her pole and checked to make sure the bait was still attached. "We're not worth their trouble." She smiled in grim recollection. "We gave them some gruesome reminders of that. Besides, I've never seen English here before, not this far north. We're not likely to see any again."

Her nonchalance was frustrating. "Heed me well, my lady. Things are not as they were. There's a new King in England and unrest in the country."

"This is not England. 'Tis Scotland. We're still under King David's rule. Just because we ran across a band of English outlaws—"

"English outlaws," he pointed out, "where there never were before."

She shrugged, then picked up the pair of trout she'd caught earlier and began wrapping them in grass.

He sighed. 'Twas not his way to bore women with discussions about the workings of government. But his leg didn't feel capable of supporting a wayward, struggling wench all the way back to the hovel. Mayhap he could make her comprehend the danger so she'd cooperate. "This new King doesn't have the support of all of the nobles. Dissenters have been stripped of their wealth and holdings, their castles given to Henry's favorites. These indigents, with nowhere to go, have begun to look elsewhere for land. A lot of them have headed north. They're laying siege to castles, *Scots* castles."

He had her attention now. "But King David won't let them lay claim to Scots holdings."

"Exactly. 'Tis the reason Sir Pagan was sent to Rivenloch."

She arched a dubious brow. "To claim my keep before the English could?"

"Nay. To help *protect* your keep from the English."

"Oh." She looked mildly surprised. Then the deeper significance of that sank in, and he could almost see the hackles rise on her back. "But Rivenloch is perfectly capable of defending itself."

Helena was a proud woman, and Colin didn't want to begin a long argument. "I've no doubt," he hedged, "but apparently your King did not think so."

She scowled.

He continued. "That we encountered a band of English mercenaries means they're already here, penetrating the Scots countryside. 'Tis unsafe for a damsel to go wandering about on her own."

To his astonishment, instead of launching a scathing protest, after a pensive moment, she nodded. "As unsafe as for a wounded Norman." She collected her catch and the fishing pole. "At least *I'm* armed," she said, slipping the knife into her belt. "What's that?" She nodded toward the iron spoon and arched a sly brow. "Did you plan to cook the English to death?"

~

# Chapter 13

HELENA GAVE COLIN the fishing pole to carry, knowing he could use it as a crutch. Though the proud warrior would never admit it, she was sure he'd taxed himself chasing after her.

As for the English, she wasn't truly afraid of running into them. She'd wandered these woods from the time she was a wee lass, battling outlaws and wild boars and oafs from the unruly Lachanburn clan. The English didn't frighten her.

But she had to return Colin to the cottage before he aggravated his wound. And if the only way was to feign cooperation and accompany him there, she'd do it. She'd already caught a hefty pair of trout for supper anyway.

As for treating his infection, she hoped it hadn't worsened. She was running low on wine, and moreover, she was running low on resolve for the unpleasant task.

'Twas curious. She never batted an eye when it came to doling out injury to a foe. She could be merciless, bloodthirsty, an unflinching warrior. But somehow, dribbling wine over Colin's wound, hearing him suck painful gasps between his teeth, knowing she hurt him badly, weakened her appetite for violence.

As they made their halting way back to the cottage, Helena was haunted by what Colin had said. Could it be true? Were English mercenaries setting their sights on Scots keeps? Had they found their way to Rivenloch already? Was it possible they'd lay siege to the castle?

It seemed unthinkable. Yet a lot of improbable things had happened of late. Her sister had wed a foreigner. The Shadow had been careless for the first time. And Helena had let a Norman kiss her. Twice.

Mayhap change was in the wind, blowing away the withered leaves of the past. Perchance 'twould be a new age for Rivenloch, a time of war and bloodshed, an era of newfound foes and newfound alliances. The thought sent a restless shiver of adventure up her spine.

But until she straightened out the mess she'd gotten herself into with Sir Pagan's right-hand man, that adventure would have to wait.

Back at the cottage, she discovered that Colin's thigh had thankfully begun to heal. The flesh around the stitched cut looked healthy once again.

No one was happier to hear the news than Colin. "No more of that bloody wine?"

"No more."

He grinned. "Let's drink to it."

She grinned back. "*You've* suffered the most from her sting," she said, offering him the wineskin. "You drink first."

He took a hearty pull and passed the skin back to her.

Only days before, she would've raised a disdainful brow and wiped the lip with her sleeve. How much had changed in the past sennight. They'd shared suppers, battle, pain, laughter, and even kisses. So with a salute of the wineskin, she upended it and drank deeply.

Supper was the best she'd tasted thus far. Colin was right. Normans had a gift for cooking. Somehow, with a few sprigs of rosemary and a clove of garlic, he turned the trout into a feast fit for company. She picked two generous handfuls of peas from a wild vine that had escaped the crofter's garden years ago, and he boiled them with mint. Even the pair of pathetically tiny apples she found on a shriveled old tree managed to become a delicious treat when he wrapped them in thick leaves of fern and baked them over the coals until they were soft and sweet.

Forsooth, so content was she as she listened to the well-fed fire pop and crackle on the hearth later that night that she didn't even blink when Colin called her to bed.

"Come," he said, patting the pallet beside him. "It grows late. I think we must rise early and rob a nest for breakfast."

"A nest?"

"I've seen quail in the woods."

She rose from the hearth and shook her head. "'Twould take many quail eggs to fill a belly."

"That's why we must rise early."

Why she willingly climbed into bed with him, she didn't know. After all, the air was less chill tonight, and the fire burned brightly. Mayhap Colin had slipped some Norman potion into her food to make her malleable and obliging. Or perchance 'twas simply her satiated appetite that mellowed her mood. Whatever 'twas, it seemed the most natural thing in the world to slip into the pallet beside him and let him pull the coverlet over her.

Until he murmured, "Tonight, my lady, do try to bridle your passions."

She stiffened. "My what?"

"Do not molest me, at least not until I'm fully awake."

She gave him a sharp elbow in the stomach, and he let out a satisfying oof, but she couldn't help the blush that crept into her cheeks.

Dawn sent narrow beams of light through the shifting branches, like a harlot running her fingers through her hair the morning after a tryst. But 'twas not the brightness that had awakened Colin as he lay beside the sleeping beauty on the pallet, her leg slung possessively over his hips.

Something foraged in the leaves just outside the cottage. Something bigger than a mouse or a squirrel or quail. Something that might make an even better breakfast than eggs.

Careful not to disturb her, he usurped the knife Helena kept at her side, then tried to extricate himself from her unwitting embrace. 'Twas impossible. As soon as she felt him stir, she woke.

"What is it?" she mumbled sleepily.

"I'm trying to rise."

She looked at him sharply. Then, suddenly realizing that part of him *had* risen under her trespassing thigh, she quickly withdrew her leg.

He chuckled softly and sat up. "Lusty wench."

Her frown was ruined by a yawn. "Where are you going?"

He clucked his tongue. "So eager, my lady. Do not fret. I'll return to your bed soon enough." He raked the hair back from his brow.

"Conceited varlet." She punched him lightly on the shoulder with the back of her fist. "I meant where are you going with my blade?"

He stood, testing his wounded leg. 'Twas healing fast. In another sennight, 'twould be as good as new. "I'm going to hunt whatever beast is foraging outside."

Her brows drew together as she listened. A heavy foot thudded on the earth, followed by the sound of grass being torn and chewed. "'Tis a cow."

"A cow?" He shook his head. "Nay, 'tis a goat or a sheep."

"I tell you, 'tis a cow."

He shrugged. "Then we shall dine well indeed."

"Wait." She rubbed at her eyes and swept the hair from her face with the back of her hand in a gesture that was charming and childlike. Then she rose to walk sleepily over to the window. She peered out through the shutters, scratching at her hip. "You cannot kill that cow."

"Of course I can." He sliced through the air with the knife. "One slash to the throat and—"

"Nay, you *will* not kill that cow."

"What do you mean?"

"'Tis one of Lachanburn's."

"Lachanburn's?"

"Aye. See that mark upon its flank?"

He joined her at the window. The shaggy, rust-colored beast with wide horns had a circle burned into its fur near the tail.

"'Tis Lachanburn's mark," she explained. "Rivenloch's neighboring clan."

"Ah." Colin pressed his thumb against the edge of the knife, testing its sharpness. "Then he won't mind sharing with his starving neighbors."

She seized his wrist. "Do not."

"Hold a moment. I was told that Scots go on cattle raids all the time. Is it not a sort of play among the clans, stealing each other's cows?"

"Stealing, aye. Killing, nay."

"Surely the Lord of Lachanburn would not begrudge the Lady of Rivenloch one paltry cow. We'll slaughter this one and give him one of Rivenloch's in exchange when we return."

She shook her head. "Not without his consent."

He sighed. He was hungry, and the beast outside could feed the two of them for weeks. 'Twas a shame to let all that meat go to waste.

Mayhap he could rouse that voracious appetite of hers. "You know, I can make an amazing roast over a slow fire. Juicy. Succulent. Tender enough to melt on your tongue."

But the stubborn wench wasn't biting. Instead, she looked thoughtfully out through the shutters. "You may not slaughter it. However . . ."

"Aye?"

"I suppose 'twould do no harm to *milk* the beast."

Colin's mouth was still watering over the thought of a savory roast. But her suggestion had promise. With milk, he could make any number of velvety sauces to enhance whatever game they caught. With a little patience, he might even churn butter or make soft ruayn cheese. And he could tie the cow nearby till they left for Rivenloch, giving them daily access to her bounty.

"My lady, that's a brilliant idea," he told her, handing her the dagger, hilt first. He rubbed his palms together. "'Tis been a while, but I think I can manage. I'll take a bucket and stool and set to it." He could already imagine Helena's expression of ecstasy as she tasted one of his favorite dishes, thickened cream poured over wild berries.

If he'd only known what mischief she wrought, he would have rattled her wicked little brain then and there.

Helena watched him with wide, innocent eyes as he strode confidently from the cottage, pail and stool in hand, to perform the impossible task. 'Twas an old trick, one played on every Scots child growing up. She grinned in sinful anticipation, climbing back under the coverlet to await his return.

Several moments later, when he entered the hovel, she feigned sleep, lying stiffly on the pallet, her back to the door.

The bucket hit the floor, followed by the stool.

"Very amusing," he drawled.

She braced herself, holding back laughter. His footsteps drew closer until he loomed over her.

"You are a naughty little Hel-cat." One of his knees sank into the pallet, pinning her beneath the coverlet. Her eyes flew open, and he planted his other knee on the opposite side, trapping her between his legs. "And you must pay for your devilry."

Any other man she would have thrown from the bed with a violent heave of her hips. But Colin had learned her tricks. He knew she relied upon surprise and subterfuge, so he was prepared to counter her every move.

"Get off of me," she grunted, struggling to get her arms free, which were also caught beneath the coverlet. But 'twas hard to fight Colin when she was also fighting laughter. Every time she envisioned him outside with his bucket and stool, trying to find the udders on Lachanburn's bull, giggles rose inside her like bubbles in a keg of ale.

"Oh, you think 'tis droll, do you?" His voice was stern, but his eyes sparkled with amusement.

She bit her twitching lip.

"I believe you're laughing at my expense," he chided.

She shook her head, but a squeak escaped her as she imagined the bull's surprise.

"Aha! You *are* laughing."

She shook her head again, more vehemently.

Then he discovered one of her well-kept secrets, one she tried to hide at all costs. His fingers skipped lightly up her ribs as he began to tickle her.

She had time to cry "Nay!" once before she dissolved into a torrent of giggles, her body jerking in helpless spasms.

He assailed her ruthlessly for several moments, then stopped to let her catch her breath. "Are you sorry now for your mischief?"

She mustered up her most severe glare, not an easy feat in the midst of laughter, and shook her head.

And then he began again. He seemed to know every ticklish spot, from the place under her arm and the gaps between her ribs to the crevice of her neck and the crest of her hipbone.

She writhed and giggled and tossed her head until she was near giddy with laughter.

He gave her respite again, his grin impish as he looked down his nose at her. "Apologize, captive, and I'll halt your torture."

She grinned back. "Why should I apologize? 'Twas your own fool fault that—"

She yelped as he clamped his fingers into the spot above her hip where she was especially ticklish.

"You should apologize," he said over her laughter, "because I might have been killed." He paused his torment to give a dramatic shudder. "You should have seen the beast's lusty eyes when I started pulling on his udder."

Her stifled laughter exploded out at his vulgarity, and he resumed her punishment, attacking her until she was breathless and weak. Finally, she could endure no more. "I yield!" she gasped.

He paused. "What was that?" He turned his ear to hear better. "What did you say?"

"You heard me." She blew the stray strands of hair from her face. "I yield."

"Ah. And you apologize?"

"I apologize," she agreed.

He climbed off her, grinning in triumph.

"I apologize," she repeated, turning onto her side, adding slyly, "for your stupidity."

He gave her bottom a solid whack before she could dodge.

"Come along, Hel-hound. We have eggs to hunt."

She should have been incensed. No one swatted a Warrior Maid of Rivenloch. Yet how could she take offense when he looked at her with such a convivial twinkle in his eye?

Precisely when he'd made the transformation from foe to fellow, she didn't know, but something had shifted between them. Whether because of the trick she'd managed to successfully perpetrate against him or simply the sweet release of laughing so long and hard, her mood was carefree the rest of the day. She no longer felt like an abductor with a hostage. Indeed, 'twas as if she and Colin were companions in arms, sharing this rousing adventure in the woods.

Helena found several caches of quail eggs hidden in the dense thicket, and Colin whipped them up over the fire into a frothy concoction with a sprinkling of thyme and the last bit of The Shadow's cheese. He even found some walnuts on the crofter's old tree, and they broke them open with a rock, digging out the choice treat within. As they cleaned the last morsel of egg from the pan, Helena began to wonder if she'd ever be able to eat dry oatcakes again.

After their meal, Colin took the fishing pole and refashioned it into a bird snare with milkweed fiber. Together they ventured into a part of the woods heavy with brush. While Colin hunkered behind an oak, extending the pole with its fiber loop near the ground, Helena stole up behind the adjacent bushes and shook the foliage. A pair of quail fluttered out in a panic, but Colin wasn't quick enough to catch them, and they skittered down the trail.

It took most of the day, but finally they managed to snare a couple of partridges, and on the way back to the cottage, Colin cut sprigs of mustard and picked a few handfuls of wild greens and violets. She busied herself plucking the birds, ordering him to rest his leg, for 'twas clear he had overtaxed himself. To her surprise, he didn't argue with her, and soon she heard him snoring atop the pallet.

She smiled, stopping her task for a moment to study him. His features were softer when he was asleep. His brow was smooth, his lashes thick where they swept his cheek. His hair, unkempt as always, fell in dark locks over his forehead and teased at his ears and jaw, giving him an air of devilry. His nostrils fluttered as he breathed, and his mouth, open enough to expose the slight cross of his front teeth, looked as innocent as a babe's.

He awoke while she was watching him, and in that instant of discovery, she saw that he *knew* she'd been watching him, for his eyes glimmered smugly.

"You let me sleep too long, my lady."

"Who could wake you?" she teased, returning to plucking the partridge. "You sleep like the dead."

"On the contrary," he said, stretching as languorously as a cat. "I awakened to the mere gaze of a woman's admiring eyes."

She felt her face grow warm. "I was not . . . admiring."

He smiled and carefully sat up. Lord, even taunting and disheveled, he was as handsome as Lucifer. "Why, my lady, is that a blush upon your cheek?"

She plucked with a vengeance. "Nay."

He set his feet slowly upon the floor. "You don't have to wait until I'm asleep, you know. You may feel at liberty to admire me any time of—"

"I was *not* admiring you. I was . . . calculating your worth at ransom, pound for pound."

"Pound for pound, eh?" He stood up and ambled

toward her, his grin wide. "And was that clothed . . . or unclothed?"

Her blush deepened. Bloody hell, even in a battle of wits, he seemed to best her at every turn.

Colin took mercy upon the poor flustered damsel and let his query go unanswered. Just like the tickling he'd made her endure this morn, he knew when enough was enough.

Her blush surprised him. After all, she'd spoken with shameless candor before the mercenaries, using all manner of suggestion and vulgarity. She'd swung her hips and displayed her bosom with unabashed enthusiasm. Why she should be troubled by the fact she'd been caught staring at him, he didn't know. 'Twas not as if he was unused to the stares of women.

Smiling at her curious contradiction, he busied himself with roasting the partridges in a paste of mustard and tearing the greens and violets into a salat.

He found he enjoyed impressing Helena with his cooking. She seemed so grateful, finishing every morsel with élan, licking her fingers, making those sensual sounds of pleasure deep in her throat. 'Twas almost with regret that he thought about their return to Rivenloch, when she'd no longer require his services as cook.

'Twas a pity he had no better stores. A few additions would have made the meal perfect. A cup of crisp, cold perry. Plump, sweet rastons fresh from the oven, slathered with butter. And those berries with thickened cream he'd dreamed of earlier. *Then* Helena's eyes would roll in ecstasy.

He supposed he'd just have to settle for offering her a

different kind of ecstasy. He smiled wickedly. She'd let him kiss her yesterday. He wondered what liberties she'd allow this eve.

A few hours later he found out. He stretched out on the pallet, propped on his elbows, while she examined his wound.

"The stitches should stay in for another sennight," she declared, swabbing the injury lightly with a wet rag.

She could've told him he'd have to live with them forever, and it would've made no difference. His mind was drifting to much more interesting thoughts as her forearm strayed dangerously close to his groin. Before, when she'd used the wine, he'd only been able to focus on the pain of his wound. Now he felt the brush of her sleeve upon his thigh, the gentleness of her fingers upon his flesh, the warmth of her body as she sat beside him on the pallet.

As she prepared to rewrap the bandage, he let out a forlorn sigh. She looked askance at him.

"No kiss?" he asked.

She lifted a dubious brow.

He looked at her, all innocence. "I'm sure that's why it's healed so quickly."

"Indeed?"

"Oh, aye." He added soberly, "Naught is more powerful than the kiss of a beautiful woman."

"Oh, I'm beautiful now, am I?" She might have said it sardonically, but her blush betrayed her. She enjoyed his compliment.

"Fairer than an English morn. Lovelier than a rose in bloom. More graceful than a dove on—"

"If I kiss your injury, will you stop spewing verse at me?"

He pretended hurt, then slowly nodded.

She leaned forward to give him a quick kiss upon his cut, and her soft hair brushed the inside of his thigh. He shivered, wondering if she knew what she did to him.

As she rewrapped the bandage, he pointed to his knuckle, scraped in the fight with the mercenaries. "I have another injury here."

She gave him a knowing glare. "I suppose that one needs a kiss as well?"

He nodded.

She smirked, but obliged him.

Then he tapped a finger on his cheekbone, grazed by an English fist.

Shaking her head at his mischief, she gave him a light kiss there as well.

Then he pointed to his lips.

She wagged a finger at him. "Valiant try, but nay."

He shrugged. "At least I spared you my bruised arse."

She gave him a chiding shove in the chest, knocking him off his elbows.

He returned with a light push at her shoulder.

Her jaw dropped, and she shoved him again.

He tugged at her hair.

Fighting laughter, she grabbed his wrist.

He rose up to give her a quick peck on the lips.

She growled at him.

He kissed her again.

"Stop it, you—"

He interrupted her with another peck.

"You knave, what are you—"

Then another.

"Cease!" Her words belied her grin.

And another.

She tried to clamp her lips shut, but laughter burst from between them.

The sixth kiss was nearly impossible, she was laughing so hard. He moved instead to her neck. But the clever wench got her revenge while he was nuzzling the sweet skin beneath her ear. Her devilish fingers found his ribs and began tickling away.

His arms instantly clamped against his sides as he made an unsuccessful grab for her wrists, and he gasped against her neck. He tried to catch her hands again, but she was as fleet as a bee, stinging him here and there, finding his most vulnerable spots. Soon his breathless laughter joined hers until finally he managed to trap her wrists. He rolled her onto her back and beamed down in victory.

"You," he said, grinning, "are a wicked, wicked wench."

She twisted against his hold, but without much effort, and 'twas then he realized the secret of her pleasure. She wasn't a lover. She was a warrior. What heated Helena's blood was battle. The key to winning her affections was to spar with her, with words, with actions. She liked to fight, liked the excitement, the aggression. He smiled. He could give her the battle of her life.

## Chapter 14

DRUNK ON LAUGHTER, Helena couldn't muster up proper outrage at the varlet for kissing her against her will. True, she'd gotten her vengeance, discovering to her glee that Colin was as ticklish as she. But now, giddy and breathless, she found his advances not so unwelcome. Indeed, a part of her, probably that "wicked, wicked" part, perversely longed to nestle even closer to the trespassing knave.

Her blood had grown warm, and her heart throbbed. She grinned, feeling the way she did after a good sword fight, as if she glowed with the light of a hundred candles.

She could have escaped him if she'd wanted to. But she only half wanted to. There was naught Helena loved better than battling a worthy foe.

She squirmed as he lowered his head to hers, and his moist breath teased at her ear. "You," she murmured, "are a vile beast."

He answered with a growl and a bite to her neck.

She gasped in surprise.

"Beast I am, my lady," he agreed, "and I shall devour you."

He gnawed playfully at her throat. She writhed beneath him, caught in a strange place between laughter and longing, and not entirely sure she sought escape.

"I shall sniff out your most delectable parts." He snuffled about her neck and ears, making her squeal. "And feed on your quivering flesh." He nipped at the lobe of her ear, sparking her desire like flint striking iron. "I'll sink my teeth into your delicate neck and drink the very life from you." He ran his tongue along the pulsing vein beneath her ear, and she shivered as the sparks burst into quick flame.

"Nay," she gasped.

"Oh, aye," he said, licking lightly around the rim of her ear. She stiffened as fire instantly infused her blood.

She fought him then, or at least she *thought* she fought him. She twisted beneath him, making fists of her hands. Yet when he released her wrists and she might have shoved him away, instead she pushed against his chest with no more force than a child brushing aside a curtain. "Nay."

"Aye." His fingers tangled in her hair as he nibbled along her jaw. "Ah, here's a choice morsel." He lapped at the corner of her mouth, as if tasting her. Then he caught her lower lip gently between his teeth.

She didn't mean to kiss him. 'Twas an accident. She nipped tentatively at his lips, once, twice, innocently enough. But then her tongue slipped out to taste his mouth, and he lapped at hers in return. Suddenly she couldn't stop. If he was a hungry beast, she was just as voracious. She slanted her mouth over his, pressing and sucking and licking, smashing her lips against his, demanding his response with such vehemence that she unwittingly bit him.

He jerked back. "Soft, my lady," he said on a chuckle. "Who is the beast now?"

His remark stunned her for a moment. Mother of God, what had possessed her? She should be fighting him off. Were those her fists tangled in his shirt?

Then his mouth descended upon hers again, tender, inviting, and her concerns faded into a haze of desire.

As if the touch of his lips was not enough to send her senses careening, he let one of his hands drift down along her neck, over her shoulder, down her sleeve. Everywhere he made contact, her skin seemed to waken, like the fur of a cat in a windstorm. He caressed the curve of her waist, and even through her gown she could feel the heat of his palm. While she held her breath, his hand stole slowly upward along her ribs until his thumb reached the crease below her breast.

She broke away from the kiss. "Nay," she gasped, sensing his intent.

"Aye," he assured her. Yet he lingered there, gazing into her eyes, smiling, stroking deliberately back and forth beneath her breast, teasing her until she thought she would go mad with longing, for her nipple began to ache for his touch.

And God help her, eventually she arched up toward him, hungry for that contact.

Only then did he proceed. With a gentle hand, he cupped the underside of her breast, hefting its malleable weight in his palm.

"So appetizing," he murmured.

Then he at last brushed his thumb across the fabric over her straining nipple.

She gasped as desire exploded through her body like a shower of sparks, targeting her breasts and the burning spot betwixt her thighs.

Yet 'twas only the beginning. He lowered his head to whisper in her ear. "Ah, another delicious place."

Still rasping his thumb over her nipple, he slipped the tip of his tongue into the shell of her ear, and 'twas as if she'd touched a sword hot from the forge. She twitched with the shock of it. She squeezed her eyes shut, craving yet abhorring the intense sensation, writhing and wallowing between ecstasy and despair.

Beyond thought, she moaned and reveled and suffered, yet grew desperate somehow for more. His breath, blown gently into her ear, sent intoxicating quivers through her. Her nipple stiffened to an almost painful tension. And her skin grew so hot that she plucked urgently at her clothes, eager to dispense with them.

He must have read her mind, for in the next moment, his hand left off its torment to loosen the ties of her gown.

"Nay," she said, clutching at her bodice, even as her rebellious fingers helped to spread the laces.

"Oh, aye, my lady."

She'd thought his touch warm before, but naught compared to the heat of flesh upon flesh as he let his hand delve within. Though his hands were callused from the sword, his caress was amazingly gentle as he cradled her breast, then tenderly squeezed her nipple.

Her fingers clawed and tangled in his shirt, and she

clung to him as if to a wild warhorse as yearning engulfed and overwhelmed her.

He murmured against her mouth. "Oh, my lady, you are most delectable there."

She thought to say him nay, but the word wouldn't form upon her lips. She could only manage a quiet mewl of protest.

"Aye, most delectable."

He left a trail of kisses along her neck and over her bosom, then slipped her loosened surcoat down. She quivered as the fabric rasped across her flesh. She'd thought no greater bliss could be endured until he licked lightly across her nipple, then lowered his lips and took sweet suckle.

She sobbed out, moving her hands to the back of his head, as if she might hold him to her bosom forever. Waves of pleasure washed over her as he used his lips and tongue to suck in a rhythm that simultaneously calmed and aroused her.

Anon her other breast yearned for the sorcery of his touch. Instinctively, she guided his head there, shivering as his lusty chuckle tickled her belly, moaning as his mouth claimed that nipple as well, kindling in her a fresh shock of euphoria.

Still she was not fully satisfied. She squirmed beneath him, thwarted, feeling as helpless as an unseasoned warrior, unable to choose the weapon that would vanquish her foe.

But Colin chose for her, and he chose expertly.

With a final brush of his tongue, he released her breast and moved up to kiss her mouth again. If 'twas possible, his lips had grown even softer. Or mayhap 'twas her own willing response that made them seem so. Their lips coupled, and their tongues intertwined, yet all the while, the fire increased betwixt her legs. She whimpered softly against his mouth.

"I know, love, I know," he murmured.

He began gathering her skirts in his fist, inching her hem slowly upward, baring her legs. Though 'twas what she desired, her hands moved out of habit to block him.

"Shh." He gently lifted her hand to his lips, kissing the back of her knuckles in reassurance.

Against her instincts, she let him proceed. He slipped his hand beneath her skirts, caressing the inside of her thigh. Her muscles twitched, unaccustomed to such contact, until his soothing strokes calmed them.

And yet this arousing touch did naught to slake her thirst. An ache grew in her womb that somehow his hand was not quite satisfying.

She grunted in frustration and eased her hips forward, willing his fingers . . . there. And yet they skipped elusively away. She arched up, trying to force his hand.

"So eager," he teased.

Searing need overrode her pride. She sobbed in dismay as he withheld what she craved most.

At long last, he yielded to her unspoken demands. "Is this what you desire?" he whispered.

His fingers smoothed the curls of her woman's mound and brushed lower, delving into the moist folds and pressing against the core of her need. She cried out and pushed against his palm, rocking instinctively against his hand.

His mouth returned to hers then, and he kissed her tenderly as he began to use his fingers upon her in a most exquisite dance.

"Oh, Helena, my sweet," he breathed against her mouth, as if he suffered along with her. "So warm. So wet."

His words spurred her to new passions. Soon, like a rising flood, lust swept her away faster than she could swim. Breathless, she grabbed for purchase, seizing his shoulders as the tide climbed higher and higher.

"Oh, my lady," he panted, "I would devour you wholly now."

She dared not even think of what he meant.

But he didn't give her time to think.

"Nay!" she cried, her eyes wide as he slipped down her body.

"Aye," he growled softly.

Panicked, she seized handfuls of his hair, half-trying to prevent him. But he moved inexorably downward until his breath stirred the soft curls guarding her womanhood.

Devour didn't begin to describe what he did. With his lips and tongue, he tasted her, savored her, feasted upon her, suckled tenderly at the core of her need until she thought she would die from the pleasure of it. Sounds came from her throat that she'd never made before, sounds of primal hunger, of womanly distress. She squeezed her eyes shut and clenched her teeth as he honed her desire to a sharper and sharper point.

And then a wave of incredible heat enveloped her, as powerful as fire, as sweet-hot as victory. She snarled her fingers in his hair, afraid he might abandon her in her time of need. But he stayed with her, easing his hands beneath her hips to lift her for his final devouring. When sweet release coursed through her, she thrust up, giving herself to him completely, letting him feed upon her while she shook in the throes of surrender.

Afterward, drained of all her strength and will and pride, she half dozed upon the pallet. Colin's head lay heavy upon her belly, and his hand covered the curls below, as if to protect them.

But 'twas too late for that.

He'd already violated her.

She swallowed hard and closed her eyes tightly. Nay, she thought. 'Twas not the truth. She'd wanted this as much as he did. And it had been pleasurable, immensely pleasurable.

Yet somehow, as the day wore on and they gradually resumed their normal activities, Helena felt as if she'd lost a contest of arms. They'd battled, and she'd fallen. It stung her to know she'd been vanquished so easily.

Thankfully, Colin seemed particularly careful not to gloat over his victory. Whenever their glances met, his gaze softened, as if he looked upon her with new eyes. Gone was his ruthless teasing. Vanished were his lusty grins and sly stares. Forsooth, if she didn't know any better, she'd suspect 'twas affection she read in his face. Still, she was haunted by the fact she'd left herself completely vulnerable to him.

By nightfall, she decided there was but one way to erase her shame. 'Twas what any bested knight would do to recover his honor. She intended to meet Colin on the field of battle again. But this time, she planned to emerge the victor.

She approached him after supper, as he reclined upon the pallet, watching her put away the last of the pots. She'd been notably nervous, thinking about what she'd plotted. Even now she wiped sweaty palms upon her skirts.

Helena had little experience when it came to trysting.

Everything she knew, she'd learned from watching maid-servants and stable lads. But a Warrior Maid of Rivenloch never shied away from a challenge, and so she was determined to carry out her mission.

Steeling herself as for a tournament, she smoothed her skirts, then straightened to her full height and walked directly to the pallet. She cleared her throat. He lifted his brows. She opened her mouth to speak, then forgot what she intended to say.

"Aye?" he asked, clearly amused.

"I wish . . ."

"You wish . . . ," he prompted.

Bloody hell, 'twas hard to talk to him when he lay there, looking so handsome and desirable and delicious. "I wish to . . ." Her gaze darted unwittingly to his groin.

The corner of his mouth curved up. "Would you like me to feed on your flesh again?"

"Nay!"

"Because you need only ask, my lady."

"Nay, 'tis not that at all." God's bones, why was this so difficult? She could seduce mercenaries all night. Why should one paltry Norman give her so much trouble?

"Perchance you'd like to play a different game?" he guessed, his eyes sparkling softly in the firelight.

"Aye. Nay! That is . . ." She blew out a hard breath. This was ridiculous. She was a Warrior Maid of Rivenloch. Bold. Strong. Fearless. "I wish to . . . to return the favor."

His brow creased. "The favor?"

"Aye."

After a moment, his expression cleared. "Ah. You wish to," he said, his voice cracking, "you wish to devour *me?*"

\* \* \*

Colin's cock might have sprung to instantaneous attention at her blushing nod, but he was still sane enough to think with his brain. Barely.

All day long he'd savored the taste of Helena upon his lips. All day long he'd imagined the further delights they might share this eve. All day long he'd relived her beautiful release, so sweet, so pure, so intense. Forsooth, he'd never found himself so obsessed with a woman.

But something was not quite right. During supper, Helena had been as edgy as a bride on her wedding night. Yet this was the same woman who had openly flaunted her charms to a campful of mercenaries. It made no sense. So despite an intense yearning for her and despite her intoxicating closeness, Colin had to know her motives.

"Why?" he croaked.

"Why?"

"Why do you wish to . . . return the favor?"

"Because . . . because 'tis fair."

"Fair?" He frowned.

She lowered her gaze to her fidgeting fingers. "You . . . pleasured me. I wish to pleasure you."

He knew women well enough to know their eyes told the truth when their lips did not. "Indeed?"

She glanced up, and he locked gazes with her, seeking an answer. She flashed him a fleeting smile, one about as convincing as a harlot in a nun's habit. Then he considered the woman. She was a warrior. She thought like a warrior. In her mind, she'd lost their first bout of lovemaking by surrendering to him. She wanted a second chance to secure his defeat.

"You do not wish to pleasure me, Hel-fire." He nodded. "'Tis but retribution you seek."

He let her stammer and stutter over that. Her blush deepened, lending truth to his speculation. The little vixen wanted vengeance.

He gave her the hint of a smile. "Fortunately, I'm not a man to quarrel over motive." His smile broadened, and he spread his arms in welcome surrender. "Take your revenge, my lady."

Despite his aching groin, despite the lusty thoughts that had tormented him all day, despite the almost unbearable anticipation, Colin couldn't help but be amused by Helena's manner as she began to initiate his seduction. He wondered if 'twas some new game she'd devised wherein she serviced her lover with no emotional engagement whatsoever. Or mayhap 'twas a survival skill she'd acquired trysting with so many stable lads.

She gingerly loosened his braies as if the laces had thorns, then hauled them down with little ceremony. When she gazed down at what she'd exposed, her face took on a grave cast, as if she were about to spar with a perilous dragon. But when she took a deep breath, then dripped spittle into her right palm and frowned down at his proud staff, he stopped her.

"May I have . . . I don't know . . . mayhap a kiss first?"

She seemed startled. "Oh. Aye." She bent forward, giving him a chaste peck upon the lips.

"Nay, Hel-fire, I mean a real kiss. A kiss that says, I wish to pleasure you."

She tried again. This time he sensed the return of the passion she'd exhibited earlier. Her lips softened upon his, and she relaxed into his embrace. She sighed against his mouth, and he parted his lips, allowing her access. Her kisses started out tenuous. Then, her tongue began to mate enthusiastically with his, swirling and circling in a seductive dance. After a moment, he could almost convince himself that she *was* seeking his pleasure, not her own vengeance.

Then, too soon, she ended the kiss. With no further ado, almost as if she had to begin the daunting task before she lost her nerve, she abruptly seized him with her wet hand and started pumping. If he hadn't been so desperate, if it hadn't been so long since he'd had a woman, he might not have responded to such brusque handling. Colin was a man of romance and style. He enjoyed the lazy art of playfulness, the leisurely pace of seduction. Seldom did he engage in hasty haystack trysts.

But it *had* been a long time, and his cock cared not a whit whether 'twas stroked fast or slow, gently or firmly, by a beautiful woman or a toothless old hag, only that 'twas stroked.

Still, she pumped at him as if 'twas a race, and he feared he'd not last long if she continued.

Gently, he surrounded her hand with his own and guided her movements, slowing her pace, shuddering at the sweet friction of her flesh around him. He felt her eyes upon him, watching his face, and he gazed up at her through half-closed lids, sharing his smoldering pleasure.

His heart was already pounding and his breath coming in shallow drafts when she cautiously lowered her head. Her hair tickled as it draped across his belly and thighs. The instant she touched her tongue to the tip of him, he felt as if a bolt of lightning struck. He stiffened, careful not to lunge upward.

But when she took him fully into her mouth, that thoughtful restraint took all his willpower. He groaned in ecstasy as she slid down his staff, inch by luscious inch. By the Saints, 'twas heavenly. Her mouth was hot and wet and slick and soft, demanding yet generous as she began to move. His nostrils flared, and his fists clenched in the coverlet as she worked her enchantment upon him. His head tossed back and forth as waves of desire threatened to drown him.

Then he made a grave mistake. A curtain of hair obscured her face, and he brushed it aside to enjoy the provocative sight. But once he glimpsed her soft pink lips wrapped around him so intimately, his control slipped away, and his passions rose faster than bubbles in ale.

"Jesu!" he gasped, fighting an unbearable need to thrust.

She spared him a glance of unmitigated triumph, but he was past care. He knew only that he needed her, desperately, and her mouth was far too delicate for the violent release he required.

Using brute strength, he lifted her off him and rolled her onto her back. Her eyes widened as he tugged up her skirts. But she didn't fight him. Instead, she sought out his mouth with hers, and the salty taste of him upon her lips drove him mad with need.

But he was not so crass as to use a woman solely for his own pleasure. As they kissed, he swept one hand through her feminine curls and delved into the secret folds beneath, using his fingers tenderly, skillfully, increasing her desires to match his own. Her passions rose so quickly and with such force that it took his breath away and taxed his restraint.

"Ah, God, Helena, I want you."

"Aye!" she gasped.

Still, fearing he would explode the moment he entered

her, he waited until she was on the verge of release. Her fingertips dug into his shoulders, and she drew in three sharp breaths. Then he plunged forward, sheathing himself fully in her warm, wet, inviting womb.

She cried out sharply.

But 'twas not in ecstasy.

'Twas in pain.

He froze in stunned disbelief, looking down at her.

"Jesu," he breathed in horror. "Sweet Jesu."

## Chapter 15

'Twas impossible. The way she'd talked, the way she'd moved, the way she'd taken him so willingly in her mouth. How could she have been a virgin? And yet he'd felt her tear as he'd pushed forward. God's blood! If only he'd known. If only he'd been able to stop himself.

He'd taken virgins before. Indeed, he was renowned for his gentleness and care where they were concerned. Many a damsel had come to him for the singular purpose of losing her maidenhead. But he'd used none of his celebrated finesse with Helena. He'd caused her pain.

He brushed the hair back from her forehead with his thumb. "Sweet Helena, why did you not . . ."

There was no way to undo what had been done. There was no way to make amends for what he'd taken. But at least he might better the ordeal for her.

Though her brow was creased, her eyes yet smoldered with passion. At least he hadn't killed all her desire.

"The sting will fade in a moment, and then I promise

I'll make it better," he murmured, resting his cheek alongside hers. "Forsooth, I'll take you to a heaven like you've never known."

She was still panting, mere moments away from climax, and he likewise hovered on the brink. But his sobering discovery had made his need less urgent. Which was useful.

"Let your muscles ease around me," he whispered. "'Twill decrease the pain if you—"

She gave a proud toss of her head. "'Tis naught," she muttered. "Your dagger is not so sharp."

Her words would have made him smile if the situation were not so grave. "I did not mean to hurt you at all, my lady. If I'd only known . . ."

"Kiss me."

He blinked. "What?"

"Kiss me."

Cautiously, wondering at her intent, he pressed his lips to hers. She returned his kiss and gradually seemed to melt at the coaxing of his mouth. She shifted her hips beneath him, adjusting to his invasion. He felt her relax around him, and he breathed a sigh of relief, knowing henceforth 'twould only get better for her.

He let his hand slip down between her breasts, then turn to follow the slight curve of her belly and fondle the curls below. "May I?"

She looked at him with smoky emerald eyes. "I insist."

He smiled. God, she was beguiling, even in the midst of this unfortunate situation. Her courage and spirit made her all the more alluring. She was no helpless maid to burst into tears at her perceived ruin. She was a true warrior, worthy of his admiration. And as Colin gradually teased the embers of her desire back to life, he began to wonder if what he felt for her could be more than mere lust, more than admiration.

Colin's dagger might not be so sharp, Helena thought, but 'twas of considerable size. He seemed to fill her completely. 'Twas not an unpleasant feeling, just an unfamiliar one. As his fingers worked their divine magic upon her, she rocked her hips gently forward and back, seeking . . . something. At first he mirrored her movements, remaining fixed within her. But anon, as his kisses deepened and her heart pummeled at her ribs and her skin began to tingle with a greater need, she arched backward, counter to his movement, forcing him to partially withdraw.

He gasped, and she, too, drew in a ragged breath at the lovely friction. But still he hesitated to move.

"Are you ready?" he whispered.

For answer, she strove upward, sheathing him again, delighting in the full sensation and the groan of pleasure she elicited from Colin.

"Oh, my lady, what you invoke." His brow creased, and his eyes squeezed shut, as if he suffered some grievous torment.

And yet she showed him no mercy. She arched back and thrust her hips forward again, and he sucked a sharp breath between his teeth.

This was victory, she thought, dizzy with power. Soon she'd have him surrendering to his passions just as she'd surrendered earlier. 'Twas a heady feeling.

Mayhap if things had continued thus, she'd have won that victory. But suddenly Colin was having no more of her manipulations. He seized the reins of her runaway desire and began steering it to his own course.

Slowly at first, he plunged forward, then retreated, and with each determined stroke, he whispered encouragements against her hair. "Aye," he breathed. "Slow. That's it. Gently."

His voice grew more ragged with each thrust, until he rasped out syllables that were no longer words, and she experienced some satisfaction as he seemed to lose control. But, curse her compliant body, she was losing control just as quickly.

A throbbing ache built inside her, deeper and more all-encompassing than the intense lightning from before. She moaned as her hips moved with a will of their own, matching his thrusts. His fingertips rubbed at her more insistently now, urging her to higher levels of sensation as he climbed the rise beside her. She clawed at his shoulders, clinging to something solid in a world that was rapidly melting beneath her. Then the fire began to blaze fiercely, spreading faster than she could douse it, and she found herself burning out of control.

Just as she reached the brink of helplessness, she heard his breath catch, once, twice. She opened her eyes to the most exquisite expression of longing and anticipation and pure need upon his face. 'Twas that expression that catapulted her beyond worldly passion to a sphere of such bliss, such euphoria, such utter satisfaction, that she cried out in joy, shuddering like a falcon diving from the highest heights.

He groaned with her, burying his face in her hair and cradling her with possessive arms as he pumped out the last of his seed.

And then the only residue of their delirious voyage was the sound of their mingled gasps. Eventually, their bodies stilled. After such chaos, the silence seemed shattering. Helena had never felt so drained, even after the fiercest battle. She lay upon the pallet like wilted seaweed washed up on the shore.

Colin had spoken truly. He'd taken her to heaven. Never had she experienced such ecstasy. Never had she felt such fire in her veins. Not even in the most rousing battle had her blood run so hot.

But most curious, she couldn't say for certain who had emerged the victor in this battle. Part of her felt triumphant. After all, Colin sprawled across her like a dead man, one leg flung over hers, his arms cast wide, his body limp, a foe defeated by her hand. And yet part of her felt he had bested her again. He'd forced her to succumb to her passions, and she'd had no strength to resist his seduction.

Nay, she amended, seduction hadn't been his idea at all. It had been born of her own thirst for revenge and her cursed impulsiveness.

Only this time she'd paid for that impulsiveness with her maidenhood.

She was not so naive as to believe 'twas his fault. She'd bear that burden. She'd encouraged him, nay, baited him. He'd never suspected she was a virgin. He couldn't be blamed for taking what she'd so willingly offered him.

Besides, she thought philosophically as she lay basking in the warm afterglow of their mating, 'twas just as well the deed was done. 'Twas no matter to her whether she was a virgin. Until Pagan's arrival, she'd never planned to marry anyway. She was a Warrior Maid.

Forsooth, she might well grow to enjoy this sort of

disport as much as she did sword fighting. After all, 'twas said that trysting was a knight's second favorite form of exercise. Even now she felt her loins awakening about him, her nipples stiffening against his firm chest, a taut vibration of anticipation singing in her blood as she prepared to reengage him.

Colin's head was filled with warring emotions—guilt and contentment, shame and ecstasy, dread and desire— to say naught of his loins. Already they hungered for her again.

But he'd made a grave mistake.

He might be a man who kept many mistresses, but he was neither philanderer nor seducer. Indeed, his morality had always been impeccable. He never forced a damsel against her will. He never trysted with married women. And he never accepted the gift of a maiden's virginity without thorough counsel beforehand.

Contrary to what Helena might think of Normans, Colin was a man of principle. He'd claimed the maidenhead of a noble lady, the daughter of a lord. Chivalry demanded he do the right thing.

But he wasn't so boorish as to speak of it now, not while he yet dwelled within her like an invader and she lay beneath him like a fallen angel. Such serious discourse required that he sit across from her, holding her hand, looking into her eyes.

He lifted himself up on his elbows and began to ease from her. But she uttered a small sound of protest and moved her hips to sheathe him again. Again, he tried to withdraw, and she foiled his attempt.

"My lady," he murmured with a rueful chuckle, "you must let me go."

"Not yet."

Her rough-voiced entreaty drew him to her like a moth to flame. God, how he longed to stay within her, to feel her passion rise again, to couple with the delectable little Hel-cat all night long. But he'd not let his cock rule his conscience.

"My lady"—he sighed—"we must talk."

But when he tried to ease from her this time, she wrapped her silken thighs about him, dug her heels into his buttocks, and held on to him with surprising strength.

"So talk," she breathed, her eyes sultry with desire.

He shivered. Lord, the woman knew not what she did to him. He couldn't talk. Bloody hell, he could hardly think.

Her lips curved into a most calculating smile then as she rocked beneath him, slowly, deliberately, teasing him with her movements.

He groaned aloud with mental anguish, knowing he had to make one last attempt at reason."My lady, have I not done enough damage?"

"Aye," she purred, "but the damage is done now."

And with that feeble assurance and a wet, passionate, breathless kiss, he found himself swept away in the power of her temptation.

For a virgin, she had an uncanny instinct for seduction, a natural talent that led her to move in the most alluring way, to touch him where he was most responsive. She tugged off his garments, and he growled with approval as her hands spread across his shoulders, squeezing at the muscles of his upper arms. But when her fingers splayed over his chest, then slid down to pluck at his nipples, lust shot through his body like a flaming arrow.

Through half-closed lids, he studied her face. Her nostrils flared in excitement, and her eyes flickered with triumph. Her smile was wicked, unabashedly wicked, and as if he could read her thoughts, he suddenly knew what she wanted. He answered her with a weak grin, only too happy to oblige.

He swiftly rolled over, taking her with him and maintaining their union as he yielded the superior position. Then he lay back and let the Warrior Maid have her way with him.

Looming over him, she rocked back till she straddled his hips, then pulled her gown off with a proud toss of her head. Sweet Saints, she was even more beautiful than he remembered. Her body was firm and lithe, her arms slim but well muscled, her belly flat, and her breasts . . . He sighed in appreciation. Her breasts were as plump and warm and inviting as loaves of cocket bread. But what drove him the most mad, what enticed him beyond reason, was not her voluptuous body, but the combination of smug victory and burning desire in her shimmering green eyes.

She wanted his unequivocal surrender.

He would give it to her gladly.

While she moved atop him, he closed his eyes and reveled in the sensuous rhythm. Her hands explored his body, gliding over his ribs, smoothing his chest, caressing his jaw, burying themselves in his hair. He reached out to softly cup her breasts, but after a light gasp of pleasure, she drew his hands away, pressing them back onto the pallet and holding him there by the wrists.

He smiled in lusty pleasure as she gazed down at him,

her eyes dark with need, her hair tickling his neck, her breasts swaying gently back and forth, tantalizingly close to his mouth.

Twice as she rode him, he was tempted to cast her hands away so he might caress her face, her breasts, her buttocks. But her grasp was firm upon his wrists. 'Twas clear she wanted complete control. And so he settled for feasting his eyes upon her creamy flesh, imagining its texture against his palms.

Too soon, too swiftly, fanned by her fervid gaze, the fires of his need flared to an all-consuming blaze. Making tight fists against the urge to enfold her in his arms and hold her close against his chest, he arched his head back and waited for the impending explosion.

And then the little witch did the unthinkable.

She stopped.

While he writhed at the edge of climax, she ceased her movements.

"Nay!" he cried, shivering with need.

He speared her with a glance and found she regarded him with breathless curiosity. Like a knight who'd never ridden a warhorse before, she was testing his limits.

She was close to his.

He grimaced with restraint and bit out a foul oath.

She moved the slightest bit, and he trembled at the sensation.

She rocked forward gently, and his hips thrust upward of their own accord.

She gasped, and her muscles squeezed around him, sending him to new heights of agony.

"Bloody hell," he said between his teeth, "have mercy. Finish me now."

She might have been wicked, but she wasn't cruel. At his bidding, she resumed her sensual ride. As fast as a wayward steed, his desires galloped, leaving him unable to steer or stop, but only fight for purchase. At last, as she lurched above him in the throes of victory, he was catapulted to his own heaven, a place higher and purer and more intensely pleasurable than any he'd visited before.

Forsooth, as she collapsed upon him and he lay exhausted beneath her, he was filled with a kind of awe.

Colin had first coupled at the age of ten and six. He'd learned quickly and become a lover of considerable renown. Since then, he'd trysted with too many women to count, and yet, impossibly, Helena had taken him to greater heights than he'd ever imagined.

Her hands now loosened upon his wrists, and he moved his arms to embrace her, relishing the warmth of her skin against his and the thrum of her beating heart. Her breath rasped along his naked shoulder, and her hair was soft against his cheek.

Who was this temptress in an angel's guise? This puzzle of a woman who was at once strong and vulnerable, wise and naive, cool and passionate? How could she know so much when she had experienced so little?

Instinct, he decided. The same instinct that made a man a gifted warrior. The same inherent talent he himself had for discerning a foe's weakness.

He smiled as he inclined his head against hers and felt her rouse, running a tentative finger around his ear, pressing her lips against his shoulder, nudging her hips forward an inch. The little vixen wanted to test him again.

He chuckled in good-natured fatigue. "Nay, my love. Not yet."

He felt her thwarted sigh upon his chest, which made him chuckle again.

"You're like a knight with a new sword, my lady," he chided, "wanting to spar past dark."

"'Tis not . . . disagreeable," she admitted.

He laughed loudly then, rattling her so that she was nearly unseated. "Not disagreeable? Is that the best you can manage?"

She stacked her fists upon his chest and rested her chin on top, glaring down at him. "Is that the best *you* can manage?"

He grabbed her wrists and spread them apart, forcing her head to drop low enough for him to steal a kiss. "You, my impatient Hel-cat, will have to wait."

She stuck out her bottom lip, and he caught it gently between his teeth, turning the gesture into a fond kiss.

"Soon," he promised.

He kept his promise, and this time their joining was sweet and tender. Gone was the fiery wench, and in her place was a delicate flower. He coaxed her petals to bloom, catching her soft cries against his shoulder before he sank into her welcoming depths, where their nectars might mingle.

And as he cradled her afterward, listening to her soft sounds of slumber, savoring the silken weight of her upon him, bathing in the musky fragrance of their lovemaking, he thought this night might not be such a tragedy after all. The marriage of honor he intended might be . . . what had she called it? Not disagreeable. He grinned. Indeed, he could well imagine a lifetime of utter contentment in Helena's arms.

~

# Chapter 16

Nay?" COLIN BURST OUT. "What do you mean, nay?"

Helena almost felt sorry for him. There seemed a look of genuine shock and hurt on his face as he knelt before her.

"'Tis not that I find you . . ." She searched for the right word.

"Disagreeable?" he sulked.

'Twas not the right word. Not at all. Indeed, she found Colin du Lac intoxicating, addictive, utterly irresistible. Which was why she had to refuse his offer.

Forsooth, this morn, just glancing at him with his twinkling eyes and seductive smile and all that glorious flesh sent her heart racing. She wanted naught but to couple with him again and again.

But marriage . . .

Until Pagan had come, she'd never considered taking a husband at all. Only desperation and the need to save her sister from an unhappy union had moved her to offer herself as a sacrifice.

She didn't want to be a wife. She wanted to be a warrior.

All the best warriors were unfettered by marriage. A warrior needed a cold heart, a heart free of encumbrances. Pagan she might yet wed to save her sister, for she felt naught for the man. But Colin . . .

She swallowed hard, withdrew her hand from between his, and crossed to the hearth. This affection she'd begun to feel for the Norman bordered dangerously on infatuation, and she dared not let him see how vulnerable she was.

She spoke over her shoulder with a nonchalance she didn't feel. "You're a fine man, and I'm sure you'd make a suitable husband, but—"

"But I'm a Norman," he muttered.

"Nay, 'tisn't that."

"Is it because you believe I'm a philanderer?"

She heard him rise and take three long strides toward her. He caught her by the shoulders and spun her to face him. His face was grim and sincere. And, God help her, as handsome as a Saint's.

"If we were wed," he vowed, "I would never take another woman to my bed. I swear it on my sword and before God."

She loved and hated the way he made her feel, as if she were cherished silver melting in his gaze. And that was why she had to turn him down. Beneath his regard, she could feel herself turning from a fierce Warrior Maid to Colin's hand-tamed Hel-kitten.

She consoled herself with the fact that Colin probably felt the same way she did about marriage. She'd heard enough to know that, no matter what he said, he was not a man for whom one woman was enough. Nay, Colin only felt compelled to marry her because he was a man of chivalry, because he was loyal to his vows, and because 'twas required when one compromised a lady.

But that meant naught to Helena. She didn't feel compromised. And Colin was no longer her hostage. She'd not imprison him in a marriage neither of them wanted, just for honor's sake.

So she forced a flippant smile to her face. "I fear I might be unable to make the same promise."

He looked at her, incredulous. "You'd cuckold me?"

She shrugged, but she couldn't maintain her indifference while he stared at her with those beguiling eyes, so she wriggled out of his hold and turned away, picking up a stick to poke at the dead coals on the hearth. "'Tis a new diversion for me, this coupling. I might wish to do . . . more of it."

His voice was seductive and threatening all at once. "I assure you, my lady, I'd give you all the coupling you require." He stole up behind her and murmured against her ear. "I could keep you in bed all night, my wanton witch, and satisfy you so thoroughly you'd be unable to rise in the morn."

She closed her eyes against a powerful wave of desire. She believed him. Already he'd left her as weak and breathless as a newborn pup.

But she'd not say the words to entrap either of them. No matter how great the temptation, the two of them were untamed beasts who needed to run free, Colin to his bevy of mistresses, Helena to her field of glory.

He cleared his throat. "I am of noble birth, my lady. 'Tis true I am a second son, not heir to my father's land. But I assure you, I receive ample compensation from—"

She whipped about in anger. "I need no man's coin. If ever I wed, 'twill not be for silver."

"Then why do you refuse me?"

That almost made her smile. 'Twould not occur to the self-assured knave that mayhap he wasn't comely or charming enough. Even if she used that excuse, she knew he'd not believe it. "No man can force me to wed," she hedged.

He shook his head. "Bloody Scotswomen," he said under his breath. "I should have known from the moment the three of you fought for the *disgrace* of marrying Pagan Cameliard . . ."

Her ears pricked up. "Aye, we did," she said, locking onto his words. "And we still do."

"What?"

"I may yet marry Pagan Cameliard."

"You can't be serious. It's been over a sennight. Your sister has already—"

"He swore he'd not take her against her will. Their marriage may yet be unconsummated."

He burst out laughing. "Oh, aye."

She bit her lip. Curse the man, even when he was laughing at her expense, he was as charming as the Devil. "Even if it *has*, if Deirdre is discontent in any way, I intend to take her place." She meant what she said, though she doubted after all this time that Deirdre would be amenable to such a thing.

"Indeed? And if Pagan will not have you?"

She knew what he intimated. She was no longer a virgin. What would Pagan think of that? But she raised her chin a notch and turned a bit of Colin's smugness back on him. "I can make him want me."

This time he didn't laugh. Forsooth he looked as if he

half believed her. The glow in his eyes dimmed, turned to disappointment, then silent anger, and finally resignation. He turned aside, limping back to the pallet to finish dressing.

She felt wretched then, for she could see her refusal had hurt him. She sighed ruefully. Deirdre would have been proud of her. For once in her life, Helena had curbed her impulsiveness and thought things through.

There was a long and awkward silence as Colin laced on his boots. Helena combed her tangled hair with her fingers, racking her brains for something to say.

Abruptly, he planted his feet on the ground and stood up. "Let's go."

Startled, she snagged her finger in a curl. "Go?"

"Back to Rivenloch."

"Now?" She frowned. "But your leg . . ."

"Is well enough."

"'Tis hardly healed." An inexplicable fluttering started in her heart, akin to panic.

"I cannot run, but I can walk well enough."

Her mind grasped at excuses. "What if the English attack us again? You're hardly fit to fight."

"I can defend you if need be."

"'Tis too soon." She turned her back on him and began mindlessly rearranging the cooking pots, confounded by her own reluctance to leave. What was wrong with her? Why would she *not* wish to return home? 'Twas not as if this hovel in the middle of the woods was so idyllic.

And yet in some ways, 'twas.

The two of them had shared much here—stories, suppers, kisses—and a part of her didn't want that adventure to end. If they returned to Rivenloch, she would go back to her predictable life of bland oatcakes and sisterly squabbles and keeping her father from harm.

"'Tis time," he said brusquely. "Forsooth, we're long overdue. And the longer you wait, the less likely Pagan will be amenable to your . . . arrangements."

She bit her lip, wishing she'd never mentioned marrying Pagan. Now, like a clumsy falcon, she'd been caught in her own jesses. "On the morrow, then. Surely one more—"

Her words trailed off as he pierced her with a gaze as fierce and cold as a Highland winter. "I will not sleep one more night with another man's wife."

After the first mile through the chill fog, every step was an agony for Colin. Pain knifed into his thigh as if the sword wounded him again and again. And yet 'twas not half so painful as the stabbing in his heart when he thought about Helena's coupling with another man.

Had he been but a plaything to her? A diversion? Did she have no feelings for him whatsoever?

He recalled his own first tryst. 'Twas with a kitchen maid, a woman eight years his senior. Yet while he lay recovering upon her bosom from the wonder of his first joining, his heart had been so full that for weeks afterward he believed the sun rose and set upon her.

Likewise, he'd never bedded a virgin without leaving her awestruck. Grateful. Adoring. Indeed, he sometimes had to wean the lovesick maids from his affections, for they oft confused physical pleasure with the leanings of the heart.

But not Helena.

She apparently felt naught for him. Not amazement. Not gratitude. Not even fondness.

He frowned. Mayhap he was wrong about the fondness. After all, she did have her arm around him, and she was helping him hobble along the path.

Mayhap, he consoled himself, 'twas only that she remained firm in her resolve to marry Pagan. Perchance her sense of duty overpowered all other emotions.

He intended to find out. 'Twas the reason that, despite the bite of pain in his leg, he was determined to return immediately to Rivenloch. Surely once Helena saw that Pagan and his bride were happy—and he'd wager half his silver they were—she'd reconsider his offer of marriage.

He hoped so. He'd spent a long time thinking about it last night as the damsel lay curled against his side.

His indiscretion had been but a tiny part of his decision to ask her for her hand. After all, there were at least a dozen noblewomen, Norman and English, who would have leaped at the chance to become his wife.

He hadn't realized it till now, but he'd grown bored with maids who sighed over his sweet praises and swooned into his arms. Helena of Rivenloch was an exotic island in a sea of willing wenches, a woman so fierce and yet so feminine, innocent yet self-assured, brutally honest yet kind of spirit. She excited and surprised him at every turn, keeping him sharp and on guard. Like a pinecone tossed on the hearth, she burned in a bright flash of fire and passion, spitting out curses like sparks, threatening to set the world ablaze. But once the embers died down and the fire cooled, she had the tender heart of an angel.

Only a woman so special could convince him to abandon his beloved bachelor's life, whether or not he'd compromised her, and he knew it.

So he'd drifted off to sleep with a smile on his face,

dreaming of their happy life together, the suppers he would cook for her, the babes she would give to him, and the tales they would tell the dozen little warrior children at their feet.

But she'd dashed those visions with one word this morn. *Nay.*

He winced as he stumbled over a root on the path and was forced to lean heavily upon her, a bolt of fire shooting up from his knee to his hip.

"Let's rest," she said, straining under his weight.

"I'm fine."

"I'm not," she countered, though he knew 'twas a lie for his sake. The wench had the stamina of a warhorse. She wasn't even breathing hard.

"Very well. But only for a moment."

She helped him to a fallen log. They sat on its mossy side, and though Colin was loath to admit it, 'twas a great relief to have the weight off his leg.

"Why are you in such a bloody hurry to get back?" she asked him bluntly.

"Why are you *not?*" Disappointment and discomfort made him irritable. "I'd think you'd be eager to win Pagan's heart."

She picked at the tree bark. "'Tis not a thing that can be rushed."

"What, seduction?" He chuckled humorlessly. "It certainly didn't take you long to wrap the mercenaries around your finger."

She scowled. "I wasn't looking to *wed* the mercenaries."

"Oh, aye. You only sought to *bed* them."

"I did not!" she snapped. "I sought to distract them so I could save your ungrateful arse."

"Save me?" he smirked. "For what? The ransom!"

"That's not true!"

Bitterness made him speak too freely. "But before you bartered me for your new bridegroom, you thought you'd taste what you'd be giving up."

Her jaw dropped. "I suppose last night was entirely *my* fault?"

"Mayhap if you'd told me you were a virgin . . ."

"Mayhap if you hadn't assumed I was *not* . . . !" Her voice rang out in the quiet wood, startling a bird from its perch.

"How was I to know," he sneered, "the way you minced and pranced and preened before those English bastards?"

She grabbed him by the front of his tabard and hauled him close. "I do not mince, you philanderer."

"Once and for all," he bit out, "I am *not* a philanderer."

What happened next happened so quickly that Colin had no time to move. While he glared into Helena's eyes, her gaze flitted up over his head, widening, and then, in one fluid movement, she stole the dagger from his belt and yanked him down toward her lap so she could fire it over his head.

He heard the thunk of the blade lodging in wood and then a man's gruff voice.

"Bloody . . . !"

When he wrenched loose from Helena's hold, he saw she'd pinned a man to a tree by the sleeve of his sword arm not five yards away. For the moment, the man couldn't brandish his sword, but already he rocked the knife back and forth, trying to dislodge it, and by the gleam in his eyes, he wouldn't hesitate to use either weapon against them.

"Shite!" Colin hissed. Helena had just disarmed him, and she had the only other weapon. He reached his hand out behind him. "Give me your knife."

"Nay."

Cursing her under his breath, he swept his arm back, intending to at least keep her behind him, out of harm's way. But she was no longer there. She'd sprung to her feet and was already advancing on the man.

"Nay!" His wound pulsing, he struggled to his feet.

"Where did you get that sword?" she demanded of the captive.

The man didn't reply, only wriggling the dagger all the faster as she approached.

"Answer me!"

"Tell her!" Colin yelled, fearing 'twas the only way to keep her from getting within striking range before Colin could reach him.

The man's eyes shifted to him, and he sneered, "One o' yer countrymen. I didn't ask 'is name, just killed 'im and took 'is blade."

Mother of God, 'twas another Englishman. Had the entire English army invaded Scotland?

Helena strayed closer, too close. "That's Mochrie's sword, you whoreson."

Colin's heart leaped into his throat. "Helena, get back!"

"Not until I reclaim this good Scots steel from this English bastard."

Colin had no idea who Mochrie was, but apparently 'twas a matter of honor with Helena that stripped all reason from her. She drew The Shadow's knife and held it to the man's throat. "Drop it."

The Englishman instantly seized her wrist with his free

hand, forcing the blade away from his throat. Colin intended to step in then, grab her around the waist, and drag her backward, the sword be damned. But before he could take a step, she drove her knee hard into the man's ballocks, and with a weak groan, he released both the sword and her wrist.

"Son of a . . . ," she muttered, retrieving the sword. This Mochrie must have been a friend, for at the edges of her angry gaze, sorrow burned. She turned on the Englishman. "How many of you are there?"

The man was doubled over, in too much pain to reply.

Then she locked eyes with Colin. "I'd wager gold he's a scout."

Colin nodded. The man's tabard was too fine for an outlaw. This was some noble's man.

With a scolding glance that told her he'd brook no argument, he snatched The Shadow's knife from her and approached the Englishman. With his free hand, he seized the man by the hair and forced his head back, then placed the knife point against his throat. "What's your name?"

"Wat. Walter."

"And who is your master, Walter?"

The man only grimaced in response.

Colin added slight pressure to the knife, letting a drop of blood well upon the point. "His name."

"Lord Morpeth."

"How many travel with you?"

The man shrugged, as much as he could with one arm pinned to a tree and a knife at his neck. "Don't know."

Most men-at-arms couldn't count past ten. "As many as your fingers?"

A snicker escaped the man.

"More?" Colin asked.

"Aye."

"As many as five men's fingers?"

The man managed a smug sneer. "As many as the stars."

Colin doubted that, but the fact that Lord Morpeth had sent a scout ahead meant it must be a contingent of considerable size. And if 'twas an army of any note, the commander would have heard of Cameliard.

"Heed me well, Wat," he bit out. "This land is under the protection of Sir Pagan Cameliard. If your master disturbs one stone of one castle in this realm, he will do battle with Cameliard's knights."

The man's eyes widened in recognition. Now Colin would let him go, counting on the fact that he'd pass the dire warning along to his English lord, thereby avoiding warfare.

He hadn't counted on the man panicking.

As Colin lowered the knife, Walter reached across and finally snagged the dagger from the tree, coming across with a back slash that Colin had to dodge to avoid. But in lunging back, Colin twisted his ankle and fell to one knee. His stitches pulled, and acid pain raced up his leg. As Walter made a return pass of the dagger, Colin raised the knife to block the blow, but the slim blade was no match for the larger weapon.

Walter's third thrust headed straight for Colin's heart.

❧

# Chapter 17

WHEN HELENA SAW Colin drop to his knee, time seemed to slow to an impossible lassitude. Icy sweat broke across her brow. A gasp of dread filled her lungs. A scream formed in her throat. A thousand amazing thoughts bombarded her in the space of an instant.

Colin couldn't die. Not here. Not now.

Not after she'd nursed his wound with such diligence.

Not after he'd held her in his arms all night.

Not when 'twas her fault all of this had come to pass.

Sweet Mary, he couldn't die.

She loved him. God help her, she loved him.

A sudden, fierce, impulsive instinct to protect Colin pushed her free of the prison of lethargy and made every muscle spring to life. Her heart pounding, her face grim, she raised Mochrie's sword.

By the time Walter lunged forward, her blade was already waiting for him. Before the point of his dagger could touch Colin's chest, the English scout half impaled himself upon her weapon.

As irrational and determined as a mother guarding her babe, she didn't hesitate to finish the grisly task. With a jerk of her shoulders, she thrust him through the rest of the way.

His eyes rolled as the life drained out of them, but it seemed a gruesome eternity before he fell at last with a gurgle and a sickly thud into a puddle of his own blood.

Colin struggled to his feet. Wasting no time, he wrenched the sword from the dead man's belly, wiping the blade upon the grass to clean it. Then he pried the dagger from his lifeless fist. At last he faced her, his mouth sagging open in wonder. "You saved my life."

But Helena had no time for his gratitude. She staggered off to lose her breakfast in the bushes.

By the time she'd braced herself enough to return to the scene, Colin had rolled the victim beneath the brush and spread dirt over the bloody trail. "We should make haste to Rivenloch," he said.

She nodded, grateful he didn't mention the slaying further. She was still trembling. 'Twas not often she had to kill a man.

He buckled on Mochrie's sword and sword belt. Then he handed her the dagger, hilt first.

She frowned at the smaller weapon in derision. "The *sword* is mine by rights."

"And so it shall be, once we're safe behind castle walls. Until then, 'tis mine to wield."

"By what right?" Some of her shakiness dissipated in the wake of rising ire. "I saved your life. You said it yourself."

His gaze was soft and sincere. "You should not have to

fight for my life." He reached out to gently squeeze her upper arm.

But no matter how genuine his concern was, his touch felt condescending. She shook off his hand, incredulous. "Do you doubt my skill?"

His expression hardened. "Do you doubt mine?"

She'd seen him with a blade. She knew he was an able warrior. But she'd not give him the satisfaction of telling him so.

When she didn't reply, he spit out a foul curse, then un-buckled the sword belt and let it drop to the ground. He limped over to the fallen log and sat down, crossing his arms over his chest. "'Tis yours, then. Go. Leave me."

She blinked, unsure of how to respond to this.

"If you cannot trust a Knight of Cameliard to defend you," he bit out, insulted, "then you are better off alone. I'll only slow you down."

"I'm not leaving you in the forest."

He gazed stonily off into the woods. "I'm not giving you a choice. I'm not moving from this spot."

A desperate frustration began to foment within her. She had no time for this nonsense. He was going to come with her, like it or not. She jerked the fallen sword from its sheath and advanced on him.

"You'll come with me. Now," she said, slashing a whistling threat through the air.

He faced her with an unwavering gaze. "Nay."

"Don't be a fool. I wield a sword."

He sniffed. "Then you'll just have to slay me."

For a long moment, they stared at each other, at an impasse.

Helena knew from his steady eyes that he meant it.

He'd let her lop off his head before he'd go with her un-armed, and likely never flinch from the blow. Curse his hide, he *was* giving her no choice.

"Shite!" She tossed the sword at his feet in surrender and turned her back on him, unwilling to see the triumphant gleam in his eyes. But as she walked away, a thunk sounded beside her in the sod. He'd fired the dagger toward her. With a snort of irritation, she retrieved it, shoving it into her belt. Then she fumed silently as, behind her, she heard Colin buckling on the sword, *her* sword.

This was why she'd never wished to marry, she reminded herself. With marriage came compromise and sometimes surrender, and she had no desire to do either. She was her own woman, and she was perfectly capable of making her own decisions without the interference of a man who believed himself abler and wiser simply by virtue of being a man.

She wished he'd walk fifty steps behind her, she thought as they set out again.

He must have read her mind. "You need not assist me, my lady. But stay within a step or two, for safety's sake."

"I *will* assist you," she insisted, ducking under his arm to take his weight upon her shoulders. Then, so he wouldn't misunderstand her motives, she grumbled, "If I don't, 'twill be nightfall before we reach the keep."

The closer they hobbled toward Rivenloch, the heavier the burden of impending dread became for Helena. For as long as she could remember, the only threats to her land had been the seasonal raiders from neighboring clans, an occasional miscreant passing through, and The Shadow, whose victims tended to be travelers. Rivenloch had seemed an impenetrable fortress.

But now that halcyon age was over. Despite her hopes that the enemy scout had exaggerated their number, that 'twas only chance a band of English mercenaries had wandered into the woods, that they posed no real threat to the Scots, she sensed in her gut that the foe lay as thick upon the land as mold upon year-old cheese.

The scout had overpowered Lord Mochrie. Yet Mochrie was a giant of a man with a chest like a barrel. 'Twould have taken more than just one scout to lay him low. Furthermore, if Mochrie's four brawny sons were with him, 'twould have required at least a dozen or so Englishmen to put up a good fight.

To make matters worse, Mochrie's keep was but a half a day's ride from Rivenloch. If he'd been slain on his own land, then the English army was already close, perilously close.

Forsooth, by afternoon, as she climbed to the upper branches of a tall oak to scan the misty countryside, Helena discovered just how close. Though their ranks disappeared into the thickening fog, the infestation of English knights ranged over the hills like fleas on a hound, as far as the eye could see.

Her face bloodless, her heart pounding, she scrambled down the tree.

"What is it?" Colin asked.

She shook her head. Her mouth was too dry with fear to speak.

"How many are there?"

She gulped. "A hundred. Maybe more."

He seized her by the shoulders and demanded her gaze with his own. "Hear me well. Pagan will not let Rivenloch fall. The keep is strong, and the Knights of Cameliard are the best in the land. I swear to you, I will die before I let these English bastards take your castle."

His words, heartfelt and determined, restored her strength. After a moment, she nodded. "A storm comes. We must hurry. Can you run?"

"I will."

'Twas all Helena could do to help Colin down the rise once Rivenloch at last came into view. The temptation to tear through the gates was great. But she'd not abandon him, not when he'd run himself half-dead to outpace the English to the castle. So they limped toward the barbican, Helena taking as much of his weight as she could.

Of course, like most men, once in the presence of his captain, Colin claimed his dire wound was but a scratch. Helena, however, spared no details when it came to telling Deirdre about the impending invasion. She gave her an estimate of the enemy's number, their direction of travel, and a warning about the ominous cast of the sky.

Orders were flung about like gauntlets cast in challenge as preparations for siege were begun at once.

To Helena's satisfaction, though Pagan had indeed assumed control of Rivenloch, it appeared Deirdre still held some sway over the Normans. She assigned Helena command over the archers, both Rivenloch's and Cameliard's, much to Colin's vexation, who wished her to take shelter with the other women and children.

At first, Helena was discomfited by the number of Cameliard denizens bustling about the hall. Faces she didn't recognize surrounded her, Norman knights and ladies and servants who seemed to overrun her Scots keep like mice. Yet they all seemed bent on helping to defend Rivenloch, carrying supplies hither and thither, aiding the men-at-arms with their weapons, gathering the livestock within the walls. Rivenloch's people had been drilled in siege preparations, but it appeared that Cameliard's were well versed in their execution.

She was likewise impressed by the discipline of the Cameliard archers. They never questioned her orders as she lined them up along the curtain wall, and their response was quick and accurate. 'Twas a heady feeling, being in control of such a powerful force. Mayhap this Norman-Scots alliance was not so terrible a thing after all.

Indeed, even Deirdre and Pagan seemed to have formed a partnership, at least when it came to protecting the keep. Whether that alliance extended to their bed-chamber, Helena didn't know. But it appeared that while Pagan was unquestionably in charge of the fighting forces, he did so with Deirdre's counsel.

If only, she thought, all husbands were so agreeable.

Colin was sure he'd been sent on a fool's errand. Deirdre had requested that he search for her father. Lame as Colin was, he was hardly the man to climb the tower stairs, looking for the addled lord. The high-handed wench had no doubt given Colin the task to keep him out of her way.

Why Pagan let the woman command him, Colin didn't know. He thought by now his captain would have tamed the headstrong damsel. But it seemed Pagan had fallen under the enchantment of the Warrior Maid of Rivenloch, and now he bowed to her authority. 'Twas most distaste-ful, most unwise.

But what gnawed at Colin's gut the most was the fact that while he hobbled up and down the interior stairs on this futile mission, Helena roamed the curtain wall, the castle's first line of defense, wholly exposed to the enemy.

That Pagan allowed this was a travesty. She was a maid, for the love of God. Had they not sworn upon their spurs to protect ladies? Yet Pagan posted her at the most vulnerable spot of the castle. The thought made him ill.

And as soon as he finished this task for Deirdre, he intended to climb the curtain wall and relieve Helena, forcibly if need be.

All at once, a deep thud shuddered the walls about him, shaking the very foundations of the tower. He stumbled to one knee as a shower of pebbles rained down upon him. Dust rose in thick plumes as the impact jarred loose the mortar between the ancient castle stones.

Lucifer's ballocks! Unless lightning had struck the tower, the English must have some war machine. A catapult. Or a trebuchet. The bastards didn't intend to lay siege, then. They meant to attack.

He scrambled to his feet and clambered up the stairs. Aware from the sudden damp draft sweeping past him that a good portion of the tower had been destroyed, he was eager to finish his task before the enemy reduced it completely to rubble.

As misfortune would have it, this was indeed the tower Lord Gellir had ascended. When Colin emerged upon the landing, he found the roof blasted away, completely open to the heavens, which had begun to rage with a punishing storm. And through the heavy rain pelting the splintered oak, he spied the white-haired Viking lord, lost and confused, crawling about the remains of his floor.

"Bloody hell," Colin said under his breath. Suddenly this fool's errand had turned into a matter of life and death.

"Lord Gellir!" he called above the rising roar of the storm.

The old man seemed not to hear. Or mayhap the voices in his head drowned out Colin's words.

"Lord Gellir!" he cried again. "Come!"

But, as bullheaded as his daughters, the lord turned and began creeping toward the crumbling edge of the tower.

"Nay!" Colin yelled.

But the man couldn't hear him. Or wouldn't. Which meant Colin would have to take stronger measures. Muttering a prayer for surefootedness, he limped carefully forward across the rain-slick planks.

"My lord!" he called. "Come away from the edge!"

But Lord Gellir seemed deaf to his pleas. Colin hobbled slowly forward, racking his brain for the right words to reach the old man.

"My lord! Come below!" he beckoned. "We're starting a game of dice!"

The lord froze and cocked his head.

"I've got six shillings!" he continued. "Silver I won off you a sennight ago! Do you remember?"

The world seemed to stand still, but for the incessant rain, as the lord's troubled brain struggled to untangle Colin's words. He twisted his head about, narrowing sharp blue eyes at Colin.

"Aye, 'tis I, Colin du Lac, Knight of Cameliard," he said hopefully, brushing the rain-drenched locks from his face. "The Normans need you for a game of dice, my lord."

But as quickly as the lord's visage cleared, it clouded again, and the old man resumed his perilous course.

"Nay, my lord!"

Colin cursed in frustration. He dared not follow. Already the floor listed dangerously. If he added his weight to that of Lord Gellir . . .

"I pray you, my lord, for your daughters' sake . . . ," he tried, but the old Viking was beyond hearing again.

And then the lord did the unthinkable. At the very precipice of the tower, he struggled to his feet. Colin froze, afraid to move, as the old man raised his arms to the sky like a sacrifice to Thor.

Then a movement beyond the lord, on the nearby hill, caught Colin's eye. Through the dense curtain of rain, he saw men priming a trebuchet. In another moment, 'twould fire upon the tower.

Purely on instinct, Colin dove forward, catching the lord about the ankles. But true to his fears, their combined weight caused the floor to tilt, and instead of stumbling backward, Lord Gellir was flung over the edge.

It took all Colin's strength to hold on, to keep the lord from falling. The Viking warrior was large and heavy as he dangled over the precipice. But Colin clenched the old man's ankles with a death grip, even as he felt himself slipping inexorably, inch by inch, toward the edge.

It seemed an eternity before relief arrived, and Colin's arms trembled with fatigue. But when Colin finally heard Pagan's welcome voice bellowing at him to hold on, he knew he'd succeeded. Lord Gellir was saved.

Before he could rejoice, the air was split by a horrific pounding and the shriek of splitting wood. Colin was shoved backward by an unseen hand. The last thing he remembered was his head thudding against something hard. Then the world went black.

\* \* \*

Helena had never heard such ungodly sounds. The second impact shook the entire castle, even the eastern wall where she stood with her archers. Firing off a quick command to them to keep an eye out for sappers, she scrambled down the steps to assess the damage.

Deirdre, too, had heard the noise and was crossing the courtyard toward the west tower when Helena met her. She'd never seen Deirdre look so pale, and when she beheld the destruction to the tower, she saw why.

The floors were completely splintered, leaving the stone tower a hollow shell filled with rubble. The top of the tower and part of the wall had crumbled away. Still, 'twas not the worst of it. Lord Gellir had been in the tower when it collapsed, and Deirdre wasn't certain he was still alive.

The two of them clambered up the ruined steps and were digging through the piles of debris, determined to find their father, when Deirdre revealed another chilling detail. Apparently Colin, attempting to save the lord, had climbed the tower a moment before 'twas hit.

Helena's heart lurched, and her determination turned to desperation. With treacherous speed, she bolted up the stairs to the top floor, which now lay exposed to the sky.

Splayed upon the tilted planks of the tower like a broken, lifeless quintain was Colin du Lac. His knee had snagged upon a chunk of stonework, saving him from sliding to certain death upon the rocks below. But that meant naught if he was already dead.

With a sharp cry, she hurtled forward, throwing herself down at his side. His handsome face was as pale as parchment, his wet locks making dark slashes across his cheek. She swept the hair from his face and took his head between her hands, willing him to wake.

"Come on, Colin," she muttered, giving his head a shake. "Come on, damn you."

But he was silent. Rain pelted his face, dribbling between his parted lips. She slipped one hand around the back of his head. It came away bloody.

"Don't you die on me, Norman," she bit out.

Her heart hammering at her ribs, she quickly searched for a pulse. Hot tears of anger and desperation rolled down her cheeks to mingle with the cold rain.

"Come on, you son of a—"

At last she found it—a weak heartbeat in his throat. He was alive. An involuntary sob of relief escaped her.

But there was no time now to try to revive him. From the tower's edge, Deirdre was crying out for aid.

Lord Gellir had fallen from the tower, outside the wall. Somehow, by the grace of God, he was yet alive, and Pagan had descended to rescue him. But the English were coming at a furious clip, and by the time Pagan tied a rope about Lord Gellir's waist, Helena and Deirdre had to work with breakneck speed to haul him out of the enemy's clutches.

But for Pagan, 'twas too late. The enemy descended upon him at once. While Helena and Deirdre watched helplessly from above, unable to save him, the English took him captive.

Helena had never seen such tragedy in Deirdre's eyes as they dragged him away, never heard such despair in her voice as she screamed for Pagan.

'Twas then Helena realized the truth. Her sister had fallen in love. She loved her Norman husband.

Helena clutched her sister's trembling hand as Pagan and his captors disappeared from view.

"I promise you, Deir, we'll get him back. Somehow. Some way. And we'll not let Rivenloch fall." They were rash words, she knew, but in that moment, she would have said anything to erase the hopelessness from Deirdre's eyes.

Deirdre gave her a stiff nod.

"Now," Helena continued, giving her hand a squeeze, "can you take Father below?"

She nodded again. Then her gaze caught on Colin. "Is he . . . ?"

"Alive." Helena's voice cracked on the word. "Barely."

With a quick glance of empathy, Deirdre turned then to take Lord Gellir's arm, guiding him toward the stairs.

Helena wasted no time. Colin might be alive, but he wasn't awake. His heart might be beating, but that didn't mean his body was whole. He might yet breathe, but the crack to his skull might have left him with only half his wits.

A tear wandered down her cheek at the thought.

She angrily swiped it away. 'Twas not like her to weep over such things. She was a warrior, not a worrier. This was only one more battle she must fight. And if there was one thing Helena knew how to do, 'twas wage war.

With a furious oath, she crossed to where he lay and scowled down at his pale and silent form. "Listen, you great overgrown son of a whelp!" she shouted. "You're going to live. Do you hear me?"

Blowing out a hard breath, she hunkered down and reached under his arms, hefting him up as best she could.

"I did not stitch you up . . . and nurse you . . . halfway across Scotland," she said between clenched teeth, dragging him with great effort across the slippery planks, "just so you could . . . die . . . from a stupid bump on the head."

＊

# *Chapter 18*

HELENA HAD NEVER felt more thwarted in her life. She bit her thumbnail, keeping vigil over Colin beside the hearth of the great hall. The cursed Norman was still unresponsive, despite the goading insults she'd showered upon him. Now she watched in silence for the flutter of an eyelid, the movement of a finger. But mostly she listened with disbelief to the mutiny transpiring among the ranks of Normans.

For years she'd drilled the knights of Rivenloch in castle defense. For a decade she'd trained the castle folk in siege preparation. And for all that time, Rivenloch had been blessed with naught but peace and security.

Now, when the keep was in the midst of a real attack, when those skills were most needed, a pack of Norman strangers had usurped command of the castle. Even Deirdre, distraught over her abducted husband but making a noble effort to wield her influence over the knights, could not muster the cooperation of the Normans.

They were a stubborn, cowardly lot who refused to confront the English. How could they call themselves men when they wouldn't lift a finger to save their own commander, who was even now being tortured?

She'd heard about enough of their craven mewling. If the Normans were too fainthearted to wage war, then she'd rally the men of Rivenloch. She stormed to her feet to muster her clansmen.

Unfortunately, she underestimated the willfulness of the Knights of Cameliard, in particular Sir Rauve d'Honore, the bear of a man left in charge. Even as she tried to mobilize a fighting force, he threatened death to anyone broaching the walls of Rivenloch. When she challenged his authority, he claimed to follow the orders of Pagan himself. It seemed Cameliard had insisted there be no negotiation for hostages. 'Twas Rauve's sworn duty to hold the castle, even if it meant sacrificing his own lord.

Helena's blood simmered with frustration. Forsooth, she could see that Rauve was as reluctant to follow his orders as she was. 'Twas obvious as she glanced about the great hall that, like her, the Normans itched for battle. But to a man, they were loyal to Pagan. They'd not gainsay their commander.

In any other instance, Helena would have admired such loyalty. But when she saw her sister's stricken face, knowing what the English would do to Pagan, she couldn't help but curse the Normans. Mayhap the rest of them were content to stand idly by, but she wasn't about to let Deirdre suffer such anguish. She'd made a promise to her sister, and she intended to keep it.

Before this night was over, she vowed, she'd come up with a way to rescue Pagan, hold on to Rivenloch, and destroy that great wooden beast that had attacked the castle, the machine the Normans called a *trebuchet*.

But unbeknownst to Helena, there was already such a plot afoot. And when she learned of it, sometime around midnight, she was shocked beyond words—first, that it involved a secret passageway beneath the keep of which she was completely unaware, and second, that the plan was orchestrated by none other than her little sister—sweet, innocent, passive Miriel.

'Twas a brilliant scheme. Even now, Deirdre and the Rivenloch knights were stealing out through Miriel's tunnel to waylay the English as they slept. The only flaw, as far as Helena could see, was that she herself wouldn't be able to join in the fighting beyond the walls. Within the hour, if the plan failed, she'd be required to oversee the castle defenses.

Naturally, the sisters didn't reveal their plans to the Normans. Sir Rauve would doubtless argue 'twas too great a risk. And perchance 'twas. But 'twas a risk Helena and Miriel were willing to take for Deirdre's sake.

On the hearth, a pinecone burst in a shower of sparks, illuminating Colin's face as she knelt close to him. By the Saints, even now, with the pale cast of death hovering upon his brow, he looked as handsome as a dark angel.

She pressed her fingers to his throat for the hundredth time. His pulse was faint, but she took heart in the fact it still beat. And when she touched his parted lips, his breath still stirred between them. There was hope.

She combed her fingers back through his damp hair. Then, checking to see that none of the knights slumbering nearby spied upon her, she pressed a gentle kiss to his forehead.

When she'd fallen in love with the Norman, she didn't know. Mayhap 'twas when they'd fished together on the stream bank. Or when he'd first kissed her. Or when he'd claimed her virginity. Or perchance 'twas all those delicious suppers he'd prepared. Whatever the cause, she knew now that she was inextricably bound to him, heart and soul.

If she lost him . . .

She closed her eyes. She couldn't bear to think about it. She might not wish to wed him, but she couldn't abide the thought of his absence. Never again hearing his carefree laughter. Never again melting beneath his lusty gaze. Never again feeling the comfort of his arms or the brush of his lips . . .

"Hel-fire."

She thought she'd imagined the whisper. But when she opened her eyes, Colin was peering up at her, his eyes narrow slits of reflection behind heavy lids.

"Colin?" she breathed.

By some miracle, he managed to lift one corner of his mouth in a smile, though she was certain 'twas the only muscle that possessed an ounce of strength.

Her heart leaped, and joy infused her blood. It took all her will not to throw her arms around him and shower his face with kisses. But she dared not. Already a tear threatened at the corner of her eye. She wiped it away with her thumb. "'Tis about time, you lazy Norman."

He blinked, disoriented by his surroundings. "Where's your father?"

"Safe." Lord, she wanted to hold him against her breast. "You saved him."

He nodded in satisfaction, then winced in pain. "My skull?"

"Suffered a nasty bump." She sniffed. "'Tis lucky you're a thickheaded Norman, or it might have been much worse."

He smiled, then closed his weary eyes. "And Pagan?"

She hesitated. "You must be thirsty. Would you like a drink?"

He licked parched lips. "Aye."

She filched a wineskin from a slumbering Norman, uncorked it, then eased an arm under his shoulders to lift him high enough to drink. She tipped the wineskin back to allow him small sips, then at his nod, withdrew it. But before she could cork it again, he seized her wrist.

"Where is Pagan?" he repeated.

Getting the full story out of Helena was no easy task. First of all, they had to speak in whispers, for 'twas night, and the men of Cameliard slept all around them. Second, Helena seemed reluctant to disclose what seemed to him rather relevant details. And third, with his brain still fuzzy from the blow to his head, he wasn't entirely sure he was understanding her correctly.

"She did what?"

It sounded as if Deirdre had sneaked out of the castle through some secret tunnel to single-handedly rescue Pagan from the English. But that couldn't be right. That would have been a fool's errand.

"Don't worry," Helena told him. "Miriel and I sent the men of Rivenloch after her."

He rattled his head. Surely he'd heard wrong. No one, not even the Scots, could be that reckless. "Did you *see* how many English there were?"

"We'll catch them with their trews down," she said proudly.

"Trews down or not, they outnumber us two to one."

"Three to one."

He eased his head back down onto the straw and stared up at the ceiling. He saw now why the King had enlisted Pagan to take over Rivenloch's defenses. Between Helena's impulsiveness, Deirdre's bravado, and Miriel's mischief, the sisters would lose the castle in no time.

"And once Rauve agrees to let the Knights of Cameliard join the fray—" Helena continued.

"He won't," he told her bluntly. "Not if Pagan commanded otherwise. Rauve takes his orders seriously."

"I wouldn't be too sure about that. My little sister has a convincing way about her."

"Pah!" Just because Helena had managed to seduce a campful of mercenaries didn't mean that all men were so easily swayed.

But as if lending instant credibility to Helena's claim, a rumbling erupted at the far end of the great hall. Sir Rauve began barking out orders, waking the men, readying them for battle.

Rauve claimed the command came from Lord Gellir, but Colin knew better. Lord Gellir was nowhere in sight. Besides, the old Viking could barely keep command over his own wits, let alone an army.

As Helena smiled in smug assurance, Colin lifted himself to his elbows. 'Twas a suicide mission. They were going to die, all of them. 'Twas foolhardy. And irresponsible. And ill conceived. But if the rest of the Knights of Cameliard were going to leave their bloody carcasses on the field, he supposed he might as well die with them. Blade in hand. A battle cry on his lips. In glorious warfare.

"I'll need my sword if I'm to join them," he grumbled.

"But . . ." Fear flickered briefly in Helena's eyes. "But you can't. You're injured. You're—"

He shook his head. "I won't desert my fellows."

"I need . . . I need a second-in-command."

He frowned up at her. A *second*-in-command?

"Someone must remain behind to defend the castle," she explained.

He wanted naught more than to say her nay, to lock her up somewhere, mayhap in the storeroom under the keep, somewhere far away and safe.

But he knew her well enough by now to realize that no amount of debate would change her mind. Confiscating her sword was out of the question as well. The crafty wench had already reclaimed Mochrie's blade from him, and taking it from her would be as difficult and cruel as stealing bread from a starving man. Helena of Rivenloch was a warrior maid. Battle raged in her veins. And her passion would not cool until she'd tasted the blood of her enemy. The least he could do was try to protect her as best he could.

He counted himself lucky that at least she didn't wish to join the men-at-arms outside the walls. She'd have the protection of the keep a while longer. Until the English fired their trebuchet. And the castle fell.

He sighed. "I'll be your second on one condition."

"Aye?"

"You keep vigil over the east wall."

She scowled. "The battle is at the *west* wall."

"Precisely."

"You cannot relegate me to—"

He sat up. "Then I'll join my men on the field."

"Wait! Wait." She skewered him with an ungrateful glare.

Lord, he thought, even when she was angry, she was beautiful. 'Twas tempting to spirit her away to her bed-chamber, the battle be damned.

"Fine," she reluctantly agreed. "I'll take the east wall."

By the time Colin mounted the steps to the walk of the western wall, the battle was well under way. To their advantage, the rain had stopped. Under the oil-black sky, by the blaze of a dozen English pavilions set afire, he saw the men of Rivenloch fighting beside the Knights of Cameliard. The clang of swords and shields, the screams of the wounded, the bellows of men bolstering their own courage rang out across the field, resonating against the stones of Rivenloch.

At this distance, 'twas impossible to tell who was winning, and Colin wondered if staying behind had been a wise choice on his part. Then he remembered Helena, who, thanks to that choice, safely patrolled the deserted eastern face of the castle. And he realized that having her out of danger was worth any cost.

He turned away from the battle for a moment, peering across the dark courtyard to the eastern wall, hoping to catch a glimpse of her. But though he could count the heads of the distant archers stationed between the mer-lons, he saw no sign of Helena. Perchance, he thought, she'd gone below to check on the women and children.

"On the hill!" one of the archers on the west wall called.

Colin wheeled back to a fresh horror. Cresting the

northern hills was a new line of rushlights, a line inexorably approaching the battlefield. "Bloody hell!"

He banged a fist upon the battlement. How many miscreant English armies had banded together to lay siege to Rivenloch? *All* of them?

He kept watch on the advancing line as they gathered at the top of the mound. They bore a dozen fiery brands, but the men numbered at least three times that. Studying the torchlit figures, Colin noted that the small soldier at the fore bore an uncanny resemblance to Miriel's shriveled old handmaiden, Sung Li. He blinked several times. The blow to his head must have rattled his brains. When he looked again, she was gone, dissolved into the shadows.

All at once, an unholy bellowing split the night as the men atop the hill raised their voices in a fierce battle cry. Colin clenched his jaw, watching this new threat charge down the slope.

"Wait!" one of the archers cried, lowering his bow. "'Tisn't the English! 'Tis Lachanburn!"

"Aye! Lachanburn!" another crowed.

The archers of Rivenloch began to cheer.

Colin narrowed his eyes. Could it be true? Were these Helena's neighbors, the ones who swapped cattle with Rivenloch?

Indeed, they appeared to join forces with the Scots and Normans as they collided with the English in a clamor of ferocious howls and crashing blades.

Perchance, he began to think, there was hope after all. Perchance victory was in their grasp.

Colin's muscles tensed, twitching with the instinctive urge to fight, as he watched the spectacular battle.

Below him, sparks shot out from clashing steel. Torches

lit the grimacing faces of bloodthirsty warriors. Dead men, their tabards ablaze, lay scattered like flaming brands upon the sod. And orange smoke billowed into the heavens from the burning pavilions. 'Twas a vision from hell.

Then, as if the Devil himself materialized on the field of battle, roaring with rage and lashing out with fury, there was an enormous explosion from the top of the hill where the trebuchet stood. A flash as blinding bright as lightning illuminated the sky, and a tremendous thunderbolt cracked the air. Sparks and splinters rained down over the battleground, pelting the warriors and scorching the earth.

Through the veil of smoke that enveloped the trebuchet, Colin could make out the ruins of the English war machine. What remained of its wooden beams looked like the broken mast of a storm-tossed ship. What had caused it to explode, Colin didn't know. But the archers along the wall walk wasted no time in speculation. A great cheer arose, surging like a wave all along the battlements, and soon Colin was caught up in the jubilation.

The English, dispirited and defeated, began to retreat then, hobbling off on a southerly course that Colin suspected might take them all the way back to England. As the conquering knights of Rivenloch and Cameliard and Lachanburn celebrated on the field of battle, Colin's heart swelled with triumph and pride. His only regret was that Helena wasn't there to share the sweet victory with him.

The battle was over. The English were fleeing. And tales of their horrific defeat at the hands of wild Scots savages and Norman champions would dog them for years, keeping Rivenloch and its surrounds safe from invasion for a long while to come.

Meanwhile, the gates of Rivenloch parted to welcome home the heroes. They rushed into the great hall like a flood, their bodies battered, their armor stained, but their bloody faces wreathed in smiles.

All around Helena, people laughed and cheered and sang and drank. Normans gave Lachanburns congratulatory slaps on the back. Rivenloch maids fluttered their eyes at the Knights of Cameliard. Young lads listened eagerly to old warriors' accounts of the battle. Servants passed out cheese and ale and sewed up soldiers' wounds. Pagan, battered almost beyond recognition, nonetheless managed a reassuring grin as he spoke with wide-eyed squires. Miriel weaved her way through the crowd, making certain everyone was content, while Deirdre sat with the Norman jongleur, Boniface, letting him treat her injuries. Even Lord Gellir, his mind clear at the moment, joined in the raucous celebration, congratulating the victors and conversing with the Lord of Lachanburn.

But despite the gaiety around her, despite the dearth of fatalities for Rivenloch, despite the fact that they had successfully routed the enemy, Helena was not in a mood to celebrate. For several reasons. Not the least of which was the fact that that scheming maidservant, Lucy Campbell, had sidled up to Colin du Lac and was whispering something in his ear. As she watched, his gaze dipped down to Lucy's overfat breasts, and a smile curved his lips.

Irrational fury flooded her veins. Spitting an oath, she clenched her jaw and her fists and stalked over to the spot near the pantry where Lucy was working her wiles.

Without a word, Helena snagged Colin by the arm and wrenched him forcefully away.

To her surprise, Colin seemed unperturbed by the interruption. He even greeted her with a fond, "Hel-fire."

Over his shoulder, Lucy, however, looked about as content as a wet cat.

He smiled. "I've been searching all over for you."

"Indeed?" she muttered. "Well, I wasn't nestled betwixt Lucy's breasts."

"What?" he asked, chuckling.

Shaking her head, she hauled him off toward a quiet corner of the hall. "You've a cut," she explained, though 'twas but a scratch upon his cheek, which he discovered at once with his thumb.

He shrugged, but sat down upon a bench, allowing her to attend to his injury.

"You should have seen it, Hel-cat," he said, his face lighting up.

"Aye," she groused, "I should have." She swabbed at his cut. "But I didn't, did I?"

He grabbed her wrist. "Are you angry?"

"Nay," she bit out between her teeth. "'Tis fine that I was posted on the wall *opposite* the battle." She yanked her hand free and began dabbing at his cheek again. "'Tis fine that while my countrymen were engaged below in glorious combat, I was resigned to strolling back and forth along the battlements as if—"

"Hey!" He winced from her ministrations, which had intensified with her ire. "You weren't just strolling back and forth. You were keeping watch. If the lines hadn't held, if our forces had fallen—"

"If, if, if." She huffed out an angry breath. "I've trained

most of my life for war, and for what? Bloody hell, I didn't even get to *see* the battle."

"Oh, Hel-cat"—he sighed, taking her chin in his hand—"I'm so grateful you were safe behind castle walls. I couldn't bear it if . . ." He choked on the words.

Though part of her was flattered and pleased by his confession, her blood yet simmered with wrath. She supposed 'twas her own fault. She'd only promised to stay within the castle to ensure that Colin would not leave. Wounded as he was, if he'd tried to join the battle, she feared he would have been the first to fall. And that would have devastated her.

She jerked her chin from his grasp. There were other things that troubled her. "I hear your captain is now lord of the castle."

"Aye. Your father wished it."

She glanced over at her father, sitting by the hearth, drinking ale with the Lord of Lachanburn. His fall earlier must have brought some of his wits back. But she had mixed feelings about his decision.

"Deirdre should inherit the command," she muttered.

"'Twould seem she has." He grinned. "I've never seen Pagan so smitten with a woman. No doubt he comes at her beck and call."

Helena scowled in Deirdre's direction. She was brushing away Boniface's ministrations now, and a determined fire lit her eyes as she came to her feet. Helena followed her gaze toward the buttery. To her amazement, Lucy now had her lascivious hands all over Pagan. Worse, he didn't seem to mind.

"Smitten," she sneered. "Indeed?" She nodded her head toward Lucy.

Colin's eyes began sparkling. He held up a finger, bidding her to wait, as he watched Deirdre make her way over to the couple. To Helena's chagrin, within a moment, Deirdre had successfully spirited Pagan away. "Indeed." He leaned close to murmur, "You see how happily wed they are? Do you still believe you can steal him from her?"

Helena would have said anything to get that cocksure look off his face. After all, the knave was comparing her skills to those of a common kitchen maid. She tossed her head. "I can, and I will."

৵

# Chapter 19

HELENA CLENCHED HER jaw and adjusted the shield over her forearm. Everywhere she'd looked this morn on the way to the tiltyard, Rivenloch was changed. In the space of but a fortnight, the Normans had left their mark. Half the outbuildings were newly timbered. The well's crumbling rock had been repaired. Freshly cut stone lay like giant broken teeth on the sward, ready to be stacked and mortared into some new wall or tower. Doves actually inhabited the dovecote, unfamiliar servants roamed the great hall, and strange hounds slept among the dogs of Rivenloch.

All these changes Helena had abided in silence. She supposed it could be argued that they were for the betterment of the castle. But when it came to command of the knights, the training and ordering and organizing that had always been *her* arena, she could not be silent. In her absence, the defense of the keep had swiftly shifted from Scot to Norman. Which infuriated her.

Of course, that fury was fueled by the fact that the one Norman she'd come to care for had grown as cool to her as the Norse wind.

'Twas her own fault, she knew. If she hadn't insisted that she still planned to win Pagan, she might have spent the past week in much more pleasurable activities than sulking by the tiltyard and snapping at servants. But nay, she'd sentenced herself to a hell of unrequited desire.

It seemed that everywhere were sly reminders of what she was missing. Scented oils found their way into her chamber. A new linen underdress mysteriously appeared upon her pallet, a pointed replacement for the one she'd torn into bandages. Even supper featured dishes suspiciously reminiscent of Colin's cooking. Everything seemed evocative of Colin. And to her utter frustration, she remembered in all-too-vivid detail the warmth of his skin, the caress of his gaze, the taste of his mouth.

God's eyes! What had happened to her? She had to banish him from her thoughts. If she couldn't control her own responses to one man, how was she going to regain command of Rivenloch's army?

Angry with herself, with Colin, with Pagan, with all the Normans and everything around her, she let wrath empower her movements as she began sparring with Deirdre. Gritting her teeth, she whirled and slashed forward with her blade, backing her sister across the empty practice field with increasingly violent blows.

Deirdre, finally trapped against the fence, ducked quickly beneath her finishing swing, and Helena's blade collided with the wattle crosspiece instead, hewing it in half.

"Here!" came Pagan's bark from across the field. "Do not destroy my tiltyard fence!"

Helena clenched her jaw again. *His* tiltyard fence? Her blood seethed. She was tempted to hack the fence to bits just for spite.

But Deirdre answered him in playful indignation. "Destroy the fence? What about me?"

He chuckled fondly. "Oh. Aye. Take care with my wife as well."

Helena bristled. *My* fence. *My* wife. Did Pagan think he owned all of bloody Rivenloch?

She slashed her blade downward. "Are we going to fight or flap our jaws?"

Deirdre gave her a nod and raised her sword and shield. Helena immediately charged forward. With each blow, she silently cursed Pagan for wreaking havoc with her life.

Slash! That was for stealing her command. Jab! That was for seizing the castle from Lord Gellir. Hack! Hack! Hack! And that was for turning her sister into a lovesick calf.

But as usual, her passion was her undoing. As she thrust viciously forward, Deirdre sidestepped her blade, giving her a hard push that sent her crashing into the fence.

Deirdre laughed, then held out a hand to her. "Temper, Helena."

Helena was too disgusted and enraged this morn for scolding or charity. She slapped her sister's hand away, then bolted to her feet. "Again," she snarled.

Deirdre lifted a brow, then engaged her once more, and Helena tried to control her anger, maintaining a defensive stance.

"Here's one Pagan showed me," Deirdre announced, slashing diagonally downward from the right, then abruptly reversing to a forward thrust from the left. 'Twas a clever move. There wasn't much strength in it, but the element of surprise compensated for that. If Deirdre hadn't halted her blade, Helena would have been stabbed through the ribs.

Normally she would have crowed with appreciation. Helena loved learning new tricks. But knowing this one had come from *him,* from Pagan, Deirdre's new lord and master, soured her enthusiasm.

"Want to learn it?" Deirdre asked.

Helena shook her head and went on the offensive again, her blood boiling. She slashed through the air, imagining she carved Pagan to ribbons. Deirdre retreated as the blade drew closer and closer. Finally, Helena whirled and came across with her blade, missing Deirdre's throat by inches. Deirdre recoiled, then returned with a chiding shove of her shield.

"'Tis only practice, Hel!" she scolded. "Leave me my head a while longer."

Helena frowned. She didn't mean to take her anger out on Deirdre. 'Twas Pagan she loathed. But her sister seemed blind to the fact that she was leashed now, kept like a hunting dog at Pagan's feet. The night of the great battle, Helena had believed he bore respect for Deirdre. He'd heeded her counsel and given her rule over part of the army. Now he wouldn't even let her spar with her own men. And she seemed not to mind. What had happened to her strong, resolute, commanding sister?

Once more Helena raised her sword, determined to maintain control of her emotions this time. She waited for Deirdre to make the first thrust.

"Here's another clever trick from Pagan," Deirdre informed her.

If Helena lost her temper after that, she could hardly be blamed. Pagan. Pagan. Pagan. Deirdre might as well sprinkle salt in her wound.

While Helena fumed, her fists tight around her hilt and the brace of her shield, Deirdre began a rapid attack that kept Helena's defenses off-balance. When Deirdre had backed her against the fence, she abruptly stepped in, pushed Helena's blade aside with her shield, and popped up under her wrist with the hilt of her own blade. The quick snap forced the blade from her grip, and it shuddered to the ground.

Even when Helena came around with her only remaining weapon, her shield, Deirdre was ready for it. She elbowed it back, coming up with the point of her sword aimed at Helena's throat.

"Aha!" Deirdre cried in triumph.

Helena seethed with rage. Damn that Norman! 'Twas not cleverness. 'Twas deviousness. 'Twas just such insidious moves that had felled Rivenloch. She was infuriated.

"Go ahead!" she shouted. "Finish it!"

Deirdre's grin faded, then turned to a scowl. She blinked. "What?"

"Finish it," she grated out. "Put me out of my misery."

"Helena. What the Devil . . ."

"Just kill me now so I don't have to endure any more of this."

"What the bloody hell are you talking about?"

"This!" Helena said, tossing her hands up in anger. "This slow, steady invasion of Rivenloch. Lucifer's ballocks!

The keep looks more and more Norman every day. 'Tis a damned travesty."

Deirdre's gaze turned wintry. "Go on."

"And that brute you call husband. He orders you about like a serving maid, Deirdre. 'Tis repulsive."

Deirdre's eyes glittered dangerously.

Helena glanced down at the steel hovering near her throat. "Either kill me or withdraw your blade. I'm not your enemy."

"I'm not so sure."

Helena gasped. Never had her sister said such a thing. "Oh, Deirdre," she said bleakly, "what has that devil done to you?"

Deirdre's gaze turned as hard as diamonds. She flung her sword away and seized Helena by the front of her tabard, hauling her to within inches of those biting cold eyes. "He is no devil, and I will not have you call him that, do you hear me?"

Helena returned her stare with one of fire, but 'twas not enough to melt Deirdre's icy glare.

"Do you hear me?" Deirdre repeated, giving her a hard shake. Before Helena could answer, she continued. "And 'tis not what he's done to me. 'Tis what he's done *for* me. And for *you,* you ungrateful wretch."

Shock took the words from Helena's mouth.

"You were there at the battle. Did you not see his bruises? His wounds? His broken bones?" Deirdre demanded. "He suffered those for Rivenloch. He would have . . ." She choked off the words, overcome with emotion. "He would have died for you, Helena."

Helena stood, dumbfounded, while Deirdre's eyes filled with defiant tears.

"And all you can think about," she continued, "are your own selfish desires. Aye, things have changed. Aye, I pay heed to what Pagan says. Not because I am his serving maid, but because he is wise."

"He has caused a rift between us," Helena murmured.

"If there is a rift between us, 'tis you who have caused it, not Pagan."

Helena gulped. Deirdre's words stung. And curse her raw nerves, tears began to prick at the back of her eyes.

Deirdre sighed, releasing her with a muttered curse. Then she began smoothing Helena's crumpled tabard. "Listen, Hel," she said more gently, "I ask only that you try to get along with him. For my sake."

Rebellion reared its head within Helena. Why should *she* be the one who had to do the getting along?

Deirdre arched a brow then, and for one moment, Helena glimpsed the unyielding warrior she'd once been. "Indeed," Deirdre said, "I command it."

Helena frowned, but finally, reluctantly, nodded. 'Twas not the outcome she wanted. But she supposed she'd been reassured on one count. Deirdre was still as tough and strong-willed an opponent as ever. There was yet some fight left in her.

For a sennight, Helena kept her promise. While she didn't go out of her way to befriend Pagan, she no longer complained about him. She even managed to return his smiles with polite nods. And she ceased trying to countermand his orders at every opportunity.

For a sennight, she was respectful and courteous.

For a sennight, she stayed out of his way.

Then on the eighth morn came the bad news.

"Bloody hell!"

Helena stomped down the tower steps, banging the back of her fist against the stone wall. She supposed anyone else would have been happy at the announcement. Forsooth, Miriel seemed alight with joy, Sung Li's face was wreathed in a sage smile, and Deirdre . . . Deirdre positively glowed.

But for Helena, the fact that her sister was going to give birth in the spring meant naught but trouble.

Already Deirdre had bent like a twig beneath Pagan's influence, listening to his ideas, heeding his advice, compromising and changing and surrendering to his will.

Now this . . .

Surely carrying his child would break Deirdre, destroying what was left of her leadership and reducing her to a cooing new mother who'd rather suckle a babe than wield a sword.

She pounded the wall again, this time scraping her knuckle. Tears filled her eyes, tears not of pain, but of loss, for the selfish truth was that now Helena had no sparring partner. Deirdre, the fierce warrior sister she'd looked up to, was gone forever.

Sucking on her bloody knuckle, Helena made a sober vow. She'd never let a man change her the way Pagan had changed Deirdre. Never.

The practice yard was noisier than a spring fair by afternoon, pungent with dust, straw, and the sweat of man and beast. Horses snorted in derision at their masters' commands. Gruff men barked, scolding the squires they sought to mold into warriors. Young boys practiced their vilest oaths as they battled straw targets and leather dummies.

As she stalked onto the yard toward Pagan, Helena thought of several oaths she'd like to practice.

'Twas only that she was upset about Deirdre's condition. That was all, she told herself. Her foul mood had naught to do with the fact that as she passed the buttery, she'd spotted Lucy with her hand down the front of Colin's trews.

She came up beside Pagan, who stood against the fence with his arms crossed, watching the sparring intently.

"Fight with me," she said tightly.

He didn't seem to hear her. His gaze was fixed on the fighting in the yard.

She spoke louder. "Fight with me."

"What?" he said absently, still staring toward the field, his attention riveted by the fighting. "Rauve! Get Kenneth to hold his shield higher!"

She followed his gaze. "I said, fight with me."

"Not like that!" he called out. "Use your shoulder!"

Undaunted, Helena reached across his belly and started to draw his sword. Only then did he clap a hand onto the hilt, giving her his attention. "What?"

"Fight. With. Me."

He perused her once, head to toe, as if she were a bothersome child. "Helena."

Even in that one word, she heard condescension. But she'd had enough of it. Since Pagan had arrived, he'd taken over the practices, forbidding Deirdre and Helena to fight with anyone else. Deirdre had allowed it, and Helena had kept her promise to try to cooperate. But now that Deirdre was with child and refused to spar at all, Helena could no longer remain silent.

She'd tried everything this morn. Insulting the Cameliard

knights. Bribing the men of Rivenloch. Even picking
fights with the Normans. But no amount of taunting or
daring or wheedling or belittling could get them to spar
with her.

"Are you afraid to fight with a woman?" she sneered.
"Is that why you got my sister with child? So you wouldn't
have to risk losing to a wench?"

Pagan looked stunned, and Helena wondered if she'd
said too much. But then an image of Colin and Lucy assailed her again, and fresh anger flooded her veins.

"What bloody cowards you Normans are!"

He frowned, but 'twas not a frown of anger. 'Twas an
expression of unease. Her words made him uncomfortable,
no more. "Helena. Sister. There's no need to—"

"Don't call me sister!" she spat.

The combatants on the field slowly ceased their battles,
drawn by curiosity to this new spectacle. Helena didn't
care. She'd take on all of them.

"I am a Warrior Maid of Rivenloch," she announced,
skewering him with a glare, "and I challenge you to battle!"

She drew her sword. To her dismay, Pagan did not un-
sheathe in turn, but only lifted his palms in a gesture of
peace. "I . . ." He cleared his throat, obviously ill at ease
with her challenge. "Listen, my lady," he said softly. "I
know you miss the practice field, sword fighting, sparring. But I cannot be your . . . sparring partner."

"No one else will fight me." To her mortification, her
voice cracked bitterly on the words. "Thanks to you and
your bloody new rules."

Still he seemed not to take offense. He stroked his chin,
carefully considering her words. Then he crossed his arms
decisively. "Colin," he said. "Colin will spar with you."

Her eyes suddenly welled with unwelcome tears, and 'twas all she could do to fight them back. "He's . . . he's wielding his blade elsewhere," she managed to choke out, lifting her chin defiantly.

Though she said naught more, Pagan deciphered her meaning. After a long and pensive pause, he nodded. "Very well," he said with a sigh. "I'll spar with you, but . . ."

She scowled. But what?

"You must not tell your sister. You know Deirdre will only be envious." He drew his sword. "I don't want her tempted to fight. 'Twould endanger our babe."

Helena looked into his eyes as if seeing him for the first time—there was an inherent kindness that made his actions almost forgivable.

As for his swordsmanship, he proved an excellent fighter. As Helena slashed and wheeled and dodged and thrust, as her blood grew hot from battle and her skin flushed with excitement, she began to enjoy their skirmish. Pagan held back naught, and yet she was able to catch him unawares once or twice with tricks that had him chuckling and saluting her inventiveness.

Indeed, she was having such a pleasurable time that she was almost able to forget about the philandering Norman she'd spied in the buttery. Almost.

Colin cursed that impudent wench, Lucy Campbell, all the way to the practice field. The conniving maidservant must have waited till she saw Helena to shove her hand down his braies. He should have realized the maid was up to no good when she beckoned him to come help her sugar her sweetmeats.

'Twas partly his own fault as well. He'd made a practice of visiting Lucy to direct her in cooking his favorite Norman dishes, foods he knew would remind Helena of him. 'Twas only natural that the woolly headed maid would come to see those visits as something more. And now she'd chosen the worst possible moment to take liberties.

Of course, he'd immediately extracted her hand, gently but firmly, but by then the damage had been done. He heard the door to the great hall swing open, and he glimpsed the angry swish of Helena's tawny braid before it slammed shut.

He'd suspected Helena would go to the lists. For days she'd paced the castle, as ill at ease as a caged lion. He knew just how she felt. Perchance she had no name for her restlessness, but he knew it well. 'Twas unrequited lust.

There were but two cures for such a malady. One, the preferred remedy, was *requited* lust. The other was fierce, blood-searing, bone-jarring combat. And given that she'd just found the man who'd offered her marriage in the embrace of another woman, he was reasonably sure she'd opt for the lists. Which vexed him sorely.

Curse the Fates, he'd hoped to have her in his bed soon.

He'd expected that by now she'd have given up on the idea of wedding Pagan, that she'd have come to terms with the fact that her sister was happily married. For the love of Mary, Deirdre had just this morn announced she was with child. Surely Helena didn't believe she could usurp her sister's place now.

The instant he saw her on the practice field, his heart plummeted. Helena's face was wreathed in a delighted grin as she cuffed Pagan on the shoulder. Pagan feigned great injury from her punch, staggering about, and Helena laughed at his antics. They looked as cheerful and familiar as old lovers. Then Helena engaged his blade, and they began to spar in earnest.

She leaped and rolled and dove and ducked, as entertaining as any acrobat. And Pagan seemed enthralled by her unique style, watching her in fascination even as he countered her every move.

*Almost* every move, Colin amended, as Pagan went down in a great puff of dirt.

In the clearing dust, Pagan laughed heartily as Helena planted a foot on his chest in triumph. Then she reached her arm down to help him up. For one awful moment, Colin wondered if Pagan would pull her down on top of him.

Colin would have. A damsel as beautiful and lusty and spirited as Helena would be impossible to resist.

'Twas painful to watch. He tried to tear his eyes away, but he couldn't.

He suspected 'twas more than just a friendly skirmish. Pagan himself had confided in Colin, telling him how battle heated his wife's blood, how it had proved a more effective tool of seduction than wine or kissing or honeyed words. And it seemed that Helena had stumbled upon the right combination of charm and innocence to effectively beguile Pagan as well.

In the end, Pagan resisted temptation. Still, when he came to his feet, he gave Helena's cheek a playful pat.

Colin's heart thumped woodenly in his chest. He turned his back and trod heavily away, unable to watch any longer. He'd known Helena had intended to seduce Pagan. And he'd known if she set her mind to it, she'd be able to. But he hadn't anticipated the pain of watching her succeed.

He clenched his jaw and walked purposefully toward the keep. He should be content. After all, Helena obviously didn't wish to wed him. Which meant he was no longer bound to do the honorable thing. He was at liberty to bed whomever he desired.

The sooner he began, he told himself, the sooner his heartache would disappear. He intended to swive as many maids as there were hours in the day, to bed so many wenches that Helena's cherished features would disappear in the sea of feminine faces.

He'd start with Lucy.

Helena beat the dust from her tabard as she took long strides across the courtyard toward the keep. Her senses were awakened, and her heart pounded as joyfully as a minstrel's timbrel. By the Saints, she hadn't felt so gloriously alive since . . .

Since she'd bedded Colin. The memory brought a fresh flush to her cheeks.

Forsooth, engaging in combat had done much to dispel her anger with Colin for his . . . indiscretion. Now that her blood was flowing and her mind was clear, she could look at things from a more rational point of view.

She hadn't so much as touched Colin for nearly a month now. Not that she hadn't longed to. Lord, sometimes she so yearned for his kiss that she licked her lips when he was nigh. And spying upon him on the practice field, where he oft wore only a thin linen shirt over his chest, she ached to put her hands all over those damp bulges of muscle.

But she swore she'd not end up like Deirdre, tamed by a man.

As for Colin, he'd refused to tryst with her while she yet claimed she might become Pagan's wife. But that didn't mean he wasn't inclined to bed other maids while he waited. And what right did Helena have to prevent him? She didn't own his body.

If Colin chose to swive that addlepated, fat-bosomed Lucy, he was welcome to her.

She frowned, stopping suddenly by the dovecote and slapping her gauntlets against her thigh.

Bloody hell, who was she fooling? She couldn't *abide* the idea of Colin sharing his magnificent body with another woman. Especially not a woman who could never appreciate his other fine qualities—his intellect, his wit, his kindness, his honor.

With a decisive sigh, she resumed her path across the courtyard, past the workshops and the chapel. By the time she reached the keep, she'd made up her mind. Just because she was determined not to marry Colin didn't mean she couldn't bed him. She only hoped she wasn't too late.

"Lucy!" she yelled as soon as she swung open the doors. The few servants tidying the great hall looked up, as did the hounds in the corner, but Lucy was nowhere in sight. "Lucy!" she snapped. "Come here at once!"

As Helena could have predicted, Lucy came stumbling from the buttery, her hair disheveled, her eyes dazzled, and her surcoat drooping off one shoulder.

"Aye, my lady?" she said breathlessly.

"Go clean out the dovecote."

Lucy's eyes narrowed to sullen slits, and she muttered

something under her breath, but she dared not show insolence to the lady of the castle. "Aye, my lady," she said
tightly, casting a surreptitious glance toward the buttery
before she picked up her skirts and marched to the keep
doors.

Helena watched the buttery entrance with her arms
crossed, waiting for Colin to emerge. But to her surprise,
the lad who staggered out a moment later was one of
Pagan's servants.

"Do you want me to clean the dovecote as well, my
lady?" he asked hopefully, tying up his trews.

"Hardly." She scowled as she glanced about the hall.
"Tell me, have you seen Colin du Lac?"

"Nay, my lady." He gave her a sheepish smile. "But
I've been . . . er . . . busy."

Helena gave him a dismissive frown and glanced about
the great hall. Where would he go?

She eyed the stairs leading down to the storage rooms.
After the sparring this morn, she was famished. Mayhap
she would pilfer a piece of cheese before she left to look
for him.

As she started down the steps, she heard a scrape from
the landing below. 'Twas probably Miriel. She spent a
good deal of time in her work chamber, going over the accounts. Still, Helena rested a wary hand on her hilt as she
crept down the stairs.

'Twas dark. The brands along the wall were unlit.
Miriel would have lit them.

A second scrape made her draw her sword. Who was
below? Surely no one up to any good would linger here in
the dark.

As stealthy as a cat, she descended the last three steps into shadow.

Suddenly she was seized about the waist. Her heart slammed up against her ribs. She raised her sword, but in the close quarters could do no more than bring the pommel down hard on her assailant's shoulder.

He groaned in pain, releasing her instantly. "Jesu!"

Helena frowned. "Colin?"

"Helena?" he wheezed.

"What the Devil—"

"God's eyes, wench. Why did you do that?"

"You're lucky I didn't run you through. What are you doing down here, all alone in the dark?"

There was a bitter edge to his voice. "Who said I was alone?"

"I . . ." She scowled. Perchance he *wasn't* alone. Perchance one of his mistresses was here with him in the shadows even now.

It didn't matter, she told herself. She had something to say, and she intended to say it. She was a Warrior Maid of Rivenloch, by God, and she wasn't about to flee from some tittering maidservant just because she'd intruded on her tryst.

Besides, she was fairly certain Colin was bluffing.

"Listen. I've come to tell you I've . . ." She put away her sword. "I've made up my mind. I'm not going to marry Pagan."

She heard him smirk. "Indeed?"

She was taken aback by his cool tone. "Aye, indeed. I thought you'd be pleased."

"Pleased?"

He'd drawn closer now. She still couldn't see him, but

the smell of cinnamon lingered on his skin—dark, masculine, and exotic.

"Aye," she said, breathing in the pleasant scent.

"And why should I be pleased?"

She felt the heat of his breath upon her neck. "You said you wouldn't bed another man's wife." She closed her eyes. God, she'd forgotten how alluring he was . . . his voice, his smell, his warmth. "But 'tis all right now. I don't intend to be Pagan's wife."

"Wife? Mistress? What's the difference?" he murmured, inhaling deeply against her hair. "The smell of Pagan is upon you."

A wave of lust washed over her, dizzying her, and she leaned toward him. "'Tis the scent of swordplay, no more." She turned her head, trying to kiss him, but he pulled back.

"Swordplay or love play?"

She ignored his question, telling him softly, "Ah, Colin, I've missed you. Do you not remember the taste of my lips?" She reached up to cup his jaw, murmuring, "Here. Let me remind you."

He stiffened at her touch. "I won't share you with another."

The way her skin tingled and her mouth hungered for his, she wasn't about to take nay for an answer. "By the Rood," she gasped, "did you not hear me? There *is* no other." She seized him by the back of the neck, claiming him with a deceptively gentle kiss.

For a good three heartbeats, Colin refused to fall prey to Helena's seductive manipulations. But once he tasted the honey of her tongue, smelled the curiously alluring tang of sweat and chain mail upon her, felt the sultry heat of her desire, he was a lost man.

He groaned, answering her kiss. His senses whirled about him like leaves at harvest, blown at her whim, as she pressed insistent lips to his.

Suddenly 'twas no matter that he'd sworn off her love, that he'd climbed down these steps to await Lucy. All his rational intentions fled as he was swept away in a cloud of lusty memory. Oh, aye, he remembered the taste of her lips. He remembered the taste of *all* of her.

"There's only you," she murmured.

God help him, he *did* believe her. Her words sounded sweet and pure, like a pledge of the heart.

Abstinence sharpened his craving, and her soft moans as her fingers clawed through his hair sent his desires wheeling out of control. He took her head between his hands and slanted his mouth across hers to deepen the kiss, delving his tongue within to sample her sweet nectar.

Her hands lowered then to grapple with his belt, and he growled his approval. Within a moment, the leather slid from his hips. Then, without prelude, she brushed her hand over his belly and lower, pressing her palm brazenly against him. He sucked in an astonished breath, and Helena, her desire fueled by the manifestation of his need for her, groaned in pleasure. Her kisses became urgent, then feverish, then frantic, until she carelessly chanced to bite his lip.

He recoiled, and she murmured an apology. But his appetite for her didn't diminish in the least.

Catching her by the shoulders, he pressed her up against the cool cellar wall. Holding her there with his forearm across her collarbone, he used his free hand to unbuckle her sword belt.

"Take me!" she insisted.

He chuckled. "Patience," he breathed, though he wondered how much longer *he* could wait. Her lust was driving him mad.

"But I want you now," she insisted.

He shivered with need. "Your armor . . ."

"Oh, ballocks!"

His lips curved into a weak grin. If he hadn't been so desperate himself, her impatience would have been amusing. But 'twould take considerable time to get her out of her chain mail. Longer to find a suitable place to couple. Unless . . .

"Take off your hose," he murmured.

Before he even finished the suggestion, she was rummaging beneath her coat of armor.

He stepped back to quickly untie his braies, letting them drop about his ankles. He'd never coupled with a woman in chain mail before, but he'd taken maids against a wall when time was short and the need pressing.

"Hold on to me," he told her when she'd rid herself of her undergarments.

She willingly wound her arms about his neck, and he braced her against the wall. Then he hooked one arm beneath her leg and hoisted it up about his bare waist. The chain mail slithered up her raised thigh. He lifted her other leg, and she gasped as she realized his intent, eagerly wrapping her limbs around him. The mail slid easily out of the way, enough to allow him access to that part of her that desired him most.

And then he eased forward, plunging into her welcoming softness. She cried out in surprised wonder, then tightened her heels upon his buttocks, sheathing him deeply, completely.

They danced with savage grace, accompanied by the jangle of chain mail, faster and faster, until Colin felt a steady heat infuse his veins, as if the friction sparked a slow-burning fire within him.

Helena clung to him like moss to a rock as her armor ground against the stone wall. Her gasps and moans filled the air, sweet music to his ears, as she dug her fingertips into the flesh of his shoulders. She buried her face against his neck, nuzzling his throat like a wolf with its kill. And once or twice he felt the nip of her teeth, as if she fought a primitive urge to feed upon him.

How much longer he could suppress his need, he didn't know. His legs trembled with the effort, and he blew out forceful breaths, trying to stem the tide of desire. At last, Helena emitted a sharp cry and stiffened as she found her release, and Colin followed her over the crest of the wave. He shuddered as they knocked against the cellar wall again and again. Finally, she wilted against him, and he, too, surrendered, drained of strength and seed.

As they floated in the aftermath of passion, he inclined his head and kissed her brow. "Now I remember," he murmured.

Then, as abruptly as lightning on a calm summer's eve, the shadows shifted on the wall. Someone was coming down the steps with a candle. Bloody hell!

"Psst! Sir Colin," came a whisper down the stairs.

Helena tensed against him.

"Shite!" he hissed. 'Twas Lucy. "I'm . . . occupied," he called up.

But Lucy, her jealousy roused by the prospect of competition, was already halfway down the steps. By the time he gently disengaged from Helena, lowering her to the ground, 'twas all he could do to haul up his braies before she arrived.

Lucy emerged in the passageway, a scornful scowl upon her face. She narrowed her eyes. "Occupied? Are you now?" She thrust the candle forward. "And who's the—" Her mouth formed a perfect circle of surprise as she spied her mistress. Then she began jabbering away like a nervous squirrel while the candle's flame fluttered in empathy. "Begging your pardon, my lady, my lord. I only came to tell you, Colin . . . *Sir* Colin, that I'll be unable to meet you for . . . for that . . . that . . . task you asked me about, 'cause . . . 'cause I'm busy now, cleaning out the dovecote . . . like my lady commanded."

She bobbed a few times, then fled up the stairs, taking the light with her.

Colin could already envision the blab wagging her tongue to every soul she passed, blathering about lusty Lady Helena and her tryst in the cellar.

"I'm sorry," Colin said, lacing up his braies. "I'll go after her, make certain she spreads no gossip."

But Helena's hands closed over his, stopping him at his task. "She won't. She knows I'll have her clean the dovecote every day for a year." Then, to his amazement, she peeled his hands away and loosened the ties he'd just tightened. "Now, are any other wenches arriving," she murmured, "or do we have the cellar all to ourselves?"

He grinned.

Her need was not so urgent now, and so he took his time with her, removing her chain mail, kissing her ten-

derly, stretching out upon the stone floor of the passageway so she could lie in comfort atop him. Blinded by the
darkness, he found his other senses heightened. His skin
roused to her touch, his ears stirred at her whispers and
cries, his nose quivered at the scent of her. And when they
rose together like bright angels escaping an inferno of desire, high into the heavens, he swore he could taste her
very soul.

## Chapter 20

Helena felt as if she danced on air. Indeed, every
time she and Colin made love, she was left with that
heady, vibrant, exhilarating sensation. 'Twas hard to believe it had been nigh three months since they'd first trysted
in the cottage in the wood. Since then they'd coupled
everywhere—in the dovecote, the stables, the pond, her
chamber, his chamber, the woods, and once even in a
garderobe. On this brisk September morn, the rising sun
greeted them at the top of the new west tower, where
they'd made love in soft pelts spread upon the fragrant
timbers of the restored floor.

While Colin lounged lazily among the furs, Helena
gave him a coy smile, then rose to dress. She never tired
of his attentions, even when they came at the most inop-
portune times and places. And Colin seemed willing to
oblige her every whim when it came to lovemaking.

If she spotted him emerging from the shadows with
Lucy Campbell on occasion, she tried to ignore the jeal-

ousy eating at her heart. She knew she had no right to be selfish, to claim him for her own, since she still had no plans to marry him. But in the deepest, most secret place in her soul, she prayed he found no joy in other women, and she dreamed he saved himself for her alone.

As for Helena, there was no other man for her. Colin had been her first. He would be her last. She couldn't imagine sharing herself with anyone else.

She slithered into her gown, feeling his lusty gaze upon her.

"Must you go?" he whispered.

"Greedy sot."

"Oh, aye." He drew his eyes slowly down the length of her, sending a shiver through her soul. Lord, 'twas tempting to stay with him another hour. But the morn marched on.

"Mayhap this afternoon," she suggested, "in the pond."

His eyes widened. "The pond? 'Tis covered in frost."

"Thin-skinned Norman," she teased.

"Cold-hearted Viking," he replied. "Where are those rose-scented silk pillows you keep promising me?"

She giggled. "Will you settle for a pile of straw in the stables?"

He grinned. "Aye. You know I will."

She wheeled to make her departure, giving him a wink at the door. "I'll see you later, then . . . stable lad."

As she glided happily down the stairs, she thought about everything she'd learned from the Norman. For Colin, making love was a journey, rife with adventure and exploration, with moments of intense focus and times of quiet reflection.

He could be as fierce as a wolf in one breath and as gentle as a lamb in the next. Sometimes he coupled with her as if they engaged in fast and furious battle. Other times he tormented her for hours with breathy kisses and featherlight touches. Once he let her bind his hands so she could ravish him at her leisure. And once he blindfolded her so his every caress was a sensual surprise.

He kept her as content as a cat with cream, and her greatest wish was that they continue forever like this.

But while Colin pleased her in bed, she found another kind of joy in her private battles with Lord Pagan, and that was where she was headed now.

Pagan had sworn Helena to secrecy concerning their meetings. Deirdre, because of her delicate and unwieldy condition, would have burst into tears if she'd known that Helena continued to spar while *she* was forced to suffer in confinement. So to protect Deirdre's feelings, they agreed to rendezvous each morn in a clearing in the wood. They told no one, not the men of Rivenloch, not the Knights of Cameliard, not even Colin. Helena carried her armor each day in a large basket that she claimed was full of provender for Brother Thomas.

There, in the thick cover of the pines, she would meet Pagan, who helped her to arm and worked to improve her fighting skills. He challenged her, strengthening her muscles, honing her technique, turning her into a better warrior than she'd ever been before. 'Twas a shame, she thought, that her sister was unable to fight, for Helena was sure she could beat her soundly now.

But what drove her more than the thought of defeating Deirdre was that of entering the tournament Pagan had planned for Rivenloch. Though she and Deirdre had oft sparred for exhibition's sake, Helena had never before fought with men in a real tournament. The idea of competing against knights from far and wide, of winning honors and prizes, of bringing glory to Rivenloch, sent a thrill of excitement rushing through her.

Of course, she'd have to enter as an unknown. Once men discovered she was a woman, most would either refuse to fight her or soften their blows. Pagan especially wouldn't approve. But 'twas not uncommon for knights to enter tournaments in unmarked armor. Sometimes they did it to conceal their illustrious reputations, sometimes to hide their outlaw status. Sometimes unseasoned warriors preferred to remain unknown until they could make a name for themselves. But whatever people supposed as they watched her battle in the tournament, Helena relished the moment when she would whip off her helm in triumph to the shocked gasps of the onlookers.

As she tucked the concealing linen carefully about her basket of armor and prepared to exit the front gates, she smiled, dreaming of October and the distinction she would bring then to the clan of Rivenloch.

Colin stood naked by the tower window, watching the sun gild the tender young oak leaves one by one. The sweet, feminine scent of Helena lingered in the room, but 'twas as elusive as the woman herself. Three months had passed, and still he had no word of commitment from her.

He might as well admit it. He was her paramour. Her courtesan. Her concubine. A prisoner of love.

'Twasn't by choice. He'd offered Helena marriage so many times he'd lost count. But the willful wench had denied him over and over.

What she wanted, he didn't know. He doubted if *she* knew. She seemed well contented with their frequent trysts, as was he. Yet he held out hope that one day she'd awaken to his heart, that she'd recognize the devotion in his eyes and agree to seal their love in the sacred union of marriage.

Even Colin, once a dedicated bachelor, could see that their bond was special. True, they quarreled a good deal of the time. But their words were never harsh. Helena and he were simply two opinionated people who were passionate about those opinions and had no qualms about voicing their differences.

Besides, their arguments were inevitably settled on a very different field of battle, one where shouts and stomping yielded to caresses and sighs, and they both emerged victorious.

'Twas clear to Colin that they were made for each other. Despite the lack of wedding vows between them, he remained faithful to her, and he suspected she was loyal to him. Why, then, was she so reluctant to trust him with her heart?

As he pensively scanned the dew-covered greensward, wondering how to earn her confidence, a subtle movement from the trees caught his eye.

'Twas Pagan, fully dressed and armed, entering the forest.

Colin frowned. Pagan seldom rose before the sun. Yet there he appeared, ready for the day. Perchance, he thought, he'd risen early at Lady Deirdre's bidding. Mayhap she'd made one of those strange demands common to expectant women, for a particular fruit or herb that could only be found in a certain clearing at a certain hour. And Pagan, dutiful husband that he was, had set about to fulfill her wishes.

Colin smiled ruefully. He wondered if he'd ever have the chance to grant such unreasonable requests for Helena.

Several moments later, as he finished dressing, pulling on his leather boots, he glimpsed a second figure entering the wood at the same spot.

Helena.

He blinked.

A half dozen ignoble thoughts crossed his mind—ugly, painful, impossible thoughts. But he dismissed them with a shake of his head. 'Twas coincidence, no more. Helena traveled to meet Brother Thomas every morn. And Pagan happened to have ventured into the wood at the same time.

Still, uncertainty gnawed at him as he turned away from the window. Was it a coincidence? He'd be a fool to overlook the possibility that Helena was . . .

Was what? he thought bitterly. Cuckolding him? Pah! She owed him naught. He didn't own her. Not her body, not her heart, and certainly not her loyalty. She'd made it clear she wanted no commitment.

Perchance this was the reason she'd made no distinct vows to him. Perchance she was in love with Pagan. 'Twas a wrenching thought, one that ripped at his heart.

The rest of the day was pure torment for him. He couldn't bring himself to keep his appointment with Helena in the stables. God's eyes, he could hardly look at her, couldn't speak to her, knowing she might have betrayed him. No matter how he tried to tell himself he'd been mistaken about what he'd seen and was making reckless assumptions, no matter how he tried to convince himself that what he and Helena shared was only frolic anyway, light adventure, meaningless fun, in his soul, he knew better.

Colin and Helena were as matched as Adam and Eve. And now he feared she'd let a deadly serpent into their Paradise.

For the next several days, he teetered on a blade's edge of uncertainty. He refused to question either Helena or Pagan, nor would he spy upon them, afraid of what he might learn. He kept himself in a state of ignorance that, if not blissful, was at least of some solace. He distracted himself with hard, long practices in the lists. And he guarded his heart against the painful possibility that his Eden was about to be destroyed.

But he couldn't abide in ignorance forever, and a sennight later, the vicious serpent reared its vile head again.

Lucy brought him the news, along with a flagon of ale, as he stood by the stable, taking a respite from training on the practice field.

"There's something I think you should know, Colin," she confided as he sipped at the drink.

He winced. Lucy somehow imagined that just because he'd once planned to tryst with her, she could address him by his first name. "*Sir* Colin."

She shrugged. "Your mistress . . ."

He glared sharply at her.

She smirked. "Everyone knows."

He scowled, downing a hearty swig of ale. He supposed she was right. Probably all of Rivenloch knew he was Helena's paramour. He wondered if they also knew he hadn't bedded her in a week. "What is it?"

"I fear," she said, pausing dramatically and glancing about for unwanted listeners, "your clever little hen services two cocks." She wiggled her eyebrows.

Colin swallowed hard. "I have no time for your gibberish," he muttered. "I have a tournament to train for." He gulped down the rest of the ale and pressed the empty flagon into her hands.

"Wait!" she said, grabbing his sleeve. "Don't you want to know who 'tis?"

"Nay," he said flatly, shaking off her hand.

But like a long-winded jongleur, she wouldn't be satisfied until she'd delivered her entire piece. "'Tis Lord Pagan himself," she whispered.

A chill sank into his bones as she confirmed what he already knew. But he shuttered his eyes against the hurt. 'Twould serve no good to let the castle blab know the depth of his anguish.

Despite her pitying pout, there was an eager glint in her eyes. She enjoyed spreading gossip and wreaking havoc. With this one piece of news, it seemed she was doing both.

"She goes to him most every day, your lady," Lucy confided. "They meet in the wood."

Colin felt his heart congeal into a cold, hard knot. Somehow he managed to keep his expression carefully neutral.

When she didn't get the reaction she expected, she shrugged. "I suppose he can't be blamed. After all, his own wife is fat with child." She cocked her head then and looked up at him with a speculative gaze. "But if you're ever in need of comfort, a little cuddle in the hay or a warm place to lay your head . . ." She lowered her eyes to her plump bosom. "You know where to find me."

Whatever she expected after that, he was fairly certain she didn't expect him to grab her by the throat and press her up against the wall of the stable. She yelped, her eyes bulged, and she began babbling like a startled chicken.

He didn't hurt her. He only frightened her. But he wanted to make certain she understood him plainly.

"Who else have you told?" he bit out.

She gulped. "No one," she squeaked.

"You're certain?"

She nodded rapidly.

"You will tell no one else. Not a word. If I find you've so much as whispered their names in the same breath, I'll wring your scrawny neck. Do you understand me?"

She nodded again. When he let her go, she stumbled, then picked up her skirts and fled like a hen chased by a fox.

When she'd gone, Colin slumped weakly against the wall. He felt as if his soul had been torn from him.

Betrayal burned in his veins like acid. The air deserted his lungs. His spirit felt crushed, as surely as glass beneath a saboton. He'd been right about Helena. But he'd been too smitten to believe it. She'd fooled him as easily as she'd tricked the English mercenaries so long ago. And like a sailor tempted by a Siren, he'd blindly followed her to his demise.

Part of him *did* feel dead. 'Twas easier than enduring the pain of betrayal. Eventually he began to breathe again, his rasps as harsh as frost upon the warm fall air. And with each rough breath, a new link of armor locked about his heart.

"Nay, nay, nay!" Pagan scolded. "You're dropping your wrist again. If you'd been fighting Faramond le Blanc, he would have lopped off your head."

Helena nodded. She didn't know what was wrong with her of late. Her limbs weren't cooperating properly, and she couldn't seem to focus on her swordplay. She wondered if it had anything to do with the fact that the tournament was less than a sennight away.

'Twas true, over the past few weeks she'd been caught up in the castle fervor as servants and craftsmen made preparations for the lavish event. Excitement was high, tempers were short, and Helena felt a fluttering in her belly every time she thought about the legendary battles to come. The knights ranged the keep in no less than full battle armor, sparring at all hours, and in the great hall, Boniface practiced the songs he'd perform at the feast afterward.

Colin seemed distracted by the upcoming tournament as well. He battled from dawn to dusk in the tiltyard. Consequently he hadn't slept with her in days.

'Twas not that she didn't understand. Most knights believed that a man's strength was diminished by too much lovemaking. But sometimes Colin seemed like a different man. The hardened warrior he'd become had no heart, no soul. This new Colin never laughed and seldom smiled. Forsooth, he seemed to be turned completely inward. If he passed her, he rarely spoke. And if he spoke, 'twas in curt tones, as if his mind was engaged elsewhere.

His grimness admittedly took some of the joy out of her anticipation of Rivenloch's grand tourney. She could only console herself by trusting that after the tournament, he'd transform back into the Colin she knew and loved. And she distracted herself from brooding by spending every waking moment in practice.

"Faramond likes to attack from above," Pagan continued with his advice. "You have to keep your wrist strong to block his blows."

Helena smiled to herself. Pagan never seemed to remember that she wasn't competing in the tournament. At least as far as anyone *knew*, she wasn't competing. But now that she was so much more skilled—faster, stronger, more agile—she wasn't about to miss this opportunity to test her talents against the best in the land.

If she could just keep her meals in her nervous stomach for more than an hour . . .

Helena's belly seized again, and she retched into her chamber pot.

Sung Li crossed smug arms across her chest, her wise face puckered with pensive wrinkles. "I know what ails you," she declared.

Why Miriel's pesky maidservant had followed Helena into her chamber, she didn't know. The old woman usually trailed behind Miriel like a devoted duckling. But for some reason, this morn she'd abandoned Miriel and seemed fascinated by Helena's ills.

"'Tis naught, only the excitement of the tourney," Helena muttered.

"Ah. And how long has it been so?"

Helena gave the impertinent maid a withering glare, then heaved up the last of her breakfast.

Sung Li clucked her tongue. "It is not the tournament." She handed Helena a wet cloth, then announced with her usual unmitigated candor, "You carry a child."

Helena almost choked. But she recovered, taking the cloth and dabbing her brow with shaky hands. "That's impossible." But even as she denied it, she realized 'twas not only possible. 'Twas probable. She and Colin had coupled enough times to spawn a whole brood of children.

"Impossible?" The old woman's thin white brows shot up. Then she narrowed her eyes to knowing slits. "You *do* know how children are made?"

Helena had little patience for Sung Li's insolence. "Out!" She pointed to the door.

Unintimidated by Helena's command, Sung Li slowly sauntered toward the door. "You should tell the father." The maid couldn't resist one last jab before she ducked out of the room. "If you know who he is."

Helena threw the wet rag at her, but it only slapped against the closing door.

Then she sank onto her pallet, biting at her thumbnail. What if Sung Li was right? What if she *was* with child? The old woman had an eerie gift of prophecy. She brushed her palm over her belly. Was Colin's babe growing within her?

A strange pair of emotions, joy and dread, battled in her brain.

Part of her was ecstatic at the thought of bearing Colin's child. Already she imagined a miniature version of Colin with dark, wavy hair and twinkling green eyes. Or mayhap a hot-tempered lass with tawny locks like hers. What a wonderful father Colin would make. He could take their child fishing and riding, sing silly songs and tell exciting adventures. He could share his laughter and his love, and together they could raise the child to be the finest warrior Rivenloch had ever known.

But another part of her resisted the subjugation of motherhood. She'd already decided she didn't want to be saddled with a husband. She most definitely didn't want the burden of a child. She'd already seen what it had done to Deirdre. Her poor sister waddled about the keep now with an inane grin on her face, as if she didn't mind in the least being kept like a coddled pet. But Helena was a creature of the wild, free, unfettered. She refused to be tamed and fattened like a breeding sow.

She slid her hands over her belly again. If she *did* carry Colin's child, it didn't show yet. For at least another month or two, no one would notice. Nobody would try to force her to wed or send her to bed like an ailing child.

After the tournament, after she'd proved herself on the field of battle, she'd think about announcing her condition. In the meantime, she'd continue on as if naught had changed.

After all, naught *had* changed. Except for the bouts of queasiness. And no one knew about those but Sung Li.

Sung Li.

Helena gave a little gasp. The meddlesome maid might be scurrying about even now, wagging her tongue all over the keep. She shot to her feet, clapping a hand on the pommel of her dagger.

A wave of dizziness overcame her, weakening her knees and threatening to make her collapse. Her head swam in murky waters, and black spots flickered at the edge of her vision.

"Ballocks."

She swayed, fighting to stay upright. Ultimately, pride forced her to sink back onto the bed before she could swoon to the floor.

In a moment, she told herself. In a moment, 'twould pass. Then she'd go after that wee old maidservant with the big mouth.

"I'm busy." Colin stabbed forward again at the straw target, half-burying his blade.

"This is important," the old woman insisted.

He gave Sung Li a sideways glare. She seemed incredibly undaunted by his violence, considering he could thrust a blade through her scrawny body as easily as the target. He wrenched his sword free and prepared to stab again.

But just as he drove the weapon forward, she somehow snapped him on the wrist with lightning speed, then dug her tiny fingertips between the sinews of his forearm. To his shock, the sword fell from his numb fingers.

"What the bloody hell . . . ?"

She released his arm, and he shook his wrist, trying to get the feeling back.

"Very," she said, "important."

He stared at her. How had she done that? Perchance 'twas an old woman's trick, like the way his grandmother could bring him to his knees with a tweak of his ear when he was a lad. "Mayhap we should enlist *you* to fight in the tourney," he grumbled.

She gave him one of her inscrutable smiles. "It would bring shame to the knights if the tournament champion was a maidservant."

Colin shook his head. Sung Li had no lack of self-worth, that was certain. He wondered how she had come to be a servant at all. "What do you want?"

Her answer was as swift and direct as her blow had been. And equally stunning. "Helena is with child."

His heart stood still. For a long moment, he couldn't breathe. But thoughts rushed through his head like a flurry of leaves in a rough wind.

Was he going to be a father? Would she marry him

now? When was the babe due? Was she excited? Worried? Upset? Why hadn't she told him herself?

And then a thought intruded that engulfed all the others, a thought so loathsome and repugnant that he could almost taste its bitterness at the back of his throat.

"Indeed?" he croaked. "And does she know who the father is?"

Sung Li frowned. "You are the only one—"

He interrupted with a humorless chuckle. "Do not be so certain."

She narrowed her already narrow eyes. "You are a fool if you believe there is anyone else."

Colin was too dispirited to reprimand Sung Li for her insolence. Aye, he was a fool, not because he believed there was another, but because for so long he'd *not* believed it. He was a masochistic fool for watching from his window every morn as they slipped into the forest for their rendezvous. And he was a cursed fool for still loving Helena, in spite of everything.

"The babe is yours," Sung Li decreed with a decisive nod of her head before she scurried off.

Colin wished he could be as sure. He retrieved his sword and wiped the blur from his eyes. 'Twas only sweat, he assured himself. After all, his heart was long dead.

# Chapter 21

HELENA HAD NEVER seen a more glorious tournament, nor had Rivenloch. The air was filled with the sounds of clashing swords and strumming lutes, thundering hooves and shivering timbrels. Refreshments of Scots ale and Norman pasties were proffered. Servants stood ready with herbs and bandages, needles and thread for the wounded, and the scarves of many a coy maiden fluttered upon the arms of brave young knights.

Dozens of pavilions dotted the adjoining field like giant flowers sprung up on the grassy knoll, their pennons fluttering proudly in shades of ore and azure, argent and sable, declaring the names of the knights from far and wide who fought for honor in the lists of Rivenloch.

At the top of the stands, seated in a box decked with flowers, Deirdre and Miriel flanked Lord Gellir, while Helena's place stood empty, for she'd left their company early, pleading an aching head. Surrounding them were the ladies from the local clans, squirming children, and lords too old to fight. And below the reserved noble assemblage was a huge host of peasants from all over the Borders, cheering and jeering, hoisting ale and wolfing down meat pies with disorderly enthusiasm.

Of course, the best part for Helena was the combat itself. Everyone seemed to be in top form. Sir Adric le Gris took down five opponents in a row in the joust. Young Kenneth distinguished himself with his swordplay against a more seasoned adversary. There were acts of noteworthy chivalry—one victorious Norman knight refused to take any further compensation from his vanquished opponents than a loaf of bread—and acts of memorable romance— Sir Malcolm bade all those he conquered leave an offering of flowers on his wife's grave. Two red-haired Lachanburns fought in a melee for the first time. And Mochrie's four sons fought for the glory of their father, killed so recently by the English. Even Colin, to Helena's satisfaction, dispatched his first two opponents almost immediately, though he seemed to take little joy in the victory.

But Helena's greatest thrill was that she had competed twice already and won her bouts, with no one suspecting who she was or even that she was a maid. Her first rival, one of the Lachanburn lads, proved too bumbling and slow for her swift slashes and spins. She used his sluggish weight against him, drawing his attack, then dodging so he plowed himself into the ground. The second knight, a Norman of exceptional height, proved a greater challenge, but once she slipped within the circle of his gangly arms, she managed to trip him over his own lanky legs, and he ended up helpless on his back with her sword at his throat.

She had some trepidation, however, about her next foe.

'Twas not that she doubted her skills. Her first two battles had assured her she was a worthy opponent. And to her immense relief, her sickness had subsided in the last few days, restoring her to the peak of health. But she was moving higher now in the ranks, and the competition was growing fierce.

She watched from the narrow slit in her helm as Boniface strode to the midst of the lists to announce the bout.

"Sir Rauve d'Honore fighting for Lord Pagan of Rivenloch," Boniface announced, "against the knight in the blue tabard."

Mumbles of speculation coursed through the crowd. But Helena was too busy thinking about the battle to come to pay them much heed. She blew out a hard, bracing breath. 'Twould be a difficult bout. Sir Rauve was a challenging opponent, twice her size, bold, and slow to tire. But she mustn't let fear get the best of her. As Pagan was fond of saying, David slew Goliath *without* three feet of good Spanish steel.

So she paraded brazenly onto the field, cutting a menacing X into the air before her. She would win this match. For herself. For her father. For the glory of Rivenloch.

From the first blow, she knew 'twould not be an easy victory. Rauve's blade collided with hers with a bone-jarring impact. Helena's arm dropped, all the strength drained from it as she stumbled back from the shock.

Fortunately, she was able to skirt away before he drew back for another strike. Shaking the numbness out of her arm, she sized him up. If she could get inside the reach of his arms where he couldn't strike her . . .

She dodged quickly forward, slicing at his shoulder. But though he retreated a step, her blade seemed to recoil off his epaulet like hail bouncing off a helm. His next blow, delivered across her chest, knocked her to the ground, jarring the wind from her.

He chivalrously waited for her to rise. After a moment, she caught her breath, then scrambled to her feet. Ducking under his arm, she managed to solidly clip the back of his head. But the great knight shook off the impact like a horse shaking off flies.

She skittered out of the way of his next strike to her side. Then he returned with a violent slash that had all his power behind it. At first all she felt was the bruising blow to her thigh, hard enough to break the links of her chain mail. Then the blade swiftly slid along her chausses, slicing through cloth and skin and muscle. She staggered forward, wincing at the searing agony. She bit her lip, stifling her cries. Jesu, the pain was so intense that she thought she might be sick.

From outside the lists, Colin glanced up briefly at the contestants, then sniffed, slapping his dusty gauntlets against his knee. 'Twould be a short match—Rauve's opponent was half his size. Then Colin would be up again. He was to be matched against a Highlander, some wild brute of a man with more brawn than grace, he'd heard.

A loud cheer arose from the stands, and he looked up again. As he expected, Sir Rauve had drawn blood and was pounding his opponent into the dust.

Then, amid the cacophony, he thought he heard his name. He scanned the crowd.

"Colin!" came a distant cry. He couldn't see her, but he recognized Deirdre's voice.

Another cheer exploded, and Colin's eyes were drawn

to the center of the lists. There was something chillingly familiar about that knight in the blue tabard—the turn of the blade, the shifting of balance, the way the shield dipped and . . .

The blood congealed in his veins. Sweet Christ, nay!

He tossed aside his gauntlets and unsheathed, bolting forward to stop the bout. But Sir Rauve's sword had already begun a powerful downward arc.

"Helena!" he bellowed.

Time slowed horribly. The air grew strangely silent. At the edge of the lists, Colin saw her now—Deirdre, her mouth open in a soundless plea. Pagan slogged forward from the opposite end of the field. Colin lifted his heavy sword as if he could ward off the blow from where he stood. But 'twas too late. Rauve's sword landed on Helena's helm with an awful metallic thud that Colin would remember for the rest of his life.

"Nay!" He vaulted over the fence, his legs pounding to close the distance.

Half-blind with dread, he was upon them before he realized that Pagan had already reached Helena and was easing off her dented helm with quivering hands. Her face was as pale as milk, and when her long hair spilled free across the sod, a low rumble of shock rolled through the crowd like thunder.

Grief twisted in Colin's belly like a knife.

Sir Rauve drew off his own helm and gasped, leaning heavily on the pommel of his sword. "My God!" he sobbed. "Nay!"

Pagan knelt beside Helena. He stroked her forehead, lifted her limp hand, searched her wan face for signs of life. "Ah, Helena, nay, don't surrender," he begged.

Colin couldn't move. Anguish paralyzed him. His lips were compressed so tightly together they were numb. He felt as if he'd aged ten years in an instant.

"Wake up," Pagan hissed, squeezing her hand. "Do you hear me? Wake up."

Blood from Helena's thigh dripped slowly, soundlessly onto the earth. No bird, no breeze, no whisper from the crowd intruded upon Pagan's prodding murmurs. The torture of waiting grew until Colin thought he would go mad with dread.

Finally, Helena's eyelids fluttered—once, twice. Then she gasped. The sound was like a stone tossed into a still pond, traveling outward into the crowd. It grew as it joined sighs of relief and finally culminated in a loud cheer.

Colin, his eyes filling with tears, his chin trembling despite the iron clench of his jaw, bowed his head and mouthed something that was half prayer, half curse.

And yet when he gazed down at Helena, who was shaking the cobwebs from her brain and blinking to clear her vision, she seemed not to realize how close she'd come to death. The foolhardy wench was already struggling to rise.

She pushed up to her elbows, glanced at Colin, who was too stunned to move, and took Pagan's offered arm. With his aid, she wrenched herself up, biting her lip as she put weight on her injured leg. Sweat popped out upon her brow, but she refused to cry out.

Instead, once she glimpsed Rauve, bent despondently over his sword, looking as if he might faint at any moment, she called out with forced levity, "Sir Rauve! I've never felt such buffets as yours! 'Tis glad I am to have you as an ally."

Pagan, seething with anger but eager to avoid a spectacle, assumed her flippant manner as well. "He is indeed formidable, my lady," he announced, "and it attests to your own skills that you've met him admirably."

The crowd cheered at the chivalrous exchange, and Rauve and Helena shook hands. Then, while Colin stood dumbfounded, she gave him a tremulous smile and limped off the field.

What was the little fool doing? She'd fallen hard. That slash on her thigh must be agonizing. Yet she behaved as if 'twere a flea's bite, as if she hadn't stood at death's door just moments before. Her levity made anger rise in him now.

Damn her! He'd nearly choked on his heart to see her fall. How dare she make light of her injuries? And how dare she enter the tournament in the first place? 'Twas just like the impulsive wench to ignore her own safety and the safety of her child for the fleeting pleasure of crossing swords with a Norman. It seemed that carrying a babe in her belly had done naught to curb her recklessness.

He bit out a foul oath under his breath. Helena would do no more fighting, if he had anything to say about it. Ever. He'd be damned if he'd let her endanger their baby again.

*Her* baby, he amended.

"Here, Colin," Pagan said softly. He scooped up Helena's forgotten helm and shoved it into Colin's hands. "Go to her. She's in great pain, though she denies it. Look after her injuries."

Colin studied Pagan, standing there with lines of concern etched across his face, and felt ill. Now that Helena was out of danger, there was room for other, darker emotions—jealousy, anger, hurt—and they all warred within him as he tried to block out the painfully vivid image of his friend and his mistress locked in passionate embrace.

"Perchance *you* should see to her," he finally growled, pushing the helm away. "From what I hear, she prefers your company." He wheeled and walked away, afraid of what he might do to Pagan if he stayed, afraid of the vulnerability he might reveal to him.

Every step was sheer torture, but Helena knew she had to hold her head high as she walked from the field, both to salvage her pride and to assuage Rauve's guilt. So she forced her limbs to as even a gait as she could manage until she found refuge behind the walls of Pagan's pavilion.

When Pagan arrived, she was leaning heavily upon the inner brace, her hands clenched in pain, but she turned to meet him with a brittle smile. "Rauve is very good," she said faintly.

"My God, Helena," he breathed, glancing at her blood-soaked tabard. He dropped her helm to the ground. "Lie down."

She glanced longingly at the pallet, but pride made her hesitate.

"You're sore wounded," he insisted. "Lie down."

"I'm fine. I need no . . ." was all she managed before her eyelids fluttered and she careened sideways.

The next thing she knew, Pagan was lifting her onto a straw pallet on the ground, tucking a bolster beneath her head. Then he opened the flap of the pavilion and called out, "You, lad! Go fetch Colin du Lac! Now!"

She closed her eyes and smiled weakly when he returned to her side. "We shall have matching scars, Colin and I."

"And I suppose you think that's admirable?" He drew his dagger to slash her bloody tabard out of the way. "You're a fool wench, Helena of Rivenloch," he muttered, "almost as pigheaded as your sister. And I'm a bigger fool. I should never have . . ."

"Don't blame yourself. You're right. I *am* pigheaded." She lifted her head to peer down at the injury. Where the mail at her thigh had been cut through, blood welled from the slash. It dizzied her to look at it.

Pagan unbuckled the wide belt holding up her chausses and gently pushed the mail down past the injury. Then he tore through the delicate linen of her undergarments, exposing her thigh.

"'Tis all right, isn't it?" she asked tentatively.

"The cut is deep, but 'tis clean. 'Twill heal."

"Then I'll be able to fight again?"

He scowled and wadded a piece of linen to stanch the flow of blood. "Unfortunately, aye." Then he added, "But not in this tournament, mark my words."

But despite his dire warning and the throbbing pain in her thigh, already she was planning for the next event. No Norman was going to tell a Warrior Maid of Rivenloch that she couldn't participate in Rivenloch's tournament.

Colin paced along the sidelines, punching his fist into his palm, tensing his jaw. God—the waiting was tearing him apart. But he'd be damned if he'd let anyone know it. He continued with his bouts as if his heart wasn't knifing at his ribs, making it hard to breathe.

The distraction of worry made his swordplay suffer.

He'd actually dropped his shield in the last battle. If he wasn't more attentive, he might end up dead.

Dead . . .

What if Helena died?

Unreasonable fear clutched at his gut. He smothered it with a curse. God's bones! She'd walked off the field. She wasn't going to die, he reasoned.

At least not immediately. As long as there was no iron left in the wound. And as long as the bandages were changed frequently. And as long as . . .

He began pacing again.

The page who came barreling toward him from the direction of the pavilions made him stop in his tracks. Even before the lad spoke, panic seized Colin. Something was wrong. Helena was in trouble. He had to go to her.

"Where is she?"

"Lord Pagan's pavilion, my lord."

Colin fled the field, snaking through the maze of tents until he found Pagan's. The flap of the pavilion snapped open beneath his hand like the giant wing of a startled bird.

"Helena!" he cried hoarsely.

Thank God, she was there. Alive, whole, and flinching from the harsh slap of sunlight that fell across her face. But so was Pagan. And as he stared down at them, Colin's greatest fears crystallized. They were lovers. There was no question about it. Helena lay half-naked across the pallet, her chausses lowered to reveal one silky hip and a blood-smudged length of thigh.

Pagan was bent over her. His hands and eyes moved across her flesh, touching her familiarly. Touching parts of her that once belonged to Colin. She'd gone to Pagan, sought out the one in whose arms she'd come to know solace. And he'd given it. Their guilt was as bold as the livid scar of a branded harlot.

Hurt and rage blinded Colin. He let out a fierce, territorial roar. Seizing Pagan by the front of his hauberk, he threw him across the pavilion like a mountain cat with a mouse. Pagan landed in a crumpled heap against one serge wall, stunned.

"You bloody bastard!"

That savage curse belonged to Deirdre. She'd just charged through the tent flap to see her husband tossed like so much dirty laundry into a pile upon the floor. It didn't take a sage to divine who had delivered him there. She instantly threw herself at Colin's back, beating upon him with her puny fists.

To Colin, 'twas as if a wild kitten had landed on him, hissing and spitting at him in impotent fury. 'Twas annoying, distracting. Without thought, he reached over his shoulder and pushed his tormentor gently away.

A low growl came from Pagan's quarter as he slowly came to his feet. He suddenly looked as dangerous as a cornered wolf. "Keep your hands off my wife," he said in a deadly whisper, his eyes as dark as a sea squall.

Colin yet scowled, but his gaze flitted briefly over to the pregnant woman he'd just nudged aside. Surely he hadn't hurt Deirdre. He hadn't *intended* to hurt her.

Nay, she was still glaring at him with undimmed hatred.

Then whatever remorse he felt was quickly consumed by rage. "Your wife?" he blurted. "Which one, Pagan?"

"What?"

"Deirdre or Helena?" Bitterness and hurt made his throat ache as he confronted the man he'd once called brother.

"What?" Helena and Deirdre said in unison.

Colin turned a rueful gaze on Deirdre. "Why don't you tell her, Pagan? Tell her how you and Helena meet in the woods each morn."

Helena sucked in a breath. "You know?"

Betrayal twisted Colin's heart. Hearing the admission from Helena's own lips was the worst pain of all.

"Pagan?" Deirdre said on a gasp. "Is this true?"

"Nay," Pagan said emphatically.

"Aye," admitted Helena at the same time.

Colin erupted with a short, harsh, humorless bark. "If you're going to lie together, you should at least remember to *lie* together."

"Colin," Pagan said, "listen to me. 'Tis not what you think."

"'Tis no matter, Pagan." Despair made him bitter and reckless. "As you said before, one sister is as good as another. When that one heals," he said, waving toward Helena, "I vow her lips will taste every bit as sweet as these."

He snagged Deirdre by the arm, bringing her up against his chest. Then he claimed her with a kiss that was as brutal as 'twas passionless. She might have tasted of honey. She might have tasted of onions. He didn't know. He only knew that when he pulled away, his hunger for revenge hadn't diminished in the least.

Pagan never had the chance to slug him. The last thing Colin saw before everything went blurry was a swirl of light blond hair, a pair of snapping green eyes, and the feminine fist of a pregnant woman coming toward his face.

# Chapter 22

HELENA'S FIRST INSTINCT as Deirdre's knuckles cracked across the bridge of Colin's nose was to defend him. Ignoring her injury, she fought her way to her feet, intending to go after her sister. She might go after Colin next for that kiss he'd given Deirdre, but that could wait. Unfortunately, as she raised her fists, a gray veil drooped over her eyes. She shook her head, trying to dispel the haze as she battled to keep her balance.

Pagan and Deirdre were shouting at each other, but their voices sounded muffled, as if the two of them were swaddled in thick cloth. And Colin, staggering, groaned as he cradled his injured nose.

Then the pavilion flap opened abruptly, and blinding light flooded the chaotic scene.

"What the Devil . . ."

'Twas Miriel. Her jaw dropped. Sung Li poked her head in an instant later, scowling at what she saw.

Pagan and Deirdre looked up once, then resumed their argument.

"You're making rash assumptions," he accused.

"So are you!" Deirdre fired back. "You're assuming I'm stupid enough to believe you."

"You stubborn wench! Will you not even listen—"

"What? Listen to your lies?"

"Stop it, you two!"

Everyone turned in amazed silence. Had that loud bellow come out of wee Miriel?

"Now," she said more calmly, crossing her arms, while behind her, Sung Li did the same. "Will someone tell me what's happened here?"

"A misunderstanding," Pagan volunteered.

"Aye," Deirdre said coldly. "It seems you misunderstood our wedding vows." With that, she shoved Pagan aside and exited the pavilion.

Pagan kicked at the sod and spat out a foul oath. "God's eyes! I knew 'twas a mistake." He gave Helena a look full of anger and self-condemnation. "I'm sorry we ever started this."

"Nay!" Helena felt a moment of panic. "Don't say that," she insisted, clutching the fabric wall of the pavilion as she teetered on her feet. "I'm not sorry. I'm grateful."

"Grateful," Pagan said, shaking his head. "For what? You can scarcely stand. Colin's got a bloodied nose. And Deirdre . . ." He looked bleakly at the ground. "Jesu, she'll never trust me again."

Helena slowly edged down the pavilion wall until she sat in a guilty huddle. Aye, she desperately wanted to continue sparring with Pagan, but not at the expense of Deirdre's marriage. "'Tis all my fault."

Pagan shook his head. "Nay, 'tis mine. And I've got to set things aright." He straightened and nodded to Miriel. "Can you see to their wounds?"

"Of course," Miriel said.

"Of course," Sung Li echoed.

Then Pagan left to seek out his wife.

Helena hoped she'd listen to him. And she hoped Colin would listen to *her*. How could the knave honestly believe she was committing adultery with Pagan?

"What happened to *you?*" Miriel asked Colin.

Blood dripped between his fingers where he clasped his nose. "Naught that fresh air won't mend," he said sullenly, brushing past her to make a brusque exit.

"You go after him," Sung Li said to Miriel, shooing her. "I will see to Helena."

Miriel left to follow Colin, and Sung Li helped Helena back to the pallet on the ground. The maid worked in silence a while, dabbing at her wound with small, skilled fingers and sprinkling strange herbs from her pouch into the cut.

The pavilion afforded little privacy. A pack of squires paraded by while Sung Li was bandaging her leg. But the modest maid swirled a cloak over Helena's leg, giving the lads an imperious glare.

Helena grabbed the tabard of one of the squires. "Have they started the archery?"

"Not yet, my lady."

"You should wait a day for your wound to heal," Sung Li informed her.

*And for tempers to cool,* Helena thought. Thank God Miriel and Sung Li had arrived when they did. Between

Colin's groundless rage, Pagan's black looks, and Deirdre's wicked punch, a nasty brawl might have otherwise ensued.

But she wasn't about to miss a moment of Rivenloch's tournament. "I'll be fine."

"*You* will be fine. But what about the babe?"

She frowned. She didn't want to think about it.

"If you put the child in harm's way," Sung Li persisted, "he will not be pleased."

Helena knew Sung Li meant Colin. "He doesn't know." Then she narrowed suspicious eyes. "Unless you told him."

Sung Li raised her brows. "Do you think I wish to be— what was it you said? Strung up by my braid and roasted slowly over a fire?"

Helena had issued that threat shortly after Sung Li had visited her. Still, the wily old maid might have had time before then to divulge the news to Colin.

On the other hand, if Colin knew she carried his child, he surely would have said something.

Pah! She didn't care if Colin would be pleased or not. She still stung from his unsubstantiated accusations. How could he believe her capable of adultery? God's eyes, Deirdre was with child. What kind of scheming witch did he think she was?

Besides, what right had he to suddenly play the jealous lover or to lay claim to her? And how dared he demand her fidelity? He certainly didn't return it. She'd given herself to Colin, body and heart and soul, and how had he repaid her? Too often to count, she'd seen him coming from meetings in the cellar with Lucy Campbell.

The thought of Lucy's smug smirk, her rosy bosom, her saucy glance, stuck in Helena's craw, choking her with ire.

"'Tis *my* babe," she croaked, "not his."

"I see." Sung Li arched a sly brow as she finished knotting the bandage. "You made this babe all by yourself, then."

Helena gave the sardonic maid a cold glare. "Listen, you meddlesome old trot. I don't care what he thinks. Colin du Lac can't tell me what I can and cannot do, where I may and may not go. Or who I will and will not bed. And he's certainly not going to prevent me from fighting in my own tournament."

Sung Li's wrinkled face turned grim then, and she seized Helena's forearm in a surprisingly firm grip, narrowing her dark, all-seeing eyes. "This child is destined to be a great warrior. Do not endanger her."

Her? The old woman's prediction sent a cool shiver along the nape of Helena's neck, rendering her speechless. She gulped. Could it be true? Had she and Colin made a warrior maid that might bring glory to Rivenloch? The possibility made her heart race. Even after Sung Li released her, Helena felt a tingle of strange current all along her arm.

Forsooth, she almost regretted her harsh words. "I'll do the child no harm," she assured the maid. "After all, 'tis only the archery this afternoon."

Though she'd hoped otherwise, Helena knew 'twould be at least another day before she felt hale enough to engage in swordplay again. Her leg was very painful. A deep purple bruise surrounded the cut. She couldn't walk without limping. Even standing long set her thigh to throbbing.

But she couldn't stay here. Things would only worsen if she lay idle. An unoccupied mind invited unwelcome thoughts. Thoughts of philandering Normans and misplaced jealousy.

An hour later, dressed in a surcoat of muted green, Helena nervously tightened the thong around her hair and peered between the milling bodies of horses tethered beside the field. 'Twas probably prudent to wait until the last minute to make her appearance. Neither Pagan nor Colin nor Deirdre would approve of her participation. But they'd be unlikely to protest publicly once the games had begun.

The ram's horn sounded, announcing the archery. With a deep breath, she slung the quiver over her shoulder, pulled on her well-worn archery gloves, picked up her bow, and limped forward.

Twenty or more archers stood along the shooting line several yards from two straw bales, loosening their arms, shrugging on quivers, eyeing up the targets. Colin was among them, his nose looking remarkably whole despite the punch Deirdre had given it. As soon as she stepped onto the field, their eyes met. She felt frozen in time, unable to breathe.

It took great courage for her to cross the field with Colin's condemning gaze upon her, but she was confident he wouldn't make a spectacle here. Ignoring the smoldering eyes that burned into the back of her head, she notched an arrow onto the bowstring and stretched it back, testing its balance and her strength.

The competition would require all of her concentration. She knew if she let up for a moment, if she allowed one wish, one regret, one thought of Colin du Lac to cross her mind, anger would rush in on her, ruining her aim.

* * * *

Colin's nose still throbbed from the clout he'd taken from Helena's sister. Still, 'twas not as painful as the throbbing of his broken heart.

'Twas natural Pagan would lie to preserve his marriage. Colin expected as much. But Helena . . . Helena hadn't even bothered to deny her trysts with Pagan. Jesu, she'd even said she was glad of them, grateful. She behaved as if their affair was of no consequence.

No consequence? Colin knew better. The babe growing in her belly might well be Pagan's.

As the archery commenced, Colin's gaze was drawn inexorably to Helena. There was one thing she'd been truthful about—she was indeed one of the best archers of Rivenloch. While she hadn't the strength of some of her ox-shouldered opponents, at close range, she was highly accurate. He began to suspect she might have a chance of winning the contest.

Colin, on the contrary, his shooting reflective of his sullen mood, half buried his shafts in the straw targets, but rarely did they come very close to the mark. He didn't survive the third round.

As he left the field, he pulled the archery glove from his hand and slapped it against his leg.

"She's good," Rauve murmured beside him. Then he added in relief, "That blow to her head didn't hurt her aim."

Colin grunted in reply. She *was* good. It made watching her that much more painful. Part of him still ached with betrayal. But part of him was grudgingly impressed with her talent. She looked every inch a Warrior Maid of Rivenloch, standing boldly astride as she took steady aim and released the shafts without faltering.

An ignoble part of him wanted her to fail miserably.

And yet he found his own bow arm clenching every time she shot. He wanted to forgive her. But he couldn't. Still, despite his bruised spirit, despite his keen sense of loss, he actually felt a flush of pride as he watched her fire arrow after arrow into the center of the target.

And when the competition came down to two—John Wyte, a stout bowman from a Norman retinue, and Helena—his heart fluttered with excitement. Each had shot off two arrows, well placed at an even distance from the center. A final shot would determine the champion.

John waved to quiet the cheering crowd. He planted his feet wide and pulled back on his bow, his bearded face grim with concentration. For a good score of heartbeats, he held steady. When he at last let the string go with a twang, the arrow impacted but half an inch from dead center.

The crowd came to its feet, applauding loudly. Colin took a long, slow breath. If Helena took her time and arced the shaft at the proper angle . . .

John Wyte nodded solemnly to Helena.

As the crowd hushed, Helena eyed up the target, shaking the stiffness from her arms. She pulled an arrow from her quiver and nocked it into place. The moment grew so still that Colin could hear the sinew stretch as she pulled the bowstring back with three fingers to nestle against her cheek. He tensed with her as she took taut aim, holding it, holding it . . .

Then she released the bowstring.

The shaft sailed into the exact center of the target. The spectators went wild. Helena laughed with joy. A curious pride surged up inside Colin. He felt her delight as if 'twere his own.

Then he remembered. This was the woman who had forsaken him. That same unwavering aim had guided her cruel shaft through his heart.

"Let's go," he said uncomfortably to Rauve, stuffing his glove into his belt and facing the stands. He couldn't bear to witness Helena's sweet victory, won so close on the heels of her bitter betrayal.

He never should have turned his back on her.

Helena nodded and waved to the crowd, delirious with triumph. She had won! Whatever might happen in the future, she'd won the day! Naught would change that. She'd always remember the warm glow that suffused her now as she turned her face proudly up toward her clan. By their spirited response, she knew that generations of Rivenloch folk would tell the story of Helena, Warrior Maid of Rivenloch, who'd conquered a score of Norman knights with her bow.

Forsooth, so absorbed was she in her victory that she scarcely noticed the wall of dust rising behind her.

A mare in heat had broken free of her keeper. Willie, the youngest stable lad at Rivenloch, was chasing the horse frantically across the field.

Unfortunately, before he could recover her, two tethered stallions caught the mare's scent. They began to snort, tugging at their ropes.

The mare skirted by, nodding as she pranced.

The stallions' eyes rolled. They neighed, straining their necks against their bonds, and kicked up their forelegs. Giving a powerful toss of his head, one stallion pulled his stake from the ground and reared up on his hindquarters. Fearing competition, the other wrenched free at once.

Both horses stamped at the sod, swinging their heads around to seek out the mare. The ground shook as the stallions charged across the green.

A couple of knights dashed after the steeds, whistling and shouting to distract them.

Through the whirling cloud of dust, Helena glimpsed Willie. He was trapped in the midst of the charge. The destriers raged all about him. At any moment, the lad might be trampled beneath their careless hooves.

Several squires had formed a loose circle at the edges of the field, and they were easing forward, trying to soothe the rampaging animals. But they were moving too slowly. By the time they reached the stallions, Willie could be dead.

Helena dropped her bow and let the quiver slide from her back. She turned to John, the archer beside her. "Give me your sword!"

He did as she asked. Taking a deep breath, she turned the blade in her hands once. Then, ignoring the pull of her bandages, she broke through the ranks of circling squires, bolting into the melee in the middle of the field.

At once, the mare skidded past her, her eyes wide with fright, her mouth foaming. Pebbles and dirt pelted Helena's ankles as she dodged the harsh whip of the mare's tail, and her wound stung as if it had opened again.

The stallions followed the mare in hot pursuit, an instant behind their quarry.

Between them, Willie ran screaming, trapped amid flailing hooves and spraying rocks. Helena dove for him, half-tripping, shoving him as hard as she could toward the safety of the wattle fence.

Then the two stallions charged, their nostrils flared,

their ears flat. Their heads bobbed above the roiling dust, and for a heartbeat, Helena could see the mad cast of their eyes, blinding them to everything but the mare. The thunder of the advancing hooves rumbled the earth beneath Helena's feet. She squinted against the choking dust rising before her and lifted her sword high to battle the huge beasts.

At the last instant, the stallions spooked. They screamed and pulled their heads back, their feet scrambling on the loose ground for purchase. Dust boiled up in confusion. The beasts were so close she could feel their hot, chuffing breath. Their legs stabbed at the sod all around. A shrill, angry neigh rent the air. The last thing she saw was a pair of enormous, shaggy hooves pawing at the sky before they descended toward her.

# Chapter 23

SOMETHING SLAMMED HELENA to the ground. The fall knocked the wind from her with all the force of a tumble in the joust. For a moment she lay as helpless as a stunned fly. But she was accustomed to falling. She regained her wits quickly, ducking her head protectively beneath one arm and groping blindly for her sword with the other.

Just as her fingers closed around the hilt, rough hands wrenched her to her feet, hauling her through the rubble. Her long skirts tripped her, but the brute who'd pushed her to the ground gave her no quarter. She twisted and fell to one knee, and searing pain streaked through her wounded thigh. Still her abductor yanked her onward.

At last she emerged from the bowels of churning dust to safety. Spitting a stray lock of hair from her mouth, Helena faced her captor. Pagan. His peculiar expression—as if he wished simultaneously to weep and wring her neck—froze the words of indignation in her throat. He looked furious and terrified and bereft, all at once.

Within moments, the mare was caught and led off the field. Several knights moved in to soothe the stallions with gentle voices and easy gestures. Willie was pulled to the fringes of the list, where he sat with his head between his knees. Yet Pagan still clung to her, trembling so violently that Helena wondered if he would explode with rage. Even after the stallions were captured and the dust settled, he refused to loosen his grip on her.

"Colin!" he bellowed.

Helena glimpsed Colin at the opposite side of the field, a naked blade in his hand, a look of simultaneous horror and rage on his face. He came to Pagan's summons, but Helena noted he never sheathed his sword. By the Rood, mayhap he intended to slay Pagan.

She wouldn't let him, of course. Deirdre, for all her faults, adored Pagan. The least Helena could do was protect him for her sister. So when Colin came with his blade flashing, Helena broke free of Pagan's hold, placing herself between them, and faced Colin with her own weapon.

Before Colin could launch an attack, Pagan bit out, "Take her off the field. Tie her up. Lock her up. Put her in chains if you have to. But see that she doesn't stray onto my lists again this day."

Helena's jaw dropped. She couldn't believe what she was hearing. *His* lists? Lucifer's ballocks! She'd just held her own with her sword in these lists. She'd just *won* the archery contest. And she'd saved Willie's life.

She was tempted to turn and focus her attack on Pagan. But Colin was still the one with the sword.

Then Colin snarled, "With pleasure," and Helena felt as if all the breath drained from her lungs.

God's bones! Were the Normans joining forces against her? In her own castle?

Colin made a grab for her, and she knocked his hand away with her sword arm, making it clear she'd brook none of his tyranny.

"Do not make a spectacle of this, Helena," Pagan muttered behind her.

"If you think for one moment I'll go peaceably, then you know naught about the Warrior Maids of Rivenloch," she retorted.

"Damn it, wench!" Pagan hissed. "'Tis for your own safety."

"Don't be ridic—"

"Put away your sword," Colin commanded.

"Don't tell me what to do! Not in my own—"

"Drop it."

Incensed, she swung the blade up, bringing the tip to Colin's bare throat. She heard at a distance the crowd's collective gasp.

Colin's eyes were as dark and cold as the grave, but beneath their glacial depths lurked a profound and bitter melancholy, an emotion that made her blade waver as she held him at bay.

When his sword clanged in surrender upon the ground, it startled her.

"Colin?" Pagan asked, incredulous.

"I cannot do it," Colin explained. "I won't cross swords with a . . . with a pregnant woman."

Helena sucked in an astonished breath.

"What?" Pagan reeled in surprise.

Colin's gaze was bleak as he stared at her, and said clearly, "I will not endanger Lord Pagan's child."

"My . . ." Pagan began, completely taken aback. Then he stepped between the two of them, his arms crossed. "Is this true, sister? Are you with child?"

She wanted to deny it. After all, the man she loved, the man who was responsible for the child, didn't even believe 'twas his. But her eyes filled inexplicably with tears, and her throat clogged until she couldn't speak.

"Jesu, Colin!" Pagan said. "I know what you think, but 'tis impossible."

Still Colin's face was shrouded in mistrust. It broke her heart, and she cursed her emotions of late, which refused to be mastered. She felt a stray tear trickle down her cheek.

With a vicious snap, she lowered her sword. Then summoning up all her pride, she turned to the crowd, her eyes glittering and her chin lifted.

"I thank you, people of Rivenloch, for your support. But my wound pains me now, and I must retire to the keep." At their cries of disappointment, she added, "Have no fear. I vow I will return on the morrow to even greater victory."

Then she returned the sword to its owner and marched from the field, smiling through her tears and waving at the spectators.

Colin's heart quivered in his chest like a virgin's knees. Sweet Jesu! When he'd beheld Helena facing the steeds with sword in hand, glaring at them as if they were dragons and she, St. George . . .

His gut gave a sickening lurch as he thought how close that sweet body had come to being mangled, how close the sparkling light in those emerald eyes had come to being extinguished. And he realized the wretched truth. Despite her sins, despite her betrayal, and despite all reason, Helena of Rivenloch was more precious to him than life itself. Aye, she was willful and stubborn. She was reckless and rebellious and untamed. She'd hurt him deeply, more deeply than any woman ever had. But she'd also kindled the fires of his heart and stirred his blood with her passion and pride and impulsiveness.

And now he was a man cursed, a hostage of her heart.

"Follow her," Pagan told him.

"*You* follow her," Colin said bleakly.

"Shite!" Pagan hissed.

He grabbed Colin's arm, and they made as casual an exit as they could manage from the field to the relative privacy behind the stable.

"I didn't touch her. I swear it."

Colin didn't want to have this conversation. 'Twas too painful to listen to Pagan's lies. And he *was* lying. Deirdre knew it. Helena had confessed as much. God's bones, Colin had seen them with his own eyes.

"Colin, listen to me. 'Tis Deirdre I love. And only her."

Colin's rage bubbled up. 'Twas vile enough to be deceived by a woman. But to be betrayed by his oldest friend . . . "You may love only her," he sneered, "but 'tis Helena you swive in the wood each morn."

"Do not insult me with unfounded accusations!"

"Unfounded? I've seen you, you bastard. I've *seen* you."

"What, Colin?" Pagan barked. "What have you seen?"

'Twas too painful to recount. Colin's mouth turned downward in a grim frown of defeat, and he started to turn away.

But Pagan wouldn't let him go. He seized him by the front of his tabard. "What have you seen?"

Bitterness consumed Colin. "You *know* what I've seen."

Pagan shook his head. "You've seen naught."

"I've seen enough," Colin snarled, daring Pagan to deny him. "You go off into the woods together every morn."

To his surprise, Pagan nodded. "Aye. We do."

For a long while the two of them only glared at each other, and a muscle began to tic in Colin's jaw.

Finally, Pagan asked, "And then?"

An ugly image filled Colin's mind, and he viciously broke Pagan's hold on his tabard. "You son of a—"

"And then?" Pagan repeated.

Over Pagan's shoulder, Colin saw Deirdre approach. Despite her earlier violence toward him, he realized she, too, was but a victim. He had to spare her the details of Pagan's sin. He muttered low, "You let your desires get the better of you."

"Nay, I let *her* desires get the better of me."

Quickly, before Deirdre could hear, he hissed, "You would blame this on Helena?"

"Aye," he declared, then amended, "mostly. 'Twas she who insisted we meet each morn. But 'twas not for swiving, you great fool. 'Twas for *sparring*."

"What?"

"Sparring. We practiced with the blade. That's all."

"You expect me to believe—"

Deirdre had drawn close enough now to hear him. "Sparring?" she said over his shoulder.

Pagan cringed.

Her mouth was agape. "You were . . . sparring . . . with my sister?"

Colin frowned. To look at Deirdre's wounded expression, one would think sparring a worse crime than fornication.

Pagan let out a shuddering sigh. "Colin, you meddling knave. Now see what you've wrought?"

Tears filled Deirdre's eyes, and Colin's scowl deepened. Were all Scotswomen so mad? The possibility of Pagan's adultery had moved Deirdre to irritation, but the fact that her husband had *sparred* with another woman . . .

"How could you?" Deirdre asked forlornly.

Pagan's shoulders drooped with guilt as he turned toward her. "I didn't mean to, my love. I lost my head. She caught me in a moment of weakness."

Colin looked from one to the other. This was sheer lunacy. But as they continued to converse, Deirdre in hurt tones, Pagan in placating ones, a tiny bud of hope began to sprout in Colin's chest.

Mayhap they *were* telling the truth.

Mayhap Pagan and Helena *had* only been sparring. But for the sake of Deirdre, unable to fight because of her condition, they'd kept their practices a secret to spare her feelings. Mayhap Pagan *hadn't* bedded Helena, but only crossed swords with her. Which meant . . .

His heart pounding, Colin left the couple to their negotiations. He had to catch Helena before she did something else foolish. After all, she carried a babe now . . . *their* babe.

Curse the wench! She must have known all along 'twas theirs, and yet she'd said naught to him. Instead, she'd sparred with Pagan, fought in the tournament, ran between charging horses, knowing she endangered the child. Did the reckless maid have no care for her own flesh and blood? Sweet Mary, did she *hope* to lose the babe?

Hurt and rage welled inside him. By God, he'd do as Pagan had commanded—tie her up, lock her up, put her in chains, whatever it took to ensure she could not endanger herself or the child.

It didn't take long to find her. Though she'd left the field with long, proud strides, now she favored her injured leg, hobbling slowly across the courtyard. The sight served to soften his fury, if only for a brief moment. Though part of him wanted to thrash her for her recklessness, part of him longed to scoop her up in his embrace.

A rush of emotions coursed through him with all the turbulence of a stormy sky. Relief and rage and tenderness. Frustration and impatience and adoration. Lust and anger and guilt. But mostly, God help him, fierce love. He loved Helena. And whether that meant sweeping her gently up in his arms or brutally tossing her over his shoulder, he knew that love was the cornerstone of every other emotion pulsing through his veins.

As he loped up, drawing even with her, she angrily wiped the remnant of a tear from her cheek, and snapped, "I don't want your apology. Leave me alone."

"I'm not offering an apology."

He bent and captured her behind the knees. With a mighty heave, he hoisted her into his arms.

She fought him. "Put me down!"

Colin walked toward the keep.

"You miserable Norman!" She squirmed in his grasp.

He kept walking.

"Let me go!" She pounded at his shoulder. "Or I'll summon the knights of Rivenloch!"

He continued walking. It didn't matter if her entire army came forward to murder him with pikes and poles. What he did was for her own good and his sanity. He carried her all the way, ignoring her protests, across the sward toward the keep, through the great hall, up the steps, to her bedchamber. And not a single Rivenloch soul intervened to stop him.

By the time they crossed the threshold of her bed-chamber, Helena had pummeled several bruises into his flesh, and yet he knew he was incapable of laying a violent hand on her. 'Twas just as well. He doubted a thrashing would have much effect on her anyway. Not when being nearly trampled to death by horses hadn't curbed her foolhardiness.

But his wrath hadn't cooled in the least. He set her upon her feet and gave the door a satisfying slam.

"This is where you will spend the rest of the tournament," he bit out, stabbing a commanding finger at her nose. His voice was hoarse with emotion, but he managed to keep it steady. "You may occupy yourself here with needlework or sleeping or gazing out the window, for all I care. But you'll not come to the lists."

She looked at him incredulously. "Do not deign to dictate to me! You are neither my husband nor my lord nor my commander."

"That shall be remedied soon enough," he assured her. "Now, do I need to chain you to the bed, or will you stay here on your word of honor?"

"What do you mean, remedied?"

"I have no intention of letting you bear a fatherless child."

Helena clenched her jaw. This was precisely why she'd resisted commitment of any kind. Just because she carried his offspring, the overbearing Norman thought he could dictate to her.

Still stinging from his mistrust and jealousy, she spoke with flippant cruelty. "What makes you think the child would be fatherless? You said it yourself. Pagan is the babe's father."

To her astonishment, he shook his head. "I am the babe's father. And you know it."

She bit her lip.

An almost indiscernible sorrow crept into his smoldering eyes. "Or were you never going to tell me?"

She swallowed hard, then turned her back on him. She didn't want him to see the faltering in her resolve. She dug her fingers into the ledge of the window. If only she didn't love him . . . If only she could harden her heart against him . . . Damn the Norman! He'd put her in exactly in the state she least wanted to be—cornered, vulnerable, powerless.

"I won't be forced into marriage," she warned him. "I am a Warrior Maid of Rivenloch. I refuse to be some man's chattel."

"I am not *some man*." He grabbed her elbow and wheeled her toward him. "I am the man who loves you. Who's planted a babe in your womb. Who's asked for your hand countless times. Who's been more faithful to you than a husband."

"Faithful!" she scoffed. "What about you and Lucy Campbell swiving in the buttery all those morns?"

"I wasn't swiving her."

She smirked.

"I swear it on my spurs. I was teaching her to cook. To please *you*."

She narrowed her eyes. Dinners at Rivenloch *had* seemed more palatable of late.

And yet that changed naught. Colin might have cared for her pleasure once, but now he wanted to control her. She broke free of his hold and began to pace in agitation, as restless as a caged wolf.

"You do not wish to please me now," she charged. "You would take my sword from me. Keep me from my own lists. Change me from a fierce warrior to a . . . a whimpering wife."

"Nay."

"Men only wish to tame women, to subdue them, to conquer them."

"Nay."

"You have even now threatened to chain me to the bed." Helena didn't mean to rant on and on, but once begun, she couldn't stem the tide of her grievances. "You men are not content until you've wrung the very spirit from a woman, made her meek and weak-willed, molded her to your pleasure, reduced her to a waddling, lazy, docile pet. Just as Pagan has done to Deirdre." She gasped as she realized what she'd blurted out.

"I wouldn't call Deirdre docile or weak-willed." He touched his nose, wincing at the bruise there. "At least not to her face."

He was partially right. Deirdre wasn't completely subdued. But then he hadn't known her before she'd been altered by marriage. "She used to be fierce," she remembered, "independent, uncompromising. Pagan changed her."

"And you think she did not change him as well?" Colin scoffed.

Helena narrowed her eyes.

"Before Pagan married Deirdre," he said, "he was strong, controlling, always sure of himself." He smiled briefly.

"Rather a worm at times." He shook his head. "Now he's as malleable as lead. 'Tis your sister who has tamed her husband."

Helena frowned. "Yet 'tis Pagan who has seized control of Rivenloch," she argued.

"Only by the King's command and your father's bidding."

"He's forbidden Deirdre to fight." She crossed her arms smugly.

He nodded. "As he would any of his knights not in perfect fighting form."

She cocked her chin upward. "She can't even make her own decisions without seeking his permission."

"And he makes none without seeking hers."

Her scowl deepened. She didn't believe that for a moment. Men accustomed to leadership never relinquished it. Colin didn't understand. How could she make him see?

"'Tis like a battle," she said. "There are always two sides. One loses, and one wins. One is the victor, and one is the victim. Only in the battle of marriage, 'tis always the man who wins." She held his gaze, wondering if she'd gotten through to him.

The last thing she expected was the burst of laughter that exploded from him. "The *battle* of marriage?"

She stiffened at his mockery, clenching her teeth against the instinct to plunge her fist through his amused grin.

Then he made the mistake of laying patronizing hands upon her shoulders as he tried to stifle his laughter. She threw off his arms and shoved hard at his chest, making him stumble back a step.

His laughter vanished then, but there was still a trace of

humor in his eyes. "Hel-cat, sweetheart, marriage is not a battle of foes." His gaze softened. "'Tis an alliance."

Helena raised her fists defensively. Even though she was free of his embrace, part of her felt cornered, snared in the twinkling, knowing, tempting allure of his eyes. The battle was on, and already he had the advantage.

Before she could throw a punch, he reached up, lightning fast, and seized her wrists.

"There is no conqueror, no conquered," he said gently. "Do you not remember?"

Her arms trapped, she resorted to making weapons of her legs. But he knew her too well. Before she could raise her knee, he lunged forward, crushing her with disturbing intimacy against the stone wall.

She silently cursed her mutinous body, which warmed even at this hostile contact. His scent, leather and smoke and spice, filled her nostrils. His voice rumbled like distant thunder. And his hips pressed against hers possessively.

"Sometimes 'tis the man who wields the greater power," he murmured, his breath stirring the tendrils along her cheek, tickling her ear, sending a shiver through her soul.

Then, just as she felt her bones begin to melt like iron on the forge, he released her suddenly. She staggered against the wall, catching her breath. He backed away, lifting his palms in a gesture of surrender. His eyes were smoky with lust, his mouth parted with hunger, and there was a telling bulge beneath his trews. "And sometimes," he whispered, desire roughening his voice, "he is at the woman's mercy."

Helena's head whirled in confusion. She gazed at Colin du Lac, standing before her in breathless wait, his need raw, his emotions bare. He'd stolen kisses from her, used her passions against her, claimed her body again and again. Yet just as often, she'd seduced and bewitched and overpowered him. In their bouts of lovemaking, there had never been a clear victor. Mayhap, she dared to hope, 'twould prove thus in marriage.

"Conquer," he breathed, "or be conquered. 'Tis no matter to me, Hel-fire. Only do not deprive me of your love."

After such sweet words of surrender, Helena could do naught else but show him mercy.

As she pushed off the wall, her blood already simmering with anticipation, her flesh burning for his touch, she managed to whisper, "Sir Colin du Lac, I challenge you to a tryst."

Somehow they found the pallet. But swiftly, their battle became a hazy blur of yielding and domination, yearning and gratification. Garments littered the chamber, and soft cries filled the air as their limbs twined in sensual combat. Colin steered the charger of their desire for a time; then she seized the reins, turning it along her chosen course. For a while, he towered above her like a conquering hero; then she rose to victory, commanding him from her lofty perch. He groaned out his need to her, and she moaned her passion to him, until their voices sounded together, and they cried out in mutual, blissful, undeniable triumph.

Afterward, in the peaceful wake of their tumultuous war, Helena lay curled against Colin's flank, his limbs surrounding her like the roots of a tree, locks of her hair draping him like ivy clinging to an oak.

"I warn you, I will not be your chattel," she murmured, running an idle finger down his breastbone.

He chuckled softly. "And I will not be your hostage."

"I won't give up my sword."

He smiled. "I won't give up my cooking pot."

Beyond the window, she could hear the distant dull thunder of hooves, cheers from the tournament field, and the indistinct voices of lovers quarreling, growing nearer. But she felt as if she floated a world away from all that.

Colin ran a fingertip down the ridge of her nose. "I *will* give up my philandering ways."

"Then I will give up . . ." She thought for a moment. As difficult as 'twas to make the promise around the lump in her throat, she knew 'twas the reasonable thing to do. "I won't spar until after the babe is born."

"Pah! You won't spar with *Pagan* until after the babe is born."

She turned her head to look at him.

He lifted her hand for a kiss. "Sung Li informed me that our babe is to be a great warrior."

"Aye?"

"Then he'll need to grow accustomed to battle. And for that, you deserve the *best* sparring partner," Colin boasted. "What say you? Every day at dawn?"

Helena's eyes filled with moisture as she gazed with almost unbearable fondness into his twinkling eyes. He *wouldn't* try to change her warring ways, then. Mayhap theirs would be a happy marriage.

"Of course," he warned, "that's only after your leg has healed."

"Of course."

"And only with blunted blades."

Her lips curved into a smile.

"What?"

"She."

"What?"

"She. Sung Li said 'twould be a lass."

"A lass?" A rainbow of emotions tinged Colin's features, but the prevailing one was wonder. "Another warrior maid . . ."

Then their sweet and intimate discourse was interrupted, with all the finesse of an ox crashing into a crockery shop, by a sudden solid pounding upon the door.

~⁓

# Chapter 24

HELENA SCRAMBLED UP AT ONCE, casting about for a weapon. Colin tossed her a surcoat.

"Colin du Lac!" came a muffled bellow. "Are you within?"

Helena frowned. The voice was unmistakably Deirdre's, and she sounded furious.

"Within?" Colin muttered, pulling on his trews. "Alas, no longer." He gave Helena a saucy wink.

"You savage, cowardly knave!" Deirdre yelled. "If you've laid a hand on my sister, I swear as God is my judge . . ."

Pagan's calmer voice joined Deirdre's at the door. "He'd not hurt her, my love."

"Oh, aye?" she snapped. "Well, he got her with child, didn't he?" She banged harder on the door. "Don't tell me *that* was her idea."

Helena gulped. There was apparently much that Deirdre

didn't know about her. Considering the circumstances, perchance 'twas best she don clothing.

"If you've touched one hair on her head, you spineless worm . . ."

Colin slipped a long shirt over his head. "You needn't worry," he called back. "Tell her, Pagan. She needn't worry."

"There," Pagan said. "You see? You needn't worry. Now I think 'twould be best if we leave them to—"

"I'm not leaving until I see her. Do you hear me, you bastard?" She hammered again. "Open this door."

Helena cursed under her breath, struggling with the laces of her surcoat. She tugged frantically at her skirts, trying to give them some semblance of order.

"I command you!" Deirdre bellowed. "Open this door now!"

Colin lifted a brow, silently asking Helena for permission to let her in. Lord, she thought, he was irresistibly handsome. His trews were wrinkled and the laces of his shirt undone. His hair, combed hastily with his fingers, was as unruly as the mane of a wild stallion, and his sultry eyes and the sheen of sweat dusting his skin left no doubt as to what they'd been doing. Still, Helena couldn't hide from her sister forever. Especially now that she intended to marry the Norman. She blew out a bracing breath and nodded.

"Damn you, varlet! Open the—"

Colin snatched the door open so quickly that Deirdre almost fell in.

"Deirdre," Helena said lightly, as if she'd come in to chat about the weather.

Deirdre's face was lined with worry. She shoved Colin

aside and came toward Helena. "Are you well? Has he—" Then she saw the state of Helena's dress, and an almost visible fury seemed to boil off of her. She whipped around to Colin, who was nodding a companionable greeting to Pagan. "You!"

Colin reflexively covered his nose.

Pagan stepped between them. "Deirdre, there's no need—"

"You will wed her this very day," Deirdre decreed, her ice-blue eyes snapping. "Do you understand?"

Helena's hackles rose at that. "You cannot command me to wed!"

Deirdre spoke over her shoulder. "I can, and I will. 'Tis for the best, Helena. I won't let you bear a bastard child."

Helena was outraged. It seemed her sister hadn't lost her imperious nature after all. "And what if I *choose* to bear a bastard child?"

"Don't be foolish."

"Don't call me foolish."

"You *are* being foolish."

"I am not."

"I'm only watching out for you, Helena."

"I don't need you to watch out for me." She planted her hands on her hips. "And I certainly don't need you choosing my bridegroom. Especially after you stole Miriel's."

Deirdre gasped, then narrowed her eyes. "'Twas for her own good, and you know it. You and I agreed. We would have done anything to save her from the pain of—"

Pagan cleared his throat. No doubt his pride was still wounded by the fact that the sisters had fought over who would make the *sacrifice* of wedding him. "Helena," he said, "be reasonable. 'Tis truly the best solution. You cannot raise a babe on your own. You cannot—"

Colin straightened to his full height and stabbed his finger at Pagan's chest. "She can do whatever she damn well pleases!"

"Oh, aye, Colin!" Deirdre bellowed. "God forbid you should be burdened with a wife! Better to swive your merry way through all the maids, scattering babes like dandelion seeds in the wind!"

Colin gaped, incredulous. "Did I say that?"

Pagan narrowed stern eyes at Colin. "You *will* marry her."

"Do not order him about!" Helena cried, poking Pagan in the shoulder. "'Tis our babe, and 'tis up to us what we decide to do about it."

"You're not thinking, Hel," Deirdre said. "Your condition has made you irrational."

Fury left Helena speechless.

Colin clenched his jaw. "Don't call her irrational! She's the wisest woman I know."

Deirdre arched a wicked brow. "Then why did she lie with *you?*"

Helena itched to slap her ill-mannered sister, but for once, she didn't let her impulses get the best of her.

"Deirdre!" Pagan scolded. "Enough."

Helena gritted her teeth. 'Twas one thing for *her* to snap at her sister. But it grated on her ears to hear Pagan issuing commands. "See?" she said to Colin. "See how he orders her about?"

Colin shook his head. "Dreadful."

"Exactly," she agreed.

"I would never do such a thing," he said.

"I thought not."

"But then," Colin added, "you wouldn't resort to such insults."

"Nay," she admitted. "I'd probably answer with my blade."

"And I'd be at your back, my love."

"As always."

They crossed their arms in unison and faced Pagan and Deirdre, who had fallen into stunned silence.

Pagan was the first to breach the long quiet. "I told you we should have left them alone," he muttered, shaking his head.

Deirdre sighed in disgust. "They've already decided to wed, haven't they?"

"Oh, aye, I'd say so."

"So all this was for naught?"

"Oh, nay. I'd say they have an amusing tale to tell at the wedding supper."

"Ballocks."

As it happened, the story *was* recounted at the wedding feast, in the form of an extremely long and detailed ballade delivered by Boniface and accompanied on the lute. Helena thought Deirdre deserved no less.

Rivenloch's great hall resounded with music and merrymaking, and the tables groaned with a sumptuous blend of hearty Scots dishes and savory Norman fare. The air was filled with the scents of ginger and galyngale, verjuice and mustard, cinnamon and ale. New trophies from the tournament graced the scrubbed plaster walls, captured pennants and silver spurs and the golden arrow Helena had won in the archery contest.

She could put a name to most of the Cameliard faces around her now, and she'd begun to think of them as denizens of Rivenloch. Forsooth, the only stranger in their midst this eve was Sir Rand of Morbroch, a handsome noble who claimed to be bewitched by Miriel. Helena had to smile as she watched him try to engage her little sister in conversation. Miriel might appear sweet, shy, and soft-spoken, but she was no wide-eyed maid. Indeed, Helena suspected more warrior blood ran through her veins than she admitted. Sir Rand might have more of a battle before him than he expected.

As for Helena and her beloved adversary, she knew the way ahead might be rocky. Sometimes Colin would wield his influence and fight for authority, but sometimes she would take the upper hand, demanding her way. With patience and love, they'd resolve their differences, and in the end, they'd both emerge victorious.

She didn't mind bending a little to his will, as long as he bent to hers in return. As Pagan had said when he presented them with his wedding gift, matching swords of Toledo steel, the best blades were flexible, yielding a bit to their opponent's blows.

As she finished off her second apple coffyn to the strains of a bawdy rondeau from Boniface, Helena suddenly felt Colin's fingers settle brazenly upon her leg. She held her breath while they worked their surreptitious, inexorable way between her thighs. She stiffened, wondering if anyone would notice. Her cheeks grew hot as a smug, secret smile began to curve his lips.

But two could play at that game. Just as coyly, she slipped her hand beneath the table, sliding her palm across his thigh to wreak her revenge, boldly cupping his cock. His sharp intake of breath was sweet reward.

When he'd recovered from his shock, he looked at her with lust-darkened eyes, and said with forced calm, "My love, are you fatigued? Would you care to retire to our chamber?"

"Aye," she said, pressing her fingers to her temple. "I believe the babe has drained me of strength this eve."

Their innocuous speech fooled no one. The laughter and jesting began at once. A troop of raucous, drunken well-wishers followed them as they retreated hastily up the stairs, departing only when Colin slammed the bedchamber door on them.

Once inside, Helena discovered that Deirdre had taken revenge upon her for Boniface's song. 'Twas subtle, but 'twas revenge nonetheless. Their bridal bed was fitted, not with linen, but with shimmering sheets of pale silk. A cauldron absolutely reeking of jasmine steamed on the hearth. And one of the castle hounds whimpered pathetically from beside the bed, no doubt mortified by the fact that around his neck were tied enough pungent spices to flavor a year's worth of pasties.

Colin shook his head in amusement, then hunkered down to scratch the hound under his savory chin, while Helena picked up the missive left on the bed.

" 'Hel,' " she read aloud, " 'May you learn to bend to the ways of your Norman husband. Deir.' "

Colin chuckled, brushing his hand across the pallet. "Silk? I think I could get used to this."

She tossed aside the note and flashed him a wicked grin. "And I'm already thinking of ways I could bend for you."

"Indeed?" He growled his approval and rose to face her, winding a lock of her hair around his finger to tug her closer.

But the pungent scent of the cauldron was suddenly overpowering, and before he could press his lips to hers, his nose wrinkled, and he turned his head aside with a huge sneeze. "Satan's claws! That brew stinks."

"We could pour it down the garderobe."

He nodded. "I'll do it." With a sultry promise in his gaze and another sneeze, he bid her, "Wait here. Don't move."

She complied, running an idle finger back and forth across the smooth fabric of the bedclothes and glancing at the hound, who stared dolefully up at her.

Colin was back in the wink of an eye, closing the door and half-flinging the empty cauldron across the room in his haste. "Now. Where were we?"

She grinned. "I was bending you to my will."

He smiled slyly in return as he drew near. "*Your* will, is it now?"

"Mm."

"And is this your will, my lady?" He slipped his hand along her jaw, caressing her cheek and pulling her close to kiss her softly on the mouth, once, twice. "Is it?"

"Aye." She sighed against his lips.

"And what about this?" he asked, letting his fingers drift down the side of her neck and across her bosom, teasing at the top of her surcoat, then delving farther, until shivers of anticipation tautened her skin. "Is this your will?"

"Oh, aye," she breathed.

He spread the laces of her surcoat then and tugged the

bodice down to bare one breast. She closed her eyes and caught her lip between her teeth, waiting for the delicious shock of his touch.

But it never came. Instead, he growled, "Ah, bloody hell."

Her eyes snapped open. "What?"

He scowled. "I can't do anything with that damned hound watching my every move."

She stifled a smile.

"Wait," he said. "Right here."

"Mm-hm." She wasn't nearly as impatient as Colin. After all, they had a lifetime ahead of them.

He dropped his gaze momentarily to her bared breast, and the desire that instantly glazed his eyes made her loins quiver. "Right here," he rasped.

Then he snagged the dog by its fragrant collar and dragged it toward the door, pushing it out by the haunches.

As he leaned back against the closed door, letting his gaze roam with sensual languor down her body, her heart pounded hard with desire.

"Come, husband," she beckoned. "I grow cold."

He came at her call, warming her with his gaze. And his touches. And his kisses. Forsooth, before long she thought she would burn for want of coupling.

And then she heard a scratching at the door.

She tried to ignore it. After all, anyone who would interrupt a bride and groom on their wedding night had to be either stupid or mad. She buried her face against Colin's neck, bathing him in kisses.

Scratch, scratch, scratch.

She sighed against his ear, hoping to drown out the

sound. But she could tell by the stiffening of his shoulders he heard it, too.

"Now what?" he hissed, exasperated.

The scratching grew more persistent, and this time 'twas accompanied by a whine.

Helena's lips quivered with repressed mirth. "'Tis the hound."

"Lucifer's balls! What does he want?" He broke away in aggravation and snatched open the door. "What do you want?"

The dog looked up guiltily, and Helena couldn't help but laugh at the comic sight. "Oh, Colin, put the poor beast out of his misery before he dies of shame."

Colin drew his dagger and sliced the pungent wreath from around the hound's neck. The dog shook all over once, ridding himself of whatever scent remained, then happily wagged his tail and trotted off.

Colin sheathed his knife and closed the door once more. "Now. Is that everything?"

Helena scanned the room. "There are still the silk sheets."

"Those?" One corner of his mouth lifted in a seductive grin as he sauntered near, then pulled her into his embrace. "Those can stay."

# About the Author

Born in Paradise, California, SARAH MCKERRIGAN has embraced her inner Gemini by leading an eclectic life. As a teen, she danced with the Sacramento Ballet, worked in her father's graphic arts studio, and composed music for award-winning science films. She sang arias in college, graduating with a degree in music, then toured with an all-girl rock band on CBS Records. She once played drums for a Tom Jones video and is currently a voice-over actress with credits, including *Star Wars* audio adventures, JumpStart educational CDs, Diablo and Starcraft video games, and the MTV animated series *The Maxx*. She now indulges her lifelong love of towering castles, trusty swords, and knights (and damsels) in shining armor by writing historical romances featuring kick-butt heroines. She is married to a rock star, is the proud guardian of two nerdy kids and a pug named Worf, and lives in a part of Los Angeles where nobody thinks she's weird.

Please turn the page for a preview
of Sarah McKerrigan's next novel,

*Knight's Prize*

available in mass market soon!

# Chapter 1
*Autumn 1136*

HE IS COMING."

Miriel's eyes widened, and she stumbled out of her last
Taijiquan posture. Her gaze darted anxiously about the
chamber. "Who?"

She was always on guard now, more so since the Knights
of Cameliard had insinuated themselves into the household of Rivenloch Castle. She never knew when a Norman
warrior might come barging into her bedchamber.

"The Night," Sung Li replied, continuing with the measured Taijiquan poses, moving with a youthful grace that
belied the wrinkled face and long snowy braid, shifting
slowly from left foot to right, then arcing like a bow being
drawn.

But Miriel's tranquility of a moment before was ir-
reparably shattered. "*What* knight?" she hissed.

Sung Li spoke serenely. "The Night that comes to swallow the Shadow."

Miriel lowered her shoulders. Apparently, then, there

was no imminent danger. 'Twas only that Sung Li was being intentionally obtuse again. While the old servant's prophecies were usually accurate, sometimes Miriel's wise and wizened companion seemed impossibly inscrutable. And inevitably chose the most unfortunate times to deliver the darkest omens.

Shivering out her rattled nerves, Miriel resumed her exercises, shadowing Sung Li in their daily ritual. Beyond and below the open shutters of the keep, the first slender spears of sunlight pierced through the Scots woods.

But now that Sung Li had cast a stone into her pool of calm, rippling her meditative poise, Miriel's movements grew awkward. What did that mean—the Night that comes to swallow the Shadow? A cloudy evening? A harsh winter? Another invasion by the English? Or could it mean something more . . . personal? Lost in thought, Miriel wobbled and finally lost her balance, coming down hard on one bare foot.

"God's hooks, Sung Li!" She crossed her arms, blowing a stray tendril of dark hair out of her eyes. "You know I can't concentrate when you deliver such ominous tidings."

Sung Li broke from the pose long enough to turn an amused, smug look upon her. "A true Master would not be distracted, not even by—"

"A dragon breathing its fiery breath upon his head," Miriel muttered. "I know. I *know*. But you could have told me later."

Sung Li finished the last extended movement, bowed respectfully toward the sun, then faced Miriel with a solemn expression. "Later is too late. The Night is coming *now*."

A slip of a breeze drifted through the window just then, bringing in the crisp October air, but the preternatural chill that shuddered Miriel's bones had naught to do with the season. "Now? But it's scarcely dawn."

Their gazes met, and Miriel thought she'd never seen her Xiansheng, her teacher, look so grave. 'Twas as if those ancient black eyes bored into her soul, seeking out her weaknesses and weighing her worth.

At last Sung Li took hold of Miriel's forearm in a surprisingly firm grip. "You must be strong. And brave. And clever."

Miriel slowly nodded. She may not fully understand Sung Li, who spoke often in riddles, but there was no question the warning was serious.

Then Sung Li released her abruptly and, as if naught had happened, resumed the role of Miriel's maidservant, donning a roughspun kirtle over the loose hemp garments worn for Taijiquan, pulling on stockings and slippers, then selecting a deep azure surcoat for Miriel from the great pine chest at the foot of the bed.

Miriel frowned, slithering into the soft wool gown while Sung Li dutifully turned away. They'd kept many secrets, the two of them, since the day five years ago when Miriel had deigned to purchase, along with nunchakus and a pair of sais from the Orient, a Chinese servant from a traveling merchant.

Sung Li had *insisted* on being purchased. 'Twas Destiny, the curious peasant had sagely proclaimed. At thirteen summers old, Miriel wasn't about to argue with Destiny.

Her father, Lord Gellir, had not approved, nor had her older sisters, Deirdre and Helena. For a long while, the denizens of Rivenloch turned disparaging Scots glares upon the wee foreigner with the strange eyes and impertinent tongue. But they'd grown accustomed to Sung Li now, and no one questioned the presence of the crone of a maidservant who clung as tightly to Miriel as a duckling to its mother.

Of course, if they'd known that the wee old woman was forsooth a wee old man, if they'd known that he devoted most of his hours teaching Miriel the fine art of Chinese warfare, and if they'd suspected that under his tutelage, Miriel had blossomed from a timid child into a fierce combatant to rival her warrior sisters, they might have taken exception.

But as Sung Li was fond of saying, the greatest weapon is the one no one knows you possess.

"Hmph." Sung Li was staring out the window, his narrow white brows furrowed.

"Hmph, what?" Miriel buckled her girdle and wiggled her feet into her slippers.

"A knight arrives."

"Now?" Miriel tensed instantly. "The Night that comes to swallow the Shadow?" Knees bent, arms raised, she was ready to fight this very moment, whether against a human foe or the dark forces of nature.

Sung Li turned on her with an annoyed scowl, then shook his head. "You are like a mouse today, starting at your own shadow." He left the window and began tidying the chamber, clucking his tongue. "It is only a common knight."

Miriel lowered her hands and fired a scathing glare at the old man, a glare that was wasted on his back. Then she peered out the window for herself. There *was* a knight on horseback cresting the rise above Rivenloch. He was in full battle dress, chain mail and surcoat, which was wise, because a stranger alone could make fast foes in the wilds of Scotland. As he rode down the hill toward the castle, the silver helm beneath his arm caught the light of dawn, glinting like fire.

She couldn't make out the crest upon his brown tabard or see him clearly, not with the shaggy mane of chestnut hair that obscured his face and reached almost to his shoulders.

"Who do you suppose—" She looked around to Sung Li, but the elusive servant was already gone, probably on his way to filch the best bread from the kitchen for his mistress's breakfast before any of those ravenous Normans could take it.

Miriel returned to the window. Mayhap the knight was a guest arriving early for Helena's wedding. He paused now, halfway down the rise, to scan his surroundings. As his gaze swept across the castle, Miriel felt an uncharacteristic shiver of trepidation skitter up her spine. She ducked reflexively behind a shutter, out of sight.

After a moment, mentally scolding herself for her cowardice, she peered out again. The knight had changed course. He now reined his mount into the dense forest that surrounded Rivenloch.

Miriel frowned. 'Twas most irregular. Why would a strange knight travel all the way to the remote keep of Rivenloch, only to swerve at the last moment into the woods?

She intended to find out.

Deirdre and Helena believed that Miriel had sealed up the secret exit from the castle, the one at the back of her workroom beneath the keep, after Rivenloch's soldiers had made use of the tunnel to defeat the attacking English army last spring. But Miriel had done no such thing. That passageway was too useful to close off. 'Twas the only way Miriel could leave the keep without being under the constant scrutiny of her overprotective sisters.

So she'd hung a tapestry over the entrance, pushed her desk against the opening, and piled up books of accounts to obscure the passage. 'Twas little trouble to move them out of the way whenever she needed to escape.

As she did now.

'Twas yet early morn. Later Helena would need her to help with wedding preparations. But she could spy upon the stranger in the woods for a bit and steal back to the castle before anyone was the wiser. She smiled to herself. 'Twas clandestine adventures like these that relieved her of the boredom of keeping the castle accounts.

Sir Rand le Brun sensed the instant he was no longer alone in the forest. 'Twasn't that the intruder made a sound or exuded a scent or even cast a shadow. But years of training as a mercenary had honed Rand's senses to a keen edge. By the faint prickling at the back of his neck, he felt sure he was being watched.

He casually eased one hand over the pommel of his sword and moved to the far side of his horse, placing the beast between him and where he guessed the intruder to be. Then, hunkering down as if to check the horse's girth, he peered beneath the beast's belly, scouring the bushes for some trace of a trespasser.

But aside from a few wraiths of steam chased from the wet oak trunks by the warm glare of the rising sun, the misty copse was silent. Branches of lush cedar drooped in slumber. Thick ferns stood like quiet sentinels. Not a beetle stirred the leaf fall.

He frowned. Mayhap 'twas an owl late to bed. Or mayhap some lost spirit haunted the Borders woods. Or, he thought, patting his horse's flank and rising again, mayhap 'twas his imagination, and he was only growing weary of the hunt, like an old hound whose sense of smell was failing.

Still, he'd always trusted his instincts. Just because he couldn't locate the threat at this moment didn't mean it wasn't there. He'd have to keep one eye on his surroundings and one hand on his blade as he searched the woods.

He didn't know exactly what he was looking for yet. All he'd been told when the Lord of Morbroch hired him was that the outlaw he sought was a man who worked alone, an elusive thief who roamed the forests of Rivenloch.

The task had seemed simple enough at first. In Rand's experience, robbers were seldom clever. 'Twould be an easy matter to locate the fellow's hideaway, take him by force, and convey him to Morbroch for judgment.

But when Rand learned how much the lord and several of his neighboring barons were willing to pay him to catch the thief who had lightened their purses, he began to wonder if 'twas not so simple an undertaking after all.

Apparently, the denizens of Rivenloch didn't mind their local outlaw. Even knowing the scoundrel had relieved numerous traveling noblemen of a vast quantity of silver, they refused to expend any effort to capture the man. Nor did they welcome the interference of outsiders.

Thus Rand would have to work in secret beneath the noses of one of the most formidable forces in Britain, the

Knights of Cameliard. The Norman knights had come last spring to take command of the Scots castle, and already they'd routed a huge force of rogue English lords who'd tried to lay siege to the keep. If they wished, they could easily prevent one paltry mercenary from capturing their outlaw.

So Rand would have to be clever.

He needed three things: a believable pretext for coming to Rivenloch, a reason to linger there, and access to the intimate workings of the keep. The Lord of Morbroch had offered him a deception that gave him all three.

Of course, if he could catch the robber at once, there would be no need for deception.

He scanned the path again for signs of inhabitation—footprints, discarded bones from a meal, remnants of a fire. The sooner he could find some clue as to the thief's whereabouts, the sooner he could quit this place and collect his reward. But all he sensed as his gaze ranged the woods was that eerie feeling he was being watched.

Then his ear caught a new sound intruding upon the silence of the forest. Footsteps.

'Twas not the stealthy passage of a thief he heard, but the purposeful approach of a pair of men. He'd expected as much. Rivenloch's guards had likely spotted him as he'd approached the castle, and now they'd come to investigate. They'd find him in another few moments.

Acting on instinct, Rand stepped to the side of the path and casually began to whistle. Then he hefted his chain mail out of the way and unlaced his braies, swiftly yanking them down to relieve himself upon a bush.

At the sudden loud gasp from the branches directly

above him, his heart bolted, his whistle suddenly turned to air, and he almost missed the bush.

God's eyes! There *was* a trespasser. Very near.

And, he realized in wonder, distinctly female.

But he could already see the shrubbery along the path parting to make way for the approaching men. There was no time to confront the damsel hiding in the tree. The most he could do was cast an amused grin up toward the concealing foliage.

"Wicked lass," he softly chided.

Then, shaking his head, he resumed whistling and returned unabashedly to his task. The way he looked at it, if the sight of a man pissing offended the maid, she deserved as much for her mischief.

Miriel was appalled. Not by the man's rude display, though 'twas most audacious and disconcerting. But by the way she'd gasped.

All her life she'd ranged these woods, as silent as mist, as invisible as air. Thanks to Sung Li's guidance, she knew how to make herself imperceptible, even to the keen-eyed owls that inhabited the trees. She could flit from branch to branch as nimbly as a squirrel and blend seamlessly into the foliage.

How the man had startled such a loud gasp from her, she didn't know. True, she'd never seen *that* part of a man before, but 'twas not so much different than she'd imagined.

Worse, she'd almost caught her breath again when he'd peered up in her direction with that smug grin. Not because he'd discovered her presence. Not because he was going to brazenly piss in front of her anyway. But because his handsome face—that strong jaw, those curving lips, the unruly hair, the perplexed furrow between his brows, and those dark, sparkling eyes—literally took her breath away.

"Good morn!" Sir Rauve's booming voice almost toppled her out of her perch. The giant black-bearded Knight of Cameliard, dogged by young Sir Kenneth, tromped forward, one cautious hand on the hilt of his sheathed sword.

"Good morn!" the stranger called back cheerfully. His voice was rich and warm, like honey mead. "And pardon me," he apologized, making a show of hauling up his braies. "Just taking care of a bit of business."

Sir Rauve nodded, wasting no time and mincing no words. "And what type of business do you have at Rivenloch, sir?"

The man grinned companionably. By the Saints, Miriel thought, his smile was absolutely stunning, wide and bright, complete with endearing dimples. "That depends on who is asking."

Rauve drew himself up to his impressive height. "Sir Rauve of Rivenloch, Knight of Cameliard, defender of this keep."

"Sir Rauve." The stranger wiped his right hand on his tabard, then put it forth in greeting. "I am Sir Rand of Morbroch."

Morbroch. Miriel knew that name.

When Sir Rauve only eyed him with suspicion, he added hopefully, "You might remember me from the tournament last month?"

Miriel frowned. The Lord of Morbroch had attended the tournament at Rivenloch with a half dozen knights. She recognized the crest on the man's tabard now, a boar's head on a ground of sable. But she didn't recall Sir Rand. And his was a face she wouldn't have easily forgotten.

At Rauve's lack of response, Sir Rand withdrew his hand and lowered his eyes with a sigh. "Then again, perchance not. I was knocked witless in the melee. Didn't recover for two days."

Miriel caught her lip beneath her teeth. That might be true. Someone was always getting knocked witless in a melee.

But Rauve was not convinced. "You've not answered my question."

"Why am I here?" Rand's brows wrinkled in charming discomfiture. "I'd . . . rather not say."

Rauve crossed his beefy arms over his chest. "And I'd rather not let you pass."

"I see." Rand took a deep breath and let it out in a bracing rush.

In that instant, Miriel saw his hand drift subtly yet purposefully toward the hilt of his sword. By the wink of danger in his eyes, she suddenly feared he was about to do something rash, like single-handedly challenging Rauve and Kenneth to battle.

But at the last moment, he hooked his thumb harmlessly into his leather sword belt and flashed them a sheepish grin. "If you must know, I've come . . . courting."

Miriel arched a brow.

"Courting?" Young Kenneth made a moue of displeasure, as if he'd said he'd come to swallow live eels.

Rauve only grunted.

"Aye." Sir Rand let out a lovesick sigh that would curdle honey. "I fear one of Rivenloch's bright angels has stolen my heart."

Miriel scowled. If there was one thing she despised, 'twas sappy proclamations of love. Especially when they were full of deceit. As this one was. Rand might have said the words, but she could tell by the amused glimmer in his eyes that he meant none of them. The knave was lying.

But of course, the guards didn't know the difference. Men could never smell deception the way a woman could.

"One of Rivenloch's angels?" Rauve growled, jutting out his bearded chin. "Well, it had better not be Lucy."

Both Miriel's brows shot up. Lucy? This was a surprise. Did the bearish Sir Rauve have a weakness for saucy Lucy Campbell?

Kenneth issued his own warning. "And if you've come for Lady Helena, 'tis too late. She's to wed in a sennight."

"Fear not," Rand said with a lighthearted chuckle. "'Tis neither, good sirs."

But when the varlet pressed a hand to his chest as if to still the beating there, Miriel couldn't resist rolling her eyes. Who was his alleged lady love, then? Margaret Duncan? Joan Atwater? Katie Simms?

"I fear my hapless heart has been claimed," he gushed, "by none other than the youngest Maid of Rivenloch . . ."

Miriel almost strangled on her surprise. Her? He'd come for *her*? God's blood, she didn't even know the man.

Apparently, he didn't know her either, for he finished on a sigh of pure adoration. "Lady Mirabel."

# THE DISH

*Where authors give you the inside scoop!*

♥ ♥ ♥ ♥ ♥ ♥ ♥ ♥ ♥ ♥ ♥ ♥ ♥ ♥ ♥

*From the desks of*
*Julie Anne Long and Sarah McKerrigan*

Dear Readers:

From fiery ballerinas to kidnapping hunks to marrying a rock star, Julie Anne Long and Sarah McKerrigan dish in this author-to-author interview.

**JULIE:** Hey, Sarah! What on earth are we going to do for our Dish thing? Do you want to talk about your book? Frankly, *I* want to talk about your book. Specifically, I'd like to know why your heroine is gripping a big dagger. And how do I get abs like hers? And who is that be-stubbled hunk lurking in the shadows? What's their story?

**SARAH:** That buff and brazen blonde is Helena, one of the three warrior maids of Rivenloch, and there's a very good reason she's wielding that sword. See, this cocky Norman knight, Pagan Cameliard, is about to subject Helena's little sister to a fate worse than death: marriage. In order to save poor Miriel, Helena decides to kidnap Colin du Lac, bestubbled hunk and Pagan's right-hand man, to use him as a hostage. Thus the book's title, **CAPTIVE HEART** (on sale now). Speaking of titles, I *love* yours! How did you come up with **WAYS TO BE WICKED**? How many ways are there? And can we learn them by reading your book? Tell me more.

**JULIE:** Ah, so *that's* the secret to a toned body—kidnapping hunks! (But don't try this at home, boys and girls.) It sounds like your heroine, Helena, knows a thing or two about being wicked. And *speaking* of **WAYS TO BE WICKED** (how's that for a segue?): I found that title by rifling through my '80s record collection—it's the name of a great old Lone Justice song. And there are *infinite* ways to be wicked, by the way. (You can see my hero and heroine, Sylvie Lamoreux and Tom Shaughnessy, engaged in one of the more, ahem, *popular* ones on the cover of the book.) Sylvie is a fiery ballerina and the darling of the Paris Opera when a mysterious letter sends her across the English Channel in search of a past she never knew she had. She lands—literally—in the lap of London's most notorious man, the gorgeous Tom Shaughnessy, owner of the bawdy White Lily theater, and fireworks ensue.

**WAYS TO BE WICKED** (on sale now) is the second book in my Regency-set trilogy about the Holt sisters, three girls separated when they were very young when their mother, the mistress of a famous politician, was framed for his murder and forced to flee, leaving them behind. *Beauty and the Spy* is the first book in that trilogy. Isn't **CAPTIVE HEART** part of a series, too, Sarah? Can you talk a little bit about it? And speaking of secret pasts—don't you have a little secret past of your own?

**SARAH:** Wow, Julie, it looks like we have more than a few things in common! Yes, **CAPTIVE HEART** is also my second book in a trilogy about sisters, though mine are Scots warrior maids, twelfth-century damsels in shining armor. In my first novel, *Lady Danger*, that same doomed-to-be-wed Miriel is saved from the altar by the sacrifice of her oldest sister, Deirdre, who disguises herself as Pagan's bride. Unfortunately, all this happens unbeknownst to Helena, who is already escorting Colin away at sword-point. But Colin deems wild Helena a rather captivating captor, and Helena's resolve to ransom him is somewhat compromised when she becomes, well, *compromised*. Still, it takes a return to the besieged Rivenloch castle, where they're forced to fight a common foe, to bring the lovers together at last.

As for *my* story, why yes, I *do* have a secret past! I started out as a singer in The Pinups, an all-girl rock-and-roll band, played drums once in a Tom Jones video, and married the current bass player of the classic rock band America. But I'm not the only one with a musical back-story. Hit it, Julie!

**JULIE:** OK, I confess: I wanted to be the female version of Bono when I grew up, so I played guitar, sang, and wrote songs in San Francisco bands for years. But you know, Sarah, when you think about it . . . now that we're romance authors, we still spend our days with passionate men who excel at, um, wielding their instruments. (Ha!) We just write stories about them.

Sincerely,

WAYS TO BE WICKED          CAPTIVE HEART
*www.julieannelong.com*        *www.sarahmckerrigan.com*